H IN UE'S EARTH

PHASE 1

IN HUE'S EARTH

PHASE 1

EDITH J. WILLOW

Edited by Scribendi
www.scribendi.com

Book Cover by mdcreation
michael@mdcreation.fr

Book design by Wordzworth
www.wordzworth.com

Printed by Lightning Source
www.lightningsource.com

First paperback edition November 2023

ISBN 978-1-7389666-0-8 (e-book) ISBN 978-1-7389666-1-5 (hardcover) ISBN 978-1-7389666-2-2 (paperback)

Published by Edith J. Willow
www.edithjwillow.ca

CONTENTS

PROLOGUE I

Sixteen Years Prior

INT. THE MAIN LOBBY OF THE GRAND ARNE OFFICE – AFTERNOON

Two GAO employees sit around the entrance of the Grand Arne Office as they watch the Bartlett's Piece documentary on the television above the doors. Behind them the rest of the employees rush around, preparing for the Pledge of Allegiance.

TV PROGRAMMER: (THROUGH THE TV) Welcome to Bartlett's Piece, one of the rarest finds on the planet and home to a population of thirty million since the days of the Rising Waters. Most of you may not remember those times that happened centuries before Bartlett's Piece was formed. However, the discovery of this precious land has brought us back to the old days, and it has become home to you and me. In this program, you'll learn how this gem was formed on Earth. Where did it get its name? And how did this mass of land become the hope that humanity was looking for all these –

The two GAO employees are shocked to see the television abruptly turn off as they turn to see one of the GAO leads holding the remote that controls the device.

GAO EMPLOYEE 1: (TURNS TO GAO TECHNICIAN 1) Hey, what was that for?

GAO LEAD 1: Why are you two sitting around when the Pledge of Allegiance is about to start?

GAO EMPLOYEE 2: There's no need to rush. We were just–

GAO LEAD 1: There's no point watching that documentary. It's going to be updated anyway Now c'mon – let's go, already.

The two GAO employees groan in annoyance as they get up and follow the GAO lead toward the Commander's Room while the rest of the staff continue to make final preparations for the Pledge of Allegiance.

ELISA: (NARRATES) He is right … there is no point in watching that documentary at all. Especially when the version you were watching has been outdated for many years, it won't tell you the full story of how this country was formed along with its dark history. But before I get to that, allow me to tell you what gets talked about in the documentary, as I tell you the full story of how Bartlett's Piece came to be the rarest find on the planet.

A Few Minutes Later

INT. THE HYPOTHESIS ROOM OF THE GRAND ARNE OFFICE – AFTERNOON

Two GAO employees look through old photo albums of Bartlett's Piece's history in the Hypothesis Room while remaining hidden from their co-workers during the Pledge of Allegiance preparation.

ELISA: (NARRATES) As I have been told, before Bartlett's Piece ever existed, there were more than a hundred countries along with thousands of cities that not even one person knows the half of. However, that all changed as the sea levels began to rise and slowly wiped out all those cities and countries at once. This was known as the Rising Waters Era. During the early stages, many people thought on their feet and built boats as they left their sinking homes to live out at sea. Others started later as the water reached up to their waists. The rest never left at all, hoping that the sea levels would go down soon. They perished in the waters, just like their homes and the rest of civilization. No one knew when the Rising Waters would stop, so they stayed in their aquatic homes in hopes that it would stop soon. However, living in the sea wasn't easy, especially when you're surrounded by storms, strong currents, and the animals that thrived beneath the waters. But the new sea dwellers still had hope, and they used their aquatic homes to search for land that would become their new home –hopefully high enough not to succumb to the Rising Waters. After finding land that appeared to be untouched without any indication of which country it belonged to, many people started demolishing their aquatic homes to build new shelters on that land, creating a civilization of their own. Eventually, this country got its name thanks to one man, Bernard Bartlett.

The GAO employees open an album to see old pictures of people living in aquatic houses, along with Bernard Bartlett building the country with those same people. They continue to look through the album as they think about what their lives would've been like during the Rising Waters Era.

GAO EMPLOYEE 3: Imagine living in those houses today.

GAO EMPLOYEE 4: It was a good thing this land was found – otherwise, I would've been seasick for years.

The GAO employees chuckle while they continue looking through the old albums.

ELISA: (NARRATES) Bernard was believed to be one of the first people to discover this land after decades of living in boats and floating houses. And what did he do when he found it? He became the first commander-in-chief of the country after guiding hundreds of people to this massive land and encouraging his citizens to guide thousands more people during the Rising Waters Era. Although many people were excited to finally live on land for the first time, they feared that their new homes would also sink under water, just like the rest of civilization had. So, they placed sticks around the shoreline with painted lines to indicate whether the water had begun rising again, and after years of not seeing the water rise past those lines, the entire community was happy to keep their homes. It seemed that the Rising Waters Era had ended. And why name the land Bartlett's Piece? Because the name itself means "son of earth," but Bartlett didn't want the land to belong to him, he wanted it to belong to the world – so the name actually means "World's Piece".

GAO EMPLOYEE 3: But why were we sent here in the first place? Shouldn't we be helping with the preparations?

GAO EMPLOYEE 4: The leads have already selected employees to handle the preparations, while we were selected to conduct Operation Wipeout. But I fell asleep during the entire meeting, so I don't even know what we're looking for.

GAO LEAD 1: (SHOUTS) Hey!

The GAO employees turn to see one of the GAO leads entering the Hypothesis Room as he walks up to them to see what is going on.

GAO LEAD 1: (SERIOUS) I don't know if you realized it, but we have a Pledge of Allegiance that's about to happen in a few minutes. What are you two doing alone in here?

GAO EMPLOYEE 3: (NERVOUSLY) Nothing too extraordinary – we're just conducting Operation Wipeout –

GAO LEAD 1: (SERIOUS) So nothing is what you're actually doing since this room has been combed through already! (BEGINS TO LEAVE) We need more bodies in the library, so let's go!

The GAO employees groan quietly in annoyance as they follow the GAO lead to the Orien Library.

ELISA: (NARRATES) After Mr. Bartlett's death, another man – Orien Arne, his trusted companion – decided to take his place. He created the building that you see before you today, known as the Grand Arne Office – and with his name meaning "eagle" or "ruler," it was a fitting title to call the country's first government administration.

A Few Minutes Later

INT. THE ORIEN LIBRARY OF THE GRAND ARNE OFFICE – AFTERNOON

The GAO lead brings the GAO employees to the Orien Library, where they are shocked to see several of their co-workers removing many Bartlett's Piece archives from their shelves and skimming through all of them to see if they mention the Metallic Order.

GAO LEAD 1: Start searching, boys.

The GAO lead leaves the employees in the library. They continue to be in shock with what they see as they watch one of their co-workers finish skimming through a book and putting it in a pile before opening another one.

ELISA: (NARRATES) He carried on the tradition of finding stragglers at sea and guiding them to the new country, but there was one person in particular that Mr. Arne should've left out at sea. Benelli Mete was his name.

The GAO employee grimaces after seeing a picture of Benelli Mete in the book and quickly rushes over to give the book to one of his co-workers. They do a double check on all the books that were given to them before tossing them all into the fireplace. Another of their peers approaches the employees who were just brought into the library.

ELISA: (NARRATES) Benelli Mete came to Bartlett's Piece with his dying wife and child, and Arne welcomed him with open arms, along with the community, as he saved his family from their illness. However, once they settled in, there was something about this land that Mete didn't like. Because the entire community came from different parts of the sunken earth, people came with their own cultures, traditions and languages. Now that the Rising Waters had receded, Benelli thought that Bartlett's Piece should have its own culture and that the civilians should aim to be the same at all costs. Arne knew the dangers of stripping people's individual characteristics away, so he never agreed to Mete's plan – no matter how much he begged and pleaded.

GAO EMPLOYEE 5: (UPSET) Don't just stand around here. Do something!

The two GAO employees are pushed to a corner where they are confronted with piles of books in the process of being selected for burning.

GAO EMPLOYEE 5: (UPSET) Start combing through these books! We don't have time to waste!

The GAO employees watch their co-worker walk back to the fireplace to monitor the other employees. Then, they look at each other in slight panic before each picks up a book and pretends to be working.

ELISA: (NARRATES) This caused Arne's downfall during his reign because after Mete presented his final plea to make Bartlett's Piece one pure civilization, he decided to challenge Arne's position as commander-in-chief. People were shocked that Mete would do such a thing after Arne saved his life along with his family, but they were more shocked by how many people supported his vision … and that support won him the challenge against Arne. After his victory, he recruited thousands of men who thought the same s he did; those same recruits marched through the streets of Bartlett's Piece, inviting more people who supported the vision and punishing those who didn't. This movement became known as the Metallic Order.

The two GAO employees continue to pretend to be working until, seeing two of their co-workers doing the same thing, they stop while constantly looking at the entrance to see if it is clear.

GAO EMPLOYEE 4: (WHISPERS) You guys were sent here, too?

GAO EMPLOYEE 2: (WHISPERS) Yeah. We're leaving now, so don't tell anybody.

The two GAO employees sit in shock as they watch their two co-workers put away their books before getting up to leave the Orien Library.

ELISA: (NARRATES) Mete created the authoritarian group himself to control the country's population, as he strove to make everyone be exactly like him. Many people submitted to his ideals to survive during those dark times; others fled further into the undeveloped parts of Bartlett's Piece to hide from the anguish caused by the Metallic Order. Members of the Order wore shiny metallic suits to showcase their authority. There were some individuals who resisted their attempts to homogenize the citizens – Orien Arne, to be exact. He also formed a group that helped citizens survive the abuse of the Metallic Order, though that effort caused him to be the first victim of Mete's gruesome punishment, the Loyalty Trials.

The two GAO employees manage to make it close to the door until one of their co-workers walks over to see what is going on.

GAO EMPLOYEE 5: (CONFUSED) Where are you guys going?

GAO EMPLOYEE 1: (CASUALLY LIES) The washroom, of course! And we're gonna go look for recruits afterwards – we have so much work to do here!

The GAO employees leave the library before their co-worker can say anything else. He shrugs hopelessly and returns to the fireplace before turning to the other employees, who stay back as they continue to pretend to work.

ELISA: (NARRATES) The Loyalty Trials were an extreme obstacle course that resistant citizens were forced to complete to prove their worthiness to the commander-in-chief. Survive the obstacle course, and the Metallic Order would spare your life along with your loved ones … fail to complete it, and your loved ones would die. All hope was lost when the world watched Orien Arne die while participating in the Loyalty Trials, and the rest of his followers perished afterwards. After Orien's death, the Metallic Order took over the Grand Arne Office and terminated any members who did not support Mete's vision. However, this part of our history will never be told in the documentary, as today's GAO is still trying to destroy any evidence that this event ever happened despite people's memories of living under the Metallic Order.

GAO EMPLOYEE 3: (WHISPERS) Maybe we should make a run for it as well.

GAO EMPLOYEE 4: (WHISPERS) I think so, too. (LOOKS OVER AT THE FIREPLACE) I don't wanna end up like that guy.

The two GAO employees turn to see their co-workers taking findings from everyone as they do a double check before throwing the books into the fireplace. One employee continuously throws books in the fireplace without checking them as he tries to suppress his own memories of experiencing the Metallic Order.

GAO EMPLOYEE 6: (SILENTLY) We must forget ... no matter what the cost, we must forget.

The GAO employee continues to throw away books and archives related to the Metallic Order and watches them burn in the fireplace.

A Few Minutes Later

INT. THE CORRIDOR OF THE GRAND ARNE OFFICE – AFTERNOON

ELISA: (NARRATES) But things managed to take a turn for the better during this era, as an unexpected visit prevented future generations from experiencing the same treatment.

A GAO lead monitors the entire operation as he watches two GAO employees on ladders take down Benelli Mete's portrait, which they hand off to another set of employees. These carry it carefully on its side before leaving the corridor and whisking it away from the area. Two other employees enter the corridor and rush to bring over a new portrait. However, they stop as the GAO lead rips the protective paper to see that it is the portrait of the newly elected commander-in-chief.

GAO LEAD 2: Perfect. Let's hang it up before the Pledge of Allegiance begins.

The GAO employees nod as they take the protective paper off the portrait itself and give it to their co-workers, who are still on the ladder. All four employees attempt to hang the portrait on the wall as the previous employees come back to the corridor and rush over to help them.

ELISA: (NARRATES) While Mete was enjoying his time as commander-in-chief, a group of travellers entered the land without permission, bearing no indication that they were citizens of Bartlett's Piece. When Mete addressed the individuals, they said they came from Faramund

– which was later called the Discovery Region after an alliance with Bartlett's Piece was formed, which almost failed due to an argument over which country was discovered first. But after witnessing the advanced technology each traveller used at the time and the artifacts they had discovered in a land that was larger than Bartlett's Piece, Mete decided to invite them to Bartlett's Piece and use their innovations to his advantage instead of making the travellers his enemy. Little did he know that allowing those travellers to stay would be his downfall. After letting them take shelter in the Grand Arne Office for years, creating the Grand Arne Institute of Technology, along with the three major Steels Services, and allowing the travellers to invite their companions to implement their inventions on the land, they turned against him.

The GAO lead watches the four GAO employees struggling to hold the portrait up and quickly steps in to help them. The employees on the ladders manage to successfully hang the portrait of the newly elected commander-in-chief on the wall and carefully adjust it before coming down the ladders. The rest of the employees and the lead back away from the portrait, along with their co-workers who were on the ladder as they take a moment to reflect on what they just did and contemplate whether "Operation Wipeout" was actually a good idea to begin with.

ELISA: (NARRATES) The travellers devised a plan to overthrow the commander-in-chief using their alliance and their technology against him. Many citizens believed that another election was going to happen and that one of the travellers would challenge Mete's position as commander-in-chief. But there was no challenge; their mission was not to take his position, but to eliminate him immediately. No one knew exactly what happened on the day Benelli Mete went missing ... all they heard was that a group of men snuck into the Grand Arne Office, bound him with rope and drugged him, then whisked him away while everyone was sleeping. Some say the group of men threw him into the sea with a brick tied to his feet. Others thought that he was secretly executed by his own bodyguards, who had only agreed to take the position for their own survival. But regardless of what happened to him – the commander-in-chief was gone, and there was no one to govern the country. Many of Mete's followers thought about taking his place as the next commander-in-chief, but the citizens fought back and helped their nomad companions dismantle the Metallic Order for good. Everyone was freed from the years of abuse under the Metallic Order, but this also led to a period of anarchy within the country as the citizens refused to let anyone else become commander-in-chief of Bartlett's Piece due to the fear of reliving those terrible moments in life.

GAO LEAD 2: Hopefully, we never have to do this again.

The GAO employees nod in agreement while they stare at the portrait of the newly elected commander-in-chief for a long moment. Meanwhile, the GAO employees, who snuck out of the library, hide behind a wall after witnessing what their co-workers did to Benelli's portrait.

GAO EMPLOYEE 1: (WHISPERS) But why would they take down the late leader's portrait? Do the officials know about this?

GAO EMPLOYEE 2: (WHISPERS) Never mind the officials. Does the new commander-in-chief know about this?

GAO EMPLOYEE 1: (WHISPERS) Of course he does – he probably demanded them to do this, if you ask me.

GAO EMPLOYEE 2: (WHISPERS) I don't think he would do such a thing; the Pledge of Allegiance hasn't started for him to be making such bold moves.

GAO EMPLOYEE 1: (WHISPERS) Well, whoever made this decision, he better hope that this exact scene doesn't happen to him. Because he's already doing a crappy job in my eyes, if he's doing crap like this.

The GAO employee walks away from the scene, leaving his co-worker with no choice but to follow him.

A Few Minutes Later

INT. THE PRIVATE CHAMBER OF THE COMMANDER'S ROOM – AFTERNOON

ELISA: (NARRATES) Many of the travellers and their companions tried to convince the citizens to vote for a new leader; they even held an election to see if anyone in the country would change their minds and hopefully cause a ripple effect for change. But they continued to live their lives without a commander-in-chief ruling the nation. That was when the nomads decided to stay in Bartlett's Piece permanently, take over the Grand Arne Office and create more technology that would help the country recover from its previous turmoil. All of this was thanks to a young man who wanted the best for Bartlett's Piece and hoped that his out-of-this-world gadgets, a high-tech upgrade in our clothing, and what I like to call his newly built intellectual and occupational assessment system, which also happens to be colour-coded, would help the citizens live a better, freer and more colourful life in the future. There was one catch, though. Having a high Tint Level percentage in this new system isn't as good as is usually anticipated. And if you need more clarification on that ... I'll just let the man explain that himself.

Isaim Hue (late-twenties) practices in front of the mirror while he recites the words of the Bartlett's Piece documentary while it plays in the background.

ISAIM: Now that you know everything about Bartlett's Piece, I hope you have a certain appreciation of our home – as well as a sense of pride that you get to be a part of ...

Isaim feels himself stuttering and shakes his head as he turns off the Bartlett's Piece documentary before turning back to the mirror.

ISAIM: (TO HIMSELF) Is it really necessary to include all this? They already know about this – every single person has watched this ... even the stuff they didn't include in the documentary. Maybe Dolan was right. I am overdoing it, especially when he says my presentation is enough. It should be enough, right?

Hearing a knock on the door, Isaim is slightly startled. He quickly checks the time on his watch.

GAO EMPLOYEE 7: (THROUGH THE DOOR) Mr. Hue! We need you to come out now – we're about to start in a few minutes!

ISAIM: (TURNS TO THE DOOR) I'll be right out – just give me a second!

Isaim hears footsteps leaving before turning back to the mirror to adjust his suit.

ISAIM: (TO HIMSELF) You got this … you got this.

Isaim takes a deep breath before leaving the private chamber to join everyone in the commander's room.

PROLOGUE II

A Few Minutes Later

INT. THE COMMANDER'S ROOM OF THE GRAND ARNE OFFICE – AFTERNOON

The GAO leads, employees and technicians are preparing for a nation-wide live broadcast at the Grand Arne Office. Isaim paces back and forth slowly, going over his speech while **Dolan Wenski (late-twenties)** watches from a safe distance.

DOLAN: What's wrong? Allowing nerves to get to you?

Isaim looks up and gives Dolan a brief smile while one of the GAO employees rushes to fix his cream-coloured business suit.

GAO LEAD 3: Just to remind you that we're going to start in five minutes.

DOLAN: We've gone over this a thousand times – you will do just fine.

ISAIM: (STOPS AND TURNS TO DOLAN) I know, I know I will be okay. It's just the excitement that I'm feeling right now from all this. We've come a long way to earn this chance. Everyone is going to be listening to our message.

DOLAN: (CLARIFIES) Your message, to be exact. Yes, I may have helped you prepare for this situation, but, at the end of the day, it was all you. You came up with the ideas; I just helped you put them all together – no big deal.

ISAIM: (GRATEFUL) That's the thing; there is no way in my life that I could have done all this without you. I mean, after all the attempts we've made to make this happen – all the obstacles we went through just to achieve this moment … I feel like we should share this position.

DOLAN: You know me; the presidential role never suited my interest – it looks good on you, anyway. Just don't let that excitement ruin your speech, okay?

Isaim just smirks and shakes his head while the GAO leads, employees and technicians set up the broadcast transmitters that connect to each region of Bartlett's Piece.

GAO LEAD 3: (RUSHES TO ISAIM) All right, Mr. Hue, we're going to start the nationwide live broadcast in thirty seconds. We're just going to need you to stand over there. Do you have any questions, sir?

ISAIM: Just one. When can we get this over with? Can we start before the thirty seconds?

DOLAN: Don't take his demand to heart. He's been waiting for this moment ever since he came to office – you might as well give him what he wants (TURNS TO ISAIM) and hey … (ENCOURAGING) You're going to be great.

Standing in the middle of the Grand Arne Office, Isaim nods in acknowledgement and adjusts his cream business suit. Dolan and the rest of the GAO employees move out of the way and the technicians activate the broadcast transmitters for the nationwide live broadcast.

GAO TECHNICIAN 1: And we are ready to begin in three, two, one …

EXT. THE CAPITAL COURTYARD OF BARTLETT'S PIECE – AFTERNOON

All broadcast transmitters are activated across Bartlett's Piece. A hologram of Isaim appears right in front of the Capital Courtyard (as well as in every household and public area of Bartlett's Piece), as all the citizens gather around the hologram of their location, publicly and privately, and wait for the nationwide live broadcast to begin.

ISAIM: (THROUGH THE HOLOGRAM) Ladies and gentlemen, citizens of Bartlett's Piece – greetings from the Grand Arne Office. For those who do not know me, I am pleased to introduce myself to the citizens of Bartlett's Piece – one of the greatest finds in humankind's history. My name is Isaim Hue, and I am one of the founders of the contemporary system and your newly elected commander-in-chief of Bartlett's Piece.

▌ INT. THE HOUSE OF THE GRAVES FAMILY – AFTERNOON

As the commander-in-chief begins his speech, nine-year-old **Deidre Graves** and seven-year-old **Fredrick Graves**, with their sister five-year-old **Elisa Graves**, gather around a smaller version of Isaim's hologram in the family's living room. Their father, **Garreth Graves (early-forties)**, watches them closely from the couch.

SEVEN-YEAR-OLD FREDRICK: (TURNS TO GARRETH HAPPILY) Look, Dad! (POINTS TO ISAIM'S HOLOGRAM) It's the new commander-in-chief!

NINE-YEAR-OLD DEIDRE: (TURNS TO GARRETH HAPPILY) Do you think he'll be better than the old commander-in-chief. Daddy?

GARRETH: I don't know, sweetheart. We'll just have to wait and see. (POINTS TO ISAIM'S HOLOGRAM) Now pay attention to the new leader's speech so we can pledge our allegiance later on, okay?

SEVEN-YEAR-OLD FREDRICK, NINE-YEAR-OLD DEIDRE, AND FIVE-YEAR-OLD ELISA: (HAPPILY) Okay!

Nine-year-old Deidre, seven-year-old Fredrick, five-year-old Elisa and their father listen to Isaim's speech and pay close attention to his hologram.

ISAIM: (THROUGH THE HOLOGRAM) It brings me great pleasure to take the time to speak to all of you on this lovely day. I also want to take the time to say thanks to everyone who supported me throughout my campaign and put their trust in me for the future of Bartlett's Piece. Thanks to your votes, you have helped earn me a seat in the Grand Arne Office to officially become your commander-in-chief.

▌ INT. THE GRAND ARNE OFFICE – AFTERNOON

ISAIM: Now, before I lead the Pledge of Allegiance, there are a few important things I would like to address to you all. As commander-in-chief, it is my duty to assist everyone with the changes that will occur within Bartlett's Piece. Many of you are aware that a new system will be introduced that will be a subtle substitute for what was once the Metallic Order. While going through the difficult times under the old system, a colleague and I have worked hard on this project, which will help replace the old system while giving each and every one of you a chance to earn what you have always wanted.

Isaim begins to pace around in his confined space, causing almost every GAO employee to react with silent consternation. Dolan, however, snickers briefly as Isaim continues speaking.

▌ EXT. THE CAPITAL COURTYARD OF BARTLETT'S PIECE – AFTERNOON

All the citizens watch Isaim's hologram pace back and forth, while a few spectators begin to comment during his speech.

ISAIM: (THROUGH THE HOLOGRAM) This new technology created for the sake of our home has been known as revolutionary and ground-breaking to the Grand Arne Institute of Technology – which I and my companion, Dolan Wenski, were a part of before I decided to run for office. After a few trials and focus groups, we have perfected this project that we guarantee is the answer to not only speed up the recovery of Bartlett's Piece but also achieve the well-being of this great land's citizens.

MALE CITIZEN: (WHISPERS) He's sure a restless bastard, our commander-in-chief.

FEMALE CITIZEN: (WHISPERS) Shh! Our commander-in-chief is speaking. Don't you dare interrupt!

The male spectator remains quiet as the crowd continues to watch Isaim's speech.

EXT. OUTSIDE THE HOUSE OF THE GRAVES' NEIGHBOURS – AFTERNOON

A child crouches and plays around with Isaim's smaller hologram as he watches it disappear and reappear multiple times while his mother and father watch him from the porch.

FATHER: (SLIGHTLY IRRITATED) Hey, stop playing with that thing and let us watch the speech.

The mother tries to calm the father down as the child continues to play with Isaim's hologram. He stops when he sees the hologram reappear on his hand and stares at it in awe while his father begins to get irritated.

CHILD: (EXCITEDLY) Whoa, that's awesome! Check this out, Dad!

FATHER: (SLIGHTLY SOFTENS) That's cool, what you did there, son, but can you please let us watch the speech? Come sit right here with us or just stay still right there. I can't focus with him disappearing and reappearing all the time.

The child sighs as he turns back to Isaim's hologram and stares at it in awe while his parents watch the speech.

INT. THE GRAVES' HOUSE – AFTERNOON

Nine-year-old Deidre, seven-year-old Fredrick and five-year-old Elisa take turns playing with Isaim's hologram as they watch it disappear and reappear multiple times until the hologram lands on seven-year-old Fredrick's hand and begins walking on his arm.

SEVEN-YEAR-OLD FREDRICK: (EXCITEDLY) Look, he's walking on my arm!

NINE-YEAR-OLD DEIDRE: (EXCITEDLY) That's so cool! I want to try!

FIVE-YEAR-OLD ELISA: (EXCITEDLY) I want to try, too!

SEVEN-YEAR-OLD FREDRICK: (PUSHES NINE-YEAR-OLD DEIDRE AWAY) No way! I did it first!

NINE-YEAR-OLD DEIDRE: (PUSHES SEVEN-YEAR-OLD FREDRICK) No fair, Freddy! You always have all the fun!

Nine-year-old Deidre and seven-year-old Fredrick start fighting over Isaim's hologram as five-year-old Elisa gets squished in the process.

FIVE-YEAR-OLD ELISA: (STRUGGLES TO BREAK FREE) Stop it! Get off of me! Daddy!

GARRETH: (UPSET) Hey! You two get off your sister!

Garreth rescues five-year-old Elisa from nine-year-old Deidre and seven-year-old Fredrick as they continue to fight over Isaim's hologram.

GARRETH: (BREAKS UP THE FIGHT) And would you two stop fighting! That's not how you should behave during the commander-in-chief's speech!

SEVEN-YEAR-OLD FREDRICK: (UPSET) It's not my fault that Deidre tried to fight me for the hologram.

NINE-YEAR-OLD DEIDRE: (POINTS TO FIVE-YEAR-OLD ELISA) And Elisa was in my way when I totally asked first.

FIVE-YEAR-OLD ELISA: (UPSET) Hey, why are you mad at me? You guys almost killed me when I wanted to try, as well.

GARRETH: (GENTLE) Now, now, there's no need to be upset; we can all just relax and watch the speech. You can stay right here with me while your brother and sister have the floor, okay?

FIVE-YEAR-OLD ELISA: (NODS) Okay, Daddy. (TURNS TO GARRETH) But where's Mommy? Shouldn't she be here too?

GARRETH: (THINKS) You are incredibly right, Elisa! Mommy should be here too. (YELLS TO UPSTAIRS) Carman!

CARMAN: (YELLS FROM UPSTAIRS) I'm coming!

GARRETH: (YELLS TO UPSTAIRS) Hurry up! The speech has already started!

Carman Graves (mid-thirties) rushes downstairs and stops when she sees everyone gathered around Isaim's hologram and listening to his speech.

GARRETH: (KINDLY) Come take a seat, darling. You were about to miss the speech and the Pledge of Allegiance.

CARMAN: (SITS BESIDE GARRETH) Well, if I knew he was going to start so soon, I wouldn't have started the laundry already.

GARRETH: The laundry can wait. (GESTURES TO ISAIM'S HOLOGRAM) This is more important. Also, we need to teach the kids how important these announcements are so that they will know what to do in the future.

CARMAN: (SHRUGS) Well, if you say so. Might as well take a break from chores.

FIVE-YEAR-OLD ELISA: (TURNS TO CARMAN) Mommy, do you think the new commander-in-chief will do a good job?

CARMAN: I don't know for sure, Elisa. We've been living in anarchy for quite some time, so we'll just have to see if he's actually going to bring something different or we're just going to relive the Metallic Order. (IMPATIENT) He just got elected; we don't know if he's going to do what he promised to do – these politicians are all just the same.

GARRETH: Let's give the man a chance. I believe that the new system that Mr. Hue is bringing will do wonders for this place. Now stop talking and listen to the man speak.

Carman huffs impatiently as everyone watches Isaim's speech.

ISAIM: (THROUGH THE HOLOGRAM) Now I understand that all of you have questions about the new system – especially when each and every one of you has received a small part of this new technology after the election. (GESTURES TO HIS LIFE BAND) That small part of that technology is a Life Band, of course, which is a crucial component that will help implement the new system for our homes.

Nine-year-old Deidre and seven-year-old Fredrick look at their Life Bands, as Garreth shows five-year-old Elisa hers. Carman, however, looks at hers with an expression of discomfort.

▎ EXT. OUTSIDE THE NEIGHBOURS' HOUSE – AFTERNOON

The child looks at his Life Band while his parents do the same with theirs as they continue to watch Isaim's speech.

ISAIM: (THROUGH THE HOLOGRAM) This new technology may seem difficult to understand at first, as I have heard many stories of citizens trying to figure out how to use this device by themselves.

▎ EXT. THE CAPITAL COURTYARD OF BARTLETT'S PIECE – AFTERNOON

Every person in the crowd observes their own Life Bands as they continue to watch Isaim's speech.

ISAIM: (THROUGH THE HOLOGRAM) But as we go through today's presentation, I hope to succeed at demonstrating the many wonders of this device to all of you. This small device will help you be a part of this country's recovery, but it can also help you become the best version of yourselves. You may think that it's impossible for a device to have such capabilities – that it's just a tiny bracelet that could never be as powerful as the commander-in-chief says it is. But believe me, when I tell you this, it's a whole lot more than what you think it is, and the people who have tested this device with me all agree. This device will grow with you, it will have a connection with you, and it will make you see things – learn things about yourself that you never thought about searching for using traditional methods. Now, I'm aware that there are citizens who seem very apprehensive about this new technology but just to reassure everyone that everything that is connected to you and this device will remain confidential under the Grand Arne Concealment Act, as every single one of you has the right to their own privacy.

Everyone begins cheering for joy and commenting to each other about the Grand Arne Concealment Act and Isaim himself as he smiles through his hologram.

ISAIM: (THROUGH THE HOLOGRAM) I can tell that has everyone excited. Now that, hopefully, I have cleared up any ambiguity, shall we get started?

INT. THE COMMANDER'S ROOM OF THE GRAND ARNE OFFICE – AFTERNOON

Isaim hears the cheers through the speakers as he smiles and chuckles to himself.

ISAIM: (POINTS TO THE MONOGRAM ON HIS LIFE BAND) As you can see on mine and your Life Bands, there is a monogram in the middle of your wrist that bears an I and an H – and believe me, it's not there to be aesthetically pleasing. (GENTLY PRESSES THE MONOGRAM) By pressing onto the monogram as if it were a button, it will open up the device's abilities, which will automatically be prompted to activate using your voice and your voice only. (TO HIS LIFE BAND) Activate Life Band.

LIFE BAND AI: Life Band activated.

As the monogram of Isaim's Life Band lights up, he quickly grabs a portable lamp for his demonstration.

LIFE BAND AI: Hello, Mr. Isaim Hue. What can I do for you today?

ISAIM: Access all connected devices.

LIFE BAND AI: Accessing all connected devices. What would you like to do with these connected devices, Mr. Hue?

ISAIM: Activate this lamp for me, please.

LIFE BAND AI: Activating lamp.

The portable lamp automatically turns on as Dolan celebrates silently.

EXT. THE CAPITAL COURTYARD OF BARTLETT'S PIECE – AFTERNOON

Everyone sees the portable lamp turn on as they stand there in awe and give Isaim a round of applause.

ISAIM: (THROUGH THE HOLOGRAM) Amazing, isn't it? Now I know what you're thinking: turning on a lamp using only your voice isn't as innovative as I have described this device as being capable of. However, it is one of the key features that has become a favourite of the Grand Arne Institute of Technology. I also did that simple demonstration just to show you that it's actually working.

INT. THE COMMANDER'S ROOM OF THE GRAND ARNE OFFICE – AFTERNOON

ISAIM: (PUTS THE LAMP AWAY) Plus, that's not the only thing the Life Band can do. Life Band, access personal information, please.

LIFE BAND AI: Accessing personal information.

A hologram screen of Isaim's personal information appears right in front of him, while the GAO leads, employees and technicians watch in awe.

ISAIM: Of course, this is for your own eyes only, but once registered with the new system, you will be able to have access to everything about yourself and update information just as easily as turning on this device. (CONTROLS THE HOLOGRAM SCREEN) Not only will you gain the basics.

EXT. THE CAPITAL COURTYARD OF BARTLETT'S PIECE – AFTERNOON

ISAIM: (THROUGH THE HOLOGRAM) You can also access information about your health and finances. (LOOKS AT HIS EXPENSES) Looks like I have a bill to take care of after this speech.

Everyone in the crowd laughs while they continue to watch Isaim's speech.

ISAIM: (THROUGH THE HOLOGRAM) As well as your status – just to see which phase you're in. Whether you are in your Tint Phase, your Canvas Phase, your Hue Phase or your Shade Phase.

Everyone in the audience is confused, and they begin to murmur among themselves during Isaim's speech.

INT. THE COMMANDER'S ROOM OF THE GRAND ARNE OFFICE – AFTERNOON

ISAIM: Now you're probably wondering why the commander-in-chief would mention these weird names and what significance does it have for me and this country? Allow me to demonstrate … (TO HIS LIFE BAND) Life Band, enable Roles Mode.

LIFE BAND AI: Enabling Roles Mode.

Isaim's suit turns charcoal grey as the GAO leads, employees and technicians react with shock, while Dolan smiles proudly.

EXT. OUTSIDE THE NEIGHBOUR'S HOUSE – AFTERNOON

The child watches Isaim's suit turn grey through the hologram as he gasps with excitement.

CHILD: (EXCITEDLY) Whoa! Mom! Dad! Did you see that!

MOTHER: (EXCITEDLY) His suit turned completely grey! (TURNS TO FATHER) Isn't that exciting?

The father just shrugs and sits there in slight discomfort while his wife and child watch Isaim's speech in awe.

INT. THE COMMANDER'S ROOM OF THE GRAND ARNE OFFICE – AFTERNOON

ISAIM: As you can see, this is not just a simple wardrobe change, as this is just the very beginning of the implementation of the new system. This is the Tint Phase, the phase that most of you are going to stay in for a while – especially the children. (PULLS A MODIFIER OUT OF HIS POCKET) Now, I'm going to add a Modifier to my Life Band just to demonstrate the different phases to everyone who is kindly watching. However, not everyone will have access to a device like this, as it is strictly used for this presentation.

Isaim places the Modifier on the monogram of his Life Band, causing the device itself to light up. The GAO leads, employees and technicians look on in wonder and anxiety, while Dolan waits in anticipation.

ISAIM: Everyone will start with this shade of grey – 80% grey, to be exact – but no one is going to stay like this forever. As you begin your developmental progress – or shall I say, live your life – you'll begin to notice that your tint will start to become lighter and lighter from time to time.

Isaim turns the Modifier clockwise as the colour of his grey suit turns lighter and lighter, while the GAO employees' mouths widen in shock.

INT. THE GRAVES' HOUSE – AFTERNOON

As nine-year-old Deidre, seven-year-old Fredrick and five-year-old Elisa watch Isaim's grey suit turn lighter and lighter, they gasp in excitement and their parents look on in astonishment.

SEVEN-YEAR-OLD FREDRICK AND NINE-YEAR-OLD DEIDRE: (EXCITEDLY) So cool!

FIVE-YEAR-OLD ELISA: (EXCITEDLY) Mommy, did you see that?

CARMAN: (IN DISBELIEF) What is he? A magician? I bet that thing is not actually working and he has people doing that behind the scenes.

GARRETH: (TURNS TO CARMAN) Don't say such a thing like that in front of the children. Allow them to be amazed by their new leader. Plus, I think it's cool too.

Carman just shakes her head while she and everyone else watch Isaim's speech.

ISAIM: (THROUGH THE HOLOGRAM) I can tell that has got some children excited, but it's not going to be as quick as I just demonstrated.

INT. THE COMMANDER'S ROOM OF THE GRAND ARNE OFFICE – AFTERNOON

ISAIM: Depending on the individual, some of you will reach the second phase faster, but that should never distress those individuals who will take longer than others. Growth is the key factor in helping you reach the second phase – your Life Band depends more on your mental growth than physical growth, and before you can even see it for yourself.

INT. THE GRAVES' HOUSE – AFTERNOON

Isaim turns the Modifier clockwise as his suit turns completely white, as nine-year-old Deidre and seven-year-old Fredrick watch in awe.

ISAIM: (THROUGH THE HOLOGRAM) You're already in the second phase. The Canvas Phase, of course.

NINE-YEAR-OLD DEIDRE: (EXCITEDLY) Whoa!

SEVEN-YEAR-OLD FREDRICK: (EXCITEDLY) That is awesome!

EXT. THE CAPITAL COURTYARD OF BARTLETT'S PIECE – AFTERNOON

ISAIM: (THROUGH THE HOLOGRAM) The Canvas Phase is sort of your freedom phase – a chance for you to get to know yourselves and figure out and discover the person that has been inside you for years. Let's just say that this phase is giving you a chance to explore – be reckless, be courageous, do things that you have never done before, do things that your parents told you not to do – just as long as you do it responsibly and it doesn't put you and anyone else in harm's way.

MALE CITIZEN: (TURNS TO FEMALE CITIZEN) I'm beginning to like this fella.

FEMALE CITIZEN: (TURNS TO MALE CITIZEN) There's so many things I would love to do.

The male citizen nods in agreement as they turn back to watch Isaim's speech.

ISAIM: (THROUGH THE HOLOGRAM) For you to reach the third phase, you have to really marinate yourself in the second phase.

INT. THE COMMANDER'S ROOM OF THE GRAND ARNE OFFICE – AFTERNOON

ISAIM: Nothing is more important than finding out who you truly are – that's another key component to reaching the third phase. You work at your fullest ability when you've reached your fullest potential.

Isaim continues his commentary, while some of the GAO leads, employees and technicians murmur amongst themselves.

GAO EMPLOYEE 8: (WHISPERS) He's really passionate, this one, especially about the new technology that he's bringing to the table.

GAO TECHNICIAN 2: (WHISPERS) Don't get too excited; he still has time to become worse than the other commander-in-chief.

DOLAN: (LOWLY) Don't talk during the commander-in-chief's speech. If you're not interested in sticking around, then go outside.

The GAO employees and technicians who were talking shut their mouths while the rest keep quiet during Isaim's speech.

ISAIM: Now, transferring to the third phase is a little different than the second phase – a lot different, if I must clarify – and it's not going to happen in just one shot, as the transformation will take some encouragement from nature – water, to be exact – to make that happen.

Dolan grabs a glass of water, hands it to Isaim and gives him an encouraging nod before standing by during the speech.

ISAIM: The reason water is the only thing that can activate this transformation is because it will help us determine those who are truly ready for the third phase. Those few will be the ones to help us build back the glory that Bartlett's Piece once had before it was taken away by the Metallic Order, and there's no better way to rebuild this country than by having the citizens who live here assist us in doing so. Now I did say that only a few of you will reach this phase earlier than others, as it doesn't happen in one shot. However, not to worry, everyone, as it's never a bad sign. You just need to explore more … and when you find the essence of your true self …

Isaim dips his sleeve into the glass of water and he watches part of his sleeve turn red, while Dolan tries his best to contain his excitement.

EXT. THE CAPITAL COURTYARD OF BARTLETT'S PIECE – AFTERNOON

The entire crowd gasps in shock and murmurs among themselves as they watch Isaim's hologram dip his sleeve into the glass of water, and it turns red.

ISAIM: (THROUGH THE HOLOGRAM) Every single one of you will have a chance to show your true colours.

Awestruck, the entire crowd gives Isaim a round of applause.

ISAIM: (THROUGH THE HOLOGRAM) Intriguing, isn't it? It's amazing what technology can do for us, personally and generally. I must share some precautions with you all – the last thing I need is for anyone to pour glasses of water on themselves, go swimming in lakes or oceans or deliberately take a shower with your clothes on – it's not going to work like that if you try force the transformation to happen. So, if I'm telling you not to do the things that I have listed for you, how is it possible to encounter a large amount of water to be safely promoted to the third phase? Perhaps this will give you a clue.

Isaim pulls out a small device that quickly shows an umbrella hologram, drawing exclamations of wonder from everyone in the crowd.

ISAIM: (THROUGH THE HOLOGRAM) Rain follows a natural process of its own as it goes through a water cycle that gives back what the sun has taken away by its heat. Plus, we have created this transformation to respond only to rainwater and nothing else, so you don't have to do the things I just mentioned – just wait for the rain to come and it will help you reach your third phase.

INT. THE COMMANDER'S ROOM OF THE GRAND ARNE OFFICE – AFTERNOON

ISAIM: I can't possibly guarantee that you won't get sick from this, but I can reassure you that it is less dangerous than the other options. Not only will you receive an experience you get to share with Mother Nature herself, but the creators of the Life Band would like you to have a little fun with this transformation while you enjoy the last bits of freedom in the Canvas Phase. (GIVES DOLAN THE SMALL DEVICE AND THE GLASS OF WATER) Thank you for standing by, Mr. Wenski. Do you mind giving a wave to our fellow citizens?

EXT. THE CAPITAL COURTYARD OF BARTLETT'S PIECE – AFTERNOON

Half of Dolan's body appears in the hologram as he waves hello before disappearing, and the crowd cheers in excitement.

FEMALE CITIZEN: (EXCITEDLY) Oh my goodness, he just waved to us – how exciting!

ISAIM: (THROUGH THE HOLOGRAM) Sounds like you have some fans out there, Mr. Wenski.

DOLAN: (THROUGH THE HOLOGRAM) No need to pay attention to that, Mr. Hue. Just focus on your presentation.

ISAIM: (THROUGH THE HOLOGRAM) That's right, we must continue – otherwise, the staff will be upset with us if we don't get to the Pledge of Allegiance.

Everyone lets out a genuine laugh as Isaim smiles at the crowd through the hologram.

▌ INT. THE COMMANDER'S ROOM OF THE GRAND ARNE OFFICE – AFTERNOON

ISAIM: Now that you've gotten yourself soaked in rain and have taken a moment to dry off, you have reached the most important phase of your life.

Isaim presses a button on the Modifier that causes his suit to turn fully red. All the GAO employees gasp in shock and drop whatever they have in their hands.

▌ EXT. THE CAPITAL COURTYARD OF BARTLETT'S PIECE – AFTERNOON

The entire crowd watches Isaim's suit turn fully red through the hologram as they gasp in shock and give him a round of applause.

ISAIM: (THROUGH THE HOLOGRAM) This is the Hue Phase. Not named after me, of course; the name was inspired by the invention of one of the greatest scientists who has ever existed on this earth – that is, the colour wheel. Invented by Isaac Newton, the colour wheel displays the relationships between each of the twelve hues represented in that chart.

▌ INT. THE GRAND ARNE OFFICE – AFTERNOON

ISAIM: However, in our case, they are not just primary, secondary and tertiary hues for the sake of us to remember, as we decided to add another element to solidify the significance of these hues: the PESTEL Analysis. This was created by another professor, whom we do not have time to speak about due to more important matters. During the Hue

Phase, each hue represents a different role – the role you're going to play in the recovery process of Bartlett's Piece. A hue will be chosen for you based on your personality, interests and abilities. Once you begin living your life, becoming your most authentic self, the Life Band will begin to pick up little bits of information about yourself while it tries to depict which of these twelve roles best suits you. However, since we might not have the time to explain all the roles, we'll only focus on the six main hues on the colour wheel. Like the hue I'm wearing now, for example, red – a powerful hue to receive if you're into politics, but maybe that's not the hue you might end up with.

▍ EXT. THE CAPITAL COURTYARD OF BARTLETT'S PIECE – AFTERNOON

Isaim presses the button on the Modifier to make his suit turn orange as everyone in the crowd gasps and exclaims in astonishment.

ISAIM: (THROUGH THE HOLOGRAM) Maybe orange will be your hue if you're interested in economics.

▍ EXT. OUTSIDE THE NEIGHBOUR'S HOUSE – AFTERNOON

Isaim presses the button on the Modifier to make his suit turn yellow, and the child and his parents look on in shock.

ISAIM: (THROUGH THE HOLOGRAM) How about those who are interested in technology? Yellow is definitely your hue.

CHILD: (EXCITEDLY) Whoa, cool! (TURNS TO HIS PARENTS) Mom, Dad, did you see that!

FATHER: (SHOCKED) What kind of sorcery is he using?

▍ INT. THE GRAVES' HOUSE – AFTERNOON

Isaim presses the button on the Modifier to make his suit turn green as nine-year-old Deidre, seven-year-old Fredrick and five-year-old Elisa gasp in excitement and Garreth looks impressed.

ISAIM: (THROUGH THE HOLOGRAM) Perhaps you have a green thumb – green has always been a suitable hue for environmentalists.

Nine-year-old Deidre, seven-year-old Fredrick and five-year-old Elisa clap in excitement while Carman sits there in disbelief.

SEVEN-YEAR-OLD FREDRICK: (EXCITEDLY) That's so cool! Dad, can I be green?

GARRETH: (SMILES) You can be whatever you want, son, just as long as you're happy with your hue.

FIVE-YEAR-OLD ELISA: (TURNS TO GARRETH) Daddy, can I be yellow? I think yellow is a happy hue.

GARRETH: (SMILES) Of course you can be yellow, Elisa – you've always been the happy one. But I do see you as red; you're quite the bossy type, like your mother.

CARMAN: (CURT) Now don't you go there. Aren't we supposed to be watching the speech?

Garreth and five-year-old Elisa giggle silently and go back to watching the speech with everyone else.

EXT. THE CAPITAL COURTYARD OF BARTLETT'S PIECE – AFTERNOON

Isaim presses the button on the Modifier to make his suit turn tooth as the entire crowd oohs in excitement.

ISAIM: (THROUGH THE HOLOGRAM) What about those who want to be in the legal system. Do you see yourself sporting blue in your future?

MALE CITIZEN: (TURNS TO FEMALE CITIZEN) I would love to receive that hue.

The female citizen nods in agreement as they turn back to Isaim's hologram to watch the presentation.

INT. THE COMMANDER'S ROOM OF THE GRAND ARNE OFFICE – AFTERNOON

As Isaim presses the button on the Modifier to make his suit turn purple, the GAO leads, employees and technicians look on in shock.

ISAIM: Or maybe you're more drawn to the social aspects of the country; purple definitely fits the role quite nicely.

GAO TECHNICIAN 2: (WHISPERS) Is he insane? How will we ever catch up to–

GAO EMPLOYEE 8: (WHISPERS) Shh! Mr. Wenski will get angry with us again.

Dolan shoots a stern look at the GAO employees and technicians who are talking, so they become silent and watch Isaim's speech.

EXT. THE CAPITAL COURTYARD OF BARTLETT'S PIECE – AFTERNOON

ISAIM: (THROUGH THE HOLOGRAM) As you can see, each hue on the colour wheel – especially the hues I haven't mentioned – represents a role for each of the factors of a PESTEL Analysis. Each and every one of you can be part of these six systems: the Political system, the Economic system, the Social system, the Technological system, the Environmental system and the Legal system. No role is more important than any other; no role is less important than any other. No role can function or create a relationship without the others as they all end up working together at the end of the day – just like the colour wheel itself. So, don't feel bad if you don't receive the hue of your choice, as each role is significant for Bartlett's Piece to start running like the productive country it once was.

Isaim presses the button on the Modifier to make his suit turn red-purple as the entire crowd gives him a round of applause.

ISAIM: (THROUGH THE HOLOGRAM) You might even receive a tertiary hue if you're a natural born multi-tasker – especially if you see yourself as filling more than just one role. Does that seem to fit you?

The entire crowd gives Isaim a round of applause as he smiles at the audience through the hologram.

ISAIM: (THROUGH THE HOLOGRAM) Not only will the Hue Phase enable the entire community from each region to build back what was once lost, but the entire purpose of this phase is to remove what the past brought to us and replace it with something more colourful in our future. One thing to keep in mind is that once you receive your hue, you will stay that hue for the rest of your life, and under no circumstances will you be allowed to change it. The Hue that was given to you highlights your strengths better than the Hue you wish you had received. And how would you know which Hue you will receive? You don't. You never will until you have lived through your Canvas Phase, and if you need desperately to find that out, all you have to do is stand in the rain and see your true colours for yourselves.

Each and every person in the crowd allows Isaim's words to sink in about staying one Hue in the Hue Phase. Some attempt to find peace within themselves, while others begin to have mixed emotions as they continue to watch the speech.

INT. THE COMMANDER'S ROOM OF THE GRAND ARNE OFFICE – AFTERNOON

ISAIM: Last but not least, we have entered a phase that is less exciting and quite unfortunate. And I say this because it relates to one of the greatest fears we have in life, as it gives us that kick-in-the-gut reminder of something that some of you may have been denying for quite some time ... that is, we're getting old.

The GAO leads, employees and technicians struggle to contain their laughter in front of Isaim and Dolan and instead let out a small smile while hearing laughter erupt throughout the speakers.

ISAIM: The phase I'm talking about is the Shade Phase – I repeat, not the most exciting phase of the phases, but it couldn't be excluded as it was a recurrence during our tests with the Life Band.

EXT. THE CAPITAL COURTYARD OF BARTLETT'S PIECE – AFTERNOON

ISAIM: (THROUGH THE HOLOGRAM) What happens in the Shade Phase is that you still get to keep the hue – and you still get to continue your part in the role that is based on the hue. It starts just like the Tint Phase, but has the opposite effect, because as you continue to live your life and do what you need to do for your family and Bartlett's Piece ... you will begin to notice that your hue starts to get darker and darker from time to time.

Isaim turns the Modifier counter clockwise as the colour of his red-purple suit turns darker and darker. Seeing this, the entire crowd exclaims in astonishment but can't hide their sadness as they watch Isaim's suit turn darker and darker.

EXT. OUTSIDE THE NEIGHBOUR'S HOUSE – AFTERNOON

ISAIM: (THROUGH THE HOLOGRAM) Furthermore, the Shade Phase affects others than those who are much older than us and have already started aging. Whether you are a child, a teenager or an adult – it also affects anyone who is going through an illness.

The child begins to pout while his mother and father allow Isaim's words to sink in while they hold each other's hands.

INT. THE GRAVES' HOUSE – AFTERNOON

ISAIM: (THROUGH THE HOLOGRAM) Now the last thing I want to do is scare you ... but as your commander-in-chief, I think it is important for you to know about the Shade Phase because, unlike the other phases I've discussed with you, it can come on at any time at any phase.

Garett and Carman look at each other in worry as they begin to have concerns about themselves and the children.

ISAIM: (THROUGH THE HOLOGRAM) Yes, you heard it right, ladies and gentlemen. The Shade Phase can sneak up on you at any time in your life. Whether you are a Tint, a Canvas or a Hue, once you begin to notice yourselves getting darker and darker day by day … that's when you know you're in the Shade Phase.

Garreth tightly holds onto five-year-old Elisa, while Carman encourages nine-year-old Deidre and seven-year-old Fredrick to sit on the couch.

EXT. THE CAPITAL COURTYARD OF BARTLETT'S PIECE – AFTERNOON

ISAIM: (THROUGH THE HOLOGRAM) The last thing I want is for anyone to be scared or plan a funeral anytime soon.

The entire crowd lets out a pleasant laugh to ease the tension as Isaim smiles and laughs with the audience through the hologram.

ISAIM: (THROUGH THE HOLOGRAM) That's what I like to hear – a little laughter to help brighten the mood … because the Shade Phase is not as bad as it seems. Yes, the Life Band can detect sicknesses and anything that can affect your health, which can cause the Shade Phase to activate. But if it's just a temporary ailment, then it's completely fine – you don't have to worry about the Shade Phase appearing due to a simple sneeze.

The entire crowd laughs even louder as they continue to watch Isaim's speech.

INT. THE COMMANDER'S ROOM OF THE GRAND ARNE OFFICE – AFTERNOON

ISAIM: You can go ahead and live your life and continue to work toward your phases without having the Shade Phase affect your life – and even if it has already started, it can be delayed. All you need to do is pay attention to your health … that's all there is about the Shade Phase – it's really about what you can do for yourself, health wise.

As the GAO employees take in Isaim's words, they take a moment to look at each other.

ISAIM: By understanding your limitations and taking the necessary precautions to improve your health, you are able to continue living the way you want to live and prevent the phase from going any further. The Shade Phase can also give you a chance to reflect on what you want to do after you've completed your time in the Hue Phase. Think of it as your retirement phase, when you see your hue getting darker and darker by the minute.

EXT. THE CAPITAL COURTYARD OF BARTLETT'S PIECE – AFTERNOON

ISAIM: (THROUGH THE HOLOGRAM) This will also give you a chance to think about the stuff you haven't done in life, the people you haven't talked to in years, the issues that you have yet to resolve with yourself, as well as with other people. These are the moments you should never take for granted during the Shade Phase ... because by the time the opportunity comes to you on a silver platter, it won't take long for the Shade Phase to activate, and you may see yourself turn completely black.

Isaim turns the Modifier counter clockwise as the crowd watches his suit turn completely black.

INT. THE COMMANDER'S ROOM OF THE GRAND ARNE OFFICE – AFTERNOON

Isaim removes the Modifier from his Life Band as his suit turns back to its previous cream colour. As he puts away the Modifier, he turns back to the broadcast transmitters to continue his speech.

ISAIM: I know this is a lot to take in during the first speech of the new commander-in-chief, and it is absolutely understandable if any of you missed anything that I have said to you for the past few hours. Not to worry. Once the Pledge of Allegiance has been completed, everyone will receive a copy of it.

EXT. THE CAPITAL COURTYARD OF BARTLETT'S PIECE – AFTERNOON

Isaim pulls out the small device again to show a hologram of the Laws and Regulations of the Hue System as everyone murmurs in awe.

ISAIM: (THROUGH THE HOLOGRAM) This book will offer you everything you need to know about how the Life Band works, as well as the new system itself. Think of it as a guideline for the new Bartlett's Piece. As I and my colleagues call it, the Laws and Regulations of the Hue System – or the LRHS if you like abbreviations. It's important for all citizens not only to be aware of what's about to happen in this country, but also to be a part of the change. This time, no one will have to live in fear – no one will have their rights stripped away and have to suppress their true selves to live a life that brings no benefits whatsoever. This time, you have control over the outcome of your life. This time, you get to achieve what you've always wanted to achieve. This time ... you can finally get what you want, and this new system will help you get whatever you want.

Everyone in the crowd begins to cheer as Isaim takes a brief break from his speech.

INT. THE COMMANDER'S ROOM OF THE GRAND ARNE OFFICE – AFTERNOON

ISAIM: Now, with that being said, I would like to ask each and every one of you to press the monogram on your Life Bands to begin the Pledge of Allegiance.

EXT. OUTSIDE THE NEIGHBOUR'S HOUSE – AFTERNOON

The child presses the monogram on his Life Band, as the mother and father do the same on theirs.

ISAIM: (THROUGH THE HOLOGRAM) And for the parents out there, I ask that you assist your children to do the same as they get to be a part of this transformation as well.

INT. THE GRAVES' HOUSE – AFTERNOON

Garreth and Carman press the monogram on their Life Bands and help nine-year-old Deidre, seven-year-old Fredrick and five-year-old Elisa do the same with theirs.

ISAIM: (THROUGH THE HOLOGRAM) Things are going to be different from now on, as I hope to continue this new system for years and centuries to come.

EXT. THE CAPITAL COURTYARD OF BARTLETT'S PIECE – AFTERNOON

Everyone in the crowd presses the monogram on their Life Bands as they continue to listen to Isaim's speech.

ISAIM: (THROUGH THE HOLOGRAM) But I promise you, I will be there for you the entire way and help guide you through this change that will bring us to a better place.

INT. THE COMMANDER'S ROOM OF THE GRAND ARNE OFFICE – AFTERNOON

The GAO leads, employees and technicians, along with Dolan, press the monograms on their Life Bands as they wait for Isaim to do the same and begin the Pledge of Allegiance.

ISAIM: (RAISES HIS LEFT HAND) Now raise your left hand and repeat after me.

The GAO leads, employees and technicians, along with Dolan, raise their left hands as Isaim begins the Pledge of Allegiance.

ISAIM: I swear wholeheartedly on my own life.

DOLAN, GAO LEADS, EMPLOYEES AND TECHNICIANS: (IN UNISON) I swear wholeheartedly on my own life.

ISAIM: That I will be a responsible law-abiding citizen of Bartlett's Piece.

DOLAN, GAO LEADS, EMPLOYEES AND TECHNICIANS: (IN UNISON) That I will be a responsible law-abiding citizen of Bartlett's Piece.

▌ EXT. OUTSIDE THE NEIGHBOUR'S HOUSE – AFTERNOON

ISAIM: (THROUGH THE HOLOGRAM) I promise to serve my purpose to help continue the productivity of this country.

CHILD, MOTHER AND FATHER: (IN UNISON) I promise to serve my purpose to help continue the productivity of this country.

ISAIM: (THROUGH THE HOLOGRAM) And participate in every event and regional action that has been ordered by the commander-in-chief.

CHILD, MOTHER AND FATHER: (IN UNISON) And participate in every event and regional action that has been ordered by the commander-in-chief.

▌ INT. THE GRAVES' HOUSE – AFTERNOON

ISAIM: (THROUGH THE HOLOGRAM) I promise to protect the moral values and regional cultures of this country.

GARRETH, CARMAN, NINE-YEAR-OLD DEIDRE, SEVEN-YEAR-OLD FREDRICK AND FIVE-YEAR-OLD ELISA: (IN UNISON) I promise to protect the moral values and regional cultures of this country.

ISAIM: (THROUGH THE HOLOGRAM) And protect all the citizens that live in it.

GARRETH, CARMAN, NINE-YEAR-OLD DEIDRE, SEVEN-YEAR-OLD FREDRICK AND FIVE-YEAR-OLD ELISA: (IN UNISON) And protect all the citizens that live in it.

Five-year-old Elisa giggles as she holds onto Garreth tightly, while he makes sure she pays attention to the Pledge of Allegiance.

▌ EXT. THE CAPITAL COURTYARD OF BARTLETT'S PIECE – AFTERNOON

ISAIM: (THROUGH THE HOLOGRAM) I promise to obey every law and regulation set by the commander-in-chief and the Grand Arne Office itself.

EVERYONE: (IN UNISON) I promise to obey every law and regulation set by the commander-in-chief and the Grand Arne Office itself.

ISAIM: (THROUGH THE HOLOGRAM) And if ever broken, to face the consequences of every wrongdoing I commit.

EVERYONE: (IN UNISON) And if ever broken, to face the consequences of every wrongdoing I commit.

▌ INT. THE COMMANDER'S ROOM OF THE GRAND ARNE OFFICE – AFTERNOON

ISAIM: As the lives, the land and the well-being of Bartlett's Piece depend on every action I take.

DOLAN, GAO LEADS, EMPLOYEES AND TECHNICIANS: (IN UNISON) As the lives, the land and the well-being of Bartlett's Piece depend on every action I take.

ISAIM: With the hope for peace and love for our beloved home ...

Isaim closes his eyes and performs the commencement ritual for the Grand Arne Office, as everyone present does the same to accept his leadership. As Isaim finishes performing the commencement ritual, he opens his eyes and smiles.

▌ EXT. THE CAPITAL COURTYARD OF BARTLETT'S PIECE – AFTERNOON

ISAIM: (THROUGH THE HOLOGRAM) Let the change begin!

Everyone in the crowd begins to cheer for Isaim as confetti cannons go off and scatter multi-coloured confetti everywhere. Everyone starts jumping up and down as they get excited about the changes that will occur in Bartlett's Piece.

ELISA: (NARRATES) That was the scene in every part of the country ... in every household after we had pledged allegiance to Isaim Hue and his new creation, the Hue System.

▌ EXT. OUTSIDE THE NEIGHBOUR'S HOUSE – AFTERNOON

The child jumps and dances for joy as the mother and father watch happily and get excited about the changes that are going to occur in Bartlett's Piece.

ELISA: (NARRATES) Everyone seemed to be excited about what was about to come.

▌ INT. THE COMMANDER'S ROOM OF THE GRAND ARNE OFFICE – AFTERNOON

Dolan claps aggressively for Isaim, as do the GAO leads, employees and technicians. Isaim turns to Dolan with a big smile on his face, excited for the changes that he will bring to Bartlett's Piece.

ELISA: (NARRATES) But did it actually work?

▌ INT. THE GRAVES' HOUSE – AFTERNOON

Garreth watches nine-year-old Deidre, seven-year-old Fredrick and five-year-old Elisa jump on the couch happily as Carman tries to get them to calm down.

ELISA: (NARRATES) However, did everyone get what they wanted?

Sixteen Years Later

▌INT. ELISA'S BEDROOM – MORNING

As the alarm clock sounds, **Elisa Graves (early-twenties)** wakes slowly from her sleep before putting it on snooze.

HOUSE AI: Alarm set on Snooze Mode. Your alarm will reactivate in sixty seconds.

Elisa covers herself with a blanket and turns away from the alarm clock as the House AI begins the countdown.

HOUSE AI: Alarm set on Snooze Mode. Your alarm will reactivate in thirty seconds.

Elisa growls through her pillow before she gets up from bed and stretches her arms.

HOUSE AI: Alarm set on Snooze Mode. Your alarm will reactivate in fifteen seconds.

Elisa opens the curtains to let the natural grey light in her room before turning to her alarm clock.

HOUSE AI: Your alarm will reactivate in ten, nine, eight, seven, six, five, four, three, two, one –

Elisa walks toward the bedside table to turn off the alarm before it sounds and sits on the edge of the bed.

HOUSE AI: Alarm dismissed. Good morning, Elisa Graves.

Elisa sighs to herself as she thinks about going to work today.

▌ INT. THE BATHROOM OF ELISA'S BEDROOM – MORNING

Elisa brushes her teeth while listening to the House AI's route updates on the Tint Valley Transit Services.

HOUSE AI: Route 311 is temporarily out of service for maintenance purposes. Route 422 is open for service; however, users can expect to experience delays.

The House AI continues to give route updates on the Tint Valley Transit Services as Elisa rinses her mouth in the sink before looking at herself in the mirror and making a subtle change to her hair.

▌ INT. ELISA'S BEDROOM – MORNING

Elisa looks through all the clothes in her closet as she tries to figure out what to wear for work.

ELISA: House, what's the weather for today?

HOUSE AI: Today's temperature is eighteen degrees, with a slight chance of rain. An umbrella and a light raincoat are the most suitable for such conditions.

Elisa pulls out one of her favourite fall coats and sees it changing to her current Tint Level before grabbing other items to complete her outfit.

▌ INT. ELISA'S APARTMENT – MORNING

Elisa grabs her purse and the keys to her apartment and attempts to leave until she hears a Notification Alert go off.

HOUSE AI: Notification Alert! Your Life Band has detected low nutrient levels in your body. It is advised that you start the day with a meal to bring up your nutrient levels.

ELISA: House, how much time do I have to get to work?

HOUSE AI: You have two hours and fifty-five minutes to arrive at WORK. It is advised that you start the day with a meal to bring up your nutrient levels.

ELISA: (HUFFS IMPATIENTLY) All right. What's in the fridge?

HOUSE AI: The refrigerator contains eggs, cheese, milk, tomatoes, lettuce, green peppers, red peppers, sausage, deli meats and mushrooms. Suggested recipes that include these items are the Classic Omelette; oil, salt and pepper must be included in this recipe. The Classic Breakfast Sandwich; bread, oil, salt and pepper must be included in this recipe. Ham and Cheese Breakfast Rollups; bread and butter must be included in this recipe.

The House AI continues to give breakfast recipes as Elisa stands there contemplating having breakfast before work.

A Few Minutes Later

❙ INT. ELISA'S APARTMENT – MORNING

Elisa eats her omelette as she watches the news to pass the time.

NEWS REPORTER: Thank you, Pat, for that weather forecast. We will definitely be bundling up for the next few days. This just in: another missing person report has been issued to Steels Protection Services. Family members of Heather Grace said that she was last seen at a local playground near Tint Valley.

The news reporter continues to talk about the missing person report as Elisa slowly begins to become anxious about the time while finishing up her omelette.

ELISA: House, how much time do I have to get to work?

HOUSE AI: You have an hour and fifty-seven minutes to arrive at WORK. (NOTIFICATION ALERT GOES OFF) Notification Alert! Your Life Band continues to detect low nutrient levels in your body; it is advised that you start the day with –

ELISA: (GETS UP AND PUTS AWAY HER PLATE) Turn the TV off.

HOUSE AI: Television off.

▌ EXT. OUTSIDE THE TINT VALLEY RESIDENCE – MORNING

Elisa leaves the residence building and quickly jogs her way to the Route 533 bus stop before it arrives. Everyone who is already at the bus stop chats amongst themselves, as the Route 533 bus pulls over to pick them up. Elisa gets slightly distracted, watching everyone talk among themselves until she feels the rush in the crowds. She quickly gets on and pays her fare with her Life Band.

▌ INT. INSIDE THE ROUTE 533 BUS – MORNING

Everyone in the bus minds their own business as they chat amongst themselves and their Life Bands, while the bus driver continues to drive the usual route.

FEMALE PASSENGER 1: Life Band. Check what shows are playing nearby.

LIFE BAND AI: Here are the results of shows now playing near your location.

MALE PASSENGER 1: Life Band, how much time do I have to get to work?

LIFE BAND AI: You have twenty-five minutes to arrive at WORK.

The male passenger grimaces worriedly, while Elisa silently watches everyone on the bus talking to their Life Bands. She continues to look around the bus mindlessly until she notices a male passenger whose Tint Level is lighter than the rest of the passengers.

MALE PASSENGER 2: Life Band, check my current Phase Status.

LIFE BAND AI: Here are the results of your Phase Status. Your Phase Status is Tint, and your current Tint Level is 35%.

MALE PASSENGER 2: (SMILES HAPPILY) Nice. Just a few more days and I will be out of this Tint Valley for good.

Elisa quickly looks away and stares at her clothes, which reveal her current Tint Level. For the rest of the ride, she tries her best not to think about the past and to just enjoy her freedom.

▌ EXT. OUTSIDE THE REGIONAL HEADQUARTERS – MORNING

Outside of Regional Headquarters, everyone talks amongst themselves and their Life Bands as they quickly make their way inside the building. Route 533 pulls over to the last bus stop; everyone inside, including Elisa, quickly exits the bus and rushes to get inside the building.

▌ INT. REGIONAL HEADQUARTERS – MORNING

Once inside the building, everyone forms a line near the entrance portals. The RH security guards make sure that everyone scans their Life Bands before entering the building even further.

RH SECURITY GUARD 1: All right, everyone, let's arrive safely. There's no need to rush!

RH SECURITY GUARD 2: Just make sure you scan your Life Band so you can enter safely. (STOPS MALE EMPLOYEE 1 MIDWAY) Hey, I need to see your bag first.

MALE EMPLOYEE 1: (SLIGHTLY HOSTILE) Okay, take it easy. (TAKES OFF HIS BAG) Just let me get myself organized first.

The RH security guard searches through the bag before giving it back to the male employee as he lets him scan his Life Band.

ENTRANCE PORTAL AI: Attendance confirmed. Welcome, Employee #486.

RH SECURITY GUARD 2: (LETS MALE EMPLOYEE 1 IN) All right, you can go in. Next person in line.

MALE EMPLOYEE 2: (SHEEPISHLYLY SURRENDERS) I got nothing on me.

RH SECURITY GUARD 2: Then just scan your Life Band, sir.

MALE EMPLOYEE 2: (SCANS HIS LIFE BAND) Okay then.

ENTRANCE PORTAL AI: Attendance confirmed. Welcome, Employee #947.

The male employee quickly makes his way to his department, as everyone else waits in line to scan their Life Bands. Elisa looks around and watches the mixed emotions happening around her while the female employee in front of her scans her Life Band.

ENTRANCE PORTAL AI: Attendance confirmed. Welcome, Employee #570.

FEMALE EMPLOYEE 1: (BEGINS WALKING AWAY) Thank you.

RH SECURITY GUARD 1: You're welcome. Have a good day. (TURNS TO ELISA) Excuse me, Miss?

ELISA: (SNAPS INTO FOCUS) I'm sorry?

RH SECURITY GUARD 1: I need to see your purse, please.

ELISA: (SLINGS OFF HER PURSE) Oh, right. Sorry about that.

Elisa gives the RH security guard her purse, and he carefully inspects it for safety measures while she waits patiently.

RH SECURITY GUARD 1: (GIVES ELISA HER PURSE) All right, looks good to me. Just scan your Life Band.

Elisa takes back her purse before scanning her Life Band to gain entrance into the building.

ENTRANCE PORTAL AI: Attendance confirmed. Welcome, Employee #263.

ELISA: (BEGINS WALKING AWAY) Have a good day.

RH SECURITY GUARD 1: You too. (TURNS TO THE NEXT PERSON) Next person in line.

Elisa makes her way to her department while everyone else waits in line to gain entrance to the building.

INT. THE RH-C DEPARTMENT OFFICE OF REGIONAL HEADQUARTERS – MORNING

Elisa rushes inside the office and quickly goes to her cubicle, where she takes off her coat and hangs it on the chair before taking a seat. She gets herself situated while everyone already in the office talks amongst themselves until **Mr. Van-Earl Popkin (mid-fifties)** walks into the office.

MR. POPKIN: (SMILES HAPPILY) Ah! Smells like a full room in here! Don't lollygag for too long because work is going to start in five minutes!

Everyone in the office rushes into their cubicles and gets themselves situated as Mr. Popkin watches the time on the Countdown Clock go down. **Thomas Dewberry (mid-thirties)** walks in and happily goes to his cubicle, where he gets himself situated.

THOMAS: (HAPPILY) Oh, what a lovely morning to start a full day of work. How are my wonderful colleagues doing?

Everyone around him groans in annoyance as Thomas scoffs at them and takes off his jacket in annoyance. Elisa puts her headset around her neck, while everyone else gets prepared for the day. **Daniel Morin (early-thirties)** walks into the office and quickly takes a sip of his coffee before going up to Mr. Popkin.

DANIEL: Good thing I got here just in time. The coffee lines are crazy down there. Are you ready for today, Boss?

MR. POPKIN: (CLASPS HIS HANDS HAPPILY) Yes, I definitely am. I can't wait to see what today's results will look like – especially if they can beat those pompous bastards from the other departments.

(TURNS TO EVERYONE) All right, everyone, listen up! We have a nine-hour workload ahead of us and I expect it to be done in eight hours! So, you better get yourselves prepared and awake as work starts in thirty seconds!

The Countdown Clock continues to go down as everyone finishes their drinks and snacks before settling down in their cubicles. Everyone begins to sign onto their systems and prepare themselves for work, while Mr. Popkin continues to watch the Countdown Clock go down.

MR. POPKIN: (TURNS TO EVERYONE) Is everyone ready?

EVERYONE: (IN UNISON) Yes, sir!

MR. POPKIN: (CONFIDENTLY) Good, because your jobs begin in three! Two! One!

The Countdown Clock buzzer goes off as everyone simultaneously puts their headsets on and begins answering calls, answering emails, completing previous documents and writing reports. Daniel heads to his personal office while Mr. Popkin watches his employees work in sync and smiles to himself until **Xavier Cunes (early-twenties)** rushes into the office, carrying a takeout latte.

XAVIER: (PANTS) Sorry, I'm late … (STOPS AND LOOKS AROUND) Has everyone already started working?

MR. POPKIN: (SLOWLY WALKS UP TO XAVIER) Yes, they have, Employee #784. They have taken the necessary precautions to be here at the appropriate time (GRADUALLY GETS ANGRY) while you were busy wasting time and not following the instructions of the organization. What's the meaning of your tardiness this time?

XAVIER: (APOLOGETIC) I'm sorry I'm late. I was going to come early … (GESTURES TO THE LATTE) but the coffee line was so long, and I needed my coffee fix –

MR. POPKIN: (SLAMS THE LATTE OUT OF XAVIER'S HAND) Screw your coffee fix!

Everyone goes quiet and turns to see Xavier's latte splatter on the floor, most having stopped what they are doing to see what is going on.

MR. POPKIN: (ANGRILY) Mark my words when I say no food and drinks are allowed during work hours. And if you really needed to have some coffee early in the morning, then you could've just gone to the kitchen and made it yourself instead of wasting time in that damn coffee line!

Daniel quickly leaves his office to go up to Mr. Popkin while Xavier stands there, frightened and ashamed.

DANIEL: Mr. Popkin, please –

MR. POPKIN: (ANGRILY) The staff that are responsible for the kitchen made sure that there are plenty of fixings so that you can prepare your coffee the way you like it. What's the need to stand in that line?

DANIEL: (COMES BETWEEN MR. POPKIN AND XAVIER) Mr. Popkin, it's okay – just let him go to work –

MR. POPKIN: (ANGRILY) Why should I when I'm going to have to hear about this from the other supervisors! This department has been the laughingstock for too long and if I'm going to have to hear from those bastards again because of this idiot –

DANIEL: (CALMLY) It's not going to happen. I can guarantee you that it won't happen.

MR. POPKIN: (GROWLS) You better be right, 'cause your life and your job depend on it. (TURNS TO XAVIER) And what are you still standing here for? (SCREAMS) Get to work!

Xavier scurries to his cubicle as Daniel tries his best to calm Mr. Popkin down.

DANIEL: (CALMLY) Okay now – it's going to be fine –

MR. POPKIN: (ANGRILY) Damn imbecile – must have come from a Blank Slate family.

DANIEL: (FIRMLY) That's enough, Mr. Popkin. Let's go – let's take a breather, all right? (TURNS TO EVERYONE) Get back to work, everyone!

Everyone immediately goes back to work as Daniel brings Mr. Popkin to the conference room. Xavier begins to sign onto his system while Thomas looks at him with annoyance and just shakes his head while everyone else continues to work. Elisa notices Xavier's solemn behavior and just sighs in empathy before returning to her work.

Several Hours Later

INT. THE RH-C DEPARTMENT OFFICE OF REGIONAL HEADQUARTERS – AFTERNOON

Everyone in the office continues to answer phone calls, answer emails, complete previous documents and write reports under Daniel's supervision. Everyone does their work simultaneously until the Countdown Clock finishes going down and the Break Bell rings.

DANIEL: (TURNS TO EVERYONE) All right, you know what time it is! It's breaktime!

MALE COLLEAGUE 1: Sweet.

Many employees waste no time in temporarily shutting down their systems and making their way out of the office.

DANIEL: You all get an hour before you come back for your afternoon shift – and I expect everyone to be back on time!

Xavier rushes out of the office while everyone else meets up with whomever and makes their way to the cafeteria. Elisa takes her time to shut down her system temporarily before she leaves the office.

INT. THE REGIONAL HEADQUARTERS CAFETERIA – AFTERNOON

Xavier pays for another latte, while everyone else pays for their lunch and sits with whomever they choose to hang out with. All the employees from different departments mingle with each other. Elisa, however, pays for her lunch and walks around looking for a place to sit by herself. She finally finds a seat near a window and goes to sit there before anyone else can take it. She looks out the window and sees the sky getting slightly brighter until a Notification Alert goes off on her Life Band.

LIFE BAND AI: Notification Alert! It has been detected that you have low nutrient levels in your body; it is advised that you start the day with –

ELISA: (PRESSES THE MONOGRAM) Dismiss all notifications.

LIFE BAND AI: Notifications dismissed.

Elisa begins eating her sandwich as she looks around and watches everyone else go about their day. She relaxes for a while and gets lost into her people watching until she overhears Thomas and a few of her colleagues chatting among themselves.

MALE COLLEAGUE 1: I can't believe we're going to work overtime again.

FEMALE COLLEAGUE 1: C'mon, don't be such a Debby Downer. I doubt that's the case.

MALE COLLEAGUE 1: Not the case? Because of what that Xavier kid did this morning, we're obviously gonna have to pick up where he left off. I swear, these damn Slates are so annoying –

FEMALE COLLEAGUE 1: Don't you dare use that word. There are plenty of them in here who are just like him –

MALE COLLEAGUE 1: So what? Is that supposed to be my problem? At least they are improving by pulling their own weight. Xavier is probably still at 80%, which makes him more useless than the rest of them!

THOMAS: I can't help but agree. I'm surprised he hasn't been transferred yet.

MALE COLLEAGUE 1: Like anyone else wants him.

FEMALE COLLEAGUE 1: C'mon guys, don't you think you're being a bit cruel?

THOMAS: How is it being cruel when it's the truth? It's an everyday inconvenience that Mr. Popkin has to hear from the other supervisors. I think the office would be three times more efficient if they weren't around.

Thomas and the rest of the colleagues continue to chat as Elisa tries her best not to get too upset by their conversation.

Thirteen Years Prior

▌ EXT. OUTSIDE THE GRAVES' HOUSE – AFTERNOON

Eight-year-old Elisa sits on the porch with tears in her eyes as her cupped hands catch the blood dripping from her bruised lip. Twelve-year-old Deidre and ten-year-old Fredrick run around the front yard playing Tag, while they ignore eight-year-old Elisa's soft crying as she sits by herself.

TWELVE-YEAR-OLD DEIDRE: (HAPPILY) Tag! You're it!

TEN-YEAR-OLD FREDRICK: (HAPPILY) No! You're it!

Twelve-year-old Deidre and ten-year-old Fredrick continue to play Tag with each other until they see Garreth's car pull up on the driveway before he gets out of the car to greet them.

TWELVE-YEAR-OLD DEIDRE AND TEN-YEAR-OLD FREDRICK: (HAPPILY) Daddy!

GARRETH: (HAPPILY) Hey kids! How have you been?

Twelve-year-old Deidre and ten-year-old Fredrick quickly run up to Garreth for a big hug while he tries his best to carry them both with his own strength. Eight-year-old Elisa remains seated on the porch as she tunes out the voices and begins to question her existence.

TWELVE-YEAR-OLD DEIDRE: (HAPPILY) Dad, come play with us!

GARRETH: (TURNS TO TWELVE-YEAR-OLD DEIDRE) Right after I greet your mother and sister! (TURNS TO EIGHT-YEAR-OLD ELISA) And how's my little princess doing –

Garreth stops and freezes in shock as he sees eight-year-old Elisa's bloody lip and the rest of her bruises as she remains silent.

GARRETH: (WORRIED) Elisa, what happened? Are you okay? (CROUCHES TO EIGHT-YEAR-OLD ELISA) Talk to me and tell me what happened – who did this to you?

Eight-year-old Elisa remains silent as Garreth looks over all her bruises until he stops and turns to twelve-year-old Deidre and ten-year-old Fredrick for answers.

GARRETH: (SERIOUSLY) Can one of you please tell me what happened to your sister?

TWELVE-YEAR-OLD DEIDRE: She got beaten up by one of the kids at school.

GARRETH: (SERIOUSLY) And you two did nothing to help her? Or at least stop it from happening in the first place?

TEN-YEAR-OLD FREDRICK: It wasn't our problem.

TWELVE-YEAR-OLD DEIDRE: We weren't the ones who got Stacy Danvers upset. She did that all by herself.

GARRETH: (PAUSES IN ANGER) Both of you get inside.

TEN-YEAR-OLD DEIDRE: (WHINES) But Dad –

GARRETH: (ANGRILY) I said get inside now! We're going to have a little talk once I'm done with your sister.

Twelve-year-old Deidre and ten-year-old Fredrick pout in frustration as they make their way inside the house. Eight-year-old Elisa remains seated on the porch until ten-year-old Fredrick pushes her out of the way.

TEN-YEAR-OLD FREDRICK: (UPSET) Nice going, you stupid Slate. Now you got us both in trouble –

GARRETH: (ANGRILY) What did you just say?

Ten-year-old Fredrick stops and turns to Garreth as he stands up and stares at him with lividness in his eyes. Twelve-year-old Deidre and eight-year-old Elisa turn to Garreth, fearing he might hurt ten-year-old Fredrick.

GARRETH: (ANGRILY) Come here. (GRABS TEN-YEAR-OLD FREDRICK'S ARM) Get your little ass over here right now!

EIGHT-YEAR-OLD ELISA: (WORRIED) Dad, stop –

TWELVE-YEAR-OLD DEIDRE: (PROTESTS) You're going to hurt him –

GARRETH: (YELLS AT TWELVE-YEAR-OLD DEIDRE) Don't you dare intervene when it comes to me and your brother! And how dare you protect him when you didn't even try to protect your little sister! (YELLS AT EIGHT-YEAR-OLD ELISA) And how dare you protect him when he didn't do the same for you! Is that something you should be proud of? Does that make any sense to you at all?

Twelve-year-old Deidre and eight-year-old Elisa go silent, while Garreth continues to have a firm hold on ten-year-old Fredrick.

GARRETH: (PULLS TEN-YEAR-OLD FREDRICK TOWARD HIM) And as for you! We have never used that word in this house, and we never will. Even if you're within the same perimeter as this house, that word should never be spoken by any of my children. We are not strangers, we are family – and not even strangers should be treated this way! And if you think you can get away with treating your little sister like that, then expect to be treated the same way by the rest of us!

As Garreth aggressively pushes ten-year-old Fredrick away from him, the boy stumbles and falls to the ground. Twelve-year-old Deidre and eight-year-old Elisa remain frozen in fear.

GARRETH: (ANGRILY) Now the both of you do as I say and get inside.

TWELVE-YEAR-OLD DEIDRE: (APOLOGETIC) Dad, we're sorry –

GARRETH: (SCREAMS) I said now!

Twelve-year-old Deidre and ten-year-old Fredrick scurry inside the house as Garreth tries to calm himself but remains angry at the same time.

GARRETH: (ANGRILY) Things are going to be different around here. Just because your Tints are lighter doesn't make you better than everyone else!

Thirteen Years Later

▌ INT. THE REGIONAL HEADQUARTERS CAFETERIA – AFTERNOON

GARRETH: (IN ELISA'S HEAD) As long as I'm alive, you will remember that to this day!

Elisa takes a moment to remember Garreth's words as she quickly but thoroughly finishes her lunch before leaving the cafeteria.

▌ INT. THE RH-C DEPARTMENT OFFICE OF REGIONAL HEADQUARTERS – AFTERNOON

Elisa returns to the office early and goes to her cubicle to sign onto her system before putting on her headset and completing one of her reports. **Hank Wilson (early-sixties)** goes around the office with his janitor cart and empties the garbage cans in every cubicle. When he sees Elisa working, he stops to talk.

HANK: (KINDLY) Ms. Graves, I see you've come back early again.

ELISA: (SMILES AND TURNS TO HANK) Yes, I have. How have you been, Hank?

HANK: I've been doing fine, just emptying these garbage cans and cleaning up coffee spills. I swear this man makes more messes than my own children.

Both Elisa and Hank laugh together, as they enjoy seeing each other for the day.

HANK: How you been, Ms. Graves?

ELISA: (SHRUGS) I've been okay. Just writing reports for the time being.

HANK: (CHUCKLES) I see that. I can tell that you're a very hard worker. But you sure look a lot skinnier than the last time I saw you. Is everything okay?

ELISA: Everything's fine. I just ate lunch before I came back.

HANK: Well, okay then – you could've fooled me. It's a shame that we don't have the same breaktime. You would've been invited to a feast that would've lasted for hours.

ELISA: (THINKS ABOUT IT AND NODS) Sounds tempting. I'll see what I can do next time.

HANK: (SMILES AND BEGINS TO LEAVE) All right, we'll be expecting you. (KINDLY) Take care of yourself, Ms. Graves – don't work too hard now.

ELISA: (KINDLY) Same goes to you, Hank.

Hank goes back to emptying all the garbage cans in the office as Elisa returns to working on her reports. She continues working, but slowly gets distracted when she starts thinking about Garreth and her memories of him.

Thirteen Years Prior

▌ EXT. OUTSIDE THE GRAVES' HOUSE – AFTERNOON

Garreth cleans eight-year-old Elisa's hands with his handkerchief as she sits still and remains quiet.

GARRETH: (CALMLY) All right, let's get you cleaned up now. It's okay – you're going to be just fine, Elisa. Don't worry about a thing. We're just going to get you back to your pretty self, okay? Now, let's move on to that face of yours.

Garreth moves on to cleaning eight-year-old Elisa's face with his handkerchief as he tries his best not to smudge blood all over her face due to her bruised lip.

GARRETH: (CALMLY) Man, that Stacy Danvers really did a number on you – I'm hoping your mother didn't see you like this. But it's okay, there's nothing to be sad about – we're going to go straight to the principal's office and deal with this situation properly, all right? (WIPES AWAY EIGHT-YEAR-OLD ELISA'S TEARS) And no more tears – you know I hate seeing you like this. It's okay. Daddy's here with you.

Eight-year-old Elisa wipes her tears away and takes the handkerchief for her lip as Garreth takes a seat beside her on the porch.

GARRETH: (CALMLY) Now that I'm done dealing with your knucklehead siblings, I think it's time for us to have a little talk. Do you mind telling me what happened?

Eight-year-old Elisa remains silent as Garreth tries his best not to become impatient with her.

GARRETH: (TICKLES EIGHT-YEAR-OLD ELISA'S NECK) I know there's a voice box in that neck of yours somewhere.

EIGHT-YEAR-OLD ELISA: (SMACKS GARRETH'S HAND AWAY) Stop it.

GARRETH: (SMILES) There it is! I knew I heard you use it earlier. Now, you're going to use it again to tell me what happened to you ... because the last thing you want is for your daddy to get mad at you. (CALMLY) Talk to me, sweetheart. You know, you can tell me anything.

EIGHT-YEAR-OLD ELISA: (PAUSES) Dad. What's the meaning of life?

Momentarily baffled, Garreth laughs out loud, causing eight-year-old Elisa to throw him an offended look and pout disappointedly.

GARRETH: (CHUCKLES) Is this what I'm hearing right now? From my own daughter?

EIGHT-YEAR-OLD ELISA: (ANNOYED) It's not funny.

GARRETH: (CHUCKLES) It sure seems funny to me! You're not even in your double digits yet and you're asking questions like that. Heck, I'm an old man and not once did that question come into my mind.

EIGHT-YEAR-OLD ELISA: (ANNOYED) I'm being serious, Dad. What is it? What's the meaning of life?

GARRETH: (PAUSES AND THINKS FOR A MOMENT) Well, sweetie, I think that's a question your father can't give you the full answer to … not that I don't know the answer. It's just a question that you need to answer on your own.

EIGHT-YEAR-OLD ELISA: (SHAKES HER HEAD) I don't understand what you're saying, Dad. Have you been hanging out with those Theodes again?

GARRETH: (CHUCKLES) No, I haven't had the time to this week. But of course, you don't understand, Elisa – you haven't lived long enough to gain a full understanding. What I can tell you is how hurt I am hearing you talk like this. The last thing a father wants is to come home to his young daughter, questioning about life. You have no idea how much that breaks my heart.

EIGHT-YEAR-OLD ELISA: (APOLOGETIC) I didn't mean to make you sad.

GARRETH: (PRETENDS TO WHIMPER) No, I'm really sad. I just can't believe my own daughter is questioning her own life. I can't help but be sad.

Garreth exaggerates his fake whimpers as eight-year-old Elisa contemplates telling him what actually happened to her at school.

EIGHT-YEAR-OLD ELISA: It was Stacy Danvers' birthday today.

Garreth stops pretending and gives eight-year-old Elisa his full attention.

EIGHT-YEAR-OLD ELISA: She was having a little get-together after school and invited me over to hang out with her and her friends. She said she had a present for me just because I accepted her invitation ... but it turned out to be a block of slate, so I threw it on the ground right in front of her.

GARRETH: So, you got beaten up because you refused to accept her present?

EIGHT-YEAR-OLD ELISA: Yes. I tried to fight back, but she is bigger than me. The only person who stopped the fight was Mrs. Cortege.

GARRETH: Well, thank goodness for Mrs. Cortege, knowing she likes to be a part of everything. Now, as for what happened, I think this entire situation is bullshit.

EIGHT-YEAR-OLD ELISA: (TURNS TO GARRETH) You keep saying that it's a bad word to use, but it doesn't stop her from using it ... (POUTS) It doesn't even stop Fredrick from using it.

GARRETH: (SERIOUSLY) Now don't worry about your brother. I'll make sure to straighten him out before I leave for work again. As for Stacy Danvers, she knew what she was doing, so she had no right to beat you up just because you rejected her gift. (HONESTLY) And I would've been just as angry with you as I was with Fredrick if I'd ever seen you with that rock in your hands.

Eight-year-old Elisa begins to feel a lot better as Garreth wraps his arm around her in comfort.

GARRETH: (CALMLY) None of this was your fault, Elisa. You did the right thing and chose not to accept that rock. You may have gotten hurt by that decision, but I can't help but be proud of you for making that decision on your own.

EIGHT-YEAR-OLD ELISA: (SULKS) But she does have a point … she just reached 50%. And Deidre is already at 49%, and Fredrick is at 52%; I'm still at 80%. How will I even get to my Canvas Phase after so long?

GARRETH: (CALMLY) Now, here's the part where your daddy can answer some part of your question.

Garreth crouches in front of eight-year-old Elisa, who sits and gives him her full attention.

GARRETH: Life is not about catching up with your peers. Nor is it about competing with them or changing yourself just to be like them. All you can ever do is be yourself, and I promise you that everything will be just fine.

EIGHT-YEAR-OLD ELISA: (PAUSES AND SULKS AGAIN) But what if nobody likes it when I'm being myself?

GARRETH: Well, sweetheart, no one comes into this life being liked by everyone, and no one comes into this life without dealing with a couple of bruises every once in a while. That's what makes you tough, so don't be too upset when it happens to you every now and again. If they don't like you, then that's just their loss. So, don't you ever worry about what everyone else thinks of you … because sooner or later, your time will come. It may not happen as fast as everyone else's, but your time will come. You just have to live a little longer to see that for yourself.

Eight-year-old Elisa thinks about Garreth's answer and nods in agreement while he smiles and takes his time to stand up straight.

GARRETH: (TAKES EIGHT-YEAR-OLD ELISA'S HAND) Now, c'mon, let's go get those bruises of yours mended, and afterwards, we're going to have a family meeting about this.

EIGHT-YEAR-OLD ELISA: (GETS UP) Please don't be too hard on them.

GARRETH: (SHAKES HIS HEAD) Oh no, I'm gonna have to be real hard on them, so this doesn't happen again. Sometimes, you have to use unpleasant methods to make sure the information sticks in their heads.

As she and Garreth make their way inside the house, eight-year-old Elisa finally laughs for the first time.

GARRETH: You have to have a firm hand if you want things to go your way.

Thirteen Years Later

▌ EXT. OUTSIDE REGIONAL HEADQUARTERS – EVENING

GARRETH: (IN ELISA'S HEAD) So, toughen up, Little Steel. You have a long way to go before your time comes.

As Elisa leaves Regional Headquarters along with everyone else, the people around her catch up with friends and take their usual routes home or to Primetime Plaza. Elisa, however, catches the Route 533 bus and heads straight home.

▌ INT. INSIDE THE ROUTE 533 BUS – EVENING

Everyone on the bus minds their own business as they chat amongst themselves and their Life Bands, while the bus driver continues to drive the usual route.

OLDER FEMALE PASSENGER: Life Band, call Daxton.

LIFE BAND AI: Calling DAXTON (RINGING) ...

DAXTON: (ON THE OTHER LINE) Hello?

OLDER FEMALE PASSENGER: Hello, Dax baby, it's Mommy! I'm just coming home from work! Did you get started on the lasagna?

The rest of the passengers get annoyed with the older female passenger as they try their best to mind their own business. Elisa sits by herself, looks out the window and watches the setting sun until it begins to rain. She notices a few kids running out of their houses to play in the rain as one mother rushes out the door to bring them back inside.

CONCERNED MOTHER: (FROM OUTSIDE) Will you kids come back inside this instant! There's no way I'm letting you two skip another day of school if this is your plan to make yourselves sick! (ANGRILY) Ooh, you're not even Canvases yet and you're out here fooling around in the rain!

Observing the scene, Elisa continues to watch the rain and the setting sun and remembers her father's words.

GARRETH: (IN ELISA'S HEAD) Your time will come … you just have to live a little longer to see that for yourself.

ELISA: (QUIETLY) I promise I'll do that, Dad.

Elisa smiles to herself as she enjoys the rest of the bus ride home.

The Next Day

▌ INT. ELISA'S BEDROOM – MORNING

The alarm clock sounds as Elisa wakes up from her sleep before she slams the alarm clock to turn it off.

HOUSE AI: Alarm dismissed. Good morning, Elisa Graves.

Elisa sighs and thinks about going back to sleep until she hears the Notification Alert go off.

HOUSE AI: Notification Alert! Your Life Band has detected an update on your financial records. A visit to the Information Hub will offer you more information on any updates received from your Life Band.

Elisa quickly sits up and freezes in confusion as she tries to remember the last transaction she made. She quickly gets out of bed to get ready for work.

▌ INT. REGIONAL HEADQUARTERS COURTYARD – MORNING

Elisa finishes scanning her Life Band through the entrance portals and goes to look for an available Information Hub while everyone else goes about their business. She looks around for an Information Hub with no line until she finally finds one and slowly goes up to it, wondering what to do. She waits for the Information Hub to do something, feeling cautious about the time.

INFORMATION HUB AI: Welcome. Please scan your Life Band through the ID slot.

Elisa finds the ID slot and puts her hand in as the Information Hub begins scanning her Life Band to grant access to her information.

INFORMATION HUB AI: Access granted. Welcome, Ms. Elisa Graves. What can I do for you today?

ELISA: Access my personal finances.

INFORMATION HUB AI: Accessing personal finances. (LOADING) Access granted. Here is an overview of your personal finances: Your current balance is –

ELISA: (CURT) Check my e-transfer status.

INFORMATION HUB AI: Accessing e-transfer status.

As the Information Hub begins to load, Elisa notices a few people staring at her.

INFORMATION HUB AI: Access granted. Here is an overview of all of your e-transfers. Your recent e-transfer status of one hundred thousand dollars sent to CARMAN GRAVES has been updated to: DECLINED.

Elisa stands there silently furious with Carman and herself as she tries her best not to get too upset.

INFORMATION HUB AI: What would you like to do with this e-transfer?

ELISA: Send the money back to my account.

INFORMATION HUB AI: Transferring funds. (LOADING) Request granted. One hundred thousand dollars has been successfully transferred to the account of ELISA GRAVES.

A few people who overheard the Information Hub stand there in shock as Elisa begins to run out of patience.

INFORMATION HUB AI: Is there anything else I can do for you today?

ELISA: (CURT) Dismiss complete access.

INFORMATION HUB AI: Dismissing complete access. (LOADING) Request granted. Please remove your Life Band from the ID slot to complete your request.

Elisa removes her hand from the ID slot as the Information Hub removes her information and resets itself for the next user.

INFORMATION HUB AI: Thank you for using the Information Hub. Have a great day.

The Information Hub repeats its greeting as Elisa rests her head and sighs in disappointment.

INFORMATION HUB AI: Welcome. Please scan your Life Band through the ID slot.

ELISA: (SILENTLY) Mother.

INT. THE RH-C DEPARTMENT OFFICE OF REGIONAL HEADQUARTERS – MORNING

Elisa walks into the office, her sour mood showing on her face as a bit of commotion goes on around her. She notices everyone talking amongst themselves and that a few colleagues are gathered around Thomas, listening to him talk.

THOMAS: (JOYFULLY) Funny how I thought yesterday was going to be a great day, but today is even better. Ah, I can just see myself in that setting now.

FEMALE COLLEAGUE 1: How do you know you're going to get it, Thomas?

THOMAS: (BRAGS) Oh please, of course I'm going to get it! Mr. Popkin would be making the biggest mistake if he gave it to someone else.

Elisa rolls her eyes and shakes her head in annoyance as she continues to scowl. However, noticing Hank, she begins to soften up.

HANK: (KINDLY) Good morning, Ms. Graves.

ELISA: (STOPS AND SMILES) Good morning, Hank. How are you today?

HANK: (KINDLY) Well, I'm doing a lot better now that I'm seeing a smile on your face. It does hurt my heart when I see you scowl like that.

ELISA: Let's just say that I'm starting to feel better myself. What time's your lunch for today?

HANK: (CHUCKLES HAPPILY) I'm glad you remember. It's at one o'clock, but I'm afraid you would be stuck here working since it's a special day for you guys.

FEMALE COLLEAGUE 2: (PASSES BY) Hey Hank, I see you're having fun with your girlfriend this morning.

HANK: (JOKINGLY) Oh, that would've been the case if my wife allowed me to bring another woman home! (TURNS TO ELISA) Don't listen to them, Ms. Graves; they just like to talk for the sake of hearing themselves. Don't you worry about a thing. You just get on with your work while I make sure the chit-chat remains low.

ELISA: (SMILES) I appreciate that, Hank.

HANK: (KINDLY) Anything for you, Ms. Graves. (BEGINS TO LEAVE) Have a nice day – and remember, smile.

Hank continues his cleaning rounds as Elisa attempts to make her way to her cubicle. However, she bumps accidentally into **Gillian Grant (late-twenties)**, who drops the stack of papers she is carrying and both women fall to the floor.

ELISA: (REMORSEFUL) Oh my goodness! I'm so sorry!

GILLIAN: (REGAINS HER BALANCE) It's okay – it's okay. There's nothing for you to worry about.

ELISA: (REMORSEFUL) I'm really sorry! Are you okay?

GILLIAN: I'm fine, really, I'm still alive – and trust me, I've been knocked down harder. Especially when it comes to this special time in the office.

Seeing the papers scattered all over the floor, Gillian stoops to pick them up, doing her best not to get angry. However, when she sees Elisa stoop to help her pick up the papers, she pauses.

GILLIAN: (GENUINELY) It's okay, love. You don't need to help me out. I can take care of this by myself.

ELISA: (GENUINELY) I insist. I really didn't mean to knock you over. If I had been paying attention to where I was going, this wouldn't have happened.

GILLIAN: (GENUINELY) Well, I wouldn't say it like that. It was a complete accident – a happy accident in fact ... and if you ask me, I think it was a blessing in disguise.

Elisa looks up and notices Gillian's Tint Level is slightly darker than hers. She smiles and continues to help her while Mr. Popkin stops by to see what happened.

MR. POPKIN: Employee #417. What happened here?

GILLIAN: (HAPPILY) Just a little accident on a busy day, Mr. Popkin, but don't worry yourself. (GESTURES TO ELISA) We're taking care of it.

MR. POPKIN: (HAPPILY) Excellent! It's a good thing to have an extra hand to help you out. Just make sure you clean up this mess before your shift starts! (TURNS TO EVERYONE) Especially since today includes a Power Hour! Five minutes!

The Countdown Clock continues to go down as everyone rushes to their cubicles, and Gillian and Elisa continue to pick up papers off the floor.

ELISA: (QUIETLY) So, no wonder Thomas was talking about himself earlier. I completely forgot that he becomes even less tolerable during Power Hours.

GILLIAN: (QUIETLY) You got that right. I literally had to hide in the kitchen just to get away from his morning monologues.

Elisa laughs briefly as she continues to help Gillian pick up the papers off the floor.

GILLIAN: (QUIETLY) But if I have to be honest, he usually does win the special prize, as he's the only one who makes the effort to be the right-hand man of Mr. Popkin. Plus, he was chosen to sit in on the special meeting with the department supervisors, so he's definitely milking it as we speak.

ELISA: (QUIETLY) I understand that, but does he really have to annoy the rest of us while he's at it?

Gillian lets out a loud laugh but tries to control it for the sake of the rest of their colleagues as she and Elisa quietly laugh it out for their own sakes.

GILLIAN: (SMILES) You know what, you're pretty funny. I never had anyone make me laugh like that before. How come I have never seen you before in my life?

ELISA: (SHRUGS) Maybe we've just been busy with work. Which could explain why I haven't seen you before. I really don't bother anyone around here. I just stay in the background for my own sake.

Gillian giggles as she and Elisa think about not having met each other on their first day on the job.

GILLIAN: I understand. I do the same thing around here – especially since this group is prone to gossip.

Elisa and Gillian both laugh until they stop collecting paper to greet each other properly.

GILLIAN: I'm Gillian, by the way.

ELISA: Elisa.

GILLIAN: (STICKS OUT HER HAND) Nice to meet you, Elisa.

Elisa and Gillian shake hands and begin to enjoy each other's company.

ELISA: (SMILES) Nice to meet you, too, Gillian. And I'm really sorry about knocking you over with these papers.

GILLIAN: (SHRUGS) Oh, it's all right! (STARTS PICKING UP PAPERS) It would've happened anyway, knowing that today's Power Hour.

ELISA: (STARTS PICKING UP PAPERS) It explains why the office is so busy. I usually see Hank during my break.

GILLIAN: (GENUINELY) I know, right? Hank is such a sweetheart – always sticking up for the little guys.

ELISA: It's funny that in a sea of people, he's the only person I talk to at the office.

Elisa and Gillian both laugh until they notice Xavier in the kitchen, searching frantically for the creamer.

GILLIAN: Yeah, you think everyone in here would be a bit friendlier since we're all in the same boat. But they're so busy picking on poor Xavier for being a late bloomer – he even took the chance to come early just so he can make his latte here. (TURNS TO XAVIER) You need a hand there, love?

XAVIER: (FRANTICALLY) I'll be at my cubicle, sir! I just need to find the creamer!

GILLIAN: (SIGHS AND SHAKES HER HEAD) Poor thing is so rattled, he doesn't even know who he's talking to.

Gillian begins to feel pity for Xavier as she and Elisa watch him searching frantically for the creamer in the kitchen. Elisa watches him closely, when suddenly she remembers where the creamer is.

XAVIER: (FRANTICALLY) All I want is some creamer. Where's the creamer? Where's the creamer?

ELISA: Bottom shelf at the back of the fridge.

Xavier stops as he and Gillian turn to Elisa in shock.

ELISA: If you want the creamer, check the bottom shelf at the back of the fridge. Unless Thomas has used it already, it should be there.

Xavier remains still until he opens the fridge and finds the creamer at the back. Impressed, Gillian turns to Elisa and exclaims in excitement.

GILLIAN: (HAPPILY) Well, would you look at that! (TURNS TO XAVIER) A colleague has finally come to your rescue; now you get to have some creamer in your coffee.

XAVIER: (TIMID) Thank you ... for the help ... but ... I don't speak to Slates.

Gillian's smile drops immediately as Xavier cowers into a corner to put some creamer in his coffee. Gillian wastes no time expressing her anger, while Elisa tries her best not to get too upset herself.

GILLIAN: (SIGHS AND SHAKES HER HEAD) Tsk, tsk, tsk ... the self-hatred has already begun – they really did a number on this guy.

ELISA: It's fine, really. It's been said more than once by many people, so ... you get used to it after a while.

GILLIAN: (TURNS TO ELISA) Really? You're going to let him get away with that? After you helped him find the damn creamer in the first place?

ELISA: Like you said before ... (TURNS TO XAVIER) He's so rattled, I don't think he even meant it in his heart.

Elisa turns to watch Xavier drink his coffee privately while Gillian huffs in protest.

GILLIAN: (TURNS TO ELISA) Well, I'm not one for second chances, so I'm definitely not giving him a hand after he used that word. (HAPPILY) But I definitely have a strong liking for you. Maybe we should have lunch this afternoon.

ELISA: (TURNS TO GILLIAN SURPRISED) Really?

GILLIAN: (HAPPILY) Sure, why not. I don't see a problem with that. Unless you're planning on sneaking out to have lunch with Hank. His lunch parties are sure tempting.

ELISA: (GIGGLES) No, I'll probably be too busy, even though a lunch party does sound tempting.

GILLIAN: You should try it one day – it will literally change your life.

ELISA: That was the plan until I found out about today's Power Hour, but since I have nothing else better to do, I don't see why not.

GILLIAN: (HAPPILY) Great! It's a date, then!

Elisa smiles genuinely as she and Gillian finish picking up the papers off the floor while they help each other up.

GILLIAN: (TAKES THE PAPERS FROM ELISA) Thank you so much for your help!

ELISA: No problem. It's the least that I can do.

GILLIAN: (HAPPILY) Well, I'm very glad I met you. For the first time, I'm actually excited about lunch. (BEGINS TO LEAVE) Just make sure to sit somewhere so I can find you, okay? (WAVES GOODBYE) I'll see you later, new buddy.

Waving goodbye to each other, Gillian takes the stack of papers to Daniel's office, where Elisa pauses and wonders about the meaning of friendship.

MR. POPKIN: Sixty seconds!

Snapping into focus, Elisa rushes to her cubicle to sign onto her system. Meanwhile, Mr. Popkin walks around the office to make sure everyone has gotten themselves situated and prepared for the Power Hour.

MR. POPKIN: (WALKS AROUND THE OFFICE) Sixty seconds! You have sixty seconds to get to work! (STOPS AND TURNS TO XAVIER) Hey, what did I tell you about the coffee? (ANGRILY) Get your ass to your cubicle now! And partner up with someone to be your mentor while you're at it!

Finishing his coffee, Xavier scurries to his cubicle to sign onto his system. Meanwhile, everyone else puts their headsets around their necks, while Mr. Popkin supervises.

MR. POPKIN: (TO EVERYONE) Your asses better be on point if you want to win this Power Hour! Is everyone ready?

EVERYONE: (IN UNISON) Yes, sir!

MR. POPKIN: (CONFIDENTLY) Good, because your jobs begin in three! Two! One!

The Countdown Clock buzzer goes off as everyone simultaneously puts their headsets on and begins working during the Power Hour.

A Few Hours Later

INT. RH-C DEPARTMENT OFFICE OF REGIONAL HEADQUARTERS – MORNING

Everyone in the office continues to answer phone calls, answer emails, complete previous documents and write reports without supervision for the day. A few employees glance at the Countdown Clock as they wait for the Break Bell to go off. A few more employees continue to work as one of their colleagues finishes up a phone call and takes off his headset to give himself a break.

FEMALE COLLEAGUE 1: (CONCERNED) Is everything okay?

MALE COLLEAGUE 1: Everything's fine. I just had a tough customer – he must be a Slate, if you ask me.

FEMALE COLLEAGUE 1: (FIRMLY) You know, I really don't like it when you use that word.

MALE COLLEAGUE 1: (SHRUGS) Unless you plan to report me, who is actually going to stop me from using that word?

Shaking her head, the female colleague goes back to work, as does the male colleague, until an Office Request goes off for his system.

SYSTEM AI: Office Request! Office Request!

The colleague clicks on the Office Request and reads it quietly until he begins to grimace in shock.

MALE COLLEAGUE 1: (UPSET) You have got to be kidding me.

FEMALE COLLEAGUE 1: (TAKES OFF HER HEADSET) What is it now?

MALE COLLEAGUE 1: (TURNS TO FEMALE COLLEAGUE 1) It's a stupid Office Request telling me to bring coffee to the conference room – I'm not doing that.

FEMALE COLLEAGUE 1: Well, if you don't want to do it, then send it to someone else.

The male colleague begins to panic until he decides to send the Office Request to the female colleague.

SYSTEM AI: Office Request! Office Request!

FEMALE COLLEAGUE 1: (UPSET) Why would you send it to me?

MALE COLLEAGUE 1: (ARGUES) You just said to send it to someone else.

FEMALE COLLEAGUE 1: (ARGUES) Like I would ever go in there. What were you thinking?

The female colleague sends the Office Request back to the male colleague.

MALE COLLEAGUE 1: (ANNOYED) Why would you send it back to me?

FEMALE COLLEAGUE 1: (UPSET) Because I'm not going to do it! So, unless you want this friendship to end, you either do it yourself or send it to someone else.

The male colleague takes the female colleague seriously and randomly sends the Office Request to someone else. The Office Request is sent around a few times until it stops at an employee who is in the middle of work.

SYSTEM AI: Office Request! Office Request!

FEMALE COLLEAGUE 2: (UPSET) No way in my life. (GETS UP AND LOOKS AROUND) Who sent this?

MALE COLLEAGUE 1: (ARGUES) If you don't want it, then send it to someone else!

FEMALE COLLEAGUE 2: (UPSET) You're so lucky I'm not going to send it back to your ass!

The other female colleague sends the Office Request to someone else, and it gets sent around a few more times around the office. When Hank arrives to do his cleaning round, he notices the silent commotion that is occurring in the office.

FEMALE COLLEAGUE 2: (COMES UP TO HANK) Hank, there's an Office Request that's going around the office. Can you please do it for the sake of all of us?

HANK: (KINDLY) Oh, I would love to help you guys out ... but since I'm just a janitor and not a representative, I don't think I'm authorized to do such a thing. Sorry.

The Office Request is continuously sent around a few times until it stops at Gillian while she is in the middle of completing a report.

SYSTEM AI: Office Request! Office Request!

GILLIAN: (BITTER) No ... there's no way in my life I'm doing that. (LOOKS AROUND) Which one of you assholes sent this?

MALE COLLEAGUE 1: (ANNOYED) Just do it already. It's not like anyone else is going to take it.

Gillian sits back and watches almost every one of her colleagues begging her to take the Office Request.

FEMALE COLLEAGUE 1: (BEGS) Please, you have to do this for us! If it were Thomas, he would've done this in a heartbeat.

GILLIAN: (BITTER) Well, I'm not Thomas … and I definitely won't do this in a heartbeat. Sorry, your problem.

MALE COLLEAGUE 1: Then send it to someone else who is willing to do it – we don't have time for this!

Gillian rolls her eyes as she turns to Xavier and watches him trying to finish his report while in the middle of a phone call. With vengeance in her heart, she sends the Office Request directly to him and watches him panic uncontrollably.

SYSTEM AI: Office Request! Office Request!

XAVIER: (SLOWLY GETS UP AND PANICS) No … no-no-no – please don't make me do this. (TAKES OFF HIS HEADSET) I messed up the last time. Please don't make me go in there!

MALE COLLEAGUE 1: (ANNOYED) Just take one for the team, Xavier.

FEMALE COLLEAGUE 1: (BEGS) Please do this for us! You might even win brownie points with Mr. Popkin!

XAVIER: (FRANTICALLY SHAKES HIS HEAD) No – no, I don't want to do this! You can't make me go in there. Who sent this?

Several of the employees point at Gillian as Xavier turns to her in shock.

XAVIER: (FRANTICALLY) But why?

GILLIAN: (BITTER) You said the word … meaning you're on my hit list.

Gillian goes back to work while Xavier exclaims in hopelessness and continues to panic. Everyone around him becomes impatient as they wait for him to take the Office Request.

MALE COLLEAGUE 1: (ANNOYED) Xavier, we literally have no time for this! Stop being such a pussy and just take the request already!

Xavier continues to panic, and then he sends the Office Request to someone else, while the rest of the employees exclaim in hopelessness. While the Office Request continues to be sent around, Elisa is on a phone call with a customer without paying attention to what is going on around her.

ELISA: (ON THE PHONE) It's okay. Just take your time. No one's here to rush you. Just letting you know that I'm right here to take you through this ... no, no, there's no need to apologize. Everyone works at their own pace; it's completely fine. I understand how you feel. That's why it's important to make sure that we take the right steps to offer the right service to our customers. You manage to find everything? Okay, let me know when you're ready.

Elisa listens carefully as she fills out the information needed for the Customer Request. She makes sure to double-check everything before she sends the Customer Request to the Head Council.

ELISA: (ON THE PHONE) Okay, your request has been sent and you can expect an update within three to ten business days. You are so welcome. Is there anything else you would like me to do? Don't you worry, Everything that's been exchanged within this phone call remains completely confidential. If you decide not to use our services for the next ninety days, we make sure that your information is removed immediately. Yes, meaning we'll have to do this all over again if you don't make a call within the next ninety days, but don't worry. Your information is safe with us. Well, thank you for using our services at Regional Headquarters, and I hope you have a great day. You, too. Bye.

Elisa ends the phone call and enters the customer's info into her Call Log before she starts working again. The Office Request continues to get sent around until it stops at Elisa, and she notices the alert on her system.

SYSTEM AI: Office Request! Office Request! (REPEATS) Office Request! Office Request!

ELISA: (CONFUSED) Office request? What in the name ...

Elisa sits there, completely puzzled, as she clicks on the Office Request to read it quietly to herself.

ELISA: (SILENTLY READS) Bring coffee to the conference room ASAP! It must be freshly made, and it must be piping hot. Also bring in all the fixings in the kitchen, including the creamer ... you must bring the creamer. (SHAKES HER HEAD) Who on earth would send this?

Elisa looks up and is shocked to see everyone staring at her while they wait patiently for her to take the Office Request.

INT. THE CONFERENCE ROOM OF THE RH-C DEPARTMENT OFFICE – MORNING

Mr. Popkin and Daniel meet with all the department supervisors, while Thomas stands in the corner and watches from afar. The five men talk about the upcoming projects as Elisa takes her time to bring in the coffee with all the fixings. Thomas remains still and watches her carefully while the meeting continues.

RH-B DEPARTMENT SUPERVISOR: (LAUGHS LOUDLY) Van-Earl – you son of a bitch! You really do know how to make a compelling argument!

RH-D DEPARTMENT SUPERVISOR: (LAUGHS) That's nothing new to us. That's just classic Van-Earl Popkin!

MR. POPKIN: (CONFIDENTLY) Well, you have to understand that it's just practical negotiation; no specialty gadgets can help change the decision. (NOTICES ELISA AND THE COFFEE) Finally, the coffee is here!

The rest of the supervisors get excited as Elisa nods hello and puts the coffee on the side table along with the fixings.

MR. POPKIN: It sure does smell fresh from where I'm sitting. (TURNS TO ELISA) Hey, Employee #263, before you go, do you mind pouring a cup for me? I usually like mine black.

ELISA: Sure thing, Mr. Popkin.

Daniel stops one of the supervisors from raising his hand for coffee, while Thomas foully watches Elisa pour a cup of coffee and give it to Mr. Popkin.

ELISA: Here you go, Mr. Popkin.

MR. POPKIN: Thank you, Employee #263, for bringing the coffee to us. But I do have to ask why it took so damn long to do it.

ELISA: I apologize for the long wait, sir. I received the Office Request at the last minute. I was just finishing a phone call when I got the request, and since everyone else was so busy during the Power Hour, I couldn't bear sending it to someone else.

Thomas stands there stunned to notice that Elisa does not break a sweat while the rest of the department supervisors begin to grow fond of her.

MR. POPKIN: (CONFIDENTLY) It's a good thing to know that some-one was out there to do the task. You know how busy people get when it comes to an Office Request.

RH-A DEPARTMENT SUPERVISOR: Yes, we have all experienced it before, but sometimes such behaviour can derive from the leadership that takes place in the office.

The other supervisors let out a snicker while Mr. Popkin tries not to take offense and takes a sip of the coffee; he is pleased that it tastes good.

MR. POPKIN: Yes, well ... (CLEARS HIS THROAT) Luckily, my group knows how to follow instructions, as this is excellent coffee, but I'll keep that in mind. (TURNS TO ELISA) Thanks again for the coffee, Employee #263.

ELISA: You're welcome, Mr. Popkin. (BEGINS TO LEAVE) If you excuse me, I have to –

RH-A DEPARTMENT SUPERVISOR: Why don't you stay for a while?

Elisa freezes in surprise while Mr. Popkin, Daniel and Thomas turn to the department supervisors, surprised as well.

ELISA: (BAFFLED) I'm sorry?

MR. POPKIN: (TAKEN ABACK) Wow, this is getting a bit weird. (PROFESSIONALLY) Listen, men, I do have to remind you that she works for me and not for anyone else, so there's no way I'm letting you distract her from work just to serve you gentlemen coffee.

RH-A DEPARTMENT SUPERVISOR: (CHUCKLES) As tempting as that may be, that's not what I meant. (TURNS TO ELISA) We're having a bit of a conflict about what project we should get started on for the next quarter. This decision is quite crucial for us supervisors, as the fate of the Regional Headquarters depends on it.

Elisa goes silent, as she remains perplexed about the entire situation, while Mr. Popkin does not even wait for her to answer.

MR. POPKIN: (LAUGHS IN DISBELIEF) Gee, this the first I'm seeing this. I don't know what's in the air today (PROFESSIONALLY), but I'm pretty sure we all have the capability to act more professionally when a lady is present. There's no need to drag her into this conversation.

RH-D DEPARTMENT SUPERVISOR: (TURNS TO MR. POPKIN) Well, I don't see a problem with it. We would like a fresh opinion to decide which project should be our best move for the organization.

RH-B DEPARTMENT SUPERVISOR: Besides, it's usually nice to have another employee in the room. Allow the young minds to understand what goes on behind the scenes – heck, we'll ask anyone if it gets us out of these chairs quicker!

Everyone laughs as Elisa lets out a small giggle.

RH-A DEPARTMENT SUPERVISOR: So, what do you say? Will you stay for a while?

ELISA: (PAUSES) I'll only stay if Mr. Popkin says it's okay.

The department supervisors turn to Mr. Popkin for an answer while he contemplates with himself.

MR. POPKIN: (CHUCKLES) Well, isn't she considerate. It's her invitation and yet she's asking for my permission. However, since you guys think it's okay, then fine … I'll let her stay. (POINTS TO THE CORNER) Just stand over there in the corner, and we'll call you when you're needed.

Elisa nods as she goes to stand in the corner but tries her best to keep her distance from Thomas, who continues to stare at her with a scowl.

MR. POPKIN: So, gentlemen, have we made a decision on –

RH-B DEPARTMENT SUPERVISOR: Wait a second here. You're already asking if we've made a decision and we haven't even asked the young lady yet. If I have to be honest, you're being quite unfair here!

RH-A DEPARTMENT SUPERVISOR: (TURNS TO ELISA) We would like to hear which project you would choose.

ELISA: And those projects are …

RH-D DEPARTMENT SUPERVISOR: Adonis or Cornelius.

ELISA: (SLIGHTLY CONFUSED) My apologies, I'm having trouble following.

Thomas stands there satisfied with Elisa's cluelessness, as Mr. Popkin and Daniel sense the impatience of the department supervisors.

DANIEL: I know that's not a straight-up answer for you all, but she has been working tremendously hard on several project reports, so she might not even remember which projects you're talking about. (TURNS TO ELISA) Adonis and Cornelius are the names of the two major projects we're deciding on. It's really important that we make a decision today. (CORDIAL) My apologies, gentlemen, I had to catch her up on the situation.

RH-A DEPARTMENT SUPERVISOR: (CORDIAL) That's fine, as long as we get to hear her opinion.

MR. POPKIN: (IN DISBELIEF) But what's the point in all of this? We've already looked at the data and made some compelling arguments about choosing the Adonis project!

THOMAS: (JUMPS IN) Yes, Mr. Popkin does have a point!

The department supervisors begin to grow impatient as Thomas leaves his corner to argue his point.

THOMAS: (CONFIDENTLY) Why bother going back and forth when Adonis is the perfect choice! It's the more exciting of the two projects; it has the bigger budget, and if we start on Adonis in the next quarter, it will put Tint Valley on the map!

MR. POPKIN: (UNINTERESTED) Yes, you said that about three times already.

THOMAS: (CONFIDENTLY) And I will say it again just to prove that Adonis is the better choice. (SLOWLY TURNS TO ELISA WHILE TALKING THROUGH HIS TEETH) So there's really no need to waste time asking for another opinion.

Elisa rolls her eyes in annoyance and is barely bothered by Thomas's threatening look as one of the department supervisors contemplates the decision.

RH-B DEPARTMENT SUPERVISOR: (FIRMLY) I still don't agree with the choice.

RH-D DEPARTMENT SUPERVISOR: (SIGHS IN HOPELESSNESS) Here we go again – you've always been indecisive making these decisions.

RH-B DEPARTMENT SUPERVISOR: (ARGUES) It's not about being indecisive! It's a risk! I don't like taking risks – and I don't want to take another risk for this organization!

MR. POPKIN: (ARGUES) You have to have the balls to take risks if you want to make more money!

RH-B DEPARTMENT SUPERVISOR: (ARGUES) But it's not just about making money! Think about the expenses we have to deal with every month! Think about the employees!

Everyone in the room starts arguing with each other as Daniel tries his best to calm everyone down. Elisa anxiously watches the fight begin to escalate until she suddenly remembers a report she did concerning the Adonis and Cornelius project.

ELISA: You should choose Cornelius.

Everyone stops fighting and turns to Elisa in shock as she stands firm with her decision.

ELISA: I believe you will have greater success if you choose Cornelius.

Mr. Popkin, Daniel and Thomas remain silent as the department supervisors seem satisfied with Elisa's answer.

RH-B DEPARTMENT SUPERVISOR: (SATISFIED) Yeah, this seems more like it – this is exactly what we've been asking for. (TURNS TO ELISA) Please explain your point to us, Ms. 263.

ELISA: Going back to all the reports I've done, I remember using the payback period on both the Adonis and Cornelius projects. From what I remember, the results were more favourable for the Cornelius project than they were for the Adonis project. However, if you still feel doubtful about the decision, I suggest that you figure out the net present value for both projects while using other criteria to finalize your decision.

Daniel frantically looks for the report she just mentioned while the department supervisors sit back, impressed with Elisa's explanation. The supervisors begin to talk amongst themselves while Daniel manages to find the report and looks through the results as he stands there astonished himself.

RH-A DEPARTMENT SUPERVISOR: (INTRIGUED) Very interesting. Would you further explain your reasons for choosing the Cornelius Project?

ELISA: The decision seemed pretty clear based on the results. Adonis had a longer payback period of five years, along with a 25% rate of return. Cornelius resulted in a shorter payback period of three point eight years, along with a 26.7% rate.

DANIEL: (BRINGS THE REPORT TO THE TABLE) She isn't mistaken. The report is right here … (LOOKS AT ELISA) submitted by Employee #263.

The department supervisors look through the report along with Mr. Popkin and Thomas, and all of them see the matching results. Mr. Popkin sits back in disbelief while the department supervisors nod to each other, impressed by Elisa's work.

RH-D DEPARTMENT SUPERVISOR: (HAPPILY) Well, I don't know about you fellas, but I feel like switching my choice! (GESTURES TO ELISA) This young lady sure knows what she's talking about!

RH-B DEPARTMENT SUPERVISOR: (CURIOUS) Why should we trust your decision?

ELISA: (GESTURES TO RH-B DEPARTMENT SUPERVISOR) You said it yourself that you didn't want to take any risks, and the Regional Headquarters does have a long history of taking risks that turned out unsuccessfully. (TURNS TO EVERYONE) If you want to stay on the safe side, I suggest you choose Cornelius. Adonis has its benefits, as it can be started anytime – even after the completion of Cornelius. However, if you choose Adonis as a starting project to begin the next quarter, you might be looking at a white elephant on your hands.

The department supervisors turn to each other in astonishment until they all start laughing uncontrollably. Mr. Popkin, Daniel and Thomas remain silent for a moment until they conform by laughing as well while Elisa stands there confused and slightly offended.

ELISA: I apologize if I said anything wrong –

RH-A DEPARTMENT SUPERVISOR: (CHUCKLES) No, that's not the case at all.

The department supervisors try their best to control their laughter, while Mr. Popkin signals Daniel and Thomas to stop laughing immediately.

RH-A DEPARTMENT SUPERVISOR: (LOOKS AT ELISA) Oh, what a shame. You bear the colours of a late Tint, but have the mind of a solid Hue.

Elisa finally flashes a slight grin as she contemplates whether to take it as a compliment or an insult.

RH-B DEPARTMENT SUPERVISOR: (HAPPILY) I'll say. I can't help but be impressed myself – not even a complete Canvas could speak like that.

RH-A DEPARTMENT SUPERVISOR: (CHUCKLES) It's very intriguing how you ended up in this department. (TURNS TO MR. POPKIN) What's going on, Van? Have you been keeping hidden gems from us all this time?

MR. POPKIN: (CORDIAL) Well, you know me, I prefer not to reveal all my secrets, especially my star employees. She's a very hard worker, and we're fortunate to have her in our department.

RH-D DEPARTMENT SUPERVISOR: (HAPPILY) How do you feel about transferring?

Elisa looks at the department supervisor in shock, along with Mr. Popkin and Daniel, while Thomas also shows signs of disbelief.

MR. POPKIN: Wait a second here. This isn't what we came here for. Yes, employees can request a transfer if they wish – we give them the absolute right to do so. However, we don't just barge into each other's offices and ask employees to transfer!

RH-D DEPARTMENT SUPERVISOR: (SHRUGS) I don't see an issue with that. (TURNS TO ELISA) Our department is usually short-staffed, and it would be great if we had an extra hand to help us out.

MR. POPKIN: (BEGINS TO ARGUE) Now you listen –

ELISA: Forgive me for interrupting, Mr. Popkin, but I do want to make one thing clear. (TURNS TO RH-D DEPARTMENT SUPERVISOR) As appreciative as I am of your offer, I believe it's best for me to stay where I am and continue to work with Mr. Popkin along with this department.

Mr. Popkin calms down while the department supervisors sit there, baffled by Elisa's loyalty.

RH-B DEPARTMENT SUPERVISOR: Wow ... Not only is she smart, but she's also very loyal to her boss. (TURNS TO RH-D DEPARTMENT SUPERVISOR) That means it's gonna be real tough, swiping her off his hands.

MR. POPKIN: (CORDIALLY) It's always a pleasure to hear your employees say such things, and you know what they say: you can't always have all the good ones ... (LOWLY) Otherwise, I would've swept through all your offices.

The department supervisors look at each other and grimace in offence, while Daniel gives Mr. Popkin a warning look.

MR. POPKIN: (CORDIALLY) But then again, I should know better than to ever downplay an employee's performance. (TURNS TO ELISA) Thank you again, Employee #263. You definitely made our decision much easier.

ELISA: (KINDLY) You're welcome, Mr. Popkin. (POINTS TO THE DOOR) And if you don't mind, I really have to go.

MR. POPKIN: (REMEMBERS) Oh yes! (TURNS TO EVERYONE) As I just remembered, today is Power Hour, and I can't have her miss out on her chance to win the special prize. (TURNS TO ELISA) You can go now – we will no longer take up your time.

RH-B DEPARTMENT SUPERVISOR: (HAPPILY) Well, it was a pleasure having you at our meeting. I definitely felt like a kid in school again.

RH-A DEPARTMENT SUPERVISOR: (CORDIAL) Thank you for giving us your input. (WAVES GOODBYE) Bye now.

Elisa waves goodbye and quickly leaves the conference room while the department supervisors begin to talk about her amongst themselves.

Thomas notices the praise Elisa is receiving from the department supervisors and begins to feel resentful toward her.

INT. THE RH-C DEPARTMENT OFFICE OF REGIONAL HEADQUARTERS – MORNING

Elisa quietly closes the door of the conference room and makes her way to her cubicle. Everyone in the office notices Elisa's return and immediately turns to her in anticipation until she gives them the "OK" gesture. Everyone exhales in relief and begins working again while Elisa puts on her headset and does the same. A few employees, confused by her calm demeanor, stare at Elisa and whisper amongst themselves.

MALE COLLEAGUE 1: (WHISPERS) I don't understand. She's not sweating, breaking out in hives – she's not even shedding one tear.

FEMALE COLLEAGUE 1: (WHISPERS) I don't get it either. How come she was able to get out of there okay? Not one single person in this room has been able to survive one sitting in a department meeting!

MALE COLLEAGUE 1: (WHISPERS) It's starting to bother me, too. What exactly happened in that conference room?

The employees who are lounging around notice the door of the conference room opening as they scurry back to their cubicles and start working again. Mr. Popkin, Daniel and Thomas exit the room along with the department supervisors who are talking about tomorrow's gathering at the Entertainment Hall.

RH-D DEPARTMENT SUPERVISOR: (HAPPILY) Well, I hope you don't mind me driving there because I like to have control of the wheel!

RH-A DEPARTMENT SUPERVISOR: (CHUCKLES) Yes, that would seriously give us a break, knowing that he's a horrible backseat driver.

Mr. Popkin laughs loudly, along with the department supervisors, while everyone in the office remains silent and continues working.

MR. POPKIN: Well, gentlemen, thank you for attending this week's meeting.

RH-B DEPARTMENT SUPERVISOR: (HAPPILY) Oh yes, it was definitely pleasurable. I'm hoping we could have another one like this week's meeting.

MR. POPKIN: (THINKS) I'll see what I can do, since this meeting was very engaging, but until then, I'll see you guys at that opera event tomorrow.

RH-D DEPARTMENT SUPERVISOR: (CORDIALLY) For sure, we will be looking forward to our small gathering at the Entertainment Hall, but for now (BEGINS TO LEAVE), we have to run.

RH-A DEPARTMENT SUPERVISOR: (WAVES GOODBYE) See you tomorrow night.

MR. POPKIN: (WAVES GOODBYE) Yeah, see you.

Mr. Popkin carefully watches the department supervisors leave the office before letting out a sigh of relief. He and Daniel begin walking around the office.

DANIEL: Well, that meeting went smoother than expected.

MR. POPKIN: (THINKS) Yes, it surely did ... because knowing if I had to sit another hour with those bastards, I would've just lost it. (COMES UP TO ELISA) Employee #263.

Elisa notices Mr. Popkin and takes off her headset to give him her full attention. He stands there silent for a moment before patting her on the shoulder.

MR. POPKIN: (GENUINELY) Great job. You really did us a solid in that meeting.

Thomas stands there stunned, while a few of the other employees sit back in shock as well.

ELISA: Thank you, Mr. Popkin.

MR. POPKIN: (GENUINELY) You're very welcome. (HAPPILY STARTS WALKING AROUND) Hold onto this moment for today because it might not come back again! Back to work, everyone!

Everyone immediately goes back to work while Elisa sits back for a moment and starts smiling to herself until Thomas comes up to her.

THOMAS: (WHISPERS ANGRILY) Don't ever think you're winning that prize by stepping out of your place!

Thomas walks away while Elisa huffs in impatience as she puts back on her headset and starts working again. Thomas walks angrily to his cubicle and signs onto his system while everyone else continues to answer phone calls, answer emails, complete previous documents and write reports.

▌ INT. REGIONAL HEADQUARTERS CAFETERIA – AFTERNOON

Elisa pays for her lunch and takes her time to search for a place to sit, as well as look for Gillian. She carefully tries her best to look through the crowd for Gillian until she gives up and sits in her usual seat near the window. Elisa starts eating her lunch and looks out the window for a moment without noticing Gillian coming slowly toward her.

GILLIAN: (KINDLY) Excuse me, Miss, is this seat taken?

Startled, Elisa stops eating and turns to see Gillian smiling at her. She relaxes and smiles back.

ELISA: (PLAYFULLY) Depends on who wants to take it. I did reserve it for a guest.

GILLIAN: (PLAYFULLY) Is that so? (PLAYFULLY LOOKS AROUND) Well, I don't see anyone else trying to take it, so it must be free … (KINDLY) Mind if I steal it from your guest to join you?

ELISA: (KINDLY) You can do whatever you please.

Elisa and Gillian smile at each other for a moment until they start laughing quietly before Gillian takes her seat.

GILLIAN: (HAPPILY) Finally, a proper lunch where I'm not accompanied by the air for once. It's good to know that there's a strong woman I can talk to in this place!

ELISA: (CONFUSED) Why would you say that?

GILLIAN: Why wouldn't I, after what you managed to pull off this morning? You got people looking at you like a superhero – or at least someone who's not from Earth.

ELISA: (SHRUGS) It was nothing, really. I just happened to remember one of the reports I did to understand what they were talking about. But from what occurred in the conference room, I understand why no one wanted to take the Office Request – I almost wanted to leave myself.

GILLIAN: Well, you could've fooled me. You came out of there like nothing had happened. Not many people in our department have the ability to sit through an entire meeting. They would come out quivering after just five minutes. But it's a good thing for Mr. Popkin. Now, he has another person to sit through meetings with.

ELISA: (SHAKES HER HEAD) You heard what he said. I doubt that's going to happen.

GILLIAN: (STUNNED) You do realize that was the first time Mr. Popkin ever said "good job" to anyone – genuinely, to be specific. You really believe that he wouldn't choose you to attend another meeting?

ELISA: (SHRUGS) I don't see any other reason not to –

GILLIAN: (HAPPILY) Don't act so coy, Elisa. If you haven't noticed, you're not as invisible as you think you are. I've been watching you.

Elisa sits there, confused as Gillian stands by her statement.

GILLIAN: (HONESTLY) Yep, ever since you got here. Believe me, I've witnessed many newcomers struggling to survive this kind of work, and they continue to have meltdowns to this day. But when you came here, you just handled things like a soldier, and from the looks of it, you must've come from a Steels background ... unless the necklace you're wearing says otherwise.

Elisa freezes as she quickly adjusts her shirt to hide the Steels dog tag necklace that once belonged to Garreth.

GILLIAN: (REASSURINGLY) Don't worry. I'm not going to tell a soul, knowing how important those dog tags are for some people.

ELISA: (SLIGHTLY RELAXED) I appreciate that … (SUSPICIOUSLY) So, you bumping into me wasn't a complete accident.

GILLIAN: (SHRUGS) You can choose to believe that if you want, but if I have to be honest, I don't think you realize how unapproachable you are. I mean, you start off your day working, as usual. You don't have any personal relationships, let alone say hello to anyone. You sit in the same spot for lunch, and you don't even stay for the full hour once you finish. Of course people are intimidated by you. No one wants to deal with rejection, since you don't talk to anybody besides Hank. (HAPPILY) But whether you think our little encounter was an accident or on purpose, I'm glad that it happened since I finally got a chance to talk to you.

Elisa flashes a brief smile, but continues to contemplate the reason for Gillian's interest in her.

ELISA: (SUSPICIOUSLY) Is there something I should know about you first, if this continues?

GILLIAN: (BLUNTLY) Oh, you'd wish I was like that. I'm surprised I've received such speculation ever since I've been here! And for the record, asking a question like that is completely rude, and you won't make any friends with that kind of mindset, as that is certainly not the case. (CURIOUS) Unless that's what you're into.

ELISA: (BLUNTLY) I don't think I like people that much for that to happen.

GILLIAN: I understand … it must've been tough growing up as a Late Tint.

ELISA: (PAUSES AND NODS) It was, but I try my best not to let it affect me … (THINKS), at least not completely.

GILLIAN: It happens to the best of us. I didn't have it any easier myself. I still continue the old habits I had back home, which could explain why I'm always cranky all the time. Mind if I ask … your Tint Level?

ELISA: 72%.

GILLIAN: (SLIGHTLY SURPRISED) Wow, lucky you. I've been at 75% for who knows how long. At least this job took me out of the 78% I'd been stuck at for years. How did you manage to get yours up so high?

ELISA: I graduated with a 72% before I came here, but I didn't start that way, that's for sure. I was stuck at 79% throughout my childhood until I reached high school. Afterward, I had never made much progress when I started working here.

GILLIAN: (SHOCKED) My goodness, it's the first that I'm hearing this ... no progress at all?

Elisa just smiles and shakes her head while Gillian sits back in disbelief.

GILLIAN: (ASTONISHED) Wow, what a shame ... and I thought I had it bad.

ELISA: It's not as bad as you think.

GILLIAN: (SERIOUSLY) Oh, it is, especially when the main purpose for Tint Valley is to improve ourselves to reach the Canvas Phase before we make it to Hue City – otherwise, you might just end up with Tint Brain. (HONESTLY) It doesn't make any sense why you haven't made any progress. From watching how you commit to your work, you should've been out of here by now ... makes you wonder if the system is actually being fair to us.

Gillian continues talking as Elisa sits there frozen in slight shock and quickly eats her lunch while she automatically remembers her mother's detestation of the Hue System.

Thirteen Years Prior

▌ INT. THE GRAVES' HOUSE – AFTERNOON

Garreth is sipping a cup of coffee in the kitchen when Carman enters the house angrily.

CARMAN: (ANGRILY TO HERSELF) Madness … just pure madness … the audacity they have to do that. It's absolute nonsense!

Carman continues to whisper angrily to herself, while Garreth watches her carefully and wonders what is going on.

GARRETH: (COMES UP TO CARMAN) What are you mumbling about this time? I see that you didn't bring any groceries today.

CARMAN: (UPSET) That's because it was your turn to pick up the groceries and you made it specifically clear that you could handle it on your own.

GARRETH: Well, I would've if I had the list – I even called the shop to see if you could tell me where it was, but they said you were unavailable.

CARMAN: (UPSET) Those bastards are usually unreliable because I heard no such thing when I left the shop.

Carman puts away her purse and her keys and goes to the kitchen to think about what to make for dinner. Garreth watches her look around the kitchen for a moment until she aggressively takes off her jacket and throws it to the floor.

CARMAN: (ANGRILY) Damn these fucking Hue Minds!

GARRETH: (SHOCKED) What on earth is wrong with you? (COMES UP TO CARMAN) Did you get bitten by the Karma Bug or something?

CARMAN: (ANGRILY) I really don't have the patience for your stupid jokes – especially when you're the reason why we agreed to this fucking system in the first place!

GARRETH: I don't know how this has turned back to me, but you know how I feel about you swearing in the house. It's not good for the kids to hear.

CARMAN: (ANGRILY) Not good for the kids? Please, they're already learning about it at school and using those words on each other! They're having way too much freedom with this new system – the Metallic Order would've straightened them out by now.

GARRETH: (ARGUES) Now don't you dare bring up those horrible times here. The Metallic Order made our lives a mess!

CARMAN: (SCREAMS) Well, this system is much worse! (ANGRILY) At least with the Metallic Order, I had a job! I never had to worry about anything until that Isaim guy brought this new system upon us! I never had to worry about what my Tint Level was to go to work! I never had to worry about being bothered, being stared at and ridiculed by my own peers while they walk around freely with their Early Tint selves. And do you know what's worse than being called a Slate? Being called a liability, as those shitheads had the audacity to look me in the eye and kick me out of the store just now! They kicked me out of the one thing I love, and I don't know what I'm going to do to keep this family alive without working ... (TEARS UP) and I never had to worry about that until this happened.

Eight-year-old Elisa sits quietly by the stairs and listens to the conversation as Carman tries her best not to cry, while Garreth remains silent and begins to understand how she feels.

GARRETH: (CALMLY) All right, let's ... (GIVES CARMAN A HUG) Let's just calm down for a second here ... I understand how you feel, and I'm sorry that happened to you. (TURNS CARMAN TOWARD HIM) But we don't have to make this our new reality, as this new system has done wonders for us. We can definitely fix this – we'll figure out a way to get your job back. I'll even take a day off for us to go to the Grand Arne Office, so we can plead our case.

CARMAN: (SMIRKS) Like those boys are going to do anything for us. (ARGUES) Who is really going to listen to a middle-aged woman who still has an 80% Tint Level? You really need to stop talking to those Theodes, if that's where your mind is going. (UPSET) Forget it. I'm not going to go to GAO just to be rejected by those bastards and be told what wonders this system has done for us – our own kids don't even get along with each other because of this system!

GARRETH: (SERIOUSLY) You know I try very hard to discipline them for such behaviour –

CARMAN: (UPSET) How effective is that? Because they're going to be confronted with such behaviour every day! From what I'm seeing, we're just wasting our voices here! How is this system benefiting anyone when only two out of our three children are progressing! Not only will I be stuck here for the rest of my life, but we'll also have another inconvenience in the house.

GARRETH: (ARGUES) Now don't you dare say that! Elisa will catch up.

CARMAN: (ARGUES) And how do you know that? The neighbours aren't saying that! Her teachers aren't saying that! The stupid AI on her Life Band isn't saying that either! And because of her Tint Level, she'll be called a dumbass for the rest of her life! So how could she possibly reach her Canvas Phase, let alone make it to Hue City with her progress?

GARRETH: (ARGUES) All I know is that putting limitations on our daughter is not going to make things any better! Now I know you're upset about all this, but don't you ever think that Elisa will never get a chance to progress! She will get a chance to go to Hue City and live a better life than everyone else!

CARMAN: (PAUSES) See … not even you know the answer.

Carman walks away from Garreth as he stands and sighs in frustration.

CARMAN: (SERIOUSLY) I'm getting sick and tired of this conversation. Call me when you have some sense in your head.

GARRETH: (SERIOUSLY) We will go to the Grand Arne Office! I believe we'll get the results we need if we try –

CARMAN: (ARGUES) Go ahead and waste your time because I'm certainly not going to do that with you.

Carman turns to make her way upstairs but stops when she sees eight-year-old Elisa sitting there, causing her to huff in frustration.

CARMAN: (UPSET) What did I tell you about eavesdropping?

Carman angrily heads upstairs to her room as Garreth comes over and sees eight-year-old Elisa on the stairs. He gradually calms down.

GARRETH: (CALMLY) Come here ... it's going to be okay.

Eight-year-old Elisa hesitates until she gets up and goes up to Garreth and he pulls her in for a hug.

Thirteen Years Later

▌ INT. REGIONAL HEADQUARTERS CAFETERIA – AFTERNOON

GILLIAN: Don't you think so?

Elisa snaps into focus and remembers that she is having lunch with Gillian.

ELISA: I guess you could say something like that.

GILLIAN: (STARES CAREFULLY AT ELISA) I see you're wearing that same look you had this morning. Mind if I ask what's going on or is it too much of a touchy topic? Did the bus driver give you a hard time today? Did a special someone forget your birthday or something? Did Mommy Dearest upset you before you went to bed last night?

Elisa stops eating and gives Gillian a firm look as she stops herself and feels slightly intimidated.

GILLIAN: (SURRENDERS) Okay, touchy topic. I promise I won't mention it again.

ELISA: (CALMLY) I apologize for that ... I just don't like talking about my personal life.

GILLIAN: It's fine, really. Everyone has their limits. Forgive me for being nosey. I'm just really excited to have lunch with someone who is willing to talk to me.

ELISA: Why would you say that?

GILLIAN: You gotta be kidding me, mate. Pay attention to the room here.

Elisa and Gillian watch quietly as several colleagues pass them without acknowledging their presence whatsoever. A few colleagues glance at Elisa and Gillian but walk away without saying hello and go about their business.

GILLIAN: (WATCHES EVERYONE) You see what's going on here? All they ever care about is the 50%s, 40%s and 30%s – not even the 60%s get such special treatment as they do. But at least they have each other, since there are a lot of them; us 70%s are not even that close. (TURNS TO ELISA) But do you see what I'm trying to say here? We're practically the smartest people in the room right now, and they pass us like we don't even exist.

ELISA: Well, technically, that's their loss. It's not our job to get them to hang out with us, so we just leave them alone and stay out of their way, since they're already doing the same for us.

GILLIAN: (CHUCKLES) Well, aren't you a shoo-in for giving people a bly. I would never have thought about it in that way. (TURNS TO EVERYONE) Those guys don't even want to sit with us but behave like babies when we don't take an Office Request.

Elisa chuckles and continues to eat her lunch. Gillian does the same until she notices Thomas sitting on the other side of the room, stressed out while a few colleagues try to calm him down.

GILLIAN: (CONCERNED) Well, isn't someone in a bad mood today. (TURNS TO ELISA) You must've really ruffled his feathers in that conference room.

Gillian turns back to see Thomas staring at Elisa angrily while she continues to calmly eat her lunch.

GILLIAN: (TURNS TO ELISA, ASTONISHED) You certainly must be wearing panties made of titanium to withstand a stare like that. It looks like you just killed his best friend right in front of him.

ELISA: (SHAKES HER HEAD) Ignore him. He's only upset that the department supervisors listened to my suggestion instead of his. And he had the nerve to threaten me to not step out of my place – as if I wanted to do that in the first place.

GILLIAN: (NONCHALANTLY) Oh, you don't have to worry about that. It's nice to see Thomas quaking in his boots for once. (SLIGHTLY CONCERNED) But you do need to be careful not to make too many enemies here. Who knows what years of being in this place would do to someone.

ELISA: I have survived here long enough without anyone bothering me. I doubt that one enemy will affect me working in this place.

GILLIAN: (SITS BACK ASTONISHED) Well, you definitely need to give me a pair of those titanium panties! There are certain times when I want to get through the day without wanting to punch someone in the face.

Elisa lets out a pleasant laugh, while Gillian enjoys lightening the mood.

GILLIAN: (IMPRESSED) That Office Request must've done something to you. Do you mind if I take the next one?

ELISA: You can go right ahead, but did you have to do that to Xavier back there?

GILLIAN: (SERIOUSLY) I had to do it – just to show him that I'm on his tail from now on! No one deserves my sympathy after saying that word. I'm not the forgiving and "look the other way" type like you are. (PLAYFULLY) And how would you know about that when you were busy with a customer?

ELISA: (PLAYFULLY) Based on your observation skills, you should already know how word gets around here.

Elisa and Gillian stare at each other for a moment until they start laughing and finish their lunch together.

A Few Hours Later

▍EXT. OUTSIDE REGIONAL HEADQUARTERS – EVENING

Everyone leaves Regional Headquarters at the end of the afternoon shift. Elisa and Gillian leave afterwards and watch everyone catch up with friends while taking their usual routes home or to Primetime Plaza.

MALE EMPLOYEE 1: (HAPPILY) Hey, we should have dinner at the Fire House tonight. I heard they brought back their famous all-you-can-eat ribs for the entire week!

MALE EMPLOYEE 2: (HAPPILY) Sounds great, man!

FEMALE EMPLOYEE 1: (CONCERNED) But wait. You know the Fire House will have trouble letting us in if we don't have eight people! (GESTURES TO ELISA AND GILLIAN) Should we ask them if they want to come with us?

MALE EMPLOYEE 1: (SHAKES HIS HEAD) Don't worry about that. I'm pretty sure we can find more of our friends if we head there now! C'mon, let's go!

The group of employees takes a large taxi to Primetime Plaza, while Elisa and Gillian stand there, unimpressed and uninterested.

GILLIAN: (SIGHS) So much for being invited to dinner.

ELISA: (REASSURINGLY) Don't worry; we'll get 'em next time.

GILLIAN: I hope so because those ribs sound so good right now. I'm contemplating whether I should head home or go to Wallace's Corner to watch a movie. (TURNS TO ELISA) Unless you want to come with me.

ELISA: (REMEMBERS) I'm actually gonna take a raincheck. There's somewhere I have to be before I head home tonight.

GILLIAN: All right, suit yourself. (TURNS TO ELISA) But don't raincheck on me for too long! I want to spend more time with my new buddy!

ELISA: (SMILES) Okay, I promise I'll be available next time.

GILLIAN: (HAPPILY) You better – you know I'll be waiting! (BEGINS TO LEAVE) Take care, Elisa!

ELISA: (STOPS AND WAVES GOODBYE) You, too! Bye, Gillian!

Gillian heads straight toward the Route 422 bus to go home, while Elisa stands there contemplating whether to go home herself or head straight to Primetime Plaza.

EXT. PRIMETIME PLAZA – EVENING

The Route 644 bus drops its passengers off at Primetime Plaza, as many people catch up with friends and family and go to their preferred stores. Elisa exits the bus and looks around for a moment until she sees Bartlett's Piece Bookstore.

INT. BARTLETT'S PIECE BOOKSTORE – EVENING

Vincent Maguire (mid-forties) is looking through a book to pass the time when he looks up to see Elisa come inside, and they both smile at each other.

ELISA: (PLEASANTLY) It's not too late, is it?

VINCENT: (SMILES) For you, it never is ... it's been a while, Ms. Graves.

ELISA: It has been, Vincent. (LOOKS AROUND) Looks like you got some new stories to fill up these shelves.

VINCENT: (LOOKS AROUND AND SMILES) New stories do have a way of finding a home here. They still haven't shut down the dig sites at the Discovery Region, even though the commander-in-chief had forbidden it years ago. (TURNS TO ELISA) But it's nice to have returning customers. You have been missed, Ms. Graves.

ELISA: (TURNS TO VINCENT) I do apologize for not visiting more often. (REMEMBERING) The last time I was here, according to the business inspector, I heard that they were closing the place down.

VINCENT: Well, luckily, there were enough readers in Tint Valley to give us enough revenue to keep this place going. And I'm glad we were able to stay open for a while longer ... especially knowing you would come when you needed a place to escape. Anything from your mother?

Elisa sighs sadly and shakes her head, while Vincent nods in understanding.

VINCENT: You're lucky that I was expecting you since I was paying attention to the calendar. (POINTS TO THE CORNER) You should be able to see a special surprise there.

Elisa goes to the corner and stops to see a shelf filled with all her favourite books, along with Garreth's favourite books, as she stands there and smiles.

VINCENT: (PLEASANTLY) Enjoy to your heart's content, Ms. Graves.

ELISA: (TURNS TO VINCENT) Thanks, Vincent.

Vincent nods and smiles before returning to his book. Elisa turns to the shelf and looks through it for a moment until she finds *Cat on a Hot Tin Roof.* She takes the book off the shelf and sits down to read it for the time being.

A Few Hours Later

▌ INT. BARTLETT'S PIECE BOOKSTORE – EVENING

Vincent checks the time and looks out the window to see Primetime Plaza quieting down. He turns to see Elisa continuing to read *Cat on a Hot Tin Roof* and then he approaches her.

VINCENT: (APOLOGETIC) I do apologize, Ms. Graves.

Elisa snaps into focus and looks up to see Vincent with a sad look on his face.

VINCENT: (APOLOGETIC) We're about to close.

Elisa takes a moment to pay attention to the time and nods in understanding as she puts the book back on the shelf. She gets up and she and Vincent walk to the front desk.

VINCENT: I hope you enjoyed your time here.

ELISA: I did. It's a shame that I didn't get to finish.

VINCENT: You're welcome to come back anytime you like – just remember that we're open all day until 8pm.

Elisa nods as she turns to the window and spots a man wearing Technological-Environmental colours standing in the middle of Primetime Plaza. She grimaces in confusion as she watches the man approaching people with a Life Pad in his hands that he tries to sell to them.

VINCENT: Are you sure you don't want to take the book home with you?

ELISA: (TURNS TO VINCENT) It's okay. I'll finish it when I come back another time. (POINTS TO A BOOK ON THE SHELF) Is that book still for sale?

VINCENT: (TURNS TO A BOOK AND PULLS IT OFF THE SHELF) Why yes, it is. (TURNS TO ELISA) You'd be surprised that I still have copies of this book. The Great Gatsby is quite popular with my small population of readers. I'm surprised you might be into it, knowing how hard I tried to sell this book to your father a gazillion times.

ELISA: My father was never into best sellers – he usually enjoyed what was in the hidden gems section. Thanks again, Vincent.

VINCENT: You're welcome, Ms. Graves. Are you sure you don't want anything else?

Elisa stands there contemplating as she turns back to the Technological-Environmental Hue selling the Life Pad in the middle of Primetime Plaza.

❚ EXT. PRIMETIME PLAZA – EVENING

Elisa leaves Bartlett's Piece Bookstore and waves goodbye to Vincent before making her way home. She tries her best to avoid the Technological-Environmental Hue trying to sell the Life Pad to a couple, as they continuously refuse him and walk away.

TECHNOLOGICAL-ENVIRONMENTAL HUE: (TO THE COUPLE) That's completely understandable. Well … I hope you have a good day. (LOOKS AROUND AND NOTICES ELISA) Hey! Mind if I talk to you for a second!

Elisa stops and gives the Technological-Environmental Hue a stern look as he comes up to her with anticipation.

TECHNOLOGICAL-ENVIRONMENTAL HUE: (EXAGGERATED) Hey there! I'm so glad you stopped for me, Miss, because I have something to show you! I just need a moment of your time.

Elisa attempts to walk away as the Technological-Environmental Hue moves to block her way.

TECHNOLOGICAL-ENVIRONMENTAL HUE: (EXAGGERATED) Now wait – I just need one moment. I promise I won't take long.

ELISA: (BLUNTLY) By any chance, are you lost?

TECHNOLOGICAL-ENVIRONMENTAL HUE: (EXAGGERATED) Of course I'm not lost. I believe I'm in the right place – especially when I want to show you this.

Elisa shields her eyes from the brightness of the Life Pad's screen as the Technological-Environmental Hue tries to hold her attention.

TECHNOLOGICAL-ENVIRONMENTAL HUE: (EXAGGERATED) Now check this out. This is the revolutionary, out-of-this-world, state-of-the-art Life Pad. While everyone is getting tired of seeing things in a hologram, the Life Pad is a great alternative to accessing information about your health and finances as well as your Phase Status.

Elisa attempts to walk away again as the Technological-Environmental Hue tries to block her way.

TECHNOLOGICAL-ENVIRONMENTAL HUE: (EXAGGERATED) Now wait–wait–wait! It can do so much more than that! All you need to do is connect your Life Pad to this device and there are all sorts of things you can do to your heart's content! You can listen to music here and watch movies here. You can even access your favourite books here if you want (GESTURES TO ELISA'S BOOK), which is so much better than purchasing a paper copy in that store!

ELISA: (BLUNTLY) Not interested.

TECHNOLOGICAL-ENVIRONMENTAL HUE: (EXAGGERATED) You haven't even given it a chance, kid – just look right here.

Elisa stands there frustrated as the Technological-Environmental Hue shows her the library that is included in the Life Pad.

TECHNOLOGICAL-ENVIRONMENTAL HUE: (EXAGGERATED) You see? It carries every single book that exists in Bartlett's Piece! We have even partnered with the GAO to publish old archives along with endless number of books available in their library – just to keep things interesting!

ELISA: And how do you know that it can carry an endless number of books in Bartlett's Piece? Did you create this thing?

TECHNOLOGICAL-ENVIRONMENTAL HUE: (EXAGGERATED) Of course I did. Why else would I be here showing this to you?

ELISA: Again, not interested.

Elisa attempts to walk away again as the Technological-Environmental Hue tries to block her way one last time.

TECHNOLOGICAL-ENVIRONMENTAL HUE: (EXAGGERATED) Now wait – just hold on for a second. I know it's something that can be hard to afford, but I'm willing to make you an offer that is brought to you by the Grand Arne Office. This allows our amazing customers to give out contributions to Bartlett's Piece to make our home a better and safer place to live, so I'm willing to let you come back tomorrow to receive this Life Pad … (POINTS TO ELISA'S BOOK) If you just give me that book in your hands.

Elisa holds on tightly to *The Great Gatsby*, while the Technological-Environmental Hue waits for her to give it to him.

ELISA: (SLIGHTLY DEFENSIVE) What if I don't want to give this to you?

TECHNOLOGICAL-ENVIRONMENTAL HUE: (EXAGGERATED) Well, that is where we run into a little problem here ... (LEANS TOWARD ELISA) You see, kid, this isn't something you can just easily walk away from – especially when the commander-in-chief has completely banned Discovery Region artifacts from entering Tint Valley. (SLIGHTLY THREATENING) So, you either have to give me the book or I'm going to have to do some not-so-nice things to pry it out of your hands, and trust me, no one out here is going to save you.

Elisa stares at the Technological-Environmental Hue angrily until she gives him *The Great Gatsby* in defeat while he goes back to salesman attitude.

TECHNOLOGICAL-ENVIRONMENTAL HUE: (EXAGGERATED) Thank you for your contribution, miss – you really did this planet a solid! I'll finalize everything when you come back tomorrow! (LOOKS AROUND AND NOTICES SOMEONE) Hey! Mind if I talk to you for a second!

The Technological-Environmental Hue goes to stop someone else to sell the Life Pad. Elisa gives him one last death stare before she walks away and heads straight home.

The Next Day

INT. THE RH-C DEPARTMENT OFFICE OF REGIONAL HEADQUARTERS – AFTERNOON

Everyone at the office continues to answer phone calls, answer emails, complete previous documents and write reports under Daniel's supervision. Everyone does their work simultaneously until the Countdown Clock finishes going down and the Break Bell rings.

DANIEL: (TURNS TO EVERYONE) All right, everyone! It's breaktime! Go ahead and relax your minds, but be back in an hour!

Everyone shuts down their systems temporarily and attempts to make their way out of the office until Mr. Popkin exits his office.

MR. POPKIN: (HAPPILY) Everyone stop where you are!

Everyone stops at once. However, a few employees start complaining and become impatient while Mr. Popkin stands there stunned by their attitude.

MR. POPKIN: What's the rush? What's this excitement about going to lunch when the winner for yesterday's Power Hour hasn't been announced yet? (HAPPILY) Especially when this week's winner gets a ticket to attend the Annual Grand Wallace Celebration Gala at the Entertainment Hall tonight.

Everyone stands in shock and claps for joy as a few employees get excited while Mr. Popkin enjoys the energy in the room.

MR. POPKIN: (HAPPILY) Yes! That's more like it! That's the energy we need when announcing this week's Power Hour winner!

Gradually, everyone stops clapping and waits in anticipation, while Mr. Popkin looks through the results.

MR. POPKIN: Now this employee has worked very hard this week – which is nothing new in the first place. This employee has worked to surpass the office's average by completing five hundred and seventy-three customer requests.

Everyone stands there astonished, as they give a round of applause. Thomas waits anxiously, his attention on Elisa, who waits casually for Mr. Popkin to announce the winner.

MR. POPKIN: Yes, this person definitely deserves that round of applause not only for their hard work but for their previous assistance with our meetings – which makes this employee a true winner, and that winner is ... Employee #158.

Thomas looks up in shock as Daniel turns to Mr. Popkin, stunned as well, while everyone turns to each other, confused but shrugs as they give Thomas a round of applause.

MR. POPKIN: Congratulations, Employee #158! You've won this week's Power Hour Prize!

Thomas remains confused for a moment until he sees Elisa clapping for him, with no resentment on her face, along with everyone else, as he acts surprised and touched by everyone's reaction.

THOMAS: (PLEASANTLY) Oh ... thank you, thank you everyone – you're far too kind. (TURNS TO MR. POPKIN) Thank you, Mr. Popkin, for giving me this opportunity to go to this gala. I promise I'll work even harder from now on and be on my best behavior for tonight's event!

MR. POPKIN: Of course you will! Just don't make us late for the event or your pay will be deducted for this week! (TO EVERYONE) That's all for now, everyone. You can go on your break – but make sure to be back in an hour sharp!

Everyone makes their way out of the office while Thomas hangs back, satisfied about winning the Power Hour prize. He notices Gillian go up to Elisa as they innocently laugh with each other and make their way to the cafeteria. Looking confused, Thomas continues to watch Gillian and Elisa until one of his colleagues pats him on the back.

MALE COLLEAGUE 1: C'mon, let's go.

THOMAS: (PLEASANTLY) I'll be right there.

Thomas loses sight of Gillian and Elisa as he huffs in annoyance and grabs his jacket before making his way to the cafeteria.

▌ INT. THE REGIONAL HEADQUARTERS CAFETERIA – AFTERNOON

GILLIAN: (SARCASTICALLY) Well, wasn't that an amazing turn of events. I can't believe Thomas has won yet again!

Elisa sits at her usual spot with Gillian, as they eat lunch together.

ELISA: C'mon, I doubt that it's anything to be upset about.

GILLIAN: (UPSET) It is, actually! It's actually pretty upsetting because it doesn't give any of us a chance to win one simple prize! (GESTURES TO THOMAS) I mean, look at him!

Elisa looks up as she and Gillian watch Thomas being his usual self as he brags to his colleagues about winning the Power Hour prize.

GILLIAN: (TURNS TO ELISA) Couldn't you have busted his balls a little harder that day? I'm getting sick and tired of this shit!

ELISA: What happened to not making any enemies in this place?

GILLIAN: (UPSET) Oh, forget ever taking me seriously when I said that. I liked it better when he was depressed and questioning himself.

ELISA: (GIGGLES) I don't think you should be upset about this. I bet you've won the Power Hour prize before.

GILLIAN: I have, but for me, it's once in a blue moon. (GESTURES TO THOMAS) For Thomas, it's the billionth fucking time! And that's something I'm not going to stand for if Mr. Popkin continues to play this rigged game with us!

ELISA: (REASSURINGLY) Why don't you have some of your lunch. It'll make you feel better.

GILLIAN: (PLAYFULLY) Yes, Mommy. Just hope I don't choke if I eat too angrily.

Elisa laughs while Gillian lets out a smile and eats her lunch until Daniel comes up to them.

DANIEL: (POLITE) Ladies, mind if I have a moment of your time?

GILLIAN: (PLAYFULLY) Depends on the moment. What exactly do you want from us, Mr. Morin?

DANIEL: (POLITE) Nothing serious. I'm just doing my job as the messenger. (TURNS TO ELISA) Mr. Popkin wanted to let you know that he went through the decision of choosing the Cornelius Project and has given you extra pay on your paycheck.

Elisa turns to Daniel in shock, while Gillian sits quietly, surprised as well.

GILLIAN: (SURPRISED) Well, how the almighty have fallen. At least something good happened today. (TURNS TO ELISA) Now you can get yourself a ticket to watch that gala tonight! (TURNS TO DANIEL) Which is another experience that Thomas has taken away from the rest of us. Why is that?

Thomas notices Daniel speaking to Elisa and Gillian as he gets up and looks for a way to approach him without them noticing.

DANIEL: All I can tell you is that it's based on the results; not everyone can exceed the office's average that easily. (TURNS TO ELISA) But Mr. Popkin did want to give you a monetary prize for your assistance that day ... (NOTICES THAT ELISA HAS ZONED OUT) Are you all right, Employee #263?

Elisa remains frozen for a moment until Gillian nudges her to pay attention.

ELISA: (SNAPS INTO FOCUS) Yes, I'm all right. I'm just shocked by all this and I'm trying my best to take it in ... (TURNS TO DANIEL) But thank you, Mr. Morin. I really appreciate it.

Gillian notices Thomas trying to sneak his way toward her, Daniel and Elisa and she prepares for the worst.

DANIEL: You deserve it after helping us in the meeting that day. I just didn't understand why he chose not to announce it earlier, as well as the most improved. (NOTICES THOMAS APPROACHING THEM) There's our Power Hour winner! I see that you came to join us!

Thomas tries his best not to be intimidated by Gillian's scowl as he slowly approaches Daniel.

DANIEL: Congrats again for winning the Power Hour prize.

THOMAS: (PLEASANTLY) Yes, thank you again for that ... I just wanted to know what I have to wear for this special event. I just wanted to make sure that I make a good impression on the supervisors and represent our RH-C department and Mr. Popkin loudly and proudly.

DANIEL: Just wear the best suit you can find. It's obviously a formal gathering, so you must dress the part if ever invited to this event.

THOMAS: (KINDLY) Right. Well, thank you for that. I really appreciate that. (TURNS TO ELISA AND GILLIAN) And I hope this inspires the rest of my colleagues to work even harder so they can get a chance to experience these opportunities.

Gillian rolls her eyes in annoyance, while Elisa nudges her arm in reassurance.

GILLIAN: (BLUNTLY) Oh, we certainly will work extremely harder the next time. (TURNS TO THOMAS) But remember this, Thomas ...

(IN FRENCH) Je ne suis que faiblesse et que fragilité … malgré moi je sens couler mes larmes … adieu, notre petite table …

THOMAS: (CONFUSED) What on earth does that mean?

ELISA: You'll find out when you get to the show.

Thomas turns to Elisa in shock and notices that both she and Gillian are giving him the same look until he huffs in annoyance and walks away. Daniel attempts to say something but ends up walking away as well, while Elisa and Gillian burst into laughter for the sake of everyone else in the room.

GILLIAN: (CHUCKLES) And to think that I was the only one who knew that. I didn't know what Mr. Popkin was thinking – you totally should've gotten that prize.

ELISA: But if I did, I would've had to beg Mr. Popkin to give me a second ticket for you to come with me.

GILLIAN: Then I should've damn well won because I would've been bold enough to ask Mr. Popkin for a second ticket for you to come with me.

Elisa and Gillian both laugh as they continue eating their lunch, while Gillian thinks about the Annual Grand Wallace Celebration Gala.

GILLIAN: Man, I would've killed to go see the Grand Wallace Celebration Gala live. It's a once-in-a-lifetime experience.

ELISA: (CONFUSED) Have they stopped broadcasting the program on all the TV channels this year?

GILLIAN: No, you can still watch it on TV (SHAKES HER HEAD AND CHUCKLES), but who wants to with that fucking Bartlett's Piece documentary interrupting the show every single time.

ELISA: (CHUCKLES) I know what you mean. My dad and I made the mistake of watching the entire documentary and completely missing out on the Grand Wallace Celebration Gala. (REMEMBERS) But you can easily pay to have that removed, so it doesn't interrupt any special airings.

GILLIAN: (SERIOUSLY) And miss out on my daily coffee fixes? No thanks. I would rather lose my voice by saying skip repeatedly than pay eight dollars a month just to not watch that documentary again. I still would rather do that than wake up early to take some stupid test just to have those assholes take that documentary off my TV. The lucky ones get to watch the Grand Wallace Celebration Gala live without any interruptions, and they don't have to pay for shit to make that happen!

Elisa giggles and continues to eat her lunch, while Gillian continues to complain.

GILLIAN: (GROWLS IN FRUSTRATION) Ah! This system fucking sucks! Why is it that only the lighter few get a chance to live their lives?

Elisa stops eating and automatically thinks about Carman and her resentment of the Hue System.

ELISA: Now you're beginning to sound like my mother.

GILLIAN: (LOOKS AT ELISA) Is that so? Well, no wonder you gave me such a look when I said Mommy Dearest – she really must've upset you that morning. (SLIGHTLY CONCERNED) What did she do to make you upset? Did she give you a tongue-lashing about not calling her often? Or did she berate you with questions about why you're not married yet?

ELISA: (SERIOUSLY) It's a lot more serious than that, since I haven't spoken to my mother in years. She keeps refusing to accept the money that I send her each month … (SIGHS IN FRUSTRATION) and I don't know if she's doing this out of spite or just seriously trying to tell me that I'm no longer her daughter.

GILLIAN: (EMPATHETIC) Well, I'm sorry to hear that, love. My mother and I have almost the exact same relationship. Except that she begs me to send her money and never refuses it – especially if it's a hundred thousand dollars.

Elisa looks at Gillian as she catches herself and looks at her apologetically.

GILLIAN: (APOLOGETIC) Sorry about that. I couldn't help but listen to the gossip when they were talking about this girl at the Information Hub … who knew that they were talking about you.

ELISA: (PAUSES AND SIGHS) It's fine, really … it's not like you started the gossip.

GILLIAN: (CERTAIN) Oh, I would never do such a thing – I wouldn't even bother to tell anyone that you tried to send a hundred thousand dollars to your mother. (CURIOUS) But I am quite tempted to know how much you have in your bank account.

ELISA: (SMILES) That I'm going to have to keep confidential.

GILLIAN: (SMILES) Fair enough. (CAUTIOUSLY CURIOUS) So what's the big deal between you and your mother? Was she part of the Anti-Hue Rallies or something?

Elisa takes a moment to remember the times when Carman took part in the Anti-Hue Rallies.

Thirteen Years Prior

▌ EXT. OUTSIDE THE GRAVES' HOUSE – AFTERNOON

EIGHT-YEAR-OLD ELISA: (CRIES) Mom, please!

Eight-year-old Elisa tries to resist Carman's aggressive pulling as she tries to bring her to the car to go to Tint Valley Hall.

CARMAN: (ANGRILY) C'mon! Let's go! We don't have time for this!

EIGHT-YEAR-OLD ELISA: (CRIES) But I don't want to go to the rally!

CARMAN: (APPROACHES EIGHT-YEAR-OLD ELISA ANGRILY) Well, we wouldn't have to, if you weren't such a deadweight on this system! Now c'mon – we have to go!

Carman grabs eight-year-old Elisa by the back of her neck and drags her inside the car, while twelve-year-old Deidre and ten-year-old Fredrick watch quietly from the window inside the house.

Thirteen Years Later

▌ INT. THE REGIONAL HEADQUARTERS CAFETERIA – AFTERNOON

ELISA: She was ... there was even a point she was the ringleader of such rallies.

GILLIAN: (TAKEN ABACK) Tragic. I actually had an encounter with anti-Hue ringleaders and they're not the nicest people, and the fact that you still send money to her?

ELISA: (SMIRKS) She's still my mother ... regardless of what happened at those rallies.

GILLIAN: Well, you must've had tougher skin than me because I would spend my mornings fighting my mother and sneaking out midway through a speech. You have to admit, it was pretty scary going to those rallies.

ELISA: (REMEMBERS) It was.

Thirteen Years Prior

▌ INT. TINT VALLEY HALL – AFTERNOON

Eight-year-old Elisa sits in a corner by herself while she watches anti-Hue members gather around and angrily express their hatred for the Hue System.

ELISA: (NARRATES) Sitting in a room full of angry people, it wasn't the best place for a kid who was trying to figure out the world ... let alone her own surroundings.

ANTI-HUE MEMBER 1: (SHOUTS) Now he will hear this message and we will have our chance to be heard! Even if we have to drag his privileged ass to the Outskirts. We will have our questions answered and our lives back to the same peace that existed before this wicked system came into our lives!

All the anti-Hue members cheer angrily and start making a ruckus in Tint Valley Hall, while eight-year-old Elisa watches fearfully.

ELISA: (NARRATES) We thought the new system was going to make things better, but there was never another time in my life when I saw so much hate in people's eyes.

Thirteen Years Later

▌ INT. THE REGIONAL HEADQUARTERS CAFETERIA – AFTERNOON

GILLIAN: (BITTER) Selfish bastards. You think they were just doing that to cause a ruckus, but they really meant business when they got the children involved. Those people were destructive – it makes me sick just thinking about those times.

ELISA: (THINKS) Yeah, I guess … but if I had to think about it, that was the most time I ever spent with my mother.

GILLIAN: (STUNNED) Really? This is what comes to your mind after being dragged to those horrible rallies? Elisa, that wasn't one of those Mommy–Daughter bonding sessions – she was basically calling you a Blank – (STOPS HERSELF AND BREATHES) … a you-know-what without saying it.

ELISA: (CALMLY) I was well aware of that. There was no doubt in my mind that she wasn't … but there were times in my childhood that I couldn't tell the difference.

Thirteen Years Prior

▎ INT. TINT VALLEY HALL – AFTERNOON

Eight-year-old Elisa stands in front of the stage in Tint Valley Hall and remains quiet as she watches Carman angrily express herself to the crowd while they take a moment to agree with what she is trying to say.

ELISA: (NARRATES) By only listening to her words, you start to think that she really hates her child.

Eight-year-old Elisa tunes out the voices and quietly watches Carman for a moment, as she recognizes the compassion and hopelessness she conveys in the delivery of her speech.

ELISA: (NARRATES) But by watching her actions alone, you begin to see things differently … then you start to wonder what her true intentions were for being part of those anti-Hue rallies. Was she a fanatic, using her daughter's Late Tint to gain a spot in the group? Or was she a mother who was truly concerned about her daughter's future and was doing whatever she could in her child's best interests?

Thirteen Years Later

▎ INT. REGIONAL HEADQUARTERS CAFETERIA – AFTERNOON

GILLIAN: I would go with the first one – there is no doubt in my mind that that group turned many good people into fanatics. I'm just so glad that the anti-Hue period is over.

Elisa smiles at Gillian's dismay with the anti-Hue group as she continues to eat her lunch.

GILLIAN: It's funny to know that you're related to a Steels officer and an anti-Hue member. There are actual anti-Hue members in this building, as we speak, and they are not as quiet and well-mannered as you are.

ELISA: I guess I never got a chance to notice them myself ... but I believe there was a point in those rallies that I let her down.

GILLIAN: Oh please, they let themselves down by believing that their screaming would get the attention of the commander-in-chief – as if Isaim Hue didn't have enough issues to deal with at Bartlett's Piece.

ELISA: To me, it worked out just fine because he was there.

GILLIAN: (SHOCKED) Wait a second. He was there?

ELISA: Yes, he was.

Thirteen Years Prior

▌INT. TINT VALLEY HALL – AFTERNOON

Isaim and Dolan sit in the front row of Tint Valley Hall and listen to Carman angrily express herself, while eight-year-old Elisa stands quietly beside her.

ELISA: (NARRATES) Front and centre, along with Vice Commander Dolan Wenski.

All the anti-Hue members express themselves aggressively, while Isaim and Dolan try their best to listen to them carefully.

ELISA: (NARRATES) Some people believed that he only came for publicity reasons.

CARMAN: (ANGRILY) And we have been living like this for the past three years and have received nothing from what this system has to offer! We have lost our jobs; our livelihoods have been taken away because of this system! How can we take care of our families? (GESTURES TO EIGHT-YEAR-OLD ELISA) How is my daughter going to survive if she's not able to find work in this system, let alone live a decent life in this place?

All the anti-Hue members jeer angrily and express themselves aggressively. Dolan whispers something in Isaim's ear, and they nod to each other before turning back to Carman and eight-year-old Elisa.

ELISA: (NARRATES) But no one can deny that he would never make a public appearance unless the problem was serious.

ISAIM: Bring the child over here.

Greatly surprised, Carman just stands there while the other anti-Hue members suddenly go quiet. Eight-year-old Elisa turns to Carman, who quickly brings her to Isaim. He greets her with a smile.

ISAIM: (KINDLY) It's okay. We just need you to stand still for a moment.

Isaim removes the new Tint Detector from his pocket and points it at eight-year-old Elisa as the device reads her current Tint Level.

CARMAN: (WORRIED) What are you doing? What are you doing to her?

ISAIM: Nothing to worry about, ma'am, I'm just reading your daughter's Tint Level … (HEARS THE BEEP AND CHECKS THE TINT DETECTOR) and according to this device, her current Tint Level is 79%.

Eight-year-old Elisa stands there in shock, along with Carman, as she turns to Isaim in disbelief.

CARMAN: (STUNNED) That's impossible … how could she be at 79%? (ARGUES) We both have been stuck at 80% throughout this entire process – that's the real reason why we're here! We both checked our Tint Levels day and night and were still confronted with 80%. How could you just come here and tell me that she's now at 79%?

ISAIM: Well, I could be wrong, since this is a new device (GESTURES TO EIGHT-YEAR-OLD ELISA), but I believe we'll both get an answer once the young lady checks herself.

Carman gives eight-year-old Elisa a warning look, while Isaim quietly encourages her to check her Tint Level as she slowly brings her Life Band toward herself.

EIGHT-YEAR-OLD ELISA: (SLIGHTLY NERVOUS) L-Life Band … check my Phase Status.

LIFE BAND AI: Here are the results of your Phase Status. Your Phase Status is Tint, and your current Tint Level is 79%.

Eight-year-old Elisa gasps in excitement and turns to see Isaim smiling gleefully, while the anti-Hue members begin to murmur amongst themselves.

ISAIM: (TURNS TO EVERYONE) As you can see, it is possible to get out of 80%. For adults, this can be quite difficult, as we have already developed habits that could possibly prevent our growth. As for children, it should be easy for them to progress and reach to a decent Tint Level toward their high school graduation … unless, as often happens, they are suppressed, left out at times by their peers, isolated in their own bubbles or constantly following their parents' teachings. We conducted a massive amount of research and saw that bullying can also prevent a child from progressing quickly, having been exposed to hostile environments. Like this one, for instance. No child should ever have to partake in such events that would cause them major stress and make them doubt themselves about their progress – especially at this tender age. I am well aware that some children may not be able to catch up with their peers as they continue their studies. (TURNS TO EIGHT-YEAR-OLD ELISA) However, with some healthy encouragement, some free time to express themselves in any way they like and a little bit of patience, they will reach the Canvas Phase in no time and will be more than qualified to reach the Hue Phase.

Eight-year-old Elisa smiles at Isaim and Dolan enjoys the silence of the entire room for a moment until one of the anti-Hue members stands up from his seat.

ANTI-HUE MEMBER 1: (ANGRILY) And why should we believe a thing you say?

Isaim turns to see the anti-Hue member standing on his seat while the rest of the members murmur in agreement.

ANTI-HUE MEMBER 2: (ANGRILY) That's right! How can we know the truth from you with all those fancy doohickies you carry in your pocket!

CARMAN: (ANGRILY) You did your whole speech switching colours like it was nothing! Why should we believe she's at 79% when you probably pointed your tech thing to change her Tint Level?

Dolan looks around anxiously to see all the anti-Hue members erupting in anger, while Isaim calmly watches them angrily express themselves.

ISAIM: Is that what you all believe?

Everyone stops shouting as Isaim points the Tint Detector at one of the Anti-Hue Members and reads the results.

ISAIM: You, 80%.

Isaim points the Tint Detector at another anti-Hue member and reads the results.

ISAIM: You, also 80%.

The rest of the anti-Hue members stand there in shock, while Dolan tries his best not to smile too widely.

ISAIM: I believe that everyone in this room is at 80% except for a few of you here – but that's just from well-trained eyes. This device is simply used to depict your current Tint Level at a faster rate, and it can be used for people who are uncomfortable speaking to their Life Band. You can simply check for yourselves if you think I'm lying.

The two anti-Hue members check their current Phase Status and see that their Tint Levels match the results of Isaim's Tint Detector.

ISAIM: But I will never offer my citizens anything that would modify or change their Phase Status, which is strictly prohibited in Bartlett's Piece. I may have created the Modifier as well as used it during my speech, but only to show you what is expected from this new system, as it was used for presentation purposes only. All the other devices I've created down the road were simply made to tell you the truth (GESTURES TO EIGHT-YEAR-OLD ELISA), and this device has simply told me that she is at 79%. (TURNS TO CARMAN) You did just say you check each other's Tint Levels day and night.

Isaim points the Tint Detector at Carman and reads the results while she stands there in disbelief.

ISAIM: But according to the Tint Detector, you might want to check again.

Eight-year-old Elisa turns to Carman for an explanation while she hesitates to bring her Life Band toward her.

CARMAN: Life Band, check my Phase Status.

LIFE BAND AI: Here are the results of your Phase Status. Your Phase Status is Tint, and your current Tint Level is 76%.

All the anti-Hue members gasp in shock, while eight-year-old Elisa looks at Carman, stunned while Isaim stands there, understanding their grief before turning back to the crowd.

ISAIM: This visit wasn't organized to bring you all down or deny your cause. We have effectively heard all of your concerns and will figure out a way for all of you to live a decent life and help your families. By the time I get back to the Grand Arne Office, you will be hearing an announcement that will happen in the next few days concerning the changes we've made. If you still have concerns, feel free to visit me at the Grand Arne Office, and we'll see what we can do from there.

DOLAN: (STANDS UP) If that's all, we should be on our way. (TURNS TO ISAIM) Commander?

Isaim nods as he and Dolan leave Tint Valley Hall while the anti-Hue members stand there in disbelief and turn to Carman for an explanation.

ANTI-HUE MEMBER 1: (IN DISBELIEF) I can't believe you would do something like this ... you said you and that child were a full 80%.

ANTI-HUE MEMBER 2: (IN DISBELIEF) We took you in as family and believed everything you said – we even made you our leader when no one else would take the task! (ANGRILY) Did you come here simply to mock us?

ANTI-HUE MEMBER 1: (ANGRILY) Did you even consider how much we have suffered living in this system!

Carman stands there worried about her safety as all the anti-Hue members start screaming and angrily expressing themselves toward her and eight-year-old Elisa.

Thirteen Years Later

▌ INT. REGIONAL HEADQUARTERS CAFETERIA – AFTERNOON

GILLIAN: So that's it? He just made a speech and left?

ELISA: Just like that. It actually became his signature move throughout the years of his reign.

GILLIAN: My goodness! And to be in close proximity to Isaim Hue. Why the heck didn't I meet you in my childhood?

Elisa bursts into laughter along with Gillian as a few colleagues turn to them, wondering what is going on.

ELISA: (HAPPILY) It would've been nice to have a friend like you in my childhood.

GILLIAN: (HAPPILY) Right? I can't believe that we have managed to find each other so late. (CURIOUS) So, what happened afterwards? Did the crowd try to swallow you up? Did they end up attacking you guys?

ELISA: No, we managed to get out of there before things began to get hectic. We didn't have time to put on our seatbelts, but it was a quiet ride back home.

GILLIAN: And your mother?

ELISA: She never went back to the group after my father found out later on. I was glad that I no longer had go there anymore ... but sad, as my mother stopped talking to me.

Gillian's smile fades as Elisa thinks solemnly about Carman's recent behaviour.

ELISA: She tried her best not to say anything to me after Isaim's visit, but I still got to hear a word from her from time to time. I would've killed to have at least a decent conversation with my mom – just once, if that's all it took. You have to cherish everything you have with your mother, even if it's as bad as you think it is ... I've been here for five years, and she hasn't given me a call once.

GILLIAN: (REMORSEFUL) Oh, my goodness ... I'm so sorry to hear that, Elisa. (PASSIONATE) I'll invite you over to my house! I'll let you come over whenever you want, if you're feeling sad or lonely. We can have a girl's night, watch all the movies available, eat popcorn and all that other junk food that's out there!

ELISA: (KINDLY) Gillian –

GILLIAN: (PASSIONATE) I'll let you talk to my mother! I'll bring the phone and let her talk to you about marriage, soap operas and everything that a woman needs to know – (TRIES NOT TO CRY) Fuck, I'll even be your mother if I have to.

ELISA: (KINDLY) Gillian, it's okay.

GILLIAN: (CRIES) No, it's not okay, Elisa – it's not okay for you to go through shit like this! You need to stop saying that such bad behaviour is okay, because it's not!

Gillian frantically tries to find the napkins on her tray and tears one in half to wipe away her tears.

GILLIAN: (WHIMPERS) Almighty, I wasn't even supposed to be sad today. Why does a poor thing like you have to be treated like this?

ELISA: (KINDLY) I appreciate your concern, Gillian. But believe me when I tell you that I'm okay. I've gotten used to it over the years, but hopefully one day, I'll strike gold ... I still have to keep trying for that day to come.

GILLIAN: (WHIMPERS) Your optimism makes me sick ... you should put a limit on such people like that. They don't deserve your loving kindness.

Elisa giggles and appreciates Gillian's words as she tries her best to get a hold of herself.

ELISA: You know, you're the first person I've ever told that to.

GILLIAN: (WIPES HER FACE) Really?

ELISA: Yeah. I've allowed myself not to get close to anyone during my time here ... I haven't even told that to Hank, and he's the only person I ever talk to. But it was nice to share that with someone who actually cares for once, and I thank you for that, Gillian.

GILLIAN: (TOUCHED) You are so welcome. (CERTAIN) You can talk to me whenever you like – you can tell me absolutely anything and I'll keep it in here! Nobody else has to know!

ELISA: (SMILES) I appreciate that, and as much as I'm flattered by that offer of being my mother, I think I like you better as my friend.

GILLIAN: (HAPPILY) Fair enough. You're lucky that the feeling is mutual, especially when you still owe me a movie date! And I'm not buying popcorn for both of us!

Elisa and Gillian start laughing loudly as a few colleagues begin to complain.

GILLIAN: (HAPPILY) Oh, shut up! We're having a good time here!

Elisa and Gillian continue to laugh as they enjoy their lunch together.

INT. RH-C DEPARTMENT OFFICE OF REGIONAL HEADQUARTERS – EVENING

Elisa continues working while everyone else in the office begins to pack their things and prepares to either go home or go to Primetime Plaza. Gillian talks to her mother through her Wireless Earpiece as she comes up to Elisa to say goodbye.

GILLIAN: (ON HER WIRELESS EARPIECE) Yes, Mother ... of course – they're definitely going to have to pay for that. (TAPS ELISA ON THE SHOULDER) Looks like I'm going to have to take a raincheck, darling … (WHISPERS) Mother is having one of her weekly meltdowns as we speak.

ELISA: (SMILES) It's fine. Maybe tomorrow will be a better time.

GILLIAN: (EXCITEDLY) I like how you think. We'll definitely go see a movie tomorrow! Don't forget, you're in charge of the popcorn. (ON HER WIRELESS EARPIECE) No, I'm not talking to you, Mother. I'm trying to make plans with a friend here … no, it's not what you think – I thought I made that clear to you already!

Gillian waves goodbye to Elisa as she continues to talk to her mother on her Wireless Earpiece and leaves the office to head home. Elisa starts working again without noticing Mr. Popkin coming up to her.

MR. POPKIN: Employee #263.

ELISA: (STARTLES SLIGHTLY AND TURNS TO MR. POPKIN) Yes, Mr. Popkin.

MR. POPKIN: (CALMLY) No need to work overtime. We're closing up the office early due to the special event tonight.

ELISA: I'll sign off as soon as I finish this report.

MR. POPKIN: Thank you, Employee #263, and you will also be getting a raise after helping us pick the Cornelius Project.

ELISA: Thank you, Mr. Popkin, but Mr. Morin already informed me during the break.

MR. POPKIN: (SLIGHTLY SURPRISED) Did he now? (SHRUGS) Well, it's better to be informed again, as you truly deserved it! (BEGINS TO LEAVE) Don't take too long with that report, as Power Hour starts again tomorrow!

ELISA: See you tomorrow, Mr. Popkin! Have fun at the Celebration Gala!

MR. POPKIN: (CONTINUES WALKING) I'll try!

Mr. Popkin heads straight to his office as Elisa turns back to her computer and finishes her report. A few other colleagues sign off their systems as they pack their things and prepare to go to Primetime Plaza.

MALE COLLEAGUE 1: I'm so hungry. Wanna go to the Fire House tonight?

FEMALE COLLEAGUE 1: You know they won't let us in if we don't have eight people.

FEMALE COLLEAGUE 2: I think we'll find more people when we get there. (GESTURES TO ELISA) Should we ask her if she wants to come as well?

FEMALE COLLEAGUE 1: (CONFUSED) I thought she already had dinner plans with someone.

MALE COLLEAGUE 1: (SCOFFS) Oh, please, like she ever has dinner plans with anyone. Let's go.

The colleagues leave the office while Elisa remains seated as she finishes her report.

ELISA: (QUIETLY TO HERSELF) They don't want me included in their dinner plans … fine, I'll make my own dinner plans.

A Few Hours Later

▎ INT. ELISA'S APARTMENT – EVENING

Elisa pours dry rigatoni pasta into a pot full of boiling water and uses a wooden spoon to mix the pasta until it settles in the pot. She then opens another pot, which contains a meat sauce but burns her hand on the steam. She quickly puts the lid back on the pot and goes to the sink to run cold water over her hand. She keeps the faucet running for a moment, then turns it off, goes back to the pot and stirs the meat sauce with a wooden spoon.

A Few Minutes Later

Elisa eats her Rigatoni Bolognese as she watches the news.

NEWS REPORTER: While Steels officers are out on patrol continuing their search for Heather Grace, there has been another missing person report that has been issued to Steels Protection Services.

The news reporter continues to talk about the missing person report as Elisa eats her food until she stops and thinks about Carman.

ELISA: Life Band, call Mom.

LIFE BAND AI: Calling MOM (RINGING) …

Elisa patiently waits for Carman to answer as her Life Band continues to ring.

LIFE BAND AI: Your call to MOM has exceeded the standard number of rings. Would you like to continue this call to MOM?

ELISA: Cancel call.

LIFE BAND AI: Cancelling call.

Elisa slams her hand on the table and automatically thinks about the day after the anti-Hue rally.

Thirteen Years Prior

█ INT. THE GRAVES' HOUSE – AFTERNOON

Carman and eight-year-old Elisa come inside the house as Garreth walks toward them furiously.

GARRETH: (UPSET) It's about damn time someone came through this door! Been spending the entire day walking around an empty house!

EIGHT-YEAR-OLD ELISA: (EXCITEDLY) Daddy!

Eight-year-old Elisa runs to give Garreth a hug, while Carman becomes more irritated as she takes off her coat and puts away the car keys.

EIGHT-YEAR-OLD ELISA: (EXCITEDLY) Daddy, you'll never guess what happened today!

GARRETH: (WORRIED) Tell me later. Are you okay? Did those people do anything to you?

EIGHT-YEAR-OLD ELISA: No, I'm okay, Dad. Are you mad at me?

GARRETH: No, sweetheart, I'm just glad that you're all right. (TURNS TO CARMAN ANGRILY) I thought I told you to stop taking her to those rallies!

CARMAN: (ANGRILY GOES UPSTAIRS) I don't have time to deal with you right now.

GARRETH: (ANGRILY WALKS TOWARD THE STAIRS) Don't you dare walk away from me! There's no way I should treat you like a child when I'm talking to my wife! Carman! (SCREAMS) Carman!

Carman slams the door upstairs as Garreth sighs in hopelessness. Eight-year-old Elisa comes up to him slowly.

EIGHT-YEAR-OLD ELISA: (WORRIED) Daddy, are you okay?

GARRETH: (PAUSES AND SIGHS) I'll be fine … I'll be fine. I'll just deal with your mother afterwards. (TURNS TO EIGHT-YEAR-OLD ELISA) Now come here. I'm so glad to see that you came back.

EIGHT-YEAR-OLD ELISA: I'm okay, Daddy. Nothing bad happened to me.

GARRETH: (WORRIED) Are you sure? You weren't scared at all?

EIGHT-YEAR-OLD ELISA: I was for a while. (EXCITEDLY) But you will never guess what happened today. Isaim Hue came to the rally!

GARRETH: (SURPRISED) Really? You got to meet the commander-in-chief?

EIGHT-YEAR-OLD ELISA: (EXCITEDLY) Yeah! He was super nice, and he wasn't afraid of the members at all! He created this new device that could read your Tint Level in seconds – and check this out! (TO HER LIFE BAND) Life Band, check my Phase Status.

LIFE BAND AI: Here are the results of your Phase Status. Your Phase Status is Tint, and your current Tint Level is 79%.

Garreth looks at eight-year-old Elisa in shock as he happily gives her a hug and starts lifting her up and spinning her around to celebrate while she laughs happily.

EIGHT-YEAR-OLD ELISA: (SCREAMS HAPPILY) Daddy, put me down!

GARRETH: (HAPPILY) I can't when I'm so happy! I knew this day would come! (PUTS EIGHT-YEAR-OLD ELISA DOWN) I told you that you wouldn't be stuck at 80% forever! Now you will be able to process quicker – maybe even faster than that Deidre and Fredrick!

EIGHT-YEAR-OLD ELISA: (SLIGHTLY BUMMED) I guess, but that's still a long way –

GARRETH: (FIRMLY) Now, don't you dare start with that talk! (HAPPILY) You will get there – I promise you! You will be out of this town, thriving in no time! It may seem small to you, but we're still going to celebrate it! So, c'mon, this calls for a celebration!

Garreth grabs the car keys and takes eight-year-old Elisa's hand to leave. However, they stop when they see twelve-year-old Deidre and ten-year-old Fredrick rushing in the house wearing Canvas colours.

GARRETH: (SERIOUSLY) Now where on earth have you two been?

TWELVE-YEAR-OLD DEIDRE: (EXCITEDLY) We just certified ourselves as Canvases!

Garreth and eight-year-old Elisa turn to each other in shock and both shrug as he turns back to twelve-year-old Deidre and ten-year-old Fredrick with a smile.

GARRETH: (HAPPILY) Well, congratulations to you both! Come give your old man a hug!

Twelve-year-old Deidre and ten-year-old Fredrick waste no time giving Garreth a hug, while eight-year-old Elisa feels slightly sad about her current Tint Level.

GARRETH: (HAPPILY) Now this really calls for a celebration, so c'mon. (TAKES EIGHT-YEAR-OLD ELISA'S HAND) I'm going to take you kids out for ice cream.

TEN-YEAR-OLD FREDRICK: (GRIMACES AT EIGHT-YEAR-OLD ELISA) Why is she coming?

GARRETH: (HAPPILY) Because we are going to have a celebration for her as well, because she is no longer at 80%. I'm hearing so much good news and today feels like a good day (FIRMLY), and we are going to keep this a good day, right, guys?

TWELVE-YEAR-OLD DEIDRE, TEN-YEAR-OLD FREDRICK AND EIGHT-YEAR-OLD ELISA: (IN UNISON) Right, Dad!

GARRETH: (HAPPILY) That's my children.

TWELVE-YEAR-OLD DEIDRE: (TURNS TO GARRETH) Where's Mommy? Is she not coming with us?

GARRETH: Mommy is a bit under the weather, so it's just going to be the four of us, okay. So, c'mon, let's go get some ice cream.

TWELVE-YEAR-OLD DEIDRE, TEN-YEAR-OLD FREDRICK AND EIGHT-YEAR-OLD ELISA: (IN UNISON) Okay!

Garreth makes sure that he has gotten twelve-year-old Deidre, ten-year-old Fredrick and eight-year-old Elisa's hands before they all leave the house to go get ice cream.

Thirteen Years Later

▎ INT. ELISA'S APARTMENT – EVENING

Elisa continues to think about the past as she discovers her true feelings about her current relationship with Carman.

ELISA: Maybe I'm not okay with it, after all.

Elisa goes back to eating her Rigatoni Bolognese and watching the news for the time being.

▌ EXT. OUTSIDE THE ENTERTAINMENT HALL – NIGHT

Every well-known Tint, Canvas, Hue and Shade citizen arrives at the Entertainment Hall to attend the Grand Wallace Celebration Gala. Many guests choose to either shake hands or give each other a hug or kiss to greet each other while they wait in line to get into the Entertainment Hall.

A Few Hours Later

▌ INT. THE MAIN LOBBY OF THE ENTERTAINMENT HALL – NIGHT

Mr. Popkin, Daniel and Thomas rush into the lobby looking for the department supervisors. They look around, surprised to see a few guests loitering in the lobby, while the Grand Wallace Celebration Gala waits to begin inside the auditorium.

MR. POPKIN: (UPSET) This is bad – this looks completely bad for us! And to think I yell at people every day for their tardiness – I knew I shouldn't have let you drive!

DANIEL: (ARGUES) Well, if you weren't such a backseat driver, then we wouldn't have been this late! And how can you possibly blame me when someone forgot about a certain someone who won the Power Hour!

THOMAS: (APOLOGETIC) Forgive me for taking so much time, Mr. Popkin. This was the only suit I could find that didn't remind me of work!

MR. POPKIN: (FIRMLY) Don't apologize, Employee #158. You should be thanking Mr. Morin because if I were driving, you would've been left at home wearing that suit.

THOMAS: (POLITE) Well, thank you for not leaving me at home, Mr. Popkin – and you too, Mr. Morin. If it's not too much, I would appreciate it if you called me –

DANIEL: Don't try to push it. Just be thankful that you're even here tonight. (TURNS TO MR. POPKIN) And if you were so reluctant about my driving, why didn't you take the wheel afterwards?

MR. POPKIN: (TURNS TO DANIEL ANGRILY) Because you know how much I hate the arts! I can't even stand listening to a single note of opera – it puts me to sleep every time. I would rather be golfing at home in my underwear than paying for another suit just to go to this damn show!

THOMAS: (NOTICES THE DEPARTMENT SUPERVISOR) Supervisors up ahead.

Mr. Popkin and Daniel stop arguing, and they both turn to see the department supervisors standing at the door, along with their own employees, including **Zach Vault (mid-twenties)**, who have won the Power Hour prize.

MR. POPKIN: (PROFESSIONAL) Gentlemen!

RH-B DEPARTMENT SUPERVISOR: (NOTICES MR. POPKIN AND SMILES) Well, there he is! Just in time for the actual show!

Mr. Popkin and the department supervisors go to greet each other while Daniel, Thomas, Zach and the other two employees watch from a distance.

MR. POPKIN: (PROFESSIONAL) Well, I apologize for our tardiness. I hope we haven't kept you waiting for long. (NOTICES ZACH AND

THE OTHER TWO EMPLOYEES) I see that we have others joining us this evening.

RH-D DEPARTMENT SUPERVISOR: (PROFESSIONAL) Well, we heard that you were bringing your Power Hour winner to the show, so we thought we would bring ours as well. (TURNS TO ZACH AND THE OTHER TWO EMPLOYEES) Don't be shy, gentlemen; come over and say hello.

Zach and the other two employees stop leaning against the wall, go over to Mr. Popkin, Daniel and Thomas and take turns greeting each other.

THOMAS: (EAGER) Hi there, I'm Thomas Dewberry.

ZACH: (CORDIAL) Nice to meet you, Mr. Dewberry. (NOTICES THOMAS'S SUIT) I wore that same exact suit during last year's event.

THOMAS: (GRADUALLY BECOMES OFFENDED) Oh, that's … nice to know.

MR. POPKIN: So, gentlemen, I'm surprised that you haven't gone in to check out the show yet.

RH-A DEPARTMENT SUPERVISOR: Well, everybody knows not to go in on the first act. That's when the children take over the stage, and you should know what happens when you mix children with music.

RH-D DEPARTMENT SUPERVISOR: Plus, we were waiting for you to arrive so that we could find our seats together without difficulty.

RH-A DEPARTMENT SUPERVISOR: You're lucky that you came, period; otherwise, we wouldn't hear the end of it if a certain someone missed the main act.

RH-D DEPARTMENT SUPERVISOR: (DEFENSIVELY) Hey, missing Genevieve Dinesen is a crime in itself, and I wouldn't mind putting you all in jail if we did.

RH-B DEPARTMENT SUPERVISOR: (CHUCKLES) There he goes with his fan-girl phase again (REMEMBERS ELISA). However, I'm shocked that we didn't get to see our new female friend again for this event.

RH-A DEPARTMENT SUPERVISOR: (REMEMBERS ELISA) Yes, how come she's not here tonight? She really did do us a solid during that meeting.

Thomas becomes annoyed as the department supervisors begin to rave about Elisa.

MR. POPKIN: Well, the tickets to this show are limited and last time I checked, the memo sent to us said they were supposed to be given to Power Hour winners only. But she was well rewarded with a monetary prize, so her efforts during that meeting weren't forgotten.

RH-A DEPARTMENT SUPERVISOR: Her prize should be bigger than just more money; she should be here enjoying the show with us.

RH-B DEPARTMENT SUPERVISOR: (GESTURES TO DANIEL) You could've easily swapped out Daniel for her to join us tonight. I'm pretty sure it wouldn't be a big deal for him to take the night off.

RH-D DEPARTMENT SUPERVISOR: We would've brought our own assistants as well, but they had other plans for tonight, and we surely know that we wouldn't have seen you if Daniel hadn't come. (TURNS TO DANIEL) It's nice having you join us, Mr. Morin.

DANIEL: (CORDIAL) I appreciate it. Glad to know that my presence is still valued.

Mr. Popkin nudges Daniel as everyone begins to notice the awkward silence.

ZACH: Forgive me for being blunt, but I believe we should be doing something more than just having small talk out here. How 'bout we do something else like watch the show.

THOMAS: (SLIGHTLY ANNOYED) It is traditional not to go in on the first act. I'm sure they taught you that on your first day.

ZACH: (CORDIAL) My apologies, Mr. Dewberry, but I was never one for following traditions. Anyway, I think those little kids have stopped dancing by now. (HONESTLY) I too was looking forward to meeting this female colleague of yours, as she was the rave of the A Department.

RH-A DEPARTMENT SUPERVISOR: (QUIETLY PULLS ZACH OVER) Remember Zach, what is said in the office must stay in the office.

ZACH: (QUIETLY) Yeah, you also told me to be on my best behaviour, but look at how that's working out for you guys. (TO EVERYONE) Well, I don't know about you gentlemen, but my butt is getting tired of this wall and is wanting to sit in those comfy chairs. (POINTS TO THE DOOR) Shall we head inside now?

MR. POPKIN: (AGREES) Yes! That sounds like a great idea! Why waste time out here when we can simply watch the show. That's what we're here for, right! (ENCOURAGING) So c'mon, let's go!

The department supervisors look at each other and shrug as they open the door to find their seats in the auditorium. Thomas, Zach and the other two employees follow as Mr. Popkin attempts to go inside until Daniel stops him.

MR. POPKIN: (IMPATIENT) What? What is up with you? C'mon, spit it out. What's going on?

DANIEL: (QUIETLY) You know they were right when they said she should be here.

Mr. Popkin quickly realizes what Daniel is talking about as he continues to push on the topic.

DANIEL: (QUIETLY) You know that they were exactly right when they said she deserves to be here. That prize shouldn't have gone to Employee #158. You know exactly who that prize belongs to.

MR. POPKIN: (PAUSES) Well, I don't see a problem in choosing Employee #158 ... he was part of the top five best performers.

DANIEL: (QUIETLY ARGUES) In fifth place! He didn't even come close to the employees who took third, second or first place, which was Employee #263! She tripled his score in two days, and it took an entire week for him to earn his officially.

MR. POPKIN: (QUIETLY ARGUES) All right, I see you're not willing to let this go, so I'm going to give you an answer! Did you want me to choose the winner who was going to make my blood pressure rise or your blood pressure rise? Because I know you wouldn't be standing here talking to me like this if I chose second place. And don't ask me how I know because I know everything that goes on in that office – even that janitor who throws those lunch parties in the break room! And since you asked me, what choice did I have? Especially when those privileged Tints in that room are not prepared to share the same space with a Slate, as far as I know! And even if I were to go through with the decision of choosing third, second or first place, do you really think those buffoons are going to behave properly in front of a woman?

Daniel stands there confused, terrified and shocked at the same time, as Mr. Popkin does not even wait for him to answer.

MR. POPKIN: (QUIETLY ARGUES) Nope? I thought so, too and that's the end of that discussion!

ZACH: (STEPS OUTSIDE) Are you guys coming in?

MR. POPKIN: (TURNS TO ZACH AND SMILES) Yes, we're just finishing up our conversation. We'll join you all in a minute.

Zach gives a thumb's up and heads back inside, as Mr. Popkin aggressively pushes Daniel to go inside the auditorium and he sheepishly obeys.

▌ INT. AUDITORIUM OF THE ENTERTAINMENT HALL – NIGHT

The Grand Wallace Celebration Gala begins with the Skyline Dancers opening the show as Mr. Popkin and Daniel make their way inside the auditorium. Thomas busies himself talking to the other two employees, while Mr. Popkin and Daniel carefully make the effort to sit beside one of the department supervisors. They take a seat beside each other as they watch the young performers dance to the music played by the Entertainment Hall Orchestra.

MR. POPKIN: (UNIMPRESSED) Huh. No wonder you guys chose not to watch the first act. These kids suck.

RH-A DEPARTMENT SUPERVISOR: Yes, it's a shame what these children have to go through on a night like this. (IN PITY) I wonder whose idea it was to have those poor things embarrass themselves on such a special occasion.

ZACH: (LEANS IN) Well, be prepared to cleanse your eyes because I heard the adult performances are legendary.

RH-D DEPARTMENT SUPERVISOR: (PLEASANTLY) Yes, the professionals are always a pleasant sight. Even the child prodigies are amazing to watch. These little ones were only added to entertain the children in the audience.

RH-B DEPARTMENT SUPERVISOR: (SIGHS) This is going to be a long show. (TURNS TO MR. POPKIN) I hope you're into opera, Van-Earl, because there's going to be lots of it.

MR. POPKIN: (CORDIAL) Yes, well ... it's always nice to try new things ... (QUIETLY GROWLS), though not if I die of boredom first.

RH-A DEPARTMENT SUPERVISOR: Shh! (WHISPERS) It's about to begin.

Mr. Popkin hears a round of applause erupt from the audience as the Skyline Dancers take a bow and wave to the audience before running backstage as the host of the Grand Wallace Celebration Gala walks on stage with a microphone in his hand.

GWCG HOST: (THROUGH THE MICROPHONE) Let's give another warm round of applause to our Skyline Dancers.

The audience claps for the Skyline Dancers as Mr. Popkin claps a few times with no interest in his heart.

GWCG HOST: (THROUGH THE MICROPHONE) Good evening, everyone. It's such a pleasure to have you all here. I'll be your host for tonight's event as I welcome you all to the Annual Grand Wallace Celebration Gala.

The audience gives an even louder round of applause, as the host smiles and patiently waits for the clapping to die down.

GWCG HOST: (THROUGH THE MICROPHONE) This evening will be full of amazing entertainment – exciting performances that you won't believe with your eyes. Our lovely performers have come from far and wide to showcase their incredible talents before you for the first time. However, they are not the only ones who will be performing, as they will be sharing the stage with our famous veterans, who have become proud members of the Entertainment Hall.

The audience gives another round of applause as the host smiles and patiently waits for the clapping to die down. The host continues his speech as Thomas struggles to see him from where he is sitting.

THOMAS: (LEANS IN) How come we didn't get a chance to sit closer to the stage?

MR. POPKIN: (LEANS IN) If you haven't noticed already, we are sitting in our assigned sections based on our Phase Status. (QUIETLY GROWLS) Why do you think we're sitting all the way in the balcony? Unless you're dying from an incurable disease, you can simply join the Shades at the very front!

A few guests shush Mr. Popkin as he quietly makes a fuss about it while Daniel tries to calm him down. Thomas sheepishly turns back to the stage as the host continues his speech.

GWCG HOST: (THROUGH THE MICROPHONE) Now, I would like to keep this short, as our first performer has taken on the task of continuing the tradition that our great founder has left for us to remember him by. So, in honour of the man who created this theatre and the love of the fine arts themselves, here to perform for the first time on this stage, I present to you ... Tiffany Scarlet!

One of the department supervisors claps heavily, as the audience gives a round of applause as the host leaves the stage. **Tiffany Scarlet**

(early-thirties) walks across the stage wearing a ballgown proclaiming her Social Hue, as the audience gives another round of applause. Tiffany smiles at the audience and waits for the applause to die down as the orchestra begins playing the music for *Adieu, Notre Petite Table*.

TIFFANY: (SINGS IN FRENCH) Je ne suis que faiblesse et que fragilité ... Ah! malgré moi je sens couler mes larmes ...

Thomas's eyes widen in consternation as he remembers Gillian taunting him while he sits there terrified and confused.

TIFFANY: (SINGS IN FRENCH) Devant ces rêves effaces ...

Daniel begins to slowly squirm in his seat as Mr. Popkin turns to him, confused and smacks him on the arm to stop while he shoos him away. They start arguing quietly with each other until the other guests shush them to stop as Tiffany continues to sing.

TIFFANY: (SINGS IN FRENCH) L'avenir aura-t-il les charmes ... de ces beaux jours déjà passés?

Mr. Popkin looks around to see everyone around him enjoying the performance, except Daniel. Tiffany's voice even affects the production staff as well as the cameramen who are filming the Grand Wallace Celebration Gala.

▌ INT. ELISA'S APARTMENT – NIGHT

Elisa watches the Grand Wallace Celebration Gala in the living room while eating a second helping of Rigatoni Bolognese. She tries her best not to make a mess of herself while not missing a single part of Tiffany's performance.

TIFFANY: (THROUGH THE TV) Adieu, notre petite table, qui nous réunit si souvent!

Elisa relaxes on the couch and continues to watch Tiffany's performance, smiling as she reminisces about watching the Grand Wallace Celebration Gala with Garreth.

TIFFANY: (THROUGH THE TV) Adieu, adieu, notre petite table, si grande pour nous cependant!

Thirteen Years Prior

▌ INT. THE GRAVES' HOUSE – NIGHT

GENEVIEVE: (THROUGH THE TV) On tient, c'est inimaginable ... Si peu de place ... en se serrant ...

Garreth and eight-year-old Elisa watch the Grand Wallace Celebration Gala together while eating popcorn on the couch as **Genevieve Dinesen (early-thirties)** performs Adieu, Notre Petite Table for the first time at the Entertainment Hall.

GARRETH: See? Not as boring as you thought, right?

EIGHT-YEAR-OLD ELISA: (SHAKES HER HEAD) Uh-uh.

GARRETH: I can't believe it – you're the only one who is willing to watch this with me. Not even your mother and sister would sit down and watch the Grand Wallace Celebration Gala.

EIGHT-YEAR-OLD ELISA: I don't see why not. She's so pretty and sings very well. Makes me wanna do it, too!

Eight-year-old Elisa gets off the couch, stands in the middle of the room and prepares to sing for Garreth.

EIGHT-YEAR-OLD ELISA: (TRIES TO MIMIC GENEVIEVE) Ah ... doo ... nay-to-pay – (STOPS AND SCRATCHES HER HEAD) Uh, wait, how does it go again? (TRIES TO MIMIC GENEVIEVE) Ah ... doo ... no (STOPS), that's not it. (TRIES AGAIN) Ah-dooooooooo!

Garreth laughs uncontrollably while eight-year-old Elisa stands there upset as she crosses her arms and pouts for the entire time.

GARRETH: (LAUGHS) I think you need to leave the singing to Miss Genevieve on TV.

EIGHT-YEAR-OLD ELISA: (WHINES) I'm trying, Dad.

GARRETH: (LAUGHS) Well, your trying might wake up your brother and sister. Now, you don't want that, do you?

EIGHT-YEAR-OLD ELISA: (BLUNTLY) No.

Eight-year-old Elisa climbs back on the couch and holds onto Garreth tightly as he laughs and wraps his arms around her.

GARRETH: (LAUGHS) You better hold onto someone else this tightly when I'm gone.

EIGHT-YEAR-OLD ELISA: (SLIGHTLY UPSET) Why do you keep saying that?

GARRETH: Because it might actually happen, and the last thing I want is for you to be alone.

EIGHT-YEAR-OLD ELISA: But I'm not alone. I have you.

GARRETH: I know you do, and I'll always be there for you no matter what ... but there will be a time when you're going to be on your own, and Daddy won't be there to protect you. I just want to make sure you'll be okay when that day comes.

EIGHT-YEAR-OLD ELISA: (SLIGHTLY WORRIED) Are you saying that because of your new job?

GARRETH: I know it's hard for you to hear this ... but there will be a time when I won't be here anymore. Not only am I getting old, but I also took an oath for the Steels Protection Services that I will protect the people in this country at all costs ... even if it means risking my life to do so.

Eight-year-old Elisa lowers her head sadly as Garreth holds onto her for comfort.

GARRETH: The last thing I wanted was to make you sad, but there are benefits to being a Steels officer. I get to protect the people in this town. I get to keep you guys safe. I even get to watch this show with you.

EIGHT-YEAR-OLD ELISA: (LOOKS UP) Really?

GARRETH: Yeah, I enjoy watching this with you. You have no idea how much I love spending time with you, so there's nothing for you to be sad about. All I want is for you to be strong on your own and live life to the fullest, which means you're gonna have to learn how to make friends.

EIGHT-YEAR-OLD ELISA: (POUTS) No.

GARRETH: And you're gonna have to get along with your siblings.

EIGHT-YEAR-OLD ELISA: (POUTS) Hmph.

GARRETH: And you're gonna have to give some of that love to your mother. I think she needs it more than I do.

EIGHT-YEAR-OLD ELISA: (TURNS TO GARRETH) What if she doesn't want me to?

GARRETH: She will. Your mother may behave coldly at times, but she's willing to melt when she is ready to – especially when she's sleeping and doesn't feel a thing at all.

EIGHT-YEAR-OLD ELISA: Are you sure that would work?

GARRETH: You just have to keep trying, and fortunately, she'll come around. And by doing all that stuff, you'll be able to grow and become the best Hue there is.

EIGHT-YEAR-OLD ELISA: (BLUNTLY) But I probably won't be a good purple.

GARRETH: (LAUGHS) You got that right. That's definitely not going to happen.

Eight-year-old Elisa and Garreth laugh, since they both believe her statement.

GARRETH: (CONFIDENTLY) I still believe you'll become a red. You do tend to boss people around sometimes.

EIGHT-YEAR-OLD ELISA: (PROTESTS) I'm not bossy –

GARRETH: Oh, yes, you are! You may not like to hear it, but you do have some traits of your mother in you.

EIGHT-YEAR-OLD ELISA: (TURNS TO GARRETH) I think we should be watching the show now.

GARRETH: You see? It's already been activated.

Eight-year-old Elisa giggles as she and Garreth continue to watch Genevieve's performance at the Grand Wallace Celebration Gala.

GENEVIEVE: (THROUGH THE TV) Adieu, notre petite table! Un même verre était le nôtre, chacun de nous, quand il buvait y cherchait les lèvres de l'autre ...

Thirteen Years Later

▌ INT. AUDITORIUM OF THE ENTERTAINMENT HALL – NIGHT

TIFFANY: (THROUGH THE TV) Ah! pauvre ami, comme il m'aimait! Adieu, notre petite table, adieu!

Everyone in the audience gives Tiffany a standing ovation, and the applause wakes up Mr. Popkin from his nap. He gets up and starts clapping too, along with Thomas, Zach and the rest of the department supervisors.

▌ INT. ELISA'S APARTMENT – NIGHT

Elisa watches Tiffany smile to the crowd and claps for her as well until the Annual Grand Wallace Celebration Gala is interrupted by the Bartlett's Piece documentary.

TV PROGRAMMER: (THROUGH THE TV) Welcome to Bartlett's Piece, one of the world's rarest finds on the planet.

ELISA: (GROWLS AND SHOUTS) House! Access all connected devices!

HOUSE AI: Accessing all connected devices. What would you like to do with these connected devices, Ms. Graves?

ELISA: (GETS UP ANGRILY) Remove Bartlett's Piece documentary!

HOUSE AI: Removing Bartlett's Piece documentary ... (LOADING) This course of action contains in-purchases from the host. By continuing, you will have to agree to a monthly subscription that removes any intersecting programs from any viewing device in this household.

ELISA: (ANGRILY) Subscribe to monthly subscription!

HOUSE AI: Subscribing to monthly subscription ... (LOADING) This course of action requires the host to take a written test to qualify for a monthly subscription.

ELISA: (GROWLS TO HERSELF) Almighty ...

HOUSE AI: When would you like to book your test?

ELISA: (ANGRILY) Tomorrow at 8 am!

HOUSE AI: Confirming test schedule ... (LOADING) Your written test will be activated in nine hours and fifty-three minutes. Please visit the Test Centre to complete your test. Once the test is completed, your monthly subscription will be activated. Your television has entered Free Trial Mode. Enjoy the program.

The Bartlett's Piece documentary disappears as the TV switches back to the Annual Grand Wallace Celebration Gala. Elisa collapses back on her couch and sighs in exhaustion.

A Few Hours Later

▌ INT. ELISA'S APARTMENT – EVENING

Carrying a lighter and five candles, Elisa calmly goes to the kitchen. She opens the fridge, pulls out the chocolate cake she made earlier and brings it to the table before taking a seat. She places the five candles on top of the cake before lighting each one with the lighter. She stares at the cake for a moment while she thinks about Garreth.

ELISA: (SOLEMNLY) Seventeen years celebrating with you ... five years celebrating without you, and yet still, after all this time ... I haven't found anyone to hold onto as tightly as I held onto you. I keep trying to keep the promise I made you ... but it looks like that promise doesn't want to be kept. That promise keeps hiding from me and doesn't want me to hold onto her as tightly as I held onto you. That promise doesn't even want to talk to me at all ... but I keep trying, just for your sake.

Elisa continues to stare at the cake for a moment while the wax from the candles starts to slowly melt.

ELISA: (SOLEMNLY) I wish you were here to give me an answer ... something that would help me make that promise's heart melt faster than these candles. I know you always have something up your sleeve ... I just need to find it for myself, right? You knew it was going to happen all along ... but it's okay ... today feels like a good night ... so let's keep it a good night, all right? Happy birthday, Dad.

Elisa blows the candles out before she ends the night with a piece of cake.

A teenage girl and her two younger siblings walk home after a trip to the convenience store. The little boy and little girl waste no time playing with their new ball while they jump into the shallow puddles on the street.

TEENAGE GIRL: (ANNOYED) C'mon guys, we don't have time for this! We have to get home!

LITTLE BOY: (TURNS TO TEENAGE GIRL) Why do you always have to be so bossy?

LITTLE GIRL: (TURNS TO TEENAGE GIRL) Come play with us! It's so much fun!

TEENAGE GIRL: Well, we'll see how much fun we're having when Mom doesn't see me come home with you guys!

LITTLE BOY AND LITTLE GIRL: (WHINE) Aww! Why do you always ruin the fun?

TEENAGE GIRL: (ANNOYED) You guys will have fun in the morning. This is not the time for kids to be playing around, anyway! Who knows what can happen at this time?

The teenage girl and her two younger siblings continue to walk home and the little boy starts bouncing the ball in the street.

TEENAGE GIRL: (ANNOYED) Stop playing with that thing. You might attract trouble.

The little boy continues to bounce the ball in the street until it bounces out of his reach and disappears into an alley.

LITTLE BOY: (WHINES) My ball!

TEENAGE GIRL: (STRICT) Leave it! I'll get you another one in the morning. Let's just get home –

The little boy runs off to find the ball while the teenage girl huffs in disbelief.

TEENAGE GIRL: (STRICT) Come back here this instant! I told you to leave it!

The little boy stops at the alley where the ball rolled off to. He is preparing to enter, but then he sees a man wearing a full black bodysuit with the letters "CX" etched on his helmet. The teenage girl holds onto the little girl in fear while the little boy steps back and watches **CX (age unknown)** walk slowly out of the alley with the ball in his hands.

CX: (DISTORTED) You want this? (SLOWLY KNEELS DOWN) Here … take it.

The little boy hesitates and attempts to take the ball from CX, but the man takes out a switchblade and punctures the ball with it.

CX: (DISTORTED) It will be the last thing you hold on to once we bring destruction to this world.

LITTLE BOY: (CRIES) Mommy!

The little boy runs to the teenage girl, who grabs both his hand and the little girl's while they run for their lives to make their way home.

TEENAGE GIRL: (SCARED) Let's go! Let's go!

CX slowly gets up as he watches the teenage girl and her two younger siblings run home.

CX: (DISTORTED) If only they knew what is coming for this world.

CX takes the time to think about his master plan with **General Metallic (age unknown)** as a distorted hologram of General Metallic appears in the streets.

GENERAL METALLIC: (DISTORTED) They wouldn't have run so easily if they did.

After the hologram of General Metallic disappears, CX begins to whistle and takes a stroll through the Tint Valley Residence.

The Next Day

▎ EXT. THE TEST CENTRE – MORNING

Elisa finishes completing the test for her monthly subscription and waits patiently for the Test Centre monitor to arrive.

TEST CENTRE MONITOR: (COMES UP TO ELISA) Finished with your test?

Elisa nods as the Test Centre monitor activates the program to calculate her results.

TEST CENTRE AI: Results confirmed. Your score is eight out of nine. Congratulations: You are now qualified for the monthly subscription that removes any intersecting programs from any viewing device. Your monthly subscription has now been activated. Enjoy your commercial-free programs.

TEST CENTRE MONITOR: That's crazy. You're one of the very few who has ever gotten only one wrong. Not many people get to make it to the standard six to earn these monthly subscriptions. (BEGINS TO LEAVE) Guess you've been paying attention to that documentary.

The Test Centre monitor moves on to another customer and activates the program to calculate their results, while Elisa stands there in slight shock and suddenly begins to feel proud of herself.

INT. RH-C DEPARTMENT OFFICE OF REGIONAL HEADQUARTERS – MORNING

Elisa walks into the office feeling good, but her smile slowly fades as she notices that Gillian is absent while everyone else continues to loiter around the office. She tries her best not to worry as she goes into her cubicle and prepares for work until she sees Hank beginning his cleaning rounds and stops him along the way.

ELISA: (QUIETLY) Hey Hank, do you mind if I speak to you for a second?

HANK: (STOPS AND SMILES AT ELISA) Ah, Ms. Graves. How are you doing this morning?

ELISA: (QUIETLY) I'm doing well. How about you?

HANK: (KINDLY) I'm doing just fine, but you seem to be a bit worried. What's going on?

ELISA: (QUIETLY) Nothing serious. Have you seen Gillian walk in the office today? I noticed that she wasn't here this morning and was wondering if you'd seen her.

HANK: (REMEMBERS) You mean your new friend? (KINDLY) It's nice to see you two finally starting to talk to each other. It's amazing how you two easily became friends. (SLIGHTLY SAD) But I'm starting to wonder if this is an act of replacing me.

ELISA: (REASSURINGLY) You know that will never happen – you could never be replaced.

HANK: (KINDLY) Well, it's good to hear that, knowing that I was just pulling your leg. (WONDERS) But I do find it strange not seeing Ms. Grant today. She usually comes here a lot earlier than the rest of the staff. I'm hoping she didn't get too caught up with the coffee line, knowing how she needs her coffee fix … (REASSURINGLY) But I'll keep an eye out for her before Mr. Popkin starts the Countdown Clock. You just sit tight while I take care of everything.

ELISA: (RELIEVED) Thank you, Hank.

HANK: (KINDLY) No problem. You can count on me for anything.

Elisa smiles and is attempting to sign onto her system when all the lights and computers begin acting up. Everyone in the office is freaking out when the hologram of General Metallic appears on every screen.

GENERAL METALLIC: (DISTORTED) This is a message for the faint of heart … as well as the citizens who know what is about to come.

Hank puts his arm around Elisa as she stands in her cubicle, petrified. At the same time, everyone else becomes scared and wonders what is happening.

GENERAL METALLIC: (DISTORTED) We have seen you … we have watched you live your lives through the Hue System.

EXT. THE CAPITAL COURTYARD OF BARTLETT'S PIECE – MORNING

All broadcast transmitters are activated as the hologram of General Metallic appears right in front of the Capital Courtyard. Watching the broadcast, the citizens tremble in fear. Meanwhile, the GAO leads, employees and technicians try their best to override the broadcast connection.

GENERAL METALLIC: (DISTORTED) We have watched many of you take advantage of what you call the "goodness" of what this system has brought to you.

GAO LEAD 1: (SHOUTS) Disable the connection now!

The GAO employees continue their efforts to override the broadcast, while General Metallic laughs ominously through the hologram.

GENERAL METALLIC: (DISTORTED) Don't bother wasting your time, staff. You'll never be able to stop this broadcast, as we've seen you reap the benefits of this system as well.

EXT. OUTSIDE THE TINT VALLEY RESIDENCE – MORNING

A hologram of General Metallic appears in one of the buildings of the Tint Valley Residence as citizens inside and outside watch the distorted broadcast.

GENERAL METALLIC: (DISTORTED) We've seen all of you take so much of this "goodness" that your little lives began to feel privileged for earning such benefits. Well, we're here to let you know that all that goodness is coming to an end. We are here to take down everything that bears the very existence of Isaim Hue ... and no one – not even your late commander-in-chief – can stop us from doing so.

The little boy who remembers CX starts to cry as his mother holds onto him, as well as the little girl and the teenage girl.

INT. RH-C DEPARTMENT OFFICE OF REGIONAL HEADQUARTERS – MORNING

GENERAL METALLIC: (DISTORTED) Your commander failed to fulfill his promise to give everyone what they wanted. We're here to remind you of his failures, as destruction will come upon Bartlett's Piece, and we shall rise once again! Be prepared for a revolution, as this message has been brought to you by General Metallic. You have been warned.

General Metallic's broadcast ends as the lights and computers go back to normal, leaving everyone frightened about what just happened. Elisa takes a moment to breathe, while she and Hank watch everyone else begin to question what just happened.

FEMALE COLLEAGUE 1: (SCARED) What is going on?

MALE COLLEAGUE 1: (SCARED) What on earth was that? What is happening here?

Mr. Popkin and Daniel emerge from their offices and see that everyone is freaking out about the broadcast.

MR. POPKIN: (QUIETLY, ANGRILY) Well, isn't this fantastic? What a day to pull off such a prank as this.

DANIEL: (QUIETLY ARGUES) Well, it was broadcast everywhere, so I doubt that it was a prank. (REASSURINGLY) It's all right, everyone. There's nothing you need to worry about. We have everything under control.

MR. POPKIN: (REASSURINGLY) Yes, don't let this silly prank get the better of you guys. (SLIGHTLY ANXIOUS) However, I'm afraid we're going to have to cancel today's Power Hour, as this office will go into Lockdown Mode.

Everyone stands there in shock and begins to murmur amongst themselves. Elisa and Hank turn to each other in worry and start thinking about Gillian.

A Few Hours Later

INT. RH-C DEPARTMENT OFFICE OF REGIONAL HEADQUARTERS – MORNING

Everyone simultaneously and anxiously does their work until the Countdown Clock finishes going down and the Break Bell rings. While everyone attempts to leave the office, Elisa stays in her cubicle. However, Mr. Popkin blocks the doors to prevent the workers from leaving.

MR. POPKIN: (FIRMLY) Just where does everyone think they're going? This is not the time for you to go to the cafeteria with your friends and socialize for hours. We're under Lockdown Mode, meaning we stay here at all costs, and we don't leave this office until Morning Shift ends. This also means you get a thirty-minute break instead of a full hour, and if you're hungry, we have had refreshments for everyone brought in from the cafeteria courtesy of the kitchen staff. So enjoy your break, but do not leave this office!

Everyone groans in frustration as they slowly make their way to the kitchen. Elisa stays where she is. She turns to see that Gillian's cubicle is still empty and sees Hank with a worried look on his face.

▎ INT. KITCHEN OF THE RH-C DEPARTMENT OFFICE – MORNING

Elisa takes the time to check out the refreshments from the kitchen and takes a sandwich to munch on, while the rest of the colleagues find something to eat for the break. Xavier rushes into the kitchen to find something to eat but tries his best to avoid everyone while everyone else talks amongst themselves.

MALE COLLEAGUE 1: (ANNOYED) This is ridiculous! If Mr. Popkin said this was a prank, why would he put the entire office on Lockdown Mode?

FEMALE COLLEAGUE 1: (SIGHS) He obviously did it for our own protection – plus we all saw what happened; he was just as scared as the rest of us.

MALE COLLEAGUE 1: (ANNOYED) But you know what happens when it comes to Lockdown; our hours get cut in the process! And I was really looking forward to today's Power Hour!

THOMAS: C'mon, nothing's wrong with going home early for the day.

FEMALE COLLEAGUE 2: (UPSET) That's easy for you to say, Thomas – you got to go to the Grand Wallace Celebration Gala!

FEMALE COLLEAGUE 1: (EXCITEDLY) Oh! How was it?

THOMAS: (GUSHES) Oh, it was amazing! I've never been sur-rounded by so much art in my entire life. It was a splendid experience! (ANNOYED) If only the supervisors didn't bring their Power Hour winners – especially this one guy who was so unkempt and annoying. I hope to never see him again.

FEMALE COLLEAGUE 1: (EXCITEDLY) But who did you get to see last night? Did you get to meet anyone? Did you meet Genevieve Dinesen?

THOMAS: (GUSHES) No – but I did see her performance, and it was amazing! But she may have a run from her money with that Tiffany Scarlett sticking around.

FEMALE COLLEAGUE 1: (EXCITEDLY) Ooh! She was there too?

FEMALE COLLEAGUE 2: (EXCITEDLY) What song did she perform last night?

THOMAS: (THINKS) I don't know. I left the program at home so I wouldn't be able to –

FEMALE COLLEAGUE 1: (BEGS) Oh, you must be able to remember!

THOMAS: (ASTONISHED) What do you want from me? (OPTIMISTIC) It was all in a different language! But I'll try to remember – I'll try … the lyrics went like … (TRIES TO SPEAK FRENCH) joo nay pass – no, not that. Um … joo nay sweet – that's not it either. Jooo –

ELISA: (IN FRENCH) Je ne suis que faiblesse et que fragilité … malgré moi je sens couler mes larmes … devant ces rêves effaces … l'avenir aura-t-il les charmes … de ces beaux jours déjà passés? Adieu, notre petite table …

Thomas and the rest of her colleagues, including Xavier, turn to Elisa in amazement. When she finishes singing, she looks at everyone with an innocent expression on her face.

ELISA: That's the name of the song, Adieu, notre petite table, and if you wanted it translated into English … it means Farewell, our little table.

FEMALE COLLEAGUE 2: (IRRITATED) How do you know all that?

ELISA: I watched it, of course; the song is performed every year in the show. It is derived from Manon, one of Andrew Wallace's favourite operas, which is why the Grand Wallace Celebration Gala contains so many opera performances to commemorate him.

XAVIER: (CONFIDENTLY) You should also know that was Genevieve's first performance before she became the famous singer she is now.

When Thomas and the rest of his colleagues turn to Xavier in shock, he quickly begins to lose his confidence.

XAVIER: (SHEEPISHLY) I thought I would let you guys know since I watched it, too.

Xavier turns back to the food as Thomas and the rest of the colleagues stand there, perplexed by him and Elisa.

MALE COLLEAGUE 1: (ANNOYED) What is this? A Slate attack? No one asked you to say anything. How do you two even know all this?

ELISA: This was all in the documentary. You should know that Andrew Wallace worked at the Discovery Region before the founding of the Entertainment Hall and that the Grand Wallace Celebration Gala happens every year to commemorate his efforts to bring the arts to Bartlett's Piece. I have watched it many times.

XAVIER: (SHEEPISHLY) Me, too.

FEMALE COLLEAGUE 2: (IRRITATED) But how were you able to watch the show in the first place?

ELISA: Everyone has access to watch any special event – it doesn't matter what your Tint Level is once you enter Tint Valley.

MALE COLLEAGUE 1: (ANNOYED) But Genevieve's performance happened thirteen years ago. How were you able to watch it then?

Xavier freezes in shock while Elisa just smirks at the question.

ELISA: You tell me … I was either invited to a friend's house … or watched it outside my window on someone else's TV … maybe I had someone in the family to watch the show with … as they carried a special background. I'll let you figure out the answer to that one.

Elisa walks away while Xavier takes more sandwiches before leaving the kitchen as well. The rest of the colleagues turn to each other in disbelief, while Thomas mentally brings his resentment for Elisa even further.

INT. RH-C DEPARTMENT OFFICE OF REGIONAL HEADQUARTERS – MORNING

Elisa walks back to her cubicle and takes a seat to start working, as usual. One of the female colleagues storms out of the kitchen and walks straight up to her.

FEMALE COLLEAGUE 1: (UPSET) Hey! You're not the only one who comes from a special background!

Elisa sighs silently to herself as the female colleague comes up to her.

FEMALE COLLEAGUE 1: (UPSET) I came from a Steels background, too! But it wasn't as fun as you think it was – it was the worst times of my life! And just to let you know, I actually lost my father for being a Steels officer. There was nothing fun about that! Do you think a Slate like you knows how that feels?

The male colleague walks up to the female colleague to back her up. Elisa tries her best not to lose her patience and sympathizes with her.

ELISA: My condolences for your loss ... the last thing I wanted to do was offend you.

MALE COLLEAGUE 1: (ANGRILY) Just who do you think you are? Nobody cares about what you have to say. No one is going to care that you even exist 'cause you mean nothing to us – and that's what you'll always be to us!

Elisa slowly begins to lose her patience and tries to ignore her male colleague as she continues to work.

MALE COLLEAGUE 1: (ANGRILY) Do you hear me talking to you? Well, let's see if this gets your attention!

The male colleague pulls an actual slate rock out of his pocket and slams it on Elisa's keyboard, as everyone else around her flinches in shock and they get irritated and begin to curse amongst themselves.

MALE COLLEAGUE 1: (ANGRILY) That should be a reminder that you don't belong here! How dare you think you can step out of your place when you're nothing but a Blank Slate?

The male colleague continues to scream at Elisa until she angrily gets up and throws the slate to the floor. Everyone around her flinches in even more shock. Daniel emerges frantically from his office to see what is happening.

MALE COLLEAGUE 1: (ANGRILY) Just what exactly are you going to do? No one is going to protect you.

ELISA: (LIVID) Like I need anyone here to protect me from the likes of you!

The male colleague steps back in shock, along with the female colleague. Daniel comes over and sees the broken slate rock on the floor, along with Elisa's broken keyboard and stands there in disbelief.

DANIEL: (IN DISBELIEF) What ... what is all this? We may be under Lockdown Mode, but I do expect everyone to act like civilized people! (LIVID) Not animals who attack each other and break office equipment! Just what went through your damn head to do something like this? Let alone use that disgusting word in this office!

MALE COLLEAGUE 1: (ARGUES) It's her damn fault. I'm just trying to put her in her place! And Mr. Popkin uses that word all the time in this office –

DANIEL: (POINTS TO THE WINDOW) And if Mr. Popkin were to jump out of that window, would you do the same? (LIVID) You damn privileged Tints need to realize that you're in the same position as her and everyone else in this office, and there is nothing special about any of you to justify such behavior! Mr. Popkin may have let that word slip out of his mouth at times, but he definitely doesn't promote stupidity in this office! (TO THE MALE COLLEAGUE) So, you better clean this up and leave this instant, for you are now on temporary suspension this week ... and you damn well know that you don't have the power to stop me from doing that.

The male colleague stands there in disbelief until he angrily picks up the broken pieces of the slate rock off the floor and storms out of the office. Everyone in the office becomes quiet as they look on, surprised to see Daniel this angry.

DANIEL: (ANGRILY TO EVERYONE) This should be a lesson for all of you not to bring such foolishness into this office again! So, you better get back to work or I'll have you all stay back doing the janitor's job throughout the entire building if that's what it takes to get that into your heads!

Everyone quickly goes back to work as Elisa tries to calm herself down. In frustration, the female colleague turns to Elisa. However, when Elisa shoots her a cold look, she panics and scurries to her cubicle while Daniel tries to calm down.

DANIEL: (CALMLY) Are you okay, Employee #263?

ELISA: (CALMLY) I'm fine, Mr. Morin. I apologize for the commotion – I ... just happened to lose myself at the moment.

DANIEL: (SHAKES HIS HEAD) Don't worry too much. It happens to the best of us. Look at me. I just sent an employee home without Mr. Popkin's permission. I'm going to get an earful from him when he hears about this.

Elisa finally relaxes and takes a seat to calm herself further, while Daniel looks at her broken keyboard and shakes his head.

DANIEL: (SIGHS) To think that this lockdown was supposed to ensure everyone's safety. Now we have to prevent everyone from killing each other. Why do these lockdowns bring out the worst in us?

ELISA: Not everyone likes being confined for a long time, yet they don't want to confront the unknown that everyone sees as dangerous. I don't think it was necessary to send him home like that –

DANIEL: (SERIOUSLY) Yes, it was. No one should be acting like that in the office. It makes me sick that it's a rule for Tints to be nonconfrontational and just watch shit happen. You should never have to put up with that behaviour, either.

ELISA: (GENUINELY) I appreciate that ... thank you for your interference, Mr. Morin.

DANIEL: Anything to help out a fellow Tint ... by any chance, have you seen Employee #417?

Elisa's blood runs cold and she feels guilty about forgetting about Gillian's absence.

DANIEL: She's not at work today and hasn't gone through the proper procedure to alert us. I figured you might know something, as you're the one that she's closest to.

ELISA: (SHAKES HER HEAD) I had no idea that she was going to be absent today. We made plans for later on, but she didn't tell me anything afterwards, so I don't know where she is either.

DANIEL: It's fine, but if you hear anything from her, please let me know directly.

ELISA: (NODS) I'll make sure I do that, Mr. Morin.

DANIEL: Thank you, Employee #263. I'll make sure that a new keyboard is brought to you right away – just take it easy until the supply staff arrives.

Elisa nods in understanding as Daniel goes back to his office while everyone continues their work. Elisa sighs as she attempts to start working, then remembers the broken keyboard and huffs in frustration as she waits for a new one to arrive.

INT. BARTLETT'S PIECE BOOKSTORE – AFTERNOON

As Elisa walks into Bartlett's Piece Bookstore, Vincent notices her sour mood and smiles to himself.

VINCENT: (KINDLY) You're back again, Ms. Graves. Is this for another special occasion?

ELISA: No, I just need somewhere to escape … Do you mind if I stick around?

VINCENT: (SMILES) You can take all the time you need when you're here. (POINTS TO THE CORNER) Go right ahead.

Elisa smiles in gratitude as she goes to the shelf filled with all of her and Garreth's favourite books. She picks up *Cat on a Hot Tin Roof* and starts reading.

A Few Hours Later

INT. BARTLETT'S PIECE BOOKSTORE – AFTERNOON

As Vincent organizes a few new books on the shelf, he takes the time to monitor Elisa and is surprised to see the number of books she has finished. She has gone through *Cat on a Hot Tin Roof*, *The Great Gatsby* and *Fahrenheit 451*. Vincent watches Elisa finish reading The Life of Pi and then put the book on the finished pile. She sits back on the chair and closes her eyes to take a break. She stays still for a moment as she thinks about Garreth's teachings.

GARRETH: (IN ELISA'S HEAD) And I'll always be there for you, no matter what ... but there will be a time when you're going to be on your own, and Daddy won't be there to protect you.

Thirteen Years Prior

▌ INT. THE SKYLINE DINER – AFTERNOON

Garreth and Carman have lunch at the Skyline Diner to celebrate eleven-year-old Fredrick's birthday with him, twelve-year-old Deidre and eight-year-old Elisa. The waitress brings them the family platter, and they all exclaim excitedly.

GARRETH: (HAPPILY) All right, Fredrick! Since it's your special day, you get first choice! Eat to your heart's content!

ELEVEN-YEAR-OLD FREDRICK: (HAPPILY) Awesome!

Eleven-year-old Fredrick grabs a beef slider along with fries, onion rings and chicken nuggets with his hands as Garreth, Carman and twelve-year-old Deidre share out their food with the utensils. Eight-year-old Elisa waits for everyone to finish before she grabs a beef slider and all the mozzarella sticks and attempts to take a chicken nugget until eleven-year-old Fredrick grabs it from her.

ELEVEN-YEAR-OLD FREDRICK: (ANNOYED) Hey! That's not for you!

Eight-year-old Elisa grimaces in confusion, while Garreth tries his best not to get too upset.

GARRETH: (SLIGHTLY STERNLY) C'mon, Fredrick! I thought we talked about this! Today is supposed to be a good day, so would you use this day to be nice to your little sister for once?

ELEVEN-YEAR-OLD FREDRICK: (WHINES) But I don't want her taking all the nuggets!

TWELVE-YEAR-OLD DEIDRE: (CHIMES IN) And she's supposed to pick her food last!

GARRETH: (TURNS TO TWELVE-YEAR-OLD DEIDRE) Now who came up with that rule? Because that didn't come from me or your mother, and last time I checked, you didn't give birth to Elisa, so you're not authorized to put such rules on her.

TWELVE-YEAR-OLD DEIDRE: (TURNS TO CARMAN) Mom!

CARMAN: (SERIOUSLY) Don't plan to upset your father today and do whatever he says. You must give him that respect if you don't plan on sleeping in the streets tonight – which I will make happen if this behaviour continues.

ELEVEN-YEAR-OLD FREDRICK: (NOTICES EIGHT-YEAR-OLD ELISA TAKE A NUGGET) Elisa!

Eight-year-old Elisa quickly eats the nugget as Carman tries her best not to get too upset.

CARMAN: (UPSET) Hey, stop your whining and eat your food! For crying out loud, it was just one nugget –

Carman aggressively grabs all the nuggets and puts them on eleven-year-old Fredrick's plate while Garreth, twelve-year-old Deidre and eight-year-old Elisa look on silently.

CARMAN: (UPSET) There! Now you have all the nuggets for yourself – and you better eat them all! Today is your special day and you're busy acting like a punk. You better quit that if you want all of us to stay here.

Eleven-year-old Fredrick pouts and starts eating his food, while twelve-year-old Deidre and eight-year-old Elisa do the same. Garreth shows appreciation for Carman's discipline, as they both start eating as well until eleven-year-old Fredrick takes eight-year-old Elisa's beef slider.

EIGHT-YEAR-OLD ELISA: (UPSET) Stop it, Fredrick! You have your own food!

ELEVEN-YEAR-OLD FREDRICK: (TAUNTS) And you're not supposed to have any food!

Eleven-year-old Fredrick attempts to eat the beef slider in front of eight-year-old Elisa. However, Carman slaps the back of his head before anyone has a chance to react. Garreth and twelve-year-old Deidre sit there shocked as eleven-year-old Fredrick freezes and drops the beef slider on the table.

CARMAN: (UPSET) Is that what you want on your birthday? 'Cause I can give you a lot more than that, if this is going to go on! I should've let you choke on that burger if you are going to be this stupid!

TWELVE-YEAR-OLD DEIDRE: Mom, you're going to make him cry.

Eleven-year-old Fredrick slowly begins to cry, though Garreth hesitates to intervene.

GARRETH: All right guys, let's just calm down for a sec–

ELEVEN-YEAR-OLD FREDRICK: (SHOUTS AT EIGHT-YEAR-OLD ELISA) You're ruining my birthday!

CARMAN: (UPSET) No one is ruining your birthday, but yourself! Who told you to take your sister's burger? Now, give it back to her!

EIGHT-YEAR-OLD ELISA: (SHEEPISHLYLY) Mommy, I don't want it anymore.

CARMAN: (TURNS TO EIGHT-YEAR-OLD ELISA) So now you want to waste food! Do you know how much we paid for this food for all of us to eat at this place? (UPSET) Because it's definitely not the amount for you to pick what you want and change your mind afterwards! So, you better eat that burger and stop this nonsense. If I knew my children were going to be such privileged assholes, I would've sent you all to the Debris Crest to have your asses disciplined for years!

Eight-year-old Elisa takes the beef slider on the table and fixes it before taking a bite. Garreth, twelve-year-old Deidre and eleven-year-old Fredrick begin to eat their food quietly while Carman tries her best not to eat her food too angrily.

GARRETH: (CALMLY) See? We're having a meal together as a family. Was that so hard?

TWELVE-YEAR-OLD DEIDRE: It would've been easier if you left Elisa home –

GARRETH: (UPSET) Oh, would you stop with that talk, Deidre! For crying out loud, I'm sick and tired of you and your brother continuing this nonsense!

Carman sighs in exasperation and allows Garreth to lecture twelve-year-old Deidre until she notices two anti-Hue members eating at the diner. She tries her best not to be seen until the two anti-Hue members notice her and sit there in shock.

CARMAN: (SERIOUSLY) All right, let's go.

Garreth, twelve-year-old Deidre, eleven-year-old Fredrick and eight-year-old Elisa turn to Carman in consternation as she gets up and slings her purse over her shoulder while she tries to get the waiter's attention.

CARMAN: (LOUDLY) Excuse me? Yeah, we're taking this to go! We're leaving now!

TWELVE-YEAR-OLD DEIDRE: (WHINES) But Mom –

CARMAN: (UPSET) No buts! I told you not to upset your father and you didn't listen – so, we're leaving now!

ELEVEN-YEAR-OLD FREDRICK: (WHINES) But what about my cake?

CARMAN: (TURNS ELEVEN-YEAR-OLD FREDRICK TOWARD HER) Hey! Fuck the cake and let's go!

Carman grabs eleven-year-old Fredrick by the arm and pulls him out of the diner. Twelve-year-old Deidre follows them to make sure everything is okay, while Garreth and eight-year-old Elisa remain seated, looking at each other in shock.

▌ EXT. TINT VALLEY OUTSKIRTS – AFTERNOON

Frowning, eleven-year-old Fredrick walks by himself as Carman lags behind him, holding twelve-year-old Deidre's hand. Garreth lags behind them, holding eight-year-old Elisa's hand as well as the bag of leftovers.

EIGHT-YEAR-OLD ELISA: Daddy, do you think it's my fault?

GARRETH: (SHAKES HIS HEAD) No, sweetheart, it's not your fault at all. You should know how your brother acts when he doesn't get what he wants, but it was a surprise to see your mother discipline him for the first time.

EIGHT-YEAR-OLD ELISA: Do you think Mommy will make Fredrick a cake when we get home?

GARRETH: We'll see how she feels along the way. Right now, she's in a fiery, hot mood, so it's best not to bother her.

CARMAN: (LOUDLY) Would you pick up the pace back there? You have the keys to the house!

GARRETH: (LOUDLY) Well, it's quite hard to catch up with everyone when you're carrying the leftovers!

Eight-year-old Elisa giggles as Carman tries not to smile too widely, as they all make their way home. Eleven-year-old Fredrick continues to sulk until he stops and sees a man harassing an older woman. Garreth and Carman also stop in their tracks and see that the man is actually a mugger.

ELEVEN-YEAR-OLD FREDRICK: (TURNS TO GARRETH) Dad, what's going on over there?

GARRETH: (LOUDLY) Don't worry, son, I'll go check it out! (TURNS TO EIGHT-YEAR-OLD ELISA) Go to your mother, okay.

Eight-year-old Elisa nods as she goes up to Carman, along with eleven-year-old Fredrick, as Garreth goes up to the mugger harassing an older woman.

OLDER WOMAN: (TERRIFIED) Please ... I told you I have nothing to give you –

MUGGER: (AGGRESSIVELY) And I know that you're lying, old hag!

OLDER WOMAN: (TERRIFIED) Please, I'm just trying to survive like everyone else –

MUGGER: (GRABS ONTO THE OLD WOMAN'S COLLAR) Does it look like I care about your sob story? I don't think you're going to like what I do to you if you don't give me what I want!

GARRETH: (FRIENDLY) May I ask what's going on here?

Annoyed, the mugger turns to Garreth while the older woman tries her best to signal him to leave right away.

MUGGER: (THREATENING) Who the fuck are you?

GARRETH: (FRIENDLY) I apologize for interrupting. I live in this neighbourhood just around the corner, and I would hate to go home without knowing that my neighbours are safe –

MUGGER: (THREATENING) Listen, old man, you better just head on home and mind your own business before you –

Taking a chance, the old lady hits the mugger on the head with her purse and he stumbles in shock while trying to regain his balance. The old lady makes a run for it before the mugger can recover, and Garreth stops him from chasing after her.

MUGGER: (LIVID) You let that bitch get away. She owed me money for crying out loud! Just who do you think you are anyway – a Steel or something?

GARRETH: (FIRMLY) I already told you who I am. I'm a man who lives in this neighbourhood. And I don't like coming to my neighbourhood seeing people who are not supposed to be here, especially men who don't know how to treat a woman right.

MUGGER: (LIVID) What makes you think you can tell me what to do? She owes –

GARRETH: (FIRMLY) Listen, I don't want to know what your association is with that woman, but I'm sure there are nicer ways to ask for money. I can teach you how to do that, if you'd like me to. What do you need it for anyway? Shelter? Medicine? Food? (GESTURES TO THE BAG OF LEFTOVERS) I have leftovers here, and I'm willing to give them to you, if you like.

ELEVEN-YEAR-OLD FREDRICK: What is Dad doing?

Carman covers eleven-year-old Fredrick's mouth as she keeps twelve-year-old Deidre and eight-year-old Elisa behind her, while Garreth continues to distract the mugger with the bag of leftovers.

GARRETH: (FRIENDLY) Take it. It's all yours, if you want it.

The mugger stares at the bag of leftovers for a moment, but then he knocks it out of Garreth's hands and pulls a stolen Taser Pistol on him. Seeing this, Carman, twelve-year-old Deidre, eleven-year-old Fredrick and eight-year-old Elisa exclaim in shock. With the weapon pointed at him, Garreth remains calm while Carman, twelve-year-old Deidre, eleven-year-old Fredrick and eight-year-old Elisa begin freaking out.

CARMAN: (SCREAMS) Garreth!

GARRETH: (LOUDLY) It's okay, Carman! It's okay – don't be scared! Everything will be all right!

MUGGER: (GESTURES TO CARMAN AND THE KIDS) Is that your family over there? (CHUCKLES OMINOUSLY) It'd be a shame for one of these pellets to catch any of their heads.

GARRETH: (STERNLY) Young man ... you better put that down if you know what's good for you.

MUGGER: (TAUNTS) Or what? You're going to stop me from shooting your entire family?

The mugger attempts to point his pistol at Carman, twelve-year-old Deidre, eleven-year-old Fredrick and eight-year-old Elisa, but Garreth knocks the weapon out of his hands and aggressively grapples with him while he tries to resist. Carman, twelve-year-old Deidre, eleven-year-old Fredrick and eight-year-old Elisa become frightened as they watch Garreth wrestle with the mugger.

CARMAN: (SCREAMS) Garreth! Garreth, stop!

The mugger tries to escape, but Garreth puts him in half Nelson and pins him to the ground and tries to keep him still.

GARRETH: (ANGRILY) I'm really going to have to teach you a few things, boy! You're never going to get through life with those bad manners of yours. The first lesson is never to threaten a man's family! Especially if that man is a Steels officer!

Garreth keeps the mugger pinned to the ground as a Steels squad car rushes up. Two Steels officers jump out and rush toward them with their Taser Pistols pointing at the mugger.

STEELS OFFICER 1: (SHOUTS) Freeze! Don't move! Officer Graves, is everything all right?

GARRETH: (ANGRILY) It will be once you arrest this guy!

The Steels officer takes over, pinning down the mugger. Garreth gets up and watches his two colleagues put handcuffs on the mugger and hoist him up while he wears a defeated look on his face.

STEELS OFFICER 2: (TURNS TO GARRETH) We got the call as soon as one of the neighbours mentioned that it was you. The last thing we wanted to do was bother you on your day off.

GARRETH: (BREATHES) It's okay ... I'm glad to help out so long as my family is safe.

STEELS OFFICER 1: We'll take it from here. We'll call you if we need anything.

The two Steels officers bring the mugger to the Steels squad car and Garreth takes a breather before turning to reassure Carman. She wastes no time running toward him and holds onto him tightly along with twelve-year-old Deidre, eleven-year-old Fredrick and eight-year-old Elisa. He wraps his arms around each of them tightly and holds onto everyone for reassurance.

Thirteen Years Later

▌ INT. BARTLETT'S PIECE BOOKSTORE – AFTERNOON

Elisa is sitting with her eyes closed when Vincent checks up on her one last time, when he hears the bells chiming from outside.

PRIMETIME PLAZA AI: Attention all consumers. All stores at the Primetime Plaza will officially close due to an Emergency Provincial Protocol. Please make your final purchases as the plaza will be under Lockdown Mode in the next five minutes. Thank you for shopping at Primetime Plaza and have a great day.

VINCENT: (TURNS TO ELISA) Ms. Graves.

ELISA: I heard.

Elisa opens her eyes and gets up from the chair as Vincent approaches her with an apologetic look.

VINCENT: (APOLOGETIC) I do apologize that this keeps on happening during your visits.

ELISA: It's fine; you don't have to apologize. They must be really serious about this protocol.

VINCENT: After what happened this morning, there's a reason why the GAO wants everything to be on Lockdown Mode.

ELISA: Do you think that the Metallic Order might return to Bartlett's Piece?

VINCENT: I don't know what to say about that … that's the last thing anyone wants, but this General Metallic character seems like a true threat. Who knows exactly what his true plan is?

Elisa tries her best not to think about General Metallic's message until she notices the Technological-Environmental Hue she encountered the last time and grimaces in annoyance while watching him trying to sell the Life Pad to people passing by.

VINCENT: Are you sure you don't want to pick up anything before you go?

ELISA: No thanks, I think I'll pass for now. (TURNS TO VINCENT) I'm sorry I lost a copy of one of your books.

VINCENT: Don't be too hard on yourself. It's a bookstore, not a library. I understand the reason for your refusal, but I actually want to give you something before you leave. (GOES TO THE SHELF) I was supposed to give it to you before, but clumsy me, I forgot to take it out from the safe. It's actually something from your father.

Elisa perks up as Vincent takes a small velvet box off the shelf and shows it to her as she responds with wonder and a smile.

▌ EXT. PRIMETIME PLAZA – AFTERNOON

Elisa and Vincent say their goodbyes and she leaves Bartlett's Piece Bookstore, carrying a copy of *Treasure Island* and the velvet box in her hands. She completely passes the Technological-Environmental Hue selling the Life Pad to people and confidently believes she can make her way home until she feels an arm slinging heavily onto her.

TECHNOLOGICAL-ENVIRONMENTAL HUE: (EXAGGERATES) Hey! Just the customer I wanted to see! It's been I don't know – about several hours since we've seen each other –

Elisa pushes the Technological-Environmental Hue off her and stands her ground in irritation.

ELISA: (STERNLY) What on earth is wrong with you?

TECHNOLOGICAL-ENVIRONMENTAL HUE: (EXAGGERATES) What? I thought we would pick up where we left off (SHOWS ELISA THE LIFE PAD), especially with your decision to buy this! The revolutionary, out-of-this-world, state-of-the-art Life Pad. It is the best alternative that you can find, which won't give you Hologram Astigmatism.

Boldly, Elisa walks away as the Technological-Environmental Hue stands there in shock.

TECHNOLOGICAL-ENVIRONMENTAL HUE: (EXAGGERATES) Now wait a second here – you didn't let me finish!

Elisa continues to walk away as the Technological-Environmental Hue chases after her.

TECHNOLOGICAL-ENVIRONMENTAL HUE: (EXAGGERATES) You can do so many things with this Life Pad! You can book reservations to the nicest restaurants, you can watch the latest movies before the release dates, you can even watch the commander-in-chief's speeches – past and present! You can read your books on this thing if you like!

Elisa stops and gives the Technological-Environmental Hue a stern look while he stops to face her.

TECHNOLOGICAL-ENVIRONMENTAL HUE: (EXAGGERATES) C'mon, Kid, you have to give things a chance. How are you going to live a good life if you don't try something new!

ELISA: (STERNLY) You know the plaza is closing soon, and regardless of the situation, you're not even supposed to be here.

TECHNOLOGICAL-ENVIRONMENTAL HUE: (EXAGGERATES) Well, according to my boss, I can do whatever I please – and since you Tints are supposed to be nonconfrontational, who is going to stop me? Now I know it's something that you can't afford at the moment.

Elisa sighs in annoyance as the Technological-Environmental Hue continues to ramble on.

TECHNOLOGICAL-ENVIRONMENTAL HUE: (EXAGGERATES) But I'm going to make you another offer that is brought to you by the Grand Arne Office. You remember the contributions that are given by our amazing customers and –

Elisa grabs the Technological-Environmental Hue's hand to tap her Life Band monogram onto his to complete the transaction.

LIFE BAND AI: Transaction complete. You have successfully purchased the AI Life Pad.

The Technological-Environmental Hue stands there in shock as Elisa lets go of his hand to speak to her Life Band.

ELISA: (TO HER LIFE BAND) Life Band, return recent purchases of this hour.

LIFE BAND AI: Returning recent purchases. You have successfully returned the purchase of the AI Life Pad. Your funds will be returned to your account in the next sixty seconds.

TECHNOLOGICAL-ENVIRONMENTAL HUE: (SHOCKED) W-w-wait a second – what was that?

ELISA: (FIRMLY) Just to show you that I can afford it and after all this time, I still don't want it. Now this place is going under lockdown in the next few minutes, so I suggest you pack up your things, take your contribution and let me go home!

Elisa slams *Treasure Island* onto the Technological-Environmental Hue and attempts to walk away until he blocks her way.

TECHNOLOGICAL-ENVIRONMENTAL HUE: (SLIGHTLY STAGGERED) Wait-wait – hold on for a second! (POINTS TO ELISA'S BOX) What about that box of yours?

ELISA: (UPSET) What more do you want from me? I have already given you a contribution.

TECHNOLOGICAL-ENVIRONMENTAL HUE: (EXAGGERATES) You did give a contribution, but that was only if you came back to finalize our deal the day after our last appointment. But since you didn't come back the day after that appointment, that means you have to offer another contribution, which is double the amount of the previous one.

ELISA: (UPSET) This doesn't make any sense!

TECHNOLOGICAL-ENVIRONMENTAL HUE: (EXAGGERATED) Well, I understand that it doesn't make sense to you … (LEANS TOWARD ELISA), but what makes sense is that you're coughing up that box. (SLIGHTLY THREATENING) So, you better listen –

ELISA: (COLDLY) No, you're the one who had better listen.

The Technological-Environmental Hue stands there stunned as Elisa eyes him coldly.

ELISA: (COLDLY) If it's something I don't want to do, it's something I don't have to do. I don't have to stand here and give you anything and I don't have to stand here and put up with any more of your bullshit. There was never a deal between us, and I don't owe you anything, so I'm going to leave you here to accept that while you leave me alone … (SLIGHTLY THREATENING) or I will involve the Steels Services to take care of your ass.

The Technological-Environmental Hue stands there dumbfounded and offended as Elisa walks away for the last time. She prepares to go home while holding onto the velvet box until she feels a heavy grip on her shoulder and is confronted yet again by the Technological-Environmental Hue.

ELISA: (UPSET) What are you doing?

TECHNOLOGICAL-ENVIRONMENTAL HUE: (THREATENING) Give it to me.

ELISA: (PROTESTS) No. What is wrong with you?

Everyone who is nearby in Primetime Plaza watches the Technological-Environmental Hue fighting Elisa as he tries to take the velvet box from her.

ELISA: (SHOUTS) Stop it – let go of me!

TECHNOLOGICAL-ENVIRONMENTAL HUE: (ANGRILY) Give it – give me the damn box!

ELISA: (SHOUTS) Let go of me!

Everyone nearby looks on in consternation but hesitates to intervene as Elisa tries to fight off the Technological-Environmental Hue. She holds onto the box tightly until she is thrown to the ground and loses her grip as the Technological-Environmental Hue stands over her.

TECHNOLOGICAL-ENVIRONMENTAL HUE: (ANGRILY) Damn Slate.

Elisa stares at the Technological-Environmental Hue lividly as he takes the velvet box, dusts himself off and goes back to a salesman's attitude while facing the crowd.

TECHNOLOGICAL-ENVIRONMENTAL HUE: (EXAGGERATED) My apologies, everyone! That was just a little nuisance over there. Now that that's over, who wants a –

Elisa jumps onto the Technological-Environmental Hue's back and puts him in a headlock while he struggles to throw her off him.

TECHNOLOGICAL-ENVIRONMENTAL HUE: (STRUGGLES TO BREATHE) What are you doing?

Everyone watching gasps in shock and makes a quick decision to either walk away, call the Steels Protection Services or just stay put as Elisa tightens her grip on the Technological-Environmental Hue.

TECHNOLOGICAL-ENVIRONMENTAL HUE: (STRUGGLES TO BREATHE) You – crazy bitch –

ELISA: (SCREAMS) Give it back!

The Technological-Environmental Hue manages to free himself from the headlock and attempts to hit Elisa, but she punches him in the face. She punches him again and swats him one last time with her purse, bringing him to his knees. Elisa is reaching for the velvet box when the Technological-Environmental Hue pulls her to the ground and starts choking her.

TECHNOLOGICAL-ENVIRONMENTAL HUE: (LIVID) You are going to die! Just die already! Die!

Elisa manages to release her arms and reach for the Technological-Environmental Hue's face. She jabs her thumbs into his eyes, causing him to scream in pain. He finally releases his grip to tend to his eyes and Elisa punches him again to get him off her. She notices the Life Pad on the ground and quickly grabs and uses it to hit him again over the head. The Technological-Environmental Hue looks at Elisa wildly and attempts to hit her. However, she gives him a final blow with the Life Pad and he collapses on the ground. Elisa takes a moment to breathe as she watches the Technological-Environmental Hue on the ground groaning in pain. She tosses the Life Pad aside and picks up the velvet box along with *Treasure Island*, then gets up and attempts to leave until she notices everyone staring at her. Everyone who has been watching the incident remains frozen, as Elisa notices the scared looks on every-one's faces as they slowly keep their distance from her.

CONCERNED CITIZEN: (SCARED) Life Band, call Steels Protection Services.

Elisa makes a run for it while everyone around her starts freaking out and calling the Steels Protection Services. She holds onto Treasure Island and the velvet box tightly as she attempts to catch the Route 644 bus, but the bus drives away to start its route. Elisa looks around frantically until she notices a taxi cab idling on the road. A female citizen attempts to get into the taxi cab, but Elisa pushes her aside and quickly gets in herself.

FEMALE CITIZEN: (ANNOYED) Hey!

ELISA: (TO THE TAXI DRIVER) Take me to the Tint Valley Residence. Quickly!

The taxi driver drives off as Elisa closes the door beside her, while the female citizen remains behind, looking on in disbelief.

▌ INT. INSIDE THE TAXI CAB – AFTERNOON

Elisa takes a breather and situates herself while the taxi driver takes her to the Tint Valley Residence. She tries to calm herself down until she notices a few citizens following her as they try to catch up with the taxi cab.

TAXI DRIVER: It's sure busy here – I wonder what's causing all the commotion.

Anxious about the citizens trying to catch up with the taxi cab, Elisa spots a steels officer on patrol. She quickly gets out of the taxi cab as the taxi driver stops midroad and is shocked to see her make a run for it.

TAXI DRIVER: (SHOUTS) Hey! (GETS OUT OF THE TAXI CAB) You forgot to pay!

▌ EXT. OUTSIDE THE TINT VALLEY RESIDENCE – AFTERNOON

Elisa continues to run away from vigilant citizens and makes it to her building, where she taps her life band to gain entrance.

TVR AI: Access granted.

Elisa enters the building and quickly closes the door behind her as many citizens gather around the doorway and try to gain access to the building.

▌ INT. ELISA'S APARTMENT – AFTERNOON

Elisa quickly enters her apartment, locks the door behind her and draws every curtain to prevent anyone from seeing her. She turns off any devices that emit light or sound before rushing into her bedroom.

▌ INT. ELISA'S BEDROOM – AFTERNOON

Elisa enters the bedroom and puts down *Treasure Island*, along with the velvet box and locks the bedroom door. She even draws the curtains closed to prevent anyone from seeing her and turns off any devices that give off light or sound. She starts looking for more things to turn off until she stops, begins to take in what happened and begins to tremble in fear. Elisa slowly backs up to a wall, slides down to the floor and hugs her knees while she begins to cry and continues to tremble in fear.

EIGHT

▌ INT. ELISA'S BEDROOM – EVENING

Elisa remains on the floor, half asleep, as a red light starts to blink in her bedroom and the entire apartment prepares to shut down.

HOUSE AI: Warning. There has been a system override of this host's residence. The apartment will shut down in sixty seconds due to an emergency protocol. Please enter the Resident ID Pin to resume normal services.

Elisa finally wakes up and sees the blinking light. She gets up to unlock the door and leaves the room to find the House Control Pad.

▌ INT. ELISA'S APARTMENT – EVENING

Elisa walks around for a moment to see the entire apartment blinking with red light as it prepares to shut down.

HOUSE AI: Warning. There has been a system override of this host's residence. The apartment will shut down in thirty seconds due to an emergency protocol. Please enter the Resident ID Pin to resume normal services.

Elisa slowly navigates her way through the blinking red light, looking for the House Control Pad. She tries her best not to bump into anything until she finds the House Control Pad and enters her Resident ID Pin. The blinking red light stops and the entire apartment goes completely dark until every light turns on, along with every device that was temporarily shut down.

HOUSE AI: The apartment has resumed normal services. Welcome back, Elisa Graves.

Elisa is slightly relieved but remains on edge as she thinks about the incident with the Technological-Environmental Hue.

▌ INT. THE BATHROOM OF ELISA'S BEDROOM – EVENING

Elisa is taking a long shower sitting down to relax when she hears a Notification Alert go off.

HOUSE AI: Notification Alert! Your Life Band has detected high stress levels in your body; it is advised that you –

ELISA: Dismiss all notifications.

HOUSE AI: Notifications dismissed.

Remaining seated, Elisa runs her fingers through her hair and allows the hot water to run in the shower. She tries her best not to think about the incident with the Technological-Environmental Hue until she notices the bruises on her knuckles and automatically feels ashamed of her actions as she tightly clutches the Steels dog tag necklace.

▌ INT. ELISA'S APARTMENT – EVENING

Elisa opens the chest that contains all her books and puts away *Treasure Island* along with the velvet box. She thinks about closing the chest, but then she keeps it open for a moment and picks the velvet box back up. Elisa stares at the velvet box for a moment and thinks about what is inside until she hears a heavy knock on her door. She tenses for a moment as she hears the heavy knock on her door again and puts the velvet box back in the chest. Then she gets up and prepares for the worst.

INT. THE 8TH FLOOR OF THE TINT VALLEY RESIDENCE – EVENING

Officer Caleb McEntire (late-twenties) knocks on Elisa's door repeatedly, while **Officer Vance Stanford (early-twenties)** stands by.

CALEB: (LOUDLY) This is Steels Services! (KNOCKS HEAVILY) Open up! We know you're in there!

Caleb continues to knock on Elisa's door while Vance sighs quietly and shakes his head in hopelessness.

VANCE: Maybe we should try again tomorrow – seems like no one's home.

CALEB: (TURNS TO VANCE) Of course someone is home. We got a notification that someone had reactivated the apartment a few minutes ago. She has to be in there. (KNOCKS HEAVILY) Open up! This is Steels Services!

VANCE: You're going to hurt your hand and my ears if you keep doing that.

Caleb shoots Vance an annoyed look and turns back to knock on the door again until he hears the door being unlocked. Both Caleb and Vance stay on guard as Elisa slowly opens the door and sees both of them in their Steels officer uniforms as she tries her best not to show any fear.

VANCE: Pardon the intrusion, ma'am. I'm Officer Stanford (GESTURES TO CALEB) and this is Officer McEntire. We're here tonight due to the many reports concerning the host that lives in this apartment.

CALEB: (SERIOUSLY) Show us your Life Band.

Elisa remains silent as she slowly raises her left hand while Caleb uses the ID Scanner to scan her Life Band.

CALEB: (READS THE ID SCANNER) Resident #495, name of host: Elisa Graves. (FIRMLY LOOKS AT ELISA) Seems like we're in the right place.

ELISA: (SHY) Is there a problem, Officer?

CALEB: We're here in response to the incident that happened at Primetime Plaza this afternoon, which involved you and a citizen who belongs to Hue City. With this reason for our visit, I'm afraid we're going to have to bring you to the station and take you in for questioning.

ELISA: (PAUSES) Okay … I'm willing to turn myself in.

CALEB: (SUBTLY SURPRISED) Hm … didn't seem that hard to do. (TURNS TO VANCE) C'mon, we should get going.

ELISA: (SHY) Wait …

Caleb and Vance turn back to Elisa as she remains inside her apartment.

ELISA: (SHY) Can I get dressed first? At least give me a chance to look decent before you take me in.

Both Caleb and Vance notice that Elisa is wearing nothing but a tank top and boy shorts, as they quickly look away and try their best to stay focused and not steal a few more glances at her current state.

CALEB: (SERIOUSLY) Make it quick (TURNS TO ELISA) or we will drag your ass there just the way you are.

Elisa nods as she politely closes the door. Caleb waits impatiently, making sure Vance stays focused on his job.

A Few Minutes Later

▌ INT. ELISA'S APARTMENT – EVENING

Elisa walks toward the mirror, wearing an old lounge dress and her favourite fall coat. She looks at herself in the mirror and begins to tremble in worry until she hides the Steels dog tag necklace underneath her neckline before approaching the door.

INT. THE 8TH FLOOR OF THE TINT VALLEY RESIDENCE – EVENING

Caleb and Vance both lean patiently against the wall until they notice the door opening and watch Elisa come out of her apartment in a more decent state.

VANCE: (POINTS TO THE MIDDLE OF THE HALLWAY) Stand over there, please.

Elisa nods and stands in the middle of the hallway.

VANCE: Hands behind your head.

Elisa obeys as she puts her hands behind her head and Caleb allows Vance to Mirandize her. Elisa tries to control her tension as Vance comes behind her and brings her arms down, one at a time, to put handcuffs on her.

VANCE: Elisa Graves, you are under arrest for aggravated assault. You have the right to remain silent and refuse to answer questions. Anything you say may be used against you in the Grand Arne Office.

EXT. OUTSIDE THE TINT VALLEY RESIDENCE – EVENING

VANCE: (IN ELISA'S HEAD) You have the right to request a Legal Hue for consolidation before speaking to a Steels officer and to have a Legal Hue present during questioning now or in the future. One will be appointed for you before any questioning, if you wish.

INT. INSIDE THE STEELS SQUAD CAR – EVENING

Elisa stares at the window and looks outside as Vance drives to the Steels Protection Services Station, with Caleb sitting in the passenger's seat. He takes the chance to observe Elisa through the rear-view mirror until she notices his gaze and he quickly looks away.

VANCE: (IN ELISA'S HEAD) If you decide to answer questions now without a Legal Hue present, you will still have the right to stop answering at any time until you talk to a Legal Hue.

▌ INT. THE STEELS PROTECTION SERVICES STATION – EVENING

When Caleb and Vance enter the Steels Protection Services Station with Elisa still in handcuffs, many of the Steels officers present stop what they are doing to see what is going on. Elisa notices almost every Steels officer staring at her as they wear the faces of either confusion, disappointment or shock as she believes most of them knew Garreth in the past.

VANCE: (IN ELISA'S HEAD) Knowing and understanding your rights as explained to you, are you willing to answer our questions without a Legal Hue present?

Elisa hopes that none of the Steels officers recognize her from the past as she mentally prepares herself for the worst.

ELISA: (IN HER HEAD) Yes.

▌ INT. THE INTERROGATION ROOM OF THE STEELS PROTECTION SERVICES STATION – EVENING

Elisa sits in the interrogation room by herself, while wearing handcuffs chained to the table. She takes a moment to let the silence sink in as she thinks about the worst times in her past.

Nine Years Prior

▌ INT. THE GRAVES' HOUSE – EVENING

Sixteen-year-old Deidre and fourteen-year-old Fredrick toss a ball to each other as they wait for Garreth and Carman to start the family meeting. Twelve-year-old Elisa relaxes on the couch and reads *Our Souls at Night* while she waits for the family meeting to start as well.

FOURTEEN-YEAR-OLD FREDRICK: What do you think Mom and Dad are going to talk about this time?

SIXTEEN-YEAR-OLD DEIDRE: I don't know. I wasn't the one who got them mad this time. They always want to lecture us about dumb stuff.

FOURTEEN-YEAR-OLD FREDRICK: (GESTURES TO TWELVE-YEAR-OLD ELISA) Especially when it comes to that nuisance.

Fourteen-year-old Fredrick notices the book that twelve-year-old Elisa is reading.

FOURTEEN-YEAR-OLD FREDRICK: You know Mom told you not to read that book. (WAITS FOR A RESPONSE) Hey! (ANGRILY) Do you hear me talking to you?

SIXTEEN-YEAR-OLD DEIDRE: Forget it, Fredrick. She's going to ignore you like she always does. She's already training for us to pretend that she doesn't exist.

FOURTEEN-YEAR-OLD FREDRICK: (ANGRILY) Well, I'm not getting in trouble again just because she doesn't listen.

SIXTEEN-YEAR-OLD DEIDRE: (ANNOYED) Just pass the ball so we can go to bed already. I want to get this family meeting over with.

Fourteen-year-old Fredrick nods and he and sixteen-year-old Deidre continue to toss the ball to each other. Twelve-year-old Elisa intentionally tunes everyone out as she continues to read *Our Souls at Night* until fourteen-year-old Fredrick gets the ball and whips it toward her; however, she quickly uses the book to deflect the ball's impact. Fourteen-year-old Fredrick comes up to twelve-year-old Elisa and tries to grab *Our Souls at Night* from her as she angrily resists.

TWELVE-YEAR-OLD ELISA: (UPSET) Stop it, Fredrick!

FOURTEEN-YEAR-OLD FREDRICK: (TAUNTS) Do I have your attention now – you dumb Slate?

TWELVE-YEAR-OLD ELISA: (UPSET) Just take your ball and leave me alone! What's your problem?

FOURTEEN-YEAR-OLD FREDRICK: (ANGRILY) That should be an obvious answer because it's always been you!

Fourteen-year-old Fredrick aggressively pulls *Our Souls at Night* out of twelve-year-old Elisa's hands and rips the book in front of her while both she and sixteen-year-old Deidre gasp in shock.

SIXTEEN-YEAR-OLD DEIDRE: (SHOCKED) Fredrick, what did you do? That was Dad's book!

FOURTEEN-YEAR-OLD FREDRICK: (ANGRILY) Then why does she have it? Why does she get to have any of Dad's stuff when he doesn't allow us to touch a single thing of his?

TWELVE-YEAR-OLD ELISA: (TRAUMATIZED) He trusted me to give it back to him – (CRIES) and you ripped it!

FOURTEEN-YEAR-OLD FREDRICK: (ANGRILY) So what? Like you deserve to read shit anyway, you crybaby! (MOCKS TWELVE-YEAR-OLD ELISA) Ooh, I ripped Dad's book – what a big deal – oh no! (TAUNTS) What are you going to do about it? Huh?

Fourteen-year-old Fredrick starts hitting twelve-year-old Elisa with the ripped book, while sixteen-year-old Deidre stands there clueless about what to do.

SIXTEEN-YEAR-OLD DEIDRE: (ANNOYED) Fredrick, c'mon! You're going to get us into trouble again!

FOURTEEN-YEAR-OLD FREDRICK: (TAUNTS) What are you going to do, Slate? What are you going to do?

Fourteen-year-old Fredrick continues to hit twelve-year-old Elisa with the ripped book until she gives him a punch in the face and tackles him to the ground, while sixteen-year-old Deidre stares in shock at what is happening.

SIXTEEN-YEAR-OLD DEIDRE: (FREAKS OUT) Elisa, stop! Fredrick, just apologize already and stop this!

Fourteen-year-old Fredrick and twelve-year-old Elisa continue fighting each other aggressively until twelve-year-old Elisa puts fourteen-year-old Fredrick in a headlock and squeezes hard, while sixteen-year-old Deidre continues to freak out.

SIXTEEN-YEAR-OLD DEIDRE: (FREAKS OUT) Elisa, just stop already! (SCREAMS TOWARD THE STAIRS) Mom! Dad! Come quick!

As Garreth and Carman scramble all the way downstairs, they see twelve-year-old Elisa literally choking fourteen-year-old Fredrick and they rush in to break up the fight.

SIXTEEN-YEAR-OLD DEIDRE: (FREAKS OUT) Do something, Dad! She's gonna kill him!

CARMAN: (LIVID) For Almighty sake – stop screaming, Deidre!

GARRETH: (DEMANDING) That's enough, Elisa – let go of him!

TWELVE-YEAR-OLD ELISA: (SCREAMS) Noooo!

GARRETH: (SHOUTS) Let go of him now, Elisa!

Garreth manages to pry twelve-year-old Elisa off fourteen-year-old Fredrick as Carman helps him up and tries to catch his breath. She notices the ripped book on the floor and turns to see that Garreth is upset, so she gets upset about it too.

CARMAN: (UPSET) What's the matter with you two? We're trying to live in a civilized home, and you kids choose to act like savages! Does it look like we live in an asylum?

FOURTEEN-YEAR-OLD FREDRICK: (POINTS TO TWELVE-YEAR-OLD ELISA) She's the crazy one, Mom! She tried to kill me!

TWELVE-YEAR-OLD ELISA: (SCREAMS) You deserve to die for ripping Dad's book – you bastard!

Fourteen-year-old Fredrick and twelve-year-old Elisa start fighting again. Garreth and Carman try their best to break it up. Fourteen-year-old Fredrick actually starts punching twelve-year-old Elisa until she drives him to a wall and starts banging his head against it before Garreth and Carman are able to pull them apart.

CARMAN: (LIVID) All right! Stop it – just stop fighting already!

GARRETH: (ANGRILY) That's enough out of you two!

TWELVE-YEAR-OLD ELISA: (SCREAMS) Let me go, Dad!

GARRETH: (SHOUTS) I said that's enough, Elisa!

Twelve-year-old Elisa stops resisting and stares at Garreth in shock while Carman and fourteen-year-old Fredrick go quiet themselves.

GARRETH: (DISAPPOINTED) This is not how I raised my children. We don't scream hateful words in this house. We don't start fights in this house. We don't tell people that they deserve to die in this house – not my house! For Almighty sakes – have the three of you lost your senses? Why is it so hard for you all to get along? Why is it so hard for you to start acting like a family? No matter how hard I try (UPSET), it's like you all want to bring me to an early grave with this madness! (TURNS TO TWELVE-YEAR-OLD ELISA) And you! I'm nothing but disappointed in you! I never expected you to be a contributor to this foolishness – and look what happened?

TWELVE-YEAR-OLD ELISA: (SHEEPISHLYLY) But he ripped your book, Dad.

GARRETH: (LIVID) And how could you use that as an excuse for your actions! I've raised you to be a respectable young lady and there should be no reason for you to start such behaviour in this house! He may have done something stupid, but I expected better from you, Elisa! I only taught you how to fight so you can use it to defend yourself – not to try to kill your brother and give me a heart attack at the same time! Is that what you want to do? Do you want to kill your father by killing his only son? Because there is no way in my life that I will allow that to happen and I will stop anyone from making that happen – even if it's my own daughter!

Twelve-year-old Elisa remains still and begins to shed tears as Carman reads the tension in the room and decides to break the silence.

CARMAN: (CALMLY) All right, let's calm down. Let's cancel today's meeting and go to bed.

FOURTEEN-YEAR-OLD FREDRICK: (TAUNTS) That's what you get, Slate –

CARMAN: (TURNS TO FOURTEEN-YEAR-OLD FREDRICK ANGRILY) Now don't you start with that fucking mouth of yours! I have had enough of you and your foolishness for one day!

FOURTEEN-YEAR-OLD FREDRICK: (SHOCKED) But I'm not the who made Dad mad –

CARMAN: (ANGRILY) It's not about making your father mad – it's about you being an asshole. (PUSHES FOURTEEN-YEAR-OLD FREDRICK TOWARD THE STAIRS) Now get your ass upstairs before you get your ass whooped by another female!

Fourteen-year-old Fredrick goes upstairs in defeat while Carman makes sure that he heads straight to his room.

CARMAN: (YELLS TOWARD THE STAIRS) Feel shame that you lost a fight with your younger sister! (TURNS TO SIXTEEN-YEAR-OLD DEIDRE) And you, I'm going to deal with you later in the kitchen.

SIXTEEN-YEAR-OLD DEIDRE: (PROTESTS) But I didn't do anything!

CARMAN: (SHOUTS) Kitchen, now – (GESTURES TO TWELVE-YEAR-OLD ELISA) before I have her deal with your ass, too!

Sixteen-year-old Deidre pouts as she goes into the kitchen, where Carman makes sure she stays.

CARMAN: (YELLS TOWARD THE KITCHEN) And I better not hear a peep from you when your father talks to your sister! (UNDER HER BREATH) Almighty, these damn kids.

Frustrated, Carman goes upstairs as twelve-year-old Elisa tries to fight the tears, and Garreth remains disappointed.

GARRETH: (DISAPPOINTED) What were you thinking? I expected better than this. I expected to see you taking a chance to play with your brother and sister – not the opposite that would cause a fracas! It shouldn't have to be this hard for you to get along with them – why do you always have to get into an issue with Fredrick?

TWELVE-YEAR-OLD ELISA: (UNDER HER BREATH) I ... hate ...

GARRETH: (SHOUTS) I know your voice box can go louder than that–!

TWELVE-YEAR-OLD ELISA: (SCREAMS) I hate him!

Garreth goes silent as sixteen-year-old Deidre peeps from the kitchen to know what is going on.

TWELVE-YEAR-OLD ELISA: (SCREAMS) That is your answer, Dad – you heard it loud and clear! I hate him! I hate the both of them – I can't stand either one of them! Why should I be the one to get along with them when they don't give me any peace in this house! All they ever do is pretend I don't exist – all they ever do is torment me every day. Why should I have to put up with that?

Garreth stands there speechless as sixteen-year-old Deidre begins to feel bad for how she and fourteen-year-old Fredrick treat twelve-year-old Elisa as she continues to cry.

TWELVE-YEAR-OLD ELISA: (WHIMPERS) Why me? Why does it always have to be me? I never asked for this stupid life! I never asked to be part of this family – who doesn't even want me here anyway! And if you want to protect your precious son – then you should just send me away and put me out of my misery!

GARRETH: (CALMLY) Elisa, stop –

TWELVE-YEAR-OLD ELISA: (CRIES) I hate it here! I hate being here! I hate everybody in this house!

GARRETH: (CALMLY) Elisa, please stop – you don't mean that! I know how –

TWELVE-YEAR-OLD ELISA: (SHOUTS) No, you don't, Dad! You don't know how it feels! Nobody knows how I feel! And nobody is going to care because of this stupid Tint that's on me!

Garreth stands there, heartbroken as sixteen-year-old Deidre begins to shed a few tears herself.

TWELVE-YEAR-OLD ELISA: (CRIES) I hate this system and I hate this life – and I would rather die than go through any more of this!

GARRETH: (HOLDS ONTO TWELVE-YEAR-OLD ELISA'S SHOULDERS) Elisa, stop it – (SHOUTS) stop it! (SERIOUSLY) This is not you. I know this is not you – and I can say that to your face because I know who you are! (SINCERELY) I know you, Elisa. I know that you've been upset for a long time, but you're better than this – you're tougher than this! And I believe that you can get through this. (BEGS) Just please ... bring back the little girl that I know and love ... please.

Garreth pulls twelve-year-old Elisa into a hug and holds onto her tightly while she cries uncontrollably. Sixteen-year-old Deidre leaves the kitchen and runs toward Garreth and twelve-year-old Elisa to give them a hug.

GARRETH: (HEARTBROKEN) I'm sorry that I made you feel this way ... I just wanted to show you that you can be loved.

SIXTEEN-YEAR-OLD DEIDRE: (SADLY) I'm sorry, too, Elisa.

Twelve-year-old Elisa continues to cry uncontrollably, while Garreth and sixteen-year-old Deidre give her the most loving hug they could ever give.

Nine Years Later

INT. THE INTERROGATION ROOM OF THE STEELS PROTECTION SERVICES STATION – EVENING

Elisa thinks about her estranged relationship with Deidre Graves and Fredrick Graves as she begins to miss Garreth more and sheds a few tears.

INT. THE STEELS PROTECTION SERVICES STATION – EVENING

Deputy Chief Officer Malcolm Reign (late-fifties) enters the Steels Protection Services Station after a long day of emergency patrolling, where **Officer Nolan Webber (early-forties)** notices him stop at the water cooler to grab a cup of water before going up to him.

NOLAN: Good evening, Deputy Reign.

MALCOLM: (EXHALES) Is it ever a good evening in this place? After a long day of patrolling, I would rather head home, have a nice plate of my wife's cooking and drink a glass of whisky – that's a good evening. Instead, I'm stuck with this.

Malcolm takes a drink of water while Nolan impatiently waits for him to finish.

NOLAN: Well, I hate to break it to you, Deputy Reign, but there has been a request for you in the interrogation room.

MALCOLM: (THROUGH THE CUP) Who's asking?

NOLAN: (FIRMLY) It's the suspect who was arrested for aggravated assault. She was involved in the incident at that plaza this afternoon.

MALCOLM: (STOPS DRINKING) Wait a minute. She's here?

NOLAN: (NODS) Yes. McEntire and Stanford made the arrest this evening after she turned herself in.

MALCOLM: (UPSET) Then why didn't you say anything sooner? Bring me to her this instant! Right now!

Malcolm heftily walks to the interrogation room as Nolan hesitates whether to follow him or stay put.

INT. THE INTERROGATION ROOM OF THE STEELS PROTECTION SERVICES STATION – EVENING

MALCOLM: (THROUGH THE DOOR) Why am I not allowed to see her? She requested to see me, and I want this door opened now!

Elisa perks up as she hears chatter outside the room and tries her best to distinguish the voices from behind the door.

VANCE: (THROUGH THE DOOR) Are you sure this is a good idea, Deputy Reign? Officer Webber told me not to allow anyone in there.

MALCOLM: (THROUGH THE DOOR) I don't care what he says! Open this door now! I want to see her this instant!

Elisa hears the door unlocking as Vance opens it to let Malcolm enter the interrogation room. They are relieved to see each other.

MALCOLM: (TURNS TO VANCE) How dare you treat a young lady like this? (DEMANDING) Uncuff her this instant!

Though with some hesitation, Vance quickly walks up to Elisa and takes the handcuffs off her while she remains seated.

VANCE: (TURNS TO MALCOLM) Are you sure about this, Deputy Reign? What if Webber tries to intervene?

MALCOLM: (CERTAIN) It's my decision and I'm willing to face any consequences that come along with it. But you don't need to worry about me. I know her, and I know everything will be okay.

Vance hesitates for a moment but leaves the interrogation room. Malcolm closes the door and exhales deeply before turning to Elisa in a calmer manner, though he is still shocked to see her in the interrogation room.

MALCOLM: (SUBTLY DUMBFOUNDED) In all my twenty years working as a Steels officer, I never thought I'd see a day like this.

Malcolm walks up to Elisa as she gets up to give him a warm hug while they enjoy their reunion.

ELISA: (HELPLESS) Malcolm … I'm so sorry –

MALCOLM: (SINCERELY) Don't apologize, sweetheart – I'm certain there is a reasonable explanation for this. If only Officer Graves were still here – he would probably have a cow if he saw his daughter in handcuffs, but what he did teach me is that there is always a way to resolve things. Now, sit down. (POINTS TO ELISA'S LIFE BAND) You need to relax before that thing starts talking to you.

Elisa sits back down while Malcolm takes a seat across from her.

MALCOLM: (SINCERELY) You have no idea how good it is to see you again, but I can't help but say that the circumstances are quite dire. (DUMBFOUNDED) How did you even get yourself into this situation?

ELISA: (TROUBLED) Believe me, I didn't want to intrude on you like this. It was just an act of emotion – it wasn't intentional at all. How bad is it, actually?

MALCOLM: (SIGHS) The man had to go to the hospital, Elisa.

Elisa's blood runs cold as she begins to realize the depth of trouble she has gotten herself into.

MALCOLM: I went to the scene myself to get some answers … and we're doing our very best to gather witnesses, but no one is fessing up about the situation. I can't help but say that the odds are against you, and if this situation gets any worse at this rate … (HESITANT) We might be looking at fourteen years.

ELISA: (SPEECHLESS) Fourteen years?

MALCOLM: The charges are aggravated assault. It can't be helped with this man receiving medical care, as we speak. (SINCERELY) But don't you dare worry about a thing – we will get you out of this situation! I will not let my friend's daughter spend a day in prison!

ELISA: (IN DISTRESS) Malcolm, I can't serve fourteen years … I'll take on anything else, but I'll just go crazy if I have to spend my entire life in prison. All I wanted was for him to leave me alone. I swear I really didn't mean for any of this to happen. I just lost it … I just lost myself in that moment. Malcolm, you have to help me.

Malcolm comes over to give Elisa a hug as she starts crying helplessly.

MALCOLM: (CERTAIN) Leave everything to me. I swear on my life that I'll help you through this.

▌ INT. THE STEELS PROTECTION SERVICES STATION – EVENING

Malcolm brings Elisa out of the interrogation room to put her into the holding cell while Nolan speaks to a Steels trainee.

NOLAN: Just run through the tests one more time and ... (NOTICES MALCOLM AND ELISA) Hey-hey-hey! What are you doing?

MALCOLM: My job, of course, Officer Webber. I thought you might be happy that I'm going to be putting her in this holding cell.

NOLAN: (IN DISBELIEF) So, you're just going to put her in there without letting anyone else talk to her?

MALCOLM: She did request me, so I thought there was no need to bring anyone else. (CERTAIN) And I'm the only one who could get her to talk, so you just have to be patient if you want to join us in the interrogation room. But for now, until we get this situation under control, she stays in here ... (TO EVERYONE) and no one is going to bring her out of this cell without my permission! (IMPATIENT) Now, is someone going to open this gate, or do I have to rip your pants off to find the key myself!

Nolan looks on furiously as one of the Steels trainees rushes over to unlock the gate to the holding cell and slides it open as Malcolm allows Elisa to step inside. Just looking inside the cell, she begins to grow anxious and turns to Malcolm as the Steels trainee closes the gate and locks it while Nolan comes over for answers.

NOLAN: (STERNLY) I hope you know what you're doing, Deputy.

MALCOLM: Of course ... I always know what I'm doing.

NOLAN: (STERNLY) I'm glad you feel that way now, but I will not entertain the fact that she's close to you. She's just like every other criminal that is in here and must face the consequences for her actions (TURNS TO ELISA STERNLY), and I will not hesitate to put you in prison once you're proven guilty.

Nolan storms away from the holding cell while Malcolm turns to Elisa to reassure her.

MALCOLM: (QUIETLY) Everything will be okay, Elisa.

ELISA: (QUIETLY) Thanks, Malcolm.

Malcolm nods in gratitude before walking away to talk to Nolan. Elisa backs away from the gate and tries her best to accept that she is in a holding cell.

Three Days Later

▌ EXT. OUTSIDE THE TINT VALLEY RESIDENCE – AFTERNOON

Everyone outside Tint Valley goes about their day as they take the time to catch up with friends after coming from work or school. Two residents sit by the stairs as they watch the news on their Life Pads while they wait to hear about Elisa's arrest.

NEWS REPORTER: (THROUGH THE LIFE PAD) This just in: The Grand Arne Office is preparing a weekly training session for citizens to protect themselves against cyberattacks. This was due to the incident that occurred three days ago, as the entirety of Bartlett's Piece was confronted by the vigilante, who goes by the name General Metallic.

RESIDENT 1: (ANNOYED) That's what they have been saying for the past few days. I'm getting sick and tired of this shit.

RESIDENT 2: (ANNOYED) I know. Why haven't they mentioned anything about that girl who was arrested here? This is the third time they haven't talked about her on the news.

RESIDENT 1: (SCOFFS) The news doesn't care about us Tints. All they care about are those Canvases and Hues. We've been hearing more about the guy who got beaten up than we hear about her.

RESIDENT 2: That is ridiculous. (CONFUSED) But wait, what about those Tints who have been disappearing? The news always talks about those missing person reports.

RESIDENT 1: They have no other choice, as it's happening frequently these days. We only get to be on the news if we're missing or dead. But if we ever get in trouble by the Steels Services, they could care less than to keep us informed after they drop the story.

RESIDENT 2: That is sad. I was really looking forward to hearing more about this girl, as she was all over the place on that day ... (THINKS) And if I have to be honest, I think what she did was pretty badass.

RESIDENT 1: (AGREES) Right? It was about time someone took care of those jerks – those lemonheads think they can just freely walk into our homes without facing the consequences. (GESTURES TO THE LIFE PAD) I even bought this stupid thing from one of them and it doesn't cure hologram astigmatism. Heck, it doesn't even take care of my regular astigmatism.

RESIDENT 2: Do you think we should go in there and give them Steels our testimony?

RESIDENT 1: And do what? Get arrested ourselves? You know how those Steels feel about fake testimonies – we weren't even there when the incident happened. What I do want is for those people in the plaza to start fessing up about what truly happened!

RESIDENT 2: I doubt that's going to happen. There are people who truly follow that nonconfrontational rule, and who's going to speak up when they're the reason she got arrested in the first place?

RESIDENT 1: That is true. What a sad world we live in. There are people who won't help you when you're in trouble but will turn on you when you take care of it yourself. I wish I could do something about it, but I'm glad that it happened ... humph. I'm surprised that I wasn't the first one who ever took on those disrespectful Hues.

The two residents think about the incident at Primetime Plaza while continuing to wait to hear about Elisa's arrest.

INT. THE HOLDING CELL OF THE STEELS PROTECTION SERVICES STATION – AFTERNOON

Elisa rests on the bench of the holding cell and keeps her eyes closed as two Steels officers watch her from the other side.

STEELS OFFICER 1: (SUBTLY ASTONISHED) Of all the people we've taken in, she is the quietest suspect we've ever held in this station. She hasn't said a word for the past three days. How are the guys going to get her to talk?

STEELS OFFICER 2: Deputy Reign says he has a plan, but it's certainly not going to get what Officer Webber needs from this girl. She doesn't even look like a violent person. How was she capable of beating up a man who's twice her size?

STEELS OFFICER 1: Believe me, once you've worked here long enough, you realize that everyone is capable of anything. But she doesn't present any symptoms of Tint Brain – I'm not sure if this is going to be an easy case to close.

STEELS OFFICER 2: That is true. They even brought in the guy who was involved in the incident this morning ... maybe we'll get some truth about what really happened at the plaza.

The two Steels officers notice a Steels trainee approaching the holding cell but stop to see Elisa resting on the bench as Nolan exits the interrogation room and walks over to him.

NOLAN: (CONFUSED) What's going on? I thought I had sent you here to get her. Why hasn't my request been followed?

STEELS TRAINEE: (POINTS TO ELISA) She's sleeping, sir ... and I don't think it's a good idea to disturb her.

Nolan turns to see Elisa resting on the bench with her eyes closed as he tries his best to be patient.

NOLAN: Ms. Graves. I'm going to bring you to the interrogation room so that you can answer a few questions for me. I believe it's time that we know your side of the story, so please wake up and let's get this over and done with.

Nolan waits for Elisa to move. However, she remains resting on the bench with her eyes closed, and he begins to lose his patience.

NOLAN: (SLIGHTLY FIRMLY) I am asking you to wake up, Ms. Graves, so I can ask you some questions! It won't take up too much of your time (STERNLY), but it will if you don't wake up soon! It's time for you to wake up, Ms. Graves! Ms. Graves? (SHOUTS) Ms. Graves! (TURNS TO EVERYONE ANGRILY) Isn't there someone in this room who can get this damn girl to wake up!

STEELS OFFICER 1: I thought Deputy Reign told us not to approach her without his –

NOLAN: (ANGRILY) I don't care what he says or what he has planned for this girl! I want to get to the bottom of this (TURNS TO ELISA ANGRILY) and I want it done now! (SHOUTS) So, wake up, Ms. Graves!

Elisa remains resting on the bench with her eyes closed. Malcolm leaves the interrogation room and approaches Nolan for an explanation.

MALCOLM: (CONFUSED) What's all this screaming out here? What exactly is going on!

NOLAN: (ANGRILY) Sorry if I disturbed you, Deputy Reign, but I'm just wondering if your friend is either dead or pretending to be a corpse to waste precious time!

MALCOLM: (NOTICES ELISA'S CURRENT STATE) Forgive me, Officer Webber – she's doing no such thing. Allow me to handle this. I'll be able to reach her.

Malcolm signals the Steels trainee to unlock the gate, and then he approaches Elisa while she remains resting on the bench with her eyes closed.

MALCOLM: (CALMLY) I know what you're doing, Elisa. I know you usually do this when you're scared ... but believe me when I tell you that everything will be fine. Officer Webber is just going to take you to the interrogation room so he can ask you a few questions. It will be very brief, and I know you'll be able to give him the answers he needs ... I'll even be in there with you if you need me to –

NOLAN: (ANGRILY) You will do no such thing–

MALCOLM: (STERNLY TO NOLAN) Then there won't be an interrogation if she doesn't want to talk! Please let me do what I need to do. (CALMLY TURNS TO ELISA) Just trust in the process, Elisa – I promise you that I will help you through this. (WAITS PATIENTLY AND TURNS TO NOLAN) Just give her some time, Officer. She'll be ready for you once she feels comfortable enough.

Nolan stands there, livid, while Malcolm attempts to leave the holding cell.

ELISA: Will I be able to plead my case?

Everyone outside the holding cell turns to Elisa in shock as she finally opens her eyes and turns to Malcolm for an answer.

ELISA: I heard that he's here today. Will I be able to plead my case, Deputy?

Malcolm hesitates to give Elisa an answer, while Nolan comes into the holding cell, furious with both of them.

NOLAN: (ANGRILY) This is ridiculous! I've waited all this time just to hear this nonsense! How was she able to know such private information?

MALCOLM: Believe me, Officer Webber, I wish I knew the answer to that question, but since she's requesting to plead her case ... we have no other choice but to prepare the deliberation room.

NOLAN: (SHOCKED) But sir –

MALCOLM: (STERNLY) If you want answers, then prepare the deliberation room so she can give them to you! We certainly don't have time for this, so it must be done now!

NOLAN: (STERNLY TO ELISA) I better not be receiving any tricks from you.

Nolan storms out of the holding cell, while Malcolm turns to Elisa in shock.

MALCOLM: (SLIGHTLY HESITANT) Elisa, are you sure about this?

ELISA: It's the only way I'm ever going to get out of here … I need to plead my case.

Malcolm admires Elisa's bravery as he takes the time to reminisce about Garreth.

MALCOLM: (NODS IN CERTAINTY) Okay then. We must prepare you quickly before he makes any sudden changes.

Elisa nods as she finally gets up from the bench and allows Malcolm to prepare her to plead her case.

A Few Minutes Later

INT. THE DELIBERATION ROOM OF THE STEELS PROTECTION SERVICES STATION – AFTERNOON

Caleb and Vance are on standby, along with the Steels trainee, while the Technological-Environmental Hue sits anxiously, waiting to give his testimony.

TECHNOLOGICAL-ENVIRONMENTAL HUE: (IMPATIENT) I'm surprised that it's taking so long to do this! Why am I here anyway? I thought I was brought here to give my testimony, not to stay here for hours, just to wait for you guys to do something! (UPSET) What kind of service is this? Do you know what I've been through?

Caleb begins to lose his patience as Vance gives him an understanding look and the Technological-Environmental Hue continues to ramble.

TECHNOLOGICAL-ENVIRONMENTAL HUE: (UPSET) Look at me! (POINTS TO HIS SCARS) Look at my face! I used to make women melt with this face! Now I couldn't even impress an old lady if I wanted to! Do you know how sad that is? All the doctor did was fill my face up with stitches – she couldn't even fix my face properly after being there for an entire week!

CALEB: Three days ago, the doctor confirmed that everything was fine for us to bring you in – she even mentioned that you could've been discharged yesterday.

TECHNOLOGICAL-ENVIRONMENTAL HUE: (UPSET) That doctor didn't know what she was talking about. I'm still in a lot of pain! This is ridiculous. I'm calling a Legal Hue right now! And I'm going to sue every single one of you for this horrible service. Just wait until the GAO brings this place to the ground! (TO HIS LIFE BAND) Life Band, call Secret Weapon!

LIFE BAND AI: Sorry, your call to SECRET WEAPON has been denied. Only one call is permitted when located in any Steels Protection Services Station. Please move to a location that is five hundred metres away from the station and try again.

The Technological-Environmental Hue sits there in shock, while Caleb shakes his head in annoyance.

VANCE: Must've forgotten that you used your one phone call to see if the doctor could take you back for a second examination.

TECHNOLOGICAL-ENVIRONMENTAL HUE: (UPSET) I don't care! I still want a Legal Hue here! I can't believe this – I'm the victim in this situation and here I am being treated as a suspect! You guys have no respect for us at all – they must not have paid you guys well to have you take it out on us! There's no shame in this place at all!

Everyone stops when they hear the door unlock. Nolan opens it and lets himself in while the Technological-Environmental Hue sighs in relief.

TECHNOLOGICAL-ENVIRONMENTAL HUE: (UPSET) Finally! Someone who looks to be in charge here! Can you tell these buffoons to allow me to call a Legal Hue? I'm very upset with the services here!

Nolan shoots the Technological-Environmental Hue a stern look and goes up to Caleb to whisper something into his ear that causes him to grimace in shock.

TECHNOLOGICAL-ENVIRONMENTAL HUE: (ANXIOUS) Wait a minute – what's going on here? (TURNS TO VANCE) What is happening? What is he whispering to him about?

Vance simply shrugs as Nolan and Caleb continue to have a private conversation.

CALEB: (QUIETLY) You serious?

NOLAN: (QUIETLY) That's what the deputy told me.

Caleb looks at Nolan in disbelief and storms out of the deliberation room while Vance wonders what is happening.

VANCE: What's going on, Officer Webber?

NOLAN: (POINTS TO THE TECHNOLOGICAL-ENVIRONMENTAL HUE) Keep him quiet and we'll be right back.

Nolan leaves the deliberation room while the Technological-Environmental Hue starts to become more nervous than he was previously.

INT. OUTSIDE THE DELIBERATION ROOM OF THE STEELS PROTECTION SERVICES STATION – AFTERNOON

Caleb paces back and forth furiously until Nolan comes out of the deliberation room to calm him down.

CALEB: (FURIOUS) Are you kidding me, officer?

NOLAN: Just calm down, Officer McEntire, there's no reason to make a big deal out of this –

CALEB: (FURIOUS) No reason? What does the deputy have in mind this time? I'm getting sick and tired of being idle in this case!

NOLAN: Everyone is frustrated, Caleb. But somehow, the deputy always figures out a way to pull things off, so just be patient.

Malcolm finally emerges with paperwork in his hands and notices Caleb and Nolan standing outside the deliberation room while he brings Elisa in handcuffs.

MALCOLM: I see that my request has been made … I was afraid that my team wasn't willing to move forward with this plan.

CALEB: (FIRMLY) There better be a good reason why we're delaying this interrogation, Deputy. He's demanding a Legal Hue as we speak.

MALCOLM: I'm aware of that and I do apologize for keeping you all waiting (GESTURES TO ELISA), but she requested to plead her case.

As Caleb turns to Elisa in disbelief, she notices the frustration on both his and Nolan's faces.

MALCOLM: (GESTURES TO THE PAPERS) And I thought it would be wrong for me not to bring the paperwork, if that's what she wishes to do. As for that lime-green fellow, he needs to understand that under the Act of Plea, both parties need to be on equal terms, and since she made the request and has refused consultation from a Legal Hue, he has to do the same as well.

Caleb turns away for a moment and begins to pace back and forth, while Elisa hopes that he agrees to accept the Act of Plea.

CALEB: (PAUSES AND TURNS TO MALCOLM) You know, I've been trained to trust your judgement throughout everything … especially when there are times that I believe you're making the wrong call.

MALCOLM: And you should still continue to trust my judgement, Officer McEntire, as you know that I've never been wrong before. I also believe that this Act of Plea will give us the answers we need for this case.

CALEB: (FIRMLY) Well, I hope you're right about that because I certainly won't believe it until I see it for myself.

MALCOLM: You will see it. (GESTURES TO ELISA) You can trust her on that; she has no reason to hide anything from us.

CALEB: (FIRMLY) We'll see what happens when she gets inside that room.

Caleb goes back to the deliberation room as Malcolm sighs and turns to Elisa.

MALCOLM: It's going to be a tough room in there. Are you sure you're ready for this?

ELISA: (DETERMINED) I'm not going to serve fourteen years for that man ... I'm ready for anything.

MALCOLM: (SUBTLY SURPRISED) All right then ... we should get started.

Elisa nods in agreement as Malcolm goes into the deliberation room, where Nolan gives her a suspicious look.

NOLAN: (FIRMLY) I'm aware that the two of you are close ... but I don't see why he puts so much trust in you.

ELISA: He's the only one I trust here, but I'm hoping I'll be able to trust you as well, Officer ... as I hope you're willing to do the same for me.

NOLAN: (PAUSES) We'll see what happens in that room today.

Nolan remains skeptical about Elisa while she simply sighs and mentally prepares herself for the Act of Plea.

█ INT. THE DELIBERATION ROOM OF THE STEELS PROTECTION SERVICES STATION – AFTERNOON

Caleb returns to the deliberation room, along with Malcolm, who holds the paperwork for the Act of Plea. Caleb goes to stand beside Vance as he wonders about the situation.

VANCE: (QUIETLY) What's going on?

CALEB: (QUIETLY) You'll find out.

Vance stands there confused as he and Caleb watch Malcolm go up to the Technological-Environmental Hue and place the paperwork for the Act of Plea in front of him.

TECHNOLOGICAL-ENVIRONMENTAL HUE: For a second, I thought someone had lost their job today. I was beginning to question how this place is being controlled.

MALCOLM: I apologize for the long wait, sir. We just wanted to retrieve some paperwork to get started officially. The reason you're here is that there has been a request to start an Act of Plea. Now, during this procedure, the two parties are granting the Steels Protection Services permission to access personal files from our database, as well as other information that relates to your case. Now, since the person who made the request has refused to involve a Legal Hue, we hope that you are willing to be on equal terms with this person, as we can't allow anyone to have an unfair advantage during the Act of Plea. Will you be okay to proceed without a Legal Hue present?

TECHNOLOGICAL-ENVIRONMENTAL HUE: (SCOFFS) Sure! Anything that will get me out of here sooner! I'm getting sick and tired of not being able to call anyone in this place. I'm even disgusted that you're using paper for this!

The Technological-Environmental Hue takes the pen from Malcolm and signs the paperwork for the Act of Plea. Malcolm gives Caleb a look of reassurance while he stands there a lot more calmly than usual.

MALCOLM: Well then, now that that's done, we can get started.

Malcolm opens the door and lets Nolan come in with Elisa in handcuffs. The Technological-Environmental Hue begins to freak out while Caleb and Vance try their best to hold him down.

TECHNOLOGICAL-ENVIRONMENTAL HUE: (TERRIFIED) Whoa-whoa-whoa! Why are you bringing her in here?

NOLAN: Relax. She is in handcuffs, sir. Plus, there are four trained Steels officers present, so we'll make sure that she doesn't lay a finger on you.

The Technological-Environmental Hue remains terrified, but shrugs off Caleb and Vance in the process. Nolan closes the door and brings

Elisa to sit on the other side of the table while he attempts to switch the handcuffs on her.

MALCOLM: I don't think that's necessary, Officer.

ELISA: It's okay, Deputy. I'm willing to have them on, if it makes everyone comfortable.

Malcolm stands there quietly, as he allows Nolan to take off the hand-cuffs that were on Elisa and switch them to the handcuffs that are chained to the table.

NOLAN: (TURNS TO MALCOLM) Turns out she really is cooperative – let's see if she remains that way during the Act of Plea.

TECHNOLOGICAL-ENVIRONMENTAL HUE: (CERTAIN) Yes! You better make sure she stays obedient. That girl is an animal, I tell you! She deserves to be locked up in a cage!

Elisa shoots the Technological-Environmental Hue an annoyed look while Nolan places the paperwork for the Act of Plea in front of her.

NOLAN: Today, we are here to begin the procedure of an Act of Plea (GESTURES AT ELISA), which was requested by Ms. Elisa Graves.

TECHNOLOGICAL-ENVIRONMENTAL HUE: (SHOCKED) Wait, what?

NOLAN: Now, during this procedure, the two parties are granting the Steels Protection Services permission to access personal files from our database as well as other information that relates to you and the case. (TURNS TO ELISA) Since you've made the request to plead your case, you have agreed not to involve a Legal Hue during this procedure. Do you still wish to continue without a Legal Hue present, Ms. Graves?

ELISA: I do.

NOLAN: All right, then sign the papers, please.

Nolan gives Elisa a pen to sign the paperwork of the Act of Plea while the Technological-Environmental Hue scoffs in disbelief.

TECHNOLOGICAL-ENVIRONMENTAL HUE: (UPSET) This is ridiculous! You can't just let her do this! (TURNS TO ELISA) I don't know why you have it out for me, kid! Just serve your sentence and leave me out of this!

VANCE: (SUSPICIOUSLY) Now, why would you say such a thing like that?

TECHNOLOGICAL-ENVIRONMENTAL HUE: (UPSET) Listen, she was the one who came after me! I don't even know this chick. I've never met her in my entire life!

NOLAN: From the way you were behaving earlier, it seems otherwise.

Caleb and Vance begin to feel suspicious about the Technological-Environmental Hue, who is clearly upset. The Steels trainee pulls out his Steels Tablet.

NOLAN: However, we are here to figure out why this situation happened in the first place. Now, Ms. Graves, you were arrested for aggravated assault due to an incident that happened at Primetime Plaza three days ago, where you attacked this man not only with your fists but also with your purse, as well as a Life Pad. Are all the statements I just stated true?

ELISA: Yes.

Shocked, Malcom, Nolan, Caleb and Vance look at Elisa, who shows no remorse whatsoever.

MALCOLM: (ATTEMPTS TO STEP IN) Elisa, I don't think you should –

ELISA: (TURNS TO MALCOLM) It's okay, Malcolm. I know what I'm doing. You don't have to worry about anything.

Malcolm nods in understanding and goes quiet while Nolan, Caleb and Vance become uncertain about Elisa's chances with the Act of Plea. The Technological-Environmental Hue notices the connection between Malcolm and Elisa as he tries to come up with an argument against them.

TECHNOLOGICAL-ENVIRONMENTAL HUE: (POINTS TO ELISA AND MALCOLM) Wait a second. There's obviously something going on between those two! You should kick him out right now, if he's going to give her impunity from the damage she caused to my face!

ELISA: (TURNS TO THE TECHNOLOGICAL-ENVIRONMENTAL HUE) Your face looks completely fine to me, so I don't see the damage you're talking about. (SMIRKS) Just consider yourself fortunate that you're still alive and talking to this day. I would've done a lot of favours for some people if I had taken it that far.

Frustrated, the Technological-Environmental Hue looks at Elisa, and Nolan begins to lose his patience.

NOLAN: (FIRMLY) That is enough out of both of you. We're not here to run a kindergarten session; we're here to solve a case. (TURNS TO ELISA STERNLY) And if I get any smart aleck behavior from you, Ms. Graves, I will increase your penalty and have you stuck here for life if you don't behave!

ELISA: (DOCILE) My apologies, Officer.

The Technological-Environmental Hue feels satisfied with Elisa's obedience as the Steels trainee looks through her record.

STEELS TRAINEE: (LOOKS THROUGH HIS STEELS TABLET) Now, it says right here that you were accepted into the Tint Valley Occupation Program five years ago, with no history of any criminal offenses.

CALEB: (LOOKS AT ELISA) You basically came here with a clean record under your belt. Why throw that away by attacking this man in the middle of the plaza?

ELISA: It was a poor decision arising from previous events.

MALCOLM: (STEPS IN) Previous events? Have you met this man before?

ELISA: I have. Two days before the incident.

Malcom, Nolan, Caleb and Vance look at the Technological-Environmental Hue suspiciously as he tries his best to act clueless in front of them.

MALCOLM: What actually occurred two days before the incident?

ELISA: He basically was trying to sell me a Life Pad at the plaza, which was a little later in the evening. I kept refusing because I already have a similar device at home (GESTURES TO THE TECHNOLOGICAL-ENVIRONMENTAL HUE), but he wouldn't let me leave until I made a contribution.

Confused, Malcom, Nolan, Caleb and Vance stare at the Technological-Environmental Hue for an explanation.

MALCOLM: What contribution?

TECHNOLOGICAL-ENVIRONMENTAL HUE: (EXAGGERATED) An offer that is brought to you by the Grand Arne Office, which allows our amazing customers to give out contributions to Bartlett's Piece to –

ELISA: (MOCKS THE TECHNOLOGICAL-ENVIRONMENTAL HUE) Make our home a better and safer place to live (BITTER) and all that other bullshit!

NOLAN: (SHOUTS) Language!

Elisa immediately goes quiet as Malcolm, Caleb and Vance become more suspicious of the Technological-Environmental Hue.

VANCE: (SUSPICIOUSLY) That's quite interesting to hear this, knowing that you just said that you had never met her before.

TECHNOLOGICAL-ENVIRONMENTAL HUE: (PRETENDS TO BE CLUELESS) Look, I'm a businessman. My job is to sell products to people! Anyone who's willing to buy something is an automatic win for me! So, it's easy for me to forget a face every now and again.

STEELS TRAINEE: (LOOKS THROUGH HIS STEELS TABLET) Not according to this video.

The Steels trainee brings his Steels Tablet to Nolan and Malcolm as they look to see the Technological-Environmental Hue directly approaching Elisa without her noticing. He sits, appearing slightly worried, until the video cuts off before the altercation happens.

STEELS TRAINEE: Just by simply guessing from this surveillance footage, it looks like he truly is acquainted with her. Unfortunately, the video was cut off after the plaza went under Lockdown mode. (LOOKS THROUGH HIS STEELS TABLET) And according to your record, there are twelve restraining orders against you, along with several complaints that involve harassment and potential stalking claims.

The Technological-Environmental Hue becomes increasingly nervous, while Nolan and Malcolm become more suspicious of him.

NOLAN: (UNCERTAIN) That could be a potential reason why this happened. (TURNS TO ELISA) But if all this was to avoid purchasing a Life Pad, what made this encounter different from the last one you had with him?

ELISA: I refuse to use the cyberattack as an excuse for my actions ... it was simply the feeling of me finally reaching a tipping point and fully losing myself emotionally. Even before the incident happened, I had paid for the Life Pad and returned it at the same time.

NOLAN: (SUSPICIOUSLY) Why would you do that?

ELISA: Because I wanted to determine the real reason why he was there ... because he wasn't after my money (TURNS TO THE TECHNOLOGICAL-ENVIRONMENTAL HUE); he was after the contribution.

NOLAN: (IMPATIENT) And what exactly is that?

MALCOLM: Officer Webber, please let her explain. I think she might be onto something.

Nolan becomes quiet and he, Malcolm, Caleb and Vance allow Elisa to continue.

ELISA: If you look closely at the surveillance footage, you can see that he is standing near Bartlett's Piece Bookstore. That's the only place I visit when I go to Primetime Plaza, and if you are familiar with my father's previous cases, there was a long history of Secondary and Tertiary Hues from that section alone attempting to collect books from that exact bookstore by harassing customers to give them up as contributions – he actually investigated this himself – and we went through it ourselves several times along with other people. The reason why such incidents like this happened is because the commander-in-chief refused to shut down Bartlett's Piece Bookstore – which pissed off the entire Environmental section and made them decide to take matters into their own hands.

Malcom, Nolan, Caleb and Vance are speechless at Elisa's explanation.

TECHNOLOGICAL-ENVIRONMENTAL HUE: (CONDESCENDINGLY) This is absolutely ridiculous. What does she know about our efforts at Hue City? You're forgetting that the commander-in-chief has completely banned Discovery Region artifacts from entering Tint Valley!

ELISA: (ARGUES) Which only applies to precious items that belong on the Forbidden List of the Discovery Region; books aren't on that list. If it was one copy, it would automatically be shipped to the Bartlett's Piece Museum, but if it were one of several copies that are still in good condition – they would go to Bartlett's Piece Bookstore, which was legally created to stop the smuggling of books after the Metallic Order was abolished. The Environmental section have been wanting to shut this place down for years due to the belief that these books are creating a wave of pollution in the country, which is why they have been allowed to continue their "contribution collection" at Tint Valley in the first place. I was willing to give him the book I had bought the first time. I actually gave him another book the second time – but the real reason I put those scars on his face was that he wanted the gift that my dad left for me five years ago.

Malcolm immediately empathises with Elisa along with Vance, while Nolan and Caleb find it difficult not to see the truth in her explanation.

ELISA: (ARGUES) My dad left something in there that was for my eyes only, which I never bought and never stole, and it was given to me by a friend of his at the bookstore. So, of course, I was upset when he wanted to take my present away from me. I was furious when he didn't see how important that box was to me and that he actually tried to fight me for it as a contribution; the scars on my knuckles don't lie – and neither do the bruises on my neck!

As Malcom, Nolan, Caleb and Vance notice the bruises on Elisa's neck, their faces harden in disappointment and they turn to the Technological-Environmental Hue angrily.

ELISA: (ARGUES) He literally tried to choke me and threatened to kill me after I took the chance to defend myself and fight for what was mine. And yes, I attacked him because it was the only way I saw to solve the situation. I was mad, I was angry, and I was upset – and I'm not afraid to admit it. And unlike him, I'm not afraid to admit that I did it and will even do it again if I have to! I'm willing to face any consequences you give me, but the reason I requested to plead my case is because I'm not going to serve fourteen years for a man who doesn't even respect the basic rules of Bartlett's Piece! For us Tints, you can't even set foot in Hue City if you're not accompanied by a certified Steels officer. The same rule applies to a Canvas and a Hue: they are only allowed to enter Tint Valley with the proper approval from the Grand Arne Office while wearing the appropriate colours of the Tint Valley, which he has not done during those two encounters! This is all in the LRHS!

NOLAN: (CONFUSED) And where exactly did you read this in the LRHS?

ELISA AND CALEB: (IN UNISON) Section four, paragraph five on page a hundred and seven.

Slightly astonished, Elisa and Caleb look at each other, but he quickly looks away. Nolan turns to the Steels trainee for answers.

NOLAN: Can you confirm this information?

STEELS TRAINEE: (LOOKS THROUGH HIS STEELS TABLET) Yes, there is a rule that exists on the Laws and Regulations of the Hue System, which is in the right section. It says that citizens of different Phase Statuses cannot intersect within other regions without proper permission granted from the Grand Arne Office. Tints are not allowed to enter Hue City without the company of a certified Steels officer. Canvases and Hues are not allowed to enter Tint Valley without approval from the Grand Arne Office, and citizens must wear the appropriate colours when entering Tint Valley.

NOLAN: And how many times has this man been approved?

STEELS TRAINEE: (LOOKS THROUGH HIS STEELS TABLET) None, sir … it says that he made zero requests to enter Tint Valley at the Grand Arne Office.

Nolan sighs in disappointment and shakes his head along with Malcom, Caleb and Vance. The Technological-Environmental Hue looks at everyone in disbelief.

TECHNOLOGICAL-ENVIRONMENTAL HUE: (UPSET) Now wait a minute! Don't you dare turn this on me! (GESTURES TO ELISA) She's the guilty party here! (TURNS TO THE STEELS TRAINEE) What does that book say about Tints being nonconfrontational?

STEELS TRAINEE: (LOOKS THROUGH HIS STEELS TABLET) It says that Tints are not allowed to engage physically and verbally with a Canvas or a Hue in any harmful manner and must remain nonconfrontational at all costs.

TECHNOLOGICAL-ENVIRONMENTAL HUE: (SATISFIED) Thank you!

STEELS TRAINEE: (LOOKS THROUGH HIS STEELS TABLET) But that only applies to the annual events that allow citizens to represent their Phase Statuses openly, and this rule applies equally to Canvases and Hues. And if I must remind everyone, the only celebration that occurred this month was the Annual Grand Wallace Celebration Gala, which happened the night before the incident.

The Technological-Environmental Hue immediately becomes silent and sits there in frustration. Malcom, Nolan, Caleb and Vance look at each other as they realize that the situation is far more severe than expected.

TECHNOLOGICAL-ENVIRONMENTAL HUE: (UPSET) Well, I wasn't aware of all these new rules. How does she remember any of the rules from that book?

MALCOLM: (SERIOUSLY) Well, from what I remember, the Laws and Regulations of the Hue System go through an update every year, and the Tints are given an up-to-date copy once they have been accepted into the Tint Valley Occupation Program. Once you're certified as a Canvas or even a Hue, it's your responsibility to keep yourself updated with the new rules. (TURNS TO THE TECHNOLOGICAL-ENVIRONMENTAL HUE STERNLY) What is also a rule from the book, from ancient times and also from common sense, is to never lay your hands on a woman!

Nolan gently pulls Malcolm away from the Technological-Environmental Hue.

NOLAN: Well, I believe we have everything we need for this Act of Plea, as we realize that we're dealing with a much bigger situation. (TURNS TO THE TECHNOLOGICAL-ENVIRONMENTAL HUE) I'm afraid you're going to have to stay a little longer for further investigation, but you will be granted permission to have a Legal Hue present during the investigation. (TURNS TO ELISA) As for Ms. Graves, you will be brought to a separate room for further questioning. You will also be granted permission to have a Legal Hue present during this investigation. However, knowing your previous answers, I'm aware that you would refuse. In the meantime, you will remain in the station until we decide what to do with you penalty wise, but for now, we thank you for your cooperation and we'll take everything you have said under consideration.

ELISA: (CORDIAL) Thank you, Officer. I appreciate you allowing me to plead my case.

NOLAN: All right then, that's all for now. The Act of Plea has officially ended. (TURNS TO CALEB AND VANCE) Please take her to the interrogation room.

Caleb and Vance nod as they go up to Elisa to take the handcuffs chained to the table off her and put her in regular handcuffs. They both help her up and bring her out of the deliberation room. Meanwhile, Nolan remains standing, severely angry but without expressing it.

NOLAN: (SERIOUSLY) Deputy, you should leave as well.

MALCOLM: (TURNS TO NOLAN) Are you sure, Officer?

NOLAN: (SERIOUSLY) I'm sure, and take the trainee with you. I'm going to spend some time alone with this man.

Malcolm nods and gestures to the Steels trainee to come with him. They both exit the deliberation room and leave Nolan alone with the Technological-Environmental Hue.

TECHNOLOGICAL-ENVIRONMENTAL HUE: (SIGHS IN RELIEF) I thought they would never leave. Listen, let's strike a little something, just between you and me, 'cause I trust you. (OPTIMISTIC) I'm willing to give you whatever you want while you keep this whole thing hush-hush and clean up my record to get that crazy bitch off my back. I know you don't like her that much, and I bet you want to put her away for life. I actually know a guy who can automatically put some nasty things on her record while you remove the nasty things off of mine so you can allow me to live my life. Sounds like a good deal, huh?

Nolan chuckles lowly while the Technological-Environmental Hue joins in without noticing him pulling a pair of handcuffs out of his pocket.

NOLAN: (SERIOUSLY) There is no deal.

The Technological-Environmental Hue's smile fades as Nolan takes his time to put the handcuffs on him.

NOLAN: (SERIOUSLY) I don't think you realize how stupid you are to try to bribe a Steels officer inside a Steels Protection Services Station. Now, I don't need much to put you away for life without the help of any of your friends ... (LEANS TOWARD THE TECHNOLOGICAL-ENVIRONMENTAL HUE OMINOUSLY) And I'm going to enjoy doing that, especially since I also don't appreciate men who lay their hands on a woman ... or anyone who feels entitled to abuse their power.

Nolan continues to laugh ominously while the Technological-Environmental Hue freezes in fear.

TEN

INT. INTERROGATION ROOM OF THE STEELS PROTECTION SERVICES STATION – AFTERNOON

Vance writes down some last thoughts on Elisa's testimony with Caleb on standby while Malcolm lets himself into the interrogation room.

VANCE: (FINISHES WRITING) All right, that is everything. (TURNS TO ELISA) Thank you for your cooperation, Ms. Graves. We'll let you know what our final decision is.

ELISA: (CORDIAL) Thank you, Officer.

MALCOLM: (WALKS OVER) Is everything done already?

VANCE: (GETS UP) Yep! Everything is done. I believe we have everything we need to close this case.

MALCOLM: (WALKS OVER) That's good. I'll let you guys do what you do best. I'll take over from here.

Vance nods as he waves goodbye to Elisa and leaves the interrogation room before Caleb slowly approaches Malcolm.

CALEB: (QUIETLY) You always find a way to impress … my apologies for questioning your judgement, Deputy Reign.

MALCOLM: (QUIETLY) That's all right, Caleb. It happens to the best of us. Just as long as I'm confident of gaining your trust from now on.

Caleb nods in understanding as he leaves the interrogation room. Malcolm gives a quick sigh of relief and turns to Elisa.

MALCOLM: (TAKES A SEAT) I don't know why he's impressed by me. You definitely convinced me that the best decision for you was to request an Act of Plea. You worked that room like it was nothing. It definitely reminded me how much you are Carman's daughter.

ELISA: (SLIGHTLY CONFUSED) You don't think I'm anything like my father?

MALCOLM: (CLARIFIES) No, I'm not saying that at all, as you do carry his love for learning. But that fire you had in your words – that's definitely your mother. Your father did have much more of a quiet spirit.

ELISA: (PLEASANTLY) I know. He probably would've told me the same thing, too.

Malcolm and Elisa both laugh pleasantly as they take a moment to think about Garreth.

MALCOLM: (PLEASED) He would've been so proud of you if he had been there ... It amazes me how much you've grown.

ELISA: (THINKS) I guess ... he would've waited to tell me that after he chewed me out first.

MALCOLM: (ADDS IN) Why do that himself when your mother would've done it for him? There were many things he managed to get away with because of her.

ELISA: (CHUCKLES AND PAUSES) So what's going to happen now?

MALCOLM: (SIGHS) Well ... we're probably going to be looking at some more surveillance footage, knowing that there's always one camera running during Lockdown Mode. We'll try our best to get more witnesses to talk about the scene; someone is bound to talk, one way or another. Your charges will obviously be changed and there will be a debate to confirm self-defence or excessive force. You probably will have to pay some fines along the way. But since this is your first offense, you'll likely get off with a warning, but other than that ... there's a likely chance you might walk out of here free. You just have to stay here for a while until we figure things out.

Elisa feels sudden relief and optimism about the outcome of her case.

ELISA: (SMILES) Thank you so much, Malcolm.

MALCOLM: (OPTIMISTIC) You're so welcome, Elisa. (STARTS TO GET UP) Just leave the heavy lifting to me, and I'll make sure you're out of here in no time.

ELISA: (SMILES) I'm sure you will. (REMEMBERS GILLIAN) There's one more thing I wanted to ask you.

MALCOLM: (SITS BACK DOWN) Now what would that be?

ELISA: (HONESTLY) A co-worker of mine did not show up to work one day ... and I believe that she's gone missing. Her name is Gillian Grant, and over the past few days, I've begun to have a really close friendship with her. I know it's common for people to miss a day of work, but with all the missing person reports and the recent cyberattack ... I just can't help but worry about her. I was wondering if you could help me find her.

MALCOLM: (THINKS) Hmm ... Gillian Grant. That name doesn't seem to ring a bell ... nor has a name like that occurred in the missing person reports. I have to say, this might be a tough task for me, since a relative must be the one who reports her missing, but I'll see what I can do concerning your friend. But right now, we have to focus on you if we're going to get you out of this station.

Malcolm gets up and takes the handcuffs chained to the table off Elisa and switches them for regular ones. He then takes her out of the interrogation room and returns her to the holding cell.

Four Days Later

INT. THE STEELS PROTECTION SERVICES STATION – AFTERNOON

Elisa naps in the holding cell as everyone at the Steels Protection Services Station performs their daily tasks. They mind their own business and allow her to sleep until they all stop and hear screaming coming from the other side of the station. Elisa immediately wakes up and turns to see the handcuffed Technological-Environmental Hue trying to fight off Caleb and Vance as they try their best to bring him to the prisoner transport vehicle.

TECHNOLOGICAL-ENVIRONMENTAL HUE: (UPSET) You can't do this!

VANCE: (FIRMLY) C'mon, sir. It's time to go.

TECHNOLOGICAL-ENVIRONMENTAL HUE: (LIVID) You can't do this. I have a right to fight for my freedom! I will sue every one of you in this station! I will bring this place to the ground with every single Legal Hue I know in Hue City!

CALEB: (SERIOUSLY) Yeah ... tell that to all the Legal Hues who refused to take your case. Guess that's a sign to say that Hue City does have some sense, after all.

The Technological-Environmental Hue stops resisting and looks at Caleb and Vance in defeat, realizing that they feel no sympathy for him whatsoever.

CALEB: (SERIOUSLY) Now, c'mon, the vehicle is waiting for you.

TECHNOLOGICAL-ENVIRONMENTAL HUE: (RESUMES RESISTING) No! Please – please don't do this to me. You can't be taking me to prison! (TURNS TO ELISA ANGRILY) You should be taking her!

Elisa remains quiet, as Caleb and Vance forcefully hold the Technological-Environmental Hue back as he attempts to charge at her.

TECHNOLOGICAL-ENVIRONMENTAL HUE: (LIVID) You should be the one who is in this position! You should be the one who is going to prison – not me! But don't worry; your time will come! We'll see how long you're going to stay safe in this stinkhole! You can't hide here forever! I'll find you! I'll make sure you will be found in every single corner in Bartlett's Piece! You're going to pay for this! You're going to pay for ruining my life! (RESUMES RESISTING) And I'll be waiting to show you what you deserve once I get out of these chains!

VANCE: (FIRMLY) Let's go!

TECHNOLOGICAL-ENVIRONMENTAL HUE: (PLEADS) Please don't take me – please!

Elisa watches slightly anxiously as Caleb and Vance finally manage to bring the Technological-Environmental Hue out of the Steels Protection Services Station. Nolan walks in and checks to see that they have brought him inside the prisoner transport vehicle before letting out a sigh of relief.

NOLAN: (RELIEVED) It's a good thing we got him out this afternoon. For once, we can have some peace and quiet in this station. (TURNS TO ELISA) Ms. Graves.

Elisa snaps into focus and immediately sits up as Nolan comes up to the holding cell with the keys in his hands.

NOLAN: As for you, today happens to be your lucky day.

Nolan unlocks the gate of the holding cell and opens it as Elisa sits there in shock.

ELISA: (ASTONISHED) Are you serious?

NOLAN: Yes. You're free to go once we have finalized everything for you.

Elisa gets up and hesitates to leave the holding cell as Nolan waits patiently. She almost begins to tear up until she sees Malcolm walking toward them with a satisfied look on his face.

ELISA: (ASTONISHED) Malcolm, is this true?

MALCOLM: (PLEASED) Yes, it is, Elisa. We've been working day and night to solve your case, and luckily, we found someone who didn't want you to spend a day in prison.

Elisa looks to see Vincent standing there with a smile on his face, as she immediately feels a wave of emotion coming over her.

ELISA: (HAPPILY) Vincent!

Elisa immediately leaves the holding cell and rushes to give Vincent a hug as Malcolm smiles at the scene.

ELISA: (CONFUSED) But how? You broke your vow to stay nonconfrontational? What made you decide to come here?

VINCENT: (HAPPILY) Because I knew it was the right thing to do. You should know that our friendship is more important than some silly vow I made. There was no way I was going to let you suffer for that man's wrongdoing.

Elisa smiles and hugs Vincent again. Caleb and Vance return and see them embracing each other before she lets him go and rushes to give Malcolm a hug.

ELISA: (HAPPILY) Thank you so much, Malcolm.

MALCOLM: (HAPPILY) No problem, Elisa. I told you to put your trust in me. Now you won't have to spend a day in prison.

ELISA: (RELEASES MALCOLM AND HUGS NOLAN) Thank you, Officer!

NOLAN: (SLIGHTLY TAKEN ABACK) Oh – okay.

Malcolm laughs as he watches Nolan awkwardly respond to Elisa's hug.

NOLAN: (TAPS ELISA'S SHOULDER IMPATIENTLY) All right, all right, that's enough out of you.

Elisa immediately releases Nolan, as Caleb and Vance come over to them.

VANCE: (JOKINGLY) Hey! We worked hard, too. Don't we get a hug, as well?

NOLAN: (TURNS TO VANCE) Now is not the time for jokes, Officer Stanford. You and Officer McEntire will be taking Ms. Graves back home as you prepare your next duty.

VINCENT: (WALKS OVER, CONFUSED) But I don't understand. I thought I would be able to take her home after all of this. You said that she was free.

NOLAN: (CLARIFIES) Yes, in the sense that she won't be in prison anytime soon ... but that doesn't mean that she's free entirely.

Elisa's smile fades as she turns to Nolan, confused about what is about to happen to her.

ELISA: (CONFUSED) What do you mean, Officer?

▌ INT. INSIDE THE STEELS SQUAD CAR – AFTERNOON

Elisa stares out the window and watches the scenery as Vance drives to the Tint Valley Residence with Caleb in the passenger's seat.

NOLAN: (IN ELISA'S HEAD) Even though that man has committed the bigger crime, it doesn't completely remove the charges you'll be facing.

Both Caleb and Vance take the chance to watch Elisa through the rear-view mirror, as she remains unresponsive toward them.

The Next Day

▌ INT. ELISA'S BEDROOM – MORNING

The alarm clock sounds, as Elisa takes her time to wake up before turning it off.

HOUSE AI: Alarm dismissed. Good morning, Elisa Graves.

Elisa sits up and takes the blanket off herself. She stares at the ankle monitor she is wearing while letting out a big sigh.

NOLAN: (IN ELISA'S HEAD) Instead of prison for fourteen years, you will be put under house arrest for the next two weeks. Reoccurring offenders are usually given a month for this punishment ... but since this is your first offense, we decided to lighten the sentence.

Yesterday

INT. THE STEELS PROTECTION SERVICES STATION – AFTERNOON

NOLAN: (GESTURES AT THE ANKLE MONITOR) You will have this ankle monitor on you for the entire time – and even when your house arrest has ended, this ankle monitor must not be removed. (SERIOUSLY) Even when you go back to work, you will still have this on until we say otherwise. Now, just to confirm that your occupation supervisor has already been notified about these circumstances and has allowed you to come back to work, even with the ankle monitor on. However, during your house arrest, you cannot accept any requests to leave your house. You cannot have any visitors over unless notified by the Steels Protection Services, and I have to emphasize this clearly: You cannot leave your house, period.

Stunned, Elisa stares at the ankle monitor in Nolan's hands.

The Next Day

INT. ELISA'S APARTMENT – MORNING

NOLAN: (IN ELISA'S HEAD) During your house arrest, two Steels officers will sweep your house on a daily basis.

Elisa takes the time to clean and straighten up her apartment until she hears a heavy knock on the door.

CALEB: (THROUGH THE DOOR) Are you decent, Ms. Graves?

Elisa hurries to open the door, where she sees Caleb and Vance standing outside dressed in casual Steels officer suits.

NOLAN: (IN ELISA'S HEAD) Meaning that if they find anything that is related to drugs, possession of weapons or anything that helps you escape – you will be brought back here in an instant. Afterwards, a Steels officer will monitor you for twelve hours, just to make sure that you don't do anything stupid, such as take off your ankle monitor, attempt to escape or commit another offense.

CALEB: (IRRITATED) Do you usually take this long to answer the door?

ELISA: (SUBMISSIVELY) My apologies, Officer.

Caleb huffs in annoyance as he and Vance enter Elisa's apartment while she steps aside, feeling uncomfortable with their presence.

Yesterday

INT. THE STEELS PROTECTION SERVICES STATION – AFTERNOON

Nolan continues to speak, while Elisa feels slightly defeated.

NOLAN: That same officer will escort you to work and back home once your period of house arrest has ended, and if that same officer has reported that you have presented good behaviour throughout this process, you will have the ankle monitor removed. (SERIOUSLY) However, if you ever try to escape or set foot anywhere beyond a five-hundred-kilometre radius, we will find you, you will be brought back to the station and you will be going to prison for life! Is that understood, Ms. Graves?

ELISA: (SUBMISSIVELY) Understood.

NOLAN: Good. Then we shouldn't have any problems at all.

Nolan brings out the Fingerprint Data Transmitter and takes Elisa's left hand and has her press her thumb on the screen while the device transfers her information to the Steels Protection Services Database.

The Next Day

█ INT. ELISA'S APARTMENT – MORNING

Elisa stands in a corner, slightly upset for the entire time that she waits for Caleb and Vance to finish sweeping through the house. She gets extremely irritated as she watches them both roughly handling her things during the house sweep.

ELISA: (UPSET) Hey, would you be careful, please? The last thing I need is for my place to look ransacked at the end of this.

Caleb and Vance stop and turn to see that Elisa is upset, then look at each other for a moment before turning back to her.

CALEB: (SERIOUSLY) I don't believe you have a say about how we do our job in this situation.

ELISA: (UPSET) Well, if this is going to happen every single day, the least I expect is for nothing to end up broken around here.

CALEB: (SERIOUSLY) Is that so? (POINTS TO THE CHEST) Then, what is in this chest?

Elisa suddenly freezes and turns to the chest, which contains all her books. She tries not to show any fear while she turns back to Caleb.

ELISA: (UPSET) Is it really necessary for you to look through that?

Caleb immediately loses his patience and grimaces in annoyance as he flings open the chest, which startles Elisa and Vance. Looking in the chest, Caleb sees books along with the velvet box and turns to Elisa for an explanation.

ELISA: (CLARIFIES) It's not what you think. I'm not running a book-smuggling operation here. I bought them all myself. You can use the barcode scanner to confirm it.

Caleb stares at Elisa furiously, while Vance lets out a deep sigh as he predicts what is about to happen.

A Few Hours Later

▌ INT. ELISA'S APARTMENT – MORNING

Elisa slowly paces back and forth, with Vance relaxing on the couch. Using the Barcode Scanner, Caleb scans every book that is inside the chest and takes his time doing so as Vance rolls his eyes and shakes his head in annoyance.

VANCE: (UNINTERESTED) Have you found any anomalies, Officer?

CALEB: (DETERMINED) Not yet.

Elisa huffs in annoyance as Caleb continues to scan every book until he reaches the end with Gulliver's Travels.

CALEB: (SIGHS) Turns out that you were right, Ms. Graves.

ELISA: (SLIGHTLY IRRITATED) I told you that you had nothing to worry about. I'd even let you disorganize my books just to prove that to you.

CALEB: (PICKS UP THE VELVET BOX) Then explain this to me. (TURNS TO ELISA) What's so special in here that it has to be concealed in a box?

ELISA: (CROSSES HER ARMS) That's the gift I was telling you about during my Act of Plea. The one that my dad left for me five years ago. If I didn't have a chance to open it, why should I let you do it?

VANCE: (GETS UP) Can't lie; she has a point there.

Vance takes the velvet box from Caleb and gives it to Elisa, who feels relieved.

VANCE: Plus, I believe that Ms. Graves is allowed to have one item or room that is prohibited for us to look through, and since we did a thorough sweep, we have nothing to worry about so far. (TURNS TO ELISA) Don't worry, Ms. Graves. I believe you'll feel more comfortable once one of us leaves the house.

CALEB: You go. I'll stay.

VANCE: (TURNS TO CALEB, SHOCKED) Are you serious?

CALEB: (SERIOUSLY) Yeah, I'm pretty sure Officer Webber has something for you to do back at the station while I watch over Ms. Graves for twelve hours.

VANCE: Are you sure about this?

CALEB: (STRICT) You heard me. Go.

VANCE: (SIGHS AND SURRENDERS) All right – I'll be out of your hair now. See you back in the station, okay? (TURNS TO ELISA) Take care, Ms. Graves. I hope to see you tomorrow (LEANS OVER AND WHISPERS), and don't take his attitude personally – he's like this all the time. Just read him a couple of those books of yours and you'd be surprised how much of a bookworm he is.

Elisa stands there slightly surprised and thinks about Vance's advice as she watches him leave her apartment before she turns back to Caleb.

ELISA: You didn't have to do that. I would've been okay with either one of you.

CALEB: (GETS UP AND WALKS UP TO ELISA) No, you wouldn't have, Ms. Graves – and believe me, you should be thanking me, since I know Vance very well. (SERIOUSLY) And yes, I had to do that because the last thing I needed on my mind was to leave a colleague here who's going to get easily distracted by you.

ELISA: (SLIGHTLY DEFENSIVE) I'm not as much of a threat as you think I am.

CALEB: (SERIOUSLY) We'll see what happens during these two weeks.

ELISA: (SHRUGS) Okay, then I'll let you do your job. Feel free to repack those books while you're at it.

Elisa walks away from Caleb as he stands there in disbelief.

CALEB: (TURNS TO ELISA, STUNNED) Excuse me? (HARSHLY) Hey! (GESTURES TO ELISA'S BOOKS) This is not my stuff!

ELISA: (STOPS AND TURNS TO CALEB) But that is not my mess. You said that you were going to be here for twelve hours. Might as well do something productive while you're here.

CALEB: (SMIRKS) You can't actually be –

ELISA: (FIRMLY) You heard me. (BEGINS TO WALK AWAY) Make sure they're organized in alphabetical order. By author, not by title!

Elisa goes to her room to put away the velvet box as Caleb growls in frustration before beginning to put the books back into the chest in alphabetical order.

A Few Hours Later

▌INT. ELISA'S APARTMENT – AFTERNOON

Elisa wraps herself in a blanket and sits on the couch as she watches the news. She tries her best not to be made uncomfortable by Caleb's intimidating stare. He sits at the dining table and watches her every move until they both hear a Notification Alert go off.

HOUSE AI: Notification Alert! Your Life Band has detected high stress levels in your body –

ELISA: Dismiss all notifications.

HOUSE AI: Notifications dismissed.

CALEB: (QUIETLY SMIRKS) Like you have anything to be stressed about.

Elisa shoots Caleb an annoyed look as she goes back to watching TV. Finally, she becomes uncomfortable with his intimidating stare.

ELISA: (ANNOYED) Why are you staring at me like that?

CALEB: (SERIOUSLY) Because I don't trust you, Ms. Graves.

ELISA: (HUFFS IMPATIENTLY) I haven't been able to do anything for the past few days and already, you make the decision not to trust me.

CALEB: (SERIOUSLY) First offenders will always have a reoccurrence. I don't know what you did to get Deputy Reign to trust you, but it sure didn't work on Officer Webber and it's sure not going to work on me. So, just be prepared for what will happen to you when that day happens.

Elisa silently growls to herself, then gets up from the couch and starts folding her blanket. Caleb continues to watch her carefully.

CALEB: Is there anyone we should know about who might stop by for a visit today?

ELISA: (ANNOYED) No.

Caleb grimaces in shock as he slowly starts to get up while he continues to watch Elisa carefully.

CALEB: No friends? No family members? No roommates? Not even a colleague who would drop by to give you some work to do at home? Should we expect frequent visitors during this house arrest?

ELISA: No, Officer. I live alone … I've always been alone ever since I got here. Why do you think I never made any additional reports after agreeing to this house arrest? The only other people who have been in this apartment were you and Officer Stanford … it's been just me in this house for the past five years.

CALEB: (CONFUSED) But that doesn't make any sense. There has to be someone in your life who's going –

ELISA: (LOOKS AT HER CLOTHES) Not when you're bearing this Tint Level. It's easy for people to ignore you, as if you're nothing. Plus, I don't have any friends, so you don't have to worry about any visitors coming here.

CALEB: (FIRMLY) I've seen people with your Tint Level who have thousands of people in their lives. You can't possibly tell me that you don't have any friends here. (ARGUES) And what about that guy you were hugging at the station yesterday? You don't think he might stop by for a visit?

ELISA: He owns the bookstore at Primetime Plaza. He doesn't have the freedom to come all the way here from the plaza – he could easily lose his livelihood if he ever did that.

CALEB: (ARGUES) But how would you know that if he wasn't your friend? Or what about Deputy Reign? Explain why you wanted to see him the day you got arrested, if he's not your friend. Unless there's another reason why you, Deputy Reign and that book guy are so close.

ELISA: I knew them through my dad. That's why we're so close. I do have a good relationship with both of them, but that doesn't make them my friends. The reason I said that is because I haven't been able to make them on my own, which is why I usually find friendships an inconvenience to me.

Elisa puts the folded blanket away and starts straightening up the place until she sees the picture of a male citizen on TV, which causes her to stop. The news reporter talks about another disappearance that occurred in Tint Valley, which makes her think about Gillian.

ELISA: Sometimes, when I do get the chance to make friends, they're never there when I need them the most.

Caleb notices Elisa staring at the TV as she imagines the picture of the male citizen switching to Gillian's face. Then she shakes her head to stop the thought and goes back to straightening up the living room.

ELISA: I know you're just trying to bring me back to the station to verify any potential visitors, but I can guarantee that no one is going to be coming to this address. (STOPS AND TURNS TO CALEB) And

I know my life is not like the average Late Tint, but it is what it is … you're just going to have to deal with that.

Caleb stares at her in silence, as Elisa takes a moment of silence herself.

ELISA: I just hope that during this house arrest, you will see that I'm not a bad person, and that you can truly trust me – even after this house arrest officially ends.

CALEB: (PAUSES AND REMAINS UNCONVINCED) Yeah, we'll see about that.

Elisa sighs in hopelessness as she goes back to straightening up the apartment, while Caleb continues to watch her every move.

ELEVEN

EXT. OUTSIDE THE STEELS PROTECTION SERVICES STATION – EVENING

Vance speaks to the family members of the missing male citizen, while Steels officers return to the station after a long day of emergency patrolling.

VANCE: (REASSURINGLY) Just be patient; we're going to do whatever it takes to find him. You don't have to worry about a thing – we'll try our very best to bring him back home to you.

The family members of the missing male citizen nod in understanding. As they solemnly make their way home, Malcolm approaches Vance after a long day of emergency patrolling.

MALCOLM: Long evening, Officer Stanford?

VANCE: (SIGHS) Sure was. I just spoke to the family members of our new missing person case.

MALCOLM: Yeah, I couldn't help but think about that as well – these missing person reports have gone rampant. Have any others come in?

VANCE: (SHAKES HIS HEAD) No, just that last one that aired on the news this morning. You seem to be taking a lot of interest in these missing person reports.

MALCOLM: (HONESTLY) Well, I can't help but think about it since that's the twelfth one this week ... plus I'm trying to do a favour for

Elisa; she thinks that one of her colleagues has gone missing as well.

VANCE: That's a shame, and to think so many people could go missing … (THINKS) Do you think that General Metallic guy has something to do with this?

NOLAN: (WALKS IN) Of course, that man has nothing to do with this. That incident was nothing but a stupid prank. Plus, the GAO has said that they're already on it, so it doesn't have to be our concern.

As Nolan walks away and heads straight to the station, Vance turns to see Malcolm tensing slightly for the moment.

VANCE: (CONFUSED) I don't understand. Why would he say that it was a prank?

MALCOLM: (QUIETLY) Because it only happened once, so, of course, people are going to think it's a prank. However, we still have to remain vigilant about this situation, as this person could possibly be a threat to our homes.

VANCE: I'll say … (WONDERS ABOUT ELISA) Hey, how come we only got to know about Ms. Graves now? Why didn't you ever introduce her to us before she was arrested?

MALCOLM: (TURNS TO VANCE IN DISBELIEF) Are you absolutely out of your mind?

VANCE: (COMPLAINS) C'mon, you should know how extremely hard it is to find someone decent in Tint Valley – and you know how much I hate arresting women! Why didn't you tell me that she was pretty?

MALCOLM: (STERNLY) She's the daughter of a very important friend of mine, and the last thing I ever want is to dishonor his good name by leaving her alone in a room with you.

VANCE: (SHOCKED) So you would rather have her alone with Caleb than me? How does this make any sense? He will skin her alive in a day before she gets out of house arrest! You know how intense he gets when he takes his job seriously.

MALCOLM: (FIRMLY) I understand that, but that is what she needs right now if she's going to get through this house arrest. The last thing I need is for her to be brought to the station for unnecessary reasons – especially when Officer Webber will do anything in his power to bring her back here. So it's best to keep things fair in this situation. And don't worry about Officer McEntire ... I'm certain Elisa will find a way to get through to him.

VANCE: (UNCONVINCED) Is that so? Because I have been a witness of Caleb's poor manners when it comes to women – I've seen droves of women trying to get Caleb's attention and he didn't budge for a second! How can you be so sure that Ms. Graves can get to him?

MALCOLM: (CONFIDENTLY) Believe me, Elisa has a way of reaching to people's hearts ... I'm certain that by the end of this house arrest, you will be seeing a different side of Officer McEntire.

VANCE: (SHRUGS) Well, we'll see about that ... I just really wanted to be alone with her.

Malcolm shakes his head in disbelief, while Vance continues to be upset about not monitoring Elisa during her house arrest.

▌ INT. ELISA'S APARTMENT – EVENING

Caleb falls asleep on the chair where he was sitting, while Elisa comes out of her room wearing sleepwear. She dries her hair with a towel until she notices Caleb sleeping and stops.

ELISA: (SLIGHTLY CONCERNED) Officer McEntire?

Elisa drops the towel and comes up to Caleb as he remains sleeping on the chair.

ELISA: (SLIGHTLY CONCERNED) Officer McEntire, are you okay? (GENTLY SHAKES CALEB) Officer McEntire?

Elisa continues to shake Caleb gently until he jerks awake and looks quickly around to see the sky getting dark.

CALEB: (SLIGHTLY GROGGY) Almighty … What happened just now?

ELISA: (SLIGHTLY CONCERNED) You were sleeping, Officer … I just came to see if you were okay.

CALEB: (PAUSES IN DISBELIEF) How on earth did I end up falling asleep? (TURNS TO ELISA IN DISBELIEF) And when did you change – I swear you were wearing something different.

ELISA: (CONFUSED) Was I supposed to have you monitor me while I'm showering?

Startled, Caleb pauses and quickly gets up, clearly embarrassed, while Elisa waits quietly for an answer.

CALEB: No, of course not. (CLEARS HIS THROAT) You are allowed to have your moments of privacy as long as I'm notified beforehand.

Caleb quickly puts the chair away as Elisa stands in slight confusion.

ELISA: Are you feeling all right, Officer?

CALEB: (CURT) I'm fine. I just … never fell asleep while monitoring someone during a house arrest.

ELISA: I'll try to look for some entertainment from now on if it will help keep you awake … I'll even let you read some of my books to pass the time.

Caleb gives Elisa a look until he hears his timer start beeping and checks to see what time it is.

ELISA: What's that?

CALEB: (TURNS OFF HIS TIMER) It's your ticket to freedom. Your twelve hours are up for today. However, we'll be back again tomorrow and the next few days afterwards … just accept this as your new reality, Ms. Graves.

Elisa remains slightly distraught as she goes to open the door for Caleb to leave the apartment. He turns to her with intimidation in his eyes.

CALEB: (FIRMLY) That sleeping bit won't happen again.

ELISA: We'll see how that goes. Have a good night, Officer McEntire.

Caleb remains furious until he leaves the apartment, while Elisa closes the door and locks it. She sighs in relief and stares at her ankle monitor as she thinks about the next few days of her house arrest.

The Next Day

▌ INT. ELISA'S APARTMENT – MORNING

Elisa sits on the couch reading Our Souls at Night as she waits for Caleb and Vance to sweep through the house.

VANCE: (COMES UP TO CALEB) All clean in this area. What about you?

CALEB: (COMES UP TO VANCE) Same, nothing suspicious in my area.

VANCE: Sweet. If we keep this up, we might get an upgrade on our badges.

Caleb tunes out Vance as he carefully watches Elisa reading without making any eye contact with him whatsoever.

CALEB: We might have to involve Tegan during these house sweeps.

VANCE: (FIRMLY) Absolutely not. (QUIETLY) Are you out of your damn mind? Why on Earth would you want to involve Tegan? You're clearly out to ruin this poor girl's life.

CALEB: (QUIETLY) She's the one who involved herself in this situation. I'm just doing my job, Officer. Plus, Tegan is the only person who can look through things that we can't simply touch at this moment. She has to get involved.

VANCE: (QUIETLY) Yeah, and that is why I say that's a bad idea.

CALEB: (QUIETLY) How is it a bad idea when I just want the job done right?

VANCE: (QUIETLY) That's the thing. You're crazy when you want a job done right. Tegan is also crazy when she wants a job done right. You know she'll look through every single thing in this place just to make up some story to bring her to the station. We will lose Ms. Graves if we bring two crazies together. C'mon, you don't think we did a good enough job together?

CALEB: (CLARIFIES) It's not that I don't trust you doing the job right; it's just … (REMEMBERS TEGAN'S IMPULSIVE BEHAVIOR) You're right. Tegan shouldn't get involved in this.

VANCE: (SIGHS IN RELIEF) Thank you – see? I knew there was a way to get through to you.

CALEB: (SLIGHTLY ANNOYED) Yeah, yeah, but I'm still going to watch over her.

VANCE: (SIGHS IN RELIEF) Okay, suit yourself. I'm needed back at the station to take care of these missing person reports. (QUIETLY) But for the next few days, let me take over the monitoring from now on.

CALEB: (FIRMLY) Leave.

Vance surrenders and leaves the apartment, while Caleb closes and locks the door. He turns to see Elisa still reading, and then he hears a knock on the door.

CALEB: (CONFUSED) What on Earth? Did he forget something?

Caleb opens the door to see a delivery man holding a chilled box in his hands.

DELIVERY MAN: (LOUDLY) Delivery for Ms. Graves!

Shocked, Caleb turns to Elisa, who looks up to see the delivery man standing outside. She rushes to take the chilled box from him.

ELISA: (KINDLY) Thank you so much.

DELIVERY MAN: (PULLS OUT HIS SIGNATURE PAD AND STYLUS) You're welcome. I also need your signature, please.

Elisa quickly puts the box away in the kitchen and rushes to sign the Signature Pad using the stylus. Then she gives them both back to the delivery man.

ELISA: (KINDLY) Here you go.

DELIVERY MAN: (TAKES HIS SIGNATURE PAD AND STYLUS) Thank you. Have a good day, Miss.

ELISA: (KINDLY) You too. Goodbye.

The delivery man turns to leave, while Elisa closes and locks the door. As she turns, she sees Caleb with a stern look on his face.

ELISA: What. You didn't say anything about ordering food.

Elisa walks away from Caleb and heads toward the kitchen, while he stands fuming.

CALEB: (FOLLOWS ELISA) Are you sure it's not something else I need to look through?

ELISA: I needed to stock up on a few things in the fridge. What else would I be ordering at this time?

Elisa attempts to open the chilled box, but Caleb takes it away from her and pulls out his switchblade to rip it open. Elisa stands there in shock while she watches Caleb rip off the tape with his knife and open the box to see raw meat, a few dairy products, fresh pasta, and a lot of cheese and vegetables with a few spices. He looks through the box thoroughly to see if he finds anything otherwise and even smells the spices. However, he finds nothing but groceries in the box.

CALEB: (SERIOUSLY) I'm not packing this up this time.

Caleb puts away the switchblade and walks away from Elisa, leaving her in shock before taking the groceries out of the box.

ELISA: (IN DISBELIEF) Was it really necessary for you to do that?

CALEB: (SERIOUSLY) Yes, it was. You may have the right to order stuff, but it's crucial for us to look through everything that comes into this house (TURNS TO ELISA), especially groceries. We just want to make sure that you're not smuggling any illegal items during your house arrest.

ELISA: (SLIGHTLY ANNOYED) I've already read the terms and conditions after I accepted this house arrest. Why on Earth would I take the chance to smuggle anything when I know it's going to give me life in prison?

CALEB: (SERIOUSLY) Even if you do it afterwards, you will still get life in prison if you're caught red-handed. Until you surpass the timeline for your first offense, you will remain under our radar for future arrests.

ELISA: (SCOFFS SILENTLY) Talk about next-level bullshit.

Caleb gives Elisa a stern look while she continues to unpack the groceries.

ELISA: I'm actually planning on making dinner today. Would you like to have some?

CALEB: (SERIOUSLY) No.

ELISA: Are you sure? I won't mind making you a plate.

CALEB: (SERIOUSLY) I'm not allowed to accept anything from detainees, whether it's food, gifts or anything that is presented in a hospitable manner; I will never accept it.

ELISA: Are you sure that's not just you being prejudiced? You're already thinking of me as a prisoner when I'm just serving a house arrest.

CALEB: (STERNLY) Did I say that you were a prisoner, or did you just think that I referred to you as one? For the record, anyone who is facing the consequences of their actions is guilty in my book. So, you don't get to tell me otherwise, because they're all the same to me!

Elisa is slightly taken aback, as Caleb aggressively pulls the chair from the dining table to take a seat.

CALEB: Plus, I have already made dinner plans, so you don't need to make anything for me.

ELISA: (SHRUGS) Suit yourself. Just don't get hungry while you're busy watching me cook.

Caleb looks at Elisa in shock and scoffs in disbelief as she continues to unpack the groceries from the box.

Several Hours Later

▎ INT. ELISA'S APARTMENT – EVENING

Elisa takes the ravioli casserole she made out of the oven, places it away from the stove and uses her knee to close the oven door. Caleb watches her carefully as she moves the ravioli casserole to the counter and then turns off the stove to check on her butternut-squash soup. She moves the pot of soup away from the hot burner and opens the lid. However, steam burns her hand, and she drops the lid and rushes to the sink to run cold water over her hand.

CALEB: Is everything all right, Ms. Graves? Are you in need of medical assistance?

ELISA: (CURT) I'm fine. I don't need any medical assistance. It's just a minor burn – nothing serious.

CALEB: Suit yourself then. Just remember to open the lid away from you next time.

ELISA: (SIGHS) I'll keep that in mind.

Elisa keeps the faucet running for a moment, then turns it off and goes back to properly close the pot of butternut-squash soup with the lid. Caleb continues to watch her carefully as Elisa thinks of a way to break the tension between them while she dries her hand with a dish towel.

ELISA: So, how long have you've been a Steels officer?

CALEB: (CURT) How's that any of your business?

ELISA: (TURNS TO CALEB) We both know that we started off on the wrong foot here. I thought I might take the chance to make things right between us. I figured that since we're going to be stuck here for a while, we might use this as an opportunity to get to know each other.

CALEB: (BLUNTLY) Why would I want to know anything about you? I don't want to know anything about you, and I don't want you to know anything about me.

ELISA: (APPALLED) What's with this disgusting attitude? I didn't ask for any of this.

CALEB: (ARGUES) Well, I beg to differ, Ms. Graves, because I wasn't the one who encouraged you to fight somebody in the middle of the plaza!

Elisa is speechless as Caleb gets up from his seat.

CALEB: (CONDESCENDINGLY) On second thought, I do want to know the reason for that! What possessed you to fight a man who is bigger than you, has a higher status than you and could've sent you to prison in seconds if he knew the right people? (COMES UP TO ELISA) Not to mention that this whole thing happened because of some stupid box! A box that we don't know what's inside because you won't allow us to see what's in it! And why is that, Ms. Graves? Why is it that you would put somebody in the hospital just to protect a box!

ELISA: (SHOUTS) Because I grew tired, dammit!

Caleb pauses in shock as Elisa loses her patience.

ELISA: (UPSET) Yes, you heard what I said – I grew tired. I grew tired of people treating me the way they liked because of their high status. (ANGRILY) And I'm certainly growing tired of you thinking that you can talk to me that way in my house! My home – the only place that is considered mine in this world – and I will not allow you to plague my home with your negativity! What is your problem, anyway? I'm trying my best to serve this stupid sentence, but it seems like you will do just about anything to push me to the brink! It's only been the second day and I'm already getting sick and tired of you being in my home! I know that my actions were wrong, and I know that I have to face the consequences – but the one thing I don't have to face is your filthy patronizing ass! (SLOWLY WALKS TOWARD CALEB) And what do you know, anyway?

Caleb backs away as Elisa advances toward him.

ELISA: (ANGRILY) I was already in a mood before this entire thing happened. I had to deal with a lot of things – a lot that you weren't even there to see for yourself to judge me! You think this is easy living in this world, bearing this Tint Level? It's not – it's not easy at all when even your own kind thinks they have the privilege to treat you like nothing! But I managed to bear through it all – I managed to keep all of this anger in because I knew there was nothing else I could do! And I kept it that way until that day – that one day I decided not to turn the other cheek – that one day I decided to fight for something that was mine and I wasn't only fighting for the box – I was fighting for my peace of mind! I needed some peace after dealing with a bunch of prejudiced co-workers who shout Slate every single time I'm in that office! I needed some peace after finding out that this General Metallic person wants to take over this fucking world all of a sudden! And this world could go to shit for all I care because it never gave me peace, so why should I be the one to give peace to that man when he wanted to take away something that is rightfully mine? And I don't regret doing it because there is a point at which every single one of us has reached their limit – and I certainly reached mine when that man wouldn't stop harassing me for one second, and I will reach there again when it comes to you! But, really, what makes you think I deserve a heavier punishment? If you were me, wouldn't you have done the same thing? Do you really think I would have let that man harass me, try to kill me and not do anything about it? Of course not because all you care about is putting me behind bars!

With his back against the wall, Caleb taps his head lightly as Elisa becomes overwhelmed with emotion.

ELISA: (SOLEMNLY) I just didn't want anything to be taken away from me again.

Caleb remains silent until he hears his timer start beeping and immediately turns it off. Elisa remains upset.

ELISA: (SOLEMNLY) Just go – I want to be alone. You have other things to do, so just leave me alone.

Caleb slowly looks away and starts to make his way to the door until he stops and turns to Elisa.

CALEB: You got the wrong idea about why I'm here. I didn't come here to be prejudiced toward you. I could care less about what your Tint Level is.

Elisa turns to Caleb, as he looks straight at her.

CALEB: I came here simply to do my job, which is to monitor you during a house arrest. Not only do I have to make sure that you don't commit a second offense, but I also have to make sure you don't end up harming anyone else or even killing yourself during this house arrest. So, don't make any suicidal plans during these two weeks, because I doubt that's something you want to put in the deputy's head.

Elisa scoffs in shock and shakes her head in disbelief. Caleb hears a knock on the door and opens it to see **Officer Tegan Drupal (mid-twenties)** standing outside.

TEGAN: (CHECKS HER TIMER) Well–well, just a few minutes off his schedule. (TURNS TO CALEB) Usually, you're more punctual than this.

CALEB: (SURPRISED) Tegan, what are you doing here?

TEGAN: The deputy wants us back in the station ASAP. I figured I'd pick you up after you were done with your monitoring duties, but I was expecting you to come out a little earlier than this.

CALEB: I was just on my way out. (CONFUSED) How did you even know where I was or the address of this place?

TEGAN: (CONFIDENTLY) Vance, of course. (LETS HERSELF IN) He sang like a canary after I whooped his ass a couple of times. You'd be surprised at what you can get out of him after a healthy dose of arm wrestling.

CALEB: (SLIGHTLY IRRITATED) I see. Just remind me to whoop his ass when I see him.

TEGAN: Now, now, there is no need to bring him more pain. He was already in a fragile state the last time I saw him. But don't worry. I'll give you guys a chance to duke it out. Plus, we should get going, since we all have that dinner tonight. Are we done here or are you guys still –

CALEB: (CERTAIN) No, we're done now. We just have to prepare for tomorrow; that's all.

TEGAN: (SHRUGS) Okay, if you say so. It isn't any of my business.

Tegan turns to see Elisa trying to contain her emotions as Caleb begins to feel bad about her current state.

TEGAN: (CONFUSED) What's wrong with her? Does she need medical assistance?

CALEB: It's not that – just give us a moment. (TURNS TO ELISA) Ms. Graves, I –

ELISA: (TRIES NOT TO CRY) Just leave already, you asshole. You're not needed anymore, so just go.

Caleb immediately goes quiet and looks away as Tegan sighs and shakes her head.

TEGAN: (UNIMPRESSED) Oh boy, looks like you've done it again. (BEGINS TO LEAVE) C'mon, let's go. We got work to do. (NOTICES CALEB IS NOT MOVING AND NUDGES HIS ARM) C'mon, you won't be able to wake up early if you keep stalling. Let's go.

Caleb snaps into focus and turns back to Elisa to say something, but ends up leaving the apartment while Tegan follows him and closes the door behind her. Elisa rushes to lock the door as she finally allows her emotions to release. She slowly sinks to the floor and begins to cry. She holds herself tightly and continues to cry uncontrollably as she thinks about the people who are no longer a part of her life.

TWELVE

Nine Years Prior

INT. ELISA'S CHILDHOOD BEDROOM OF THE GRAVES' HOUSE – EVENING

Twelve-year-old Elisa is reading a book under the blanket with the Light Box on when Garreth opens the door and sees that she is not sleeping.

GARRETH: (WHISPERS) Elisa? Elisa, do you hear me?

Garreth enters the room and takes the blanket off twelve-year-old Elisa to see her reading *Gulliver's Travels* while holding the Light Box in her hands.

TWELVE-YEAR-OLD ELISA: (ANNOYED) Hey!

GARRETH: (QUIETLY) Elisa, it's okay … it's just me. You have nothing to worry about.

TWELVE-YEAR-OLD ELISA: (SIGHS) For a second, I thought you were Fredrick.

GARRETH: (QUIETLY) Well, I don't think your brother is planning to bother you anytime soon, but that shouldn't stop you from trying to get along with him.

Twelve-year-old Elisa huffs in annoyance as Garreth smiles in understanding.

GARRETH: (QUIETLY) Now, I did not come in here just to lecture you, but will you tell me what you're doing up so late?

TWELVE-YEAR-OLD ELISA: (SIGHS) I don't want to go to school.

GARRETH: (QUIETLY) Why not? You're about to start high school soon. I'm surprised that you're not excited about this.

TWELVE-YEAR-OLD ELISA: (QUIETLY) Why should I be when I'm just going to see the same people again?

GARRETH: (QUIETLY) Well, you don't know that for sure. Maybe you'll meet some other people, kids who came from all sorts of parts in Bartlett's Piece. Now, I know I can't convince you to make friends, but I sure can try to prevent a fight with your mother if she finds out that you're not in bed. (TAKES THE LIGHT BOX AWAY FROM TWELVE-YEAR-OLD ELISA) And you know how I feel when it comes to you using this device. It's not safe for you.

TWELVE-YEAR-OLD ELISA: (QUIETLY) But it's the only light I can use to see the pages properly.

GARRETH: (GESTURES TO THE LIGHT BOX) But you have to understand how strong these devices were made. Holding this amount of light this close will mess up your eyes. Plus, there are far more precious things to see out there than just words in a book.

Garreth turns off the Light Box and puts it in his pocket while twelve-year-old Elisa pouts.

GARRETH: (REASSURINGLY) Now let your old man tell you a story that doesn't require you to read anything.

TWELVE-YEAR-OLD ELISA: (QUIETLY) Is this another one of your mystical stories?

GARRETH: (CHUCKLES) C'mon, you used to love those stories when you were younger. Don't tell me you've gotten too old for my stories. Now lie down, get yourself comfortable and close your eyes if you want to hear this story.

Twelve-year-old Elisa nods as she covers herself with the blanket and lies down with closed eyes while Garreth prepares for his story.

GARRETH: (QUIETLY) Now allow your mind to wander as I tell you a story about a forest. It was one of the most beautiful forests in the world – a forest everyone wished to see. You can imagine how everyone reacted when they heard about this forest. The idea of seeing the water flowing from the roots all the way up to the tree trunks and branches as every vein of those trees illuminated like the sun and the leaves sparkled like the night sky. But as beautiful as that forest was, nobody was allowed to go inside … because that forest was so protected, no one got a chance to experience its true beauty … no one got to see the forest with their own eyes, so they all thought it was just a dream.

Twelve-year-old Elisa imagines the illuminating forest as Garreth continues his story.

GARRETH: Now inside that forest, there lived a little girl –

TWELVE-YEAR-OLD ELISA: (SMIRKS) A little girl? Was her name Melisa?

GARRETH: (CHUCKLES) Malia is her name. I knew I couldn't get away with using Melisa again, but you know how I feel when you're interrupting my stories.

TWELVE-YEAR-OLD ELISA: (SUBMISSIVELY) Sorry.

GARRETH: Now, this little girl, Malia, loved this forest with her whole heart. She swore to protect it with her whole life. She'd even trained herself to become the best warrior who had ever lived on this Earth to fight any trespasser who would cause harm to the forest. However, when she wasn't busy fighting off trespassers, she would lie on the forest ground and watch the giant larks – not those tiny birds you see outside. These were big larks that were larger than a fully built house, and they came in a variety of colours, from the brightest yellows to the deepest blues. Malia would watch those magnificent creatures soaring across the sky as their wings brought an enormous amount of wind to the forest and caused all the glass seeds from the dandelion fluffs to scatter all around the forest – even touching her nose a few times. And when she wasn't watching the larks or playing with the dandelions, she just stared at the clouds, which were just as fluffy as cotton candy.

TWELVE-YEAR-OLD ELISA: (GIGGLES) Cotton candy clouds –

GARRETH: You're interrupting again.

TWELVE-YEAR-OLD ELISA: (PROTESTS) No, I wasn't this time. (SUBMISSIVELY) Okay, I'll stop talking now.

GARRETH: The forest was the one thing that Malia never wanted to give up on ... and because she loved it so much, it was the one thing she never wanted to share. Her love was so deep that she would destroy anyone who dared to enter the forest. No one got a chance to see the beauty of the forest ... and some even had to pay the ultimate price for trying. As Malia got older, she realized that the forest wasn't shining its brightest. The leaves were not sparkling like they used to ... the giant larks stopped flying over the forest ... and the dandelion seeds stopped becoming glass. Malia worried that the forest was slowly starting to die, so she left the one place she loved and went on a journey to save her precious home. She came back with the cleanest water she could possibly find to heal the forest, but nothing changed. She went on another journey and found the most powerful fruits to heal the forest, but nothing changed. She left again and came back to train the larks that stayed so they could use their wings to blow away the clouds so that the forest could receive the brightest sunlight it could ever experience ... but still, there were no changes.

Twelve-year-old Elisa remains quiet with her eyes closed as Garreth continues his story.

GARRETH: Now Malia was furious about her efforts to save the forest. She was so furious that she stopped going on journeys and did what she did best, which was to stay put and protect. But as she stayed in the forest longer, she realized that something else had changed while she was gone … someone had entered the forest. She searched and searched and searched for the intruder all day and all night until she finally found the person. It was a girl who was lying on the forest floor, and she was wearing a thin hood that covered her limbs. Pulling out the greatest weapon she could ever find, Malia wondered how the girl had managed to enter the forest. She shouted, "Who are you? What are you doing in my forest?" The young lady replied weakly, "It's okay. I'll be gone soon … I've always dreamed of being inside this forest. I thought I would take the chance to see it, since I don't have much time … I just wanted to see the forest before I go, and then I'll be on my way on a journey of no return." Malia quickly realized that the girl was dying … and that the roots remained the brightest of all the areas to keep her alive. Just seeing this made Malia so angry that she was about to kill the girl for stealing the life force of the forest when she realized that the forest was giving its life force to the girl.

TWELVE-YEAR-OLD ELISA: (POUTS) Why does this story feel sad?

GARRETH: Just hang on. I haven't reached the end yet.

Twelve-year-old Elisa nods and keeps her eyes closed as Garreth continues his story.

GARRETH: She thought that the forest loved the girl more than it loved Malia. She thought the forest loved the girl so much that it was willing to give its life force to save her … which made Malia believe that her love for the forest was one-sided, and so she made the decision to let the forest go. So, she gave the cleanest water to the girl, gave the most powerful fruit to the girl, and even ordered the larks that stayed to blow away the fluffy clouds just so the girl received the brightest sunlight. She wanted to experience the wonders of the forest one last time with the dying girl before she had to go – the dandelion seeds even turned back to glass one last time … and when she realized that this very moment was going to be her last day in the forest, she was willing to even sacrifice herself and give her life force to the girl.

TWELVE-YEAR-OLD ELISA: (POUTS) Malia died?

GARRETH: No, she did not die, Elisa. In fact, she was surprised to see that she was still alive when she woke up the next day. But when she looked around, she saw that the forest wasn't illuminating anymore. The trees were dead, the birds were gone, and the dandelion fluffs remained fluffs for the entire time. Even the clouds weren't as fluffy as they used to be. But when she turned around, she saw the brightest light she'd ever seen. It was coming from the girl, who was no longer dying. Her limbs were no longer thin; her thin hood was gone, and just the sight of her made Malia wonder in awe as she saw how truly beautiful the girl was. She was shining so brightly that her light was getting brighter and brighter and brighter until it burst all across the forest – making the trees illuminate again like the sun and the leaves sparkle like the night sky. Malia was amazed that the girl had revived the forest back to life … but not as amazed as when she saw the girl transform into the biggest lark that she had ever seen. Her wings were as tall as the trees in the forests, and each of her feathers illuminated just as brightly as the leaves, while Malia saw the energy flowing through the bird's body.

Twelve-year-old Elisa smiles with her eyes closed as Garreth continues his story.

GARRETH: She came up to Malia and said, "You were never alone in this forest, and you will never be alone … the forest loved you so much and appreciated everything you did during its time of need … but the forest knew that there's a bigger world out there for you to explore, and I became this to show you what that wonderful world looks like." She offered herself to Malia and said, "Come, let me show you what that world looks like." Malia got on her back and held on tightly as the lark shot up to the sky and soared over the forest and Malia saw how beautiful it was from afar. But that wasn't the only thing she saw … the lark took her to many places where Malia saw the coldest mountains, the hottest deserts, and the most beautiful beaches and greenest forests in the world. She saw everything that was beautiful in this world, and she began to love the lark just as much as she loved the forest. Then the lark told her, "There's one more place I want to show you … but you're going to have to hold on tightly." The lark soared even higher to the sky, so poor Malia feared that she was going to get blown away by the wind. However, she trusted the lark and held on tightly. The lark told her, "Hang on, we're going to a place where no man has ever been before … just hold on a little tighter as we're about to ascend in three … two … one."

Nine Years Later

▌ INT. ELISA'S BEDROOM – NIGHT

Elisa wakes up and quickly looks around the room until she sees that it is still dark outside. She takes a moment to breathe, as she thinks about the dream she just had. Her face hardens in anger as she sees the ankle monitor still on until she begins to cry and starts to miss Garreth's presence.

ELISA: (SOLEMNLY) Dad … Why aren't you here? I would really like to hear one of your stories right now.

Elisa pulls her knees close to her and holds them tightly as she continues to cry.

The Next Day

▌ INT. ELISA'S APARTMENT – MORNING

Elisa opens the door and allows Caleb and Vance to come inside the apartment to begin their house sweep.

CALEB: You slept well, Ms. Graves?

Elisa does not respond to Caleb as he begins to look through the bathroom and bedroom, while Vance looks through the living room and kitchen. Elisa tries her best not to get upset until Caleb steps out of the room and shows her the velvet box in his hands. She gives him a dirty look, and he surrenders and puts the box down. Vance finishes looking through the living room and kitchen.

VANCE: (TURNS TO CALEB) All clear from my end. How 'bout yours?

CALEB: All clear as well (GESTURES TO ELISA'S BEDROOM). Check to see if I missed anything.

Vance nods and goes to look through the bathroom and bedroom, while Caleb looks through the living room and kitchen. Caleb is taking the time to look through the fridge to see if he finds anything suspicious when he notices the half-eaten ravioli casserole inside. He remembers the horrible service he received at the Fire House and discreetly takes a piece of ravioli from the casserole. He quickly eats the ravioli and closes the fridge when he realizes that Elisa has been watching him for the entire time.

VANCE: (FROM ELISA'S BEDROOM) All clear in here! Anything from your side?

CALEB: (ALOUD) No! All clear as well!

VANCE: (COMES OUT OF ELISA'S BEDROOM) Great, that means everything is okay.

TEGAN: (WALKS IN) Well, hello-hello! I see that I came in at just the right time!

Elisa is confused to see Tegan letting herself into the apartment, along with Vance, who turns to Caleb furiously while he stands there, shocked himself.

TEGAN: (CONFIDENTLY) I'm glad that you guys are still here. I was afraid I'd miss the party.

CALEB: (WALKS UP TO TEGAN) What are you doing here? This is not your case.

TEGAN: (BLUNTLY) I know, but Webber worried that you guys might be doing a crappy job, so he thought it would be good for me to check things out for myself.

VANCE: (WALKS UP TO TEGAN) This doesn't make any sense. There's no reason for you to be here.

CALEB: (CALMLY) Officer, calm down.

VANCE: (ARGUES) No, I can't calm down after witnessing this nonsense!

Elisa remains quiet as she watches Vance and Caleb arguing with each other, while Tegan patiently waits to start her personal house sweep.

VANCE: (ARGUES) This is ridiculous! (POINTS TO CALEB AND TEGAN) You two are ridiculous!

CALEB: (STRICT) Stanford, we shouldn't be behaving like this in front of the detainee.

VANCE: (ARGUES) I don't care anymore because this is complete bullshit! (TURNS TO TEGAN) This case already has two officers assigned to this task. Why do you need to get involved? Does the deputy even know about this?

TEGAN: (BLUNTLY) Of course he does, and hey, I know you're still salty about your losing streak last night, but I only came here following orders. We all know that we have to answer back to Webber at the end of the day. So, are you two going to let me do my job or do I have to get Officer Webber involved in this situation?

Both Caleb and Vance go silent but remain furious about the situation, as Tegan confirms the answer to her question.

A Few Minutes Later

▌ INT. ELISA'S APARTMENT – MORNING

Tegan looks through each of the cupboards and drawers in the kitchen while Caleb and Vance stand by, watching nervously.

TEGAN: You got a nice apartment, Ms. Graves. Too bad I didn't get to know you sooner. There are a bunch of guys at our station who love a clean house.

Elisa remains quiet as she, Caleb and Vance wait for Tegan to end her personal house sweep as she finishes looking through the kitchen.

TEGAN: (WALKS AROUND THE APARTMENT) Seems like everything is okay here. (POINTS TO ELISA'S BEDROOM) Has this room been checked already?

VANCE: Yes, Officer McEntire and I both checked the room ourselves.

TEGAN: Well, consider it to be checked again, as I could imagine you boys having a hard time checking this room. (TURNS TO ELISA) Do you mind if I –

ELISA: Go ahead, I don't mind.

Tegan smiles as she willingly goes to Elisa's bedroom, while Vance turns to Caleb for an explanation.

VANCE: (QUIETLY ARGUES) I can't believe you actually got Tegan involved.

CALEB: (QUIETLY ARGUES) I swear on my life, I didn't know that she was coming.

VANCE: (QUIETLY ARGUES) And why should I believe that? After you specifically said that you were going to bring her here to do these sweeps.

CALEB: (QUIETLY ARGUES) It was just an idea. I didn't even get a chance to mention it to her! And you're one to talk, after you revealed confidential information to her.

VANCE: (QUIETLY ARGUES) What are you talking about?

CALEB: (QUIETLY ARGUES) Didn't she say that you're the one who told her where Ms. Graves lives after you lost?

VANCE: (QUIETLY ARGUES) Of course, I wouldn't do such a thing.

CALEB: (QUIETLY ARGUES) Then how did she know where I was? Why on earth did she come here last night?

VANCE: (QUIETLY ARGUES) I don't know! All I know is that I would never reveal such information to her, and I swear on my life on it! I may be a sore loser, but I would never do anything stupid like that! Why did you think I wanted to avoid a situation like this in the first place? You know how she gets when it comes to these house sweeps!

CALEB: (PAUSES IN CONSTERNATION) But if you didn't tell her, then how did she get the address?

TEGAN: (COMES OUT OF ELISA'S BEDROOM) You two better be glad that I came because you would've certainly gotten into trouble if you didn't find this.

Caleb and Vance turn to see Tegan holding a porcelain bowl containing razorblades and rubbing alcohol, as they both stand there nervously.

TEGAN: (TURNS TO ELISA) Mind explaining this to us, Ms. Graves?

ELISA: I realized that I had run out of some supplies, so I took the razorblades from a used razor I had. I was just about to clean them when you guys arrived.

TEGAN: (UNCONVINCED) Is that so? (LOOKS AT ELISA) To me, it doesn't look like you have an ounce of hair to shave off your body, but I'll leave it alone for now, since it's a common practice.

Tegan puts down the porcelain bowl and turns to see the velvet box on the table.

TEGAN: What about this box?

Elisa tenses up along with Caleb and Vance when Tegan picks up the velvet box to do a thorough examination.

TEGAN: (CURIOUS) Must be something special to be kept in a fancy box like this. I wonder what's inside.

ELISA: I'm afraid you can't open it.

Caleb and Vance turn to Elisa in shock, as Tegan gives her a look of suspicion.

TEGAN: (SUSPICIOUSLY) Now why is that? Is there something in this box that we shouldn't know about, Ms. Graves?

ELISA: (FIRMLY) I haven't had a chance to look at it myself, and I would like to keep it that way until this house arrest ends.

TEGAN: (SUSPICIOUSLY) Is that so? Well, why not just do it now? I'm certain there's no harm in everybody knowing what's inside this box.

ELISA: (FIRMLY) Officer, please. I don't want anyone else touching that box.

TEGAN: (CONDESCENDINGLY) It's just a simple task.

Caleb begins to lose his patience as he silently watches the situation between Elisa and Tegan.

TEGAN: (CONDESCENDINGLY) I'm not asking you to move a mountain; I'm just asking you to open this box for us … (SUSPICIOUSLY) unless you have something to hide.

VANCE: (STEPS IN) You're stepping out of line, Officer Drupal. She specifically told us not to –

TEGAN: (TURNS TO VANCE HARSHLY) Shut up! I wasn't asking you to talk! Especially when you two bozos fail to do your jobs correctly.

ELISA: (FIRMLY) Officer, please don't take it out on them.

TEGAN: (TURNS TO ELISA HARSHLY) Then open the damn box already! Because I'm getting sick and tired of all this stalling and waiting for someone just to do one simple task! (WAVES THE VELVET BOX AROUND) Should you do the honours, or shall I, because I don't mind.

CALEB: (SHOUTS) That's enough, Officer Drupal!

Tegan turns to Caleb in surprise as he comes over to take the velvet box away from her, while Elisa and Vance are themselves astonished.

CALEB: (STERNLY) We are doing our jobs properly, which includes giving respect to the detainee. Now, Ms. Graves specifically prohibited us from looking through this box without her permission.

Caleb walks away from Tegan as she stands there stunned while watching him hand the velvet box back to Elisa.

CALEB: (CALMLY) And since she has every right to do so, it's our job to respect that decision and leave this box alone.

Elisa hesitates for a moment before taking the velvet box from Caleb and holding it tightly to give herself reassurance.

TEGAN: (UPSET) This is ridiculous. You're jeopardizing this whole case just to protect some stupid box?

CALEB: (STERNLY) I'm not jeopardizing anything, I'm just –

Caleb stops himself as he hears a disturbance coming from outside, while Vance notices the sudden change.

VANCE: (CONCERNED) What's wrong?

Caleb rushes toward the window and looks outside to see a crowd gathering around the Tint Valley Residence while one of the citizens is screaming hysterically.

SCARED CITIZEN: (FROM OUTSIDE) Help! Somebody help, please! He's trying to kidnap my child!

Shots erupt from outside as Caleb, Vance and Tegan pull out their Taser Pistols and rush out of the apartment.

INT. THE 8TH FLOOR OF THE TINT VALLEY RESIDENCE – MORNING

TEGAN: (RUSHED) Life Band, call Emergency Squad.

LIFE BAND AI: Calling EMERGENCY SQUAD (RINGING) …

EMERGENCY SQUAD: (ON THE OTHER LINE) What's the emergency?

TEGAN: (RUSHED) I need backup to arrive at this location! Shots have been fired – repeat, shots have been fired! I need backup this instant!

Tegan, Caleb and Vance quickly leave the Tint Valley Residence and rush to the scene outside.

▌ INT. ELISA'S APARTMENT – MORNING

Frightened, Elisa remains behind until she rushes to the door but then stops as she remembers the ankle monitor. She remains frozen at the doorway until she hears the commotion going on outside and then she rushes to the window and watches the crowd scatter in fear. She watches Tegan come up to the citizen who was screaming earlier and tries to calm her down.

TEGAN: (FROM OUTSIDE) It's going to be okay –

SCARED CITIZEN: (FROM OUTSIDE) He tried to take my baby!

TEGAN: (FROM OUTSIDE) Don't worry, ma'am, reinforcements are on their way! Just stick with us. We have everything under control!

Hearing shots erupt again, Elisa ducks down and quivers in fear while she hears the crowd screaming from outside. She remains frozen in her position until she turns to see her TV acting up and the hologram of General Metallic appearing on the screen.

GENERAL METALLIC: (DISTORTED) Ah, the sound of people screaming. It's such a pleasant sound to me at least ... but don't worry ... your time will come soon to join them.

General Metallic's hologram disappears as the apartment starts to shut down and a red light starts blinking.

HOUSE AI: Warning. There has been a system override of this host's residence. Warning, there has been a system override of this host's residence.

Elisa remains frozen in fear as she sees people running across the hallway fearfully. Caleb rushes back inside and is shocked to see the apartment in its current state as the blinking red light continues.

CALEB: (LOOKS AROUND CONFUSED) What happened? Why's the place like this?

Caleb rushes to Elisa, where she remains in her trembling state.

CALEB: (CONCERNED) Hey. Talk to me – what happened?

ELISA: (UNSTEADY) He … he showed …

CALEB: (CONCERNED) Who showed? Someone showed up here? Did someone come here to attack you?

Elisa vigorously shakes her head and manages to point to the TV as Caleb looks at it in confusion.

CALEB: (TURNS BACK TO ELISA) Someone showed up on the TV; is that what happened? (GRABS ELISA'S SHOULDERS) Hey! Get a grip on yourself. (SERIOUSLY) There's nothing to be scared of! Not when I'm here, not when I'm right here to protect you.

Elisa vigorously shakes her head again, but freezes in shock as Caleb tightens his grip on her shoulders.

CALEB: (FIRMLY) Yes, I am! I'm not just here to protect the public. I'm also here to protect you! (CALMLY) You can count on me for that. You don't have to worry about a thing when I'm here. Just calm down and take a deep breath, okay?

Elisa nods as she manages to take deep breaths, though she continues to tremble and the apartment blinks a red light.

HOUSE AI: Warning. There has been a system override of this host's residence. Warning, there has been a system override of this host's residence.

CALEB: (CALMLY) That's it … just breathe, Ms. Graves. I'm right here. I promise nothing bad will happen to you.

Elisa nods again as she continues to take deep breaths. Caleb stays with her for the entire time to comfort her.

THIRTEEN

INT. THE STEELS PROTECTION SERVICES STATION – AFTERNOON

Malcolm views the surveillance footage of the Tint Valley Residence, along with Vance and sighs in agony while watching the incident over and over again.

MALCOLM: (SHAKES HIS HEAD) This is madness … (TURNS TO VANCE) Just when you think the situation couldn't get any worse, it just happens to get worse. And we were prepared to put this behind us.

VANCE: We did all that we could to control the situation before reinforcements arrived, but the suspect managed to escape during the chaos. (LOOKS DOWN) If only we had managed to catch him sooner –

MALCOLM: (REASSURINGLY) Don't beat yourself up. You should be proud of your work. You did the best you could to protect the people and that's all that matters. (TURNS TO HIS LIFE BAND) And to you, Officer McEntire, how are things on your end?

CALEB: (ON THE OTHER LINE) Everything has finally come back into order.

INT. ELISA'S APARTMENT – AFTERNOON

Elisa's apartment returns to its normal conditions as Caleb talks to Malcolm through his Life Band.

CALEB: Things have calmed down after the incident, and we were fortunate enough to report no deaths or injuries during the situation.

INT. THE STEELS PROTECTION SERVICES STATION – AFTERNOON

CALEB: (ON THE OTHER LINE) However, there is still speculation about a reoccurrence, as we fear that the suspect is still out there.

MALCOLM: Don't worry about the suspect. Just focus on the current task. We will take over from now on and make sure a situation like this doesn't happen again. What about the detainee? How is she doing with all of this?

INT. ELISA'S APARTMENT – AFTERNOON

Caleb turns to see Elisa reading *Never Let Me Go* on the couch and turns back to his Life Band.

CALEB: The detainee is doing okay at the moment. She's still a bit traumatized by the situation, but so far she hasn't had any injuries or committed any violations during her house arrest.

MALCOLM: (ON THE OTHER LINE) That's good to hear, as long as she's all right. It would crush me to know if anything had happened to her.

CALEB: I know … but I have a feeling that there has been another General Metallic incident, as he caused a system override to the apartment.

INT. THE STEELS PROTECTION SERVICES STATION – AFTERNOON

CALEB: (ON THE OTHER LINE) I'll ask around to see if any other residents experienced the same thing.

MALCOLM: You do that while we figure things out from our end – and come straight back to the station after you have finished your monitoring duties.

▌ INT. ELISA'S APARTMENT – AFTERNOON

CALEB: Understood.

MALCOLM: (ON THE OTHER LINE) And please keep an eye on Elisa. Don't be fooled by her reclusive exterior; she is very fragile, especially when it comes to these situations ... and I know I can count on you for that, as she needs to feel safe during this troubling time.

CALEB: I'll do that, sir.

MALCOLM: (ON THE OTHER LINE) Good, I know you will, with the hope that you will come to see that she's actually a good person. If Officer Drupal ever intervenes with this case again, make sure to tell her to come straight to me as she will receive a temporary suspension for her unauthorized actions. Regardless of whether they were Officer Webber's orders, you all would still have to answer to me. Is that understood?

CALEB: Understood, sir. I'll make sure she gets the message.

MALCOLM: (ON THE OTHER LINE) Now proceed with your duties, and I'll see you at the station soon.

CALEB: Will do, Deputy.

LIFE BAND AI: Call ended.

Exhausted, Caleb sighs and walks over to Elisa, where she continues to read *Never Let Me Go.*

CALEB: How are you feeling, Ms. Graves?

ELISA: (SARCASTICALLY) I'm feeling just fine, Officer. I mean, how else would I feel after seeing General Metallic show up on my TV?

CALEB: (SNICKERS) Seems like you're doing a lot better than you were earlier.

Caleb takes a seat at the table while he thinks about how he previously treated Elisa during her house arrest.

CALEB: I have a question to ask you.

ELISA: (CONTINUES READING) What would that be?

CALEB: The razorblades in the bowl. I saw them before and wanted to ask you about them. What were you planning to do with those?

ELISA: (LOOKS AT CALEB) You know I can't buy razors during house arrest, so I had to clean my old ones. I had no other choice but to go back to old habits.

CALEB: I see … are you sure there wasn't another reason?

ELISA: Even if I felt that way, I don't have the heart to kill myself or anyone in this building … and I wouldn't want to go through all that trouble in the first place. (GOES BACK TO READING) So, you don't have to worry, Officer. You won't have to jeopardize your job for me, as I'm planning to do nothing for the next few days.

CALEB: I'll definitely make sure that happens. (TURNS TO THE VELVET BOX) Also, how come you haven't opened this box yet?

ELISA: (BLUNTLY) I was hoping to do it under less serious circumstances.

Caleb lets out a snicker, while Elisa remains on edge.

ELISA: (ATTEMPTS TO REACH FOR THE VELVET BOX) Unless you want me to open it now to end my curiosity.

CALEB: (SHAKES HIS HEAD) No. I'll officially leave you alone with this box since it's so important to you, but I am starting to think that Deputy Reign was wrong about you being fragile.

Elisa tries her best not to smile as she continues to read *Never Let Me Go* while Caleb thinks about Tegan's unexpected visit.

CALEB: You know what happened this morning wasn't planned.

ELISA: (CONTINUES READING) It's nothing for you to beat yourself up over. None of us had any idea that General Metallic was going to show up again.

CALEB: Not the incident with General Metallic. I'm talking about Officer Drupal.

Elisa stops reading entirely and puts the book away to give Caleb her full attention.

CALEB: If I had known that she was planning to show up today, I would've prevented it from happening in the first place. I've already put you through enough crap, and I didn't want her to come here to make things worse for you – and she's known for doing that to pri – (STOPS HIMSELF AND BREATHES) ... people who are facing incarceration. She will look through people's houses and use anything that she finds to send someone to prison. I knew she was going to do that today and I didn't want her to do that to you because ... I knew you deserved better. There was even a point when I wanted her to get involved and I'm sorry for that.

ELISA: (PAUSES) Did you really mean what you said back there ... about protecting me?

CALEB: I took an oath to risk my life to protect the people in this country at all costs ... especially the people who are facing detention. So, when I say that I'm here to protect you ... you best believe that I meant every word I said.

ELISA: I appreciate that, Officer. (PAUSES) Do you think General Metallic had something to do with this incident?

CALEB: I can't discuss ongoing investigations with civilians ... but regardless of whether it is General Metallic's doing or someone else's, I'm confident that our team will prevent this threat from going any further. Right now, the main focus is to make sure everyone here is safe and secure.

ELISA: I believe you can ... what you guys did out there was incredibly brave. So, I trust that you have the ability to protect us, and I know that you will be able to figure this out sooner rather than later.

CALEB: Thank you, I ... (SLIGHTLY TAKEN ABACK) didn't think I needed to hear that after this situation happened. I'll make sure to take that with me when investigating this case.

Elisa gives Caleb a small smile and then they both turn, hearing a knock on the door.

CALEB: Did you make another order or something, Ms. Graves?

Caleb gets up, goes to open the door and is surprised to see a taxi driver standing there. Elisa is also surprised until she remembers that he had given her a ride a few days ago.

TAXI DRIVER: (NERVOUSLY) Hello, I'm looking for Ms. Graves.

CALEB: (TURNS TO ELISA STERNLY) I thought you said you weren't expecting any visitors!

TAXI DRIVER: (NERVOUSLY) No, I'm not here for a visit. I just came to see if I had gotten the right place. (GESTURES TO ELISA) I gave this young lady a ride the other day and she forgot to pay for her fare.

ELISA: (REMEMBERS) Oh!

Elisa puts her book away and rushes to the door, while Caleb remains on defense.

ELISA: I'm so sorry about that. Here you go.

The taxi driver allows Elisa to tap her Life Band monogram onto his to complete the transaction at a safe distance.

LIFE BAND AI: Transaction complete. You have successfully purchased a taxi fare.

TAXI DRIVER: (PLEASED) Thank you so much.

ELISA: You're so welcome. I'm very sorry about the other day.

TAXI DRIVER: (PLEASANTLY) It's all right ... Maybe, after you're done with your legal troubles, I could possibly do some favours for you.

CALEB: (TURNS TO THE TAXI DRIVER STERNLY) Leave now before I'm tempted to arrest you for sexual harassment.

The taxi driver's smile quickly fades and he scurries off. Caleb closes and locks the door before turning to Elisa.

CALEB: (STERNLY) Are there any other surprises I should know about, Ms. Graves?

ELISA: Believe me, I had no idea that he was going to show up. But I can guarantee that there won't be any more surprises.

CALEB: (STERNLY) Are you sure?

ELISA: I swear on my life it'll never happen again.

CALEB: (PAUSES AND NODS) Okay then … but I will hold this against you if it does.

ELISA: Did you really have to chase him away like that?

CALEB: Trust me. I did you a solid. Never accept favours from taxi drivers.

Caleb walks away from Elisa while she stands there, shocked and confused at the same time.

A Few Hours Later

▌ INT. ELISA'S APARTMENT – EVENING

Caleb lets out a yawn as he tries his best not to fall asleep where he sits. Turning, he sees Elisa sitting on the couch reading *Our Souls at Night* instead of the book she had been reading before.

CALEB: I see you switched to a new book.

Elisa gives Caleb a look as he immediately reads her energy.

CALEB: I also realized that we started on the wrong foot and wanted to break the ice for once.

Elisa remains silent as she goes back to reading *Our Souls at Night.*

CALEB: What are you reading this time?

ELISA: It's called Our Souls at Night. It's one of my favourite books in the world and the only thing that could put me in a good mood.

CALEB: (NODS) I see. (LOOKS AT ELISA) What chapter are you on?

ELISA: (LOOKS AT CALEB) Three … (PAUSES) Why do you ask?

Caleb gets up from where he is sitting and comes over to Elisa as she sits there, confused. He takes a seat on the edge of the couch and takes *Our Souls at Night* from Elisa and he looks at the page she is currently on.

CALEB: Where did you stop?

ELISA: (POINTS TO THE PARAGRAPH) Here.

Caleb reads silently to himself before stopping at the paragraph where Elisa has pointed out to him. He begins to read *Our Souls at Night* aloud while she sits there, astonished by what is going on. Elisa sits mesmerized by Caleb reading aloud until he finishes reading the chapter, marks the page and gives *Our Souls at Night* back to her, as she remains astonished by what has just happened.

CALEB: That should be able to keep me awake for a while.

ELISA: I didn't expect you to be into romance.

CALEB: I'm not. It was a book that was in the station's Lost 'n Found. I just simply wanted to catch up.

Elisa pouts slightly as Caleb gets up from the edge of the couch.

CALEB: Plus, you're the most boring detainee I've ever had to monitor. I needed to do something to stay awake.

ELISA: You are welcome to read some of my books, if you like.

CALEB: (TURNS TO ELISA) And I'll still continue to decline …

Caleb notices the Steels dog tag necklace that Elisa is wearing as he gradually begins to relax.

CALEB: I didn't see you wearing that necklace before. I've would've been able to recognize a former Steels officer. It's a shame that I didn't get to know that sooner.

ELISA: It's not mine; it's my dad's. (HOLDS ONTO THE DOG TAG NECKLACE) Mr. Garreth Graves – thirteen years of being a Steels officer, yet he never took the role of a deputy. He would rather be out there fighting crime than stuck in an office telling people what to do.

CALEB: I see … I guess that's why Malcolm can't stay in his office for the entire day either. But it's funny that I'm hearing about this now. How come he wasn't involved in this case or even came here for a visit?

ELISA: (SOLEMNLY) He can't. He died five years ago.

CALEB: (PAUSES IN SHOCK AND BECOMES SOLEMN) My condolences, Ms. Graves. I didn't know –

ELISA: (SOLEMNLY) It's okay; you wouldn't have known … it's been a while since I've talked about my dad to anyone.

CALEB: I hope you don't mind me asking, but how did he … ?

ELISA: (SOLEMNLY) He was killed in action … during a night patrol. My mom and I heard shots outside that night and saw him …

Elisa stops herself and tries not to remember Garreth's death. Caleb pulls out a handkerchief from his pocket and gives it to her and she uses it to wipe away the tears that manage to escape.

CALEB: It's okay to feel sad … it's never a good feeling when we lose someone, but it's worse to hold it in. I'm very sorry to hear that, Ms. Graves.

ELISA: Thank you, Officer. This was actually one of his favourite books. Although he was never much of one for best sellers, he was willing to give this book a chance. Reading this book allows me to remember him and all the good memories I have of him … as if he is still here with me. This was the last thing that he gave me before he passed away … he wanted me to keep it for him, along with a promise that became quite difficult to keep over the years. He said we would meet each other again, but … I guess I'll have to wait to see what he actually meant by that.

CALEB: It's a shame I didn't get to know him. He seems like a great guy.

ELISA: He was a great guy … the best teacher, the best parent and the best Steels officer. Malcolm could tell you all about that. He was definitely the best father I ever could have had … I doubt that I would even be here if it weren't for him.

Elisa thinks about Garreth being alive during her current situation until Caleb's Timer starts beeping. He immediately turns it off.

CALEB: Looks like it's my time to go. I'll figure things out on my end so that we can prevent any system overrides from happening again. I'll make sure to have more officers patrolling the area in the meantime … (BEGINS TO LEAVE) But for now, you should be safe while I'm gone. You just need to let us know right away if anything happens.

ELISA: (NODS) Okay then … (TURNS TO CALEB) Thank you for reading today, Officer McEntire. I really enjoyed it.

CALEB: (STOPS AND TURNS TO ELISA) You're welcome … see you tomorrow, Ms. Graves.

Caleb immediately leaves the apartment as Elisa stands there, slightly bemused before locking the door. Thinking about Caleb reading to her, she smiles to herself until she notices her cheeks getting hot and begins to worry about herself.

The Next Day

▍ INT. ELISA'S APARTMENT – MORNING

Elisa decides to linger and watch Caleb and Vance do the house sweep instead of reading a book on the couch. She watches the pair switch places as Vance looks through the bathroom and bedroom, while Caleb looks through the living room and kitchen. Elisa remains still until she silently goes to the kitchen and catches him looking through the fridge again, as she remembers what she saw yesterday.

ELISA: Find anything interesting, Officer McEntire?

Caleb slams his head on one of the shelves of the fridge and looks up quickly to see Elisa standing in the doorway while he tries to maintain his composure.

CALEB: I'm just doing my –

ELISA: (SMILES) It's okay; I won't tell anyone.

Looking slightly agitated, Caleb wonders what Elisa saw yesterday as Vance finishes looking through the bathroom and bedroom.

VANCE: (LOUDLY) Okay! All clear from my end! (TURNS TO CALEB) Is it the same for you, Officer?

CALEB: (NODS) Yeah. (GOES UP TO VANCE) Everything is clear on my end.

VANCE: Good. Now that's done, I'll be taking over the monitoring duties while you leave –

CALEB: (STUNNED) Excuse me?

VANCE: (FIRMLY) You heard me! After what happened yesterday, I can no longer trust you with monitoring duties anymore.

CALEB: (STERNLY) I already told you what happened yesterday wasn't my idea.

VANCE: (ARGUES) But you thought about it after just two days of monitoring Ms. Graves! You didn't even obey your usual one-week rule of siccing Tegan on detainees – and that was way out of line on your part.

CALEB: (ARGUES) But how was that my fault when I didn't give her the address?

VANCE: (ARGUES) I don't know how she got the address. All I know is that you're not monitoring anymore!

CALEB: (STERNLY) Leave!

VANCE: (ARGUES) You leave! Why do you always have to be so stubborn!

CALEB: (ARGUES) You're the one who's being stubborn!

Caleb and Vance continue to argue as Elisa watches quietly and wonders what to do. Finally, she quickly comes in between them to stop the argument.

ELISA: Guys, please stop arguing.

Caleb and Vance stop arguing but stare at each other intensely, with Elisa standing between them.

ELISA: (TURNS TO VANCE) Officer Stanford, it's okay. There's no need to make any changes. I'm okay with Officer McEntire monitoring me.

VANCE: (ARGUES) You don't understand, Ms. Graves. I'm doing this for your own good.

ELISA: (KINDLY) I understand that, and I appreciate your concern, Officer … but I would rather stick with the original arrangements. I'll be okay, Officer Stanford. You have nothing to worry about.

Vance looks at Elisa in shock and turns to Caleb for an explanation. He, however, stands with a calm expression on his face.

CALEB: You heard her. (GESTURES TO THE DOOR) Time to go.

Momentarily at a loss for words, Vance stands there until he starts wagging his finger angrily at Caleb. He, however, simply shrugs and remains impassive.

VANCE: (UPSET) Wait till you get back to the station. (BEGINS TO LEAVE) Just you wait, Caleb – we'll sort this out when you get back.

Upset, Vance leaves the apartment and shuts the door behind him while Caleb and Elisa turn to each other and simply laugh.

CALEB: I thought he was never going to leave. But why would you do that?

ELISA: (CONFUSED) What do you mean?

CALEB: You have every right to change the officer who gets to monitor you. Why did you decide to keep things the same?

ELISA: I figured that we had managed to work out our differences, so there wasn't a need to make any changes.

As Elisa goes to lock the door, Caleb waits, thinking about how their association with each other has changed throughout the house arrest.

ELISA: (TURNS TO CALEB) I also reread the terms and conditions, and it doesn't say anything about officers not accepting things from detainees. Are you sure there isn't anything I can get for you?

Caleb stands there, taken slightly aback, as Elisa patiently waits for him to answer.

FOURTEEN

▌ INT. ELISA'S APARTMENT – MORNING

Caleb sits at the dining table as Elisa brings him a plate of scrambled eggs and potato hash, along with some leftover baked ziti she made the night before. He takes a chance to taste everything on the plate as Elisa waits for his reaction.

ELISA: How do you like everything, Officer?

CALEB: (FINISHES CHEWING) It's good … it's far better than the food at the Fire House. I can tell you that.

Elisa smiles gleefully as Caleb continues to eat his breakfast.

CALEB: (WITH HIS MOUTH FULL) But that doesn't change a thing between us. Just because I allowed you to feed me doesn't mean I won't hesitate to arrest you if you do anything outside this house arrest.

ELISA: (SMILES) I'm aware of that, Officer. I'm just glad that you like the food.

CALEB: (WITH HIS MOUTH FULL) I do. Thank you for this.

Caleb continues eating until he stops and swallows his last mouthful, as he remembers what he brought with him today.

CALEB: I'm glad Officer Stanford is not here because this is the one thing I didn't want him to see me do, but since you're in such a giving mood.

Caleb gets up and heads to the door as Elisa stands there, confused.

ELISA: (CONFUSED) Where are you going?

CALEB: (TURNS TO ELISA) Just wait here. I'll be right back.

Elisa obeys as she watches Caleb step out of the apartment and waits patiently until he comes back carrying a big box of books.

ELISA: (SHOCKED) What's all this?

CALEB: Turns out you were right about those Hues. A few officers had just finished a stakeout mission last night and managed to solve a case that involved years of book scamming from customers. There's a lot more where these came from, but unfortunately, they became ash before we could ever get a chance to salvage them. Obviously, some arrests were made – meaning that lime-green friend of yours is going to have some company soon, but they brought back these books to the station last night and I thought I would bring them here since you have a love of books. (PUTS THE BOX AWAY AND TURNS TO ELISA) You can check them out if you like.

Elisa stands there astonished as she comes up to the box of books and looks through each book inside. Caleb tries his best not to smile too much, as he sees the excitement in Elisa's eyes while she looks through every book in the box and notices the red tags on most of them and the green tags on the rest.

CALEB: The ones with the red tags are specifically yours. I checked them myself and saw that some of them were not just purchased by you but also by your father ... I hope you don't mind that I brought them back to you.

ELISA: (EXCITEDLY) Are you kidding me? Of course, I don't mind! (STOPS AND GASPS IN EXCITEMENT) Oh, my goodness! I've always wanted to read this!

Elisa picks up *Northern Lights* from the box of books and jumps for joy. Caleb enjoys watching her until she comes over and hugs him.

CALEB: (SLIGHTLY TAKEN ABACK) O–okay. I was not expecting that. (SLIGHTLY AGITATED) Ms. Graves, please let go ... (STERNLY) Let go before I decide to put handcuffs on you.

Elisa quickly releases Caleb from her hug as he straightens out his uniform and huffs in relief.

CALEB: (FIRMLY) It was nothing, all right? I just brought over a couple of books for you to look at. There's nothing for you to be gushing over.

ELISA: (SUBMISSIVELY) I'm sorry. (SMILES) I just got really excited when I saw these books. I thought I would never see them again. Thank you, Officer.

CALEB: (CALMLY) You're welcome, Ms. Graves. Now, you stay over there while I go finish my breakfast.

Caleb sits back down at the dining table to eat his breakfast, while Elisa begins taking out the books with the red tags on them. She has already started sorting them in alphabetical order (by author, not by title), then she stops and sneaks up behind Caleb and gives him another hug.

CALEB: (UPSET) Almighty – would you stop with the hugging already! Can't you see that I'm trying to eat here? I have already said you're welcome to you!

ELISA: (RELEASES CALEB) I know. I just wanted to thank you again, Officer McEntire.

CALEB: (CURT) You're welcome again, now shoo. Let me eat in peace.

Elisa respectfully backs away from Caleb as he continues to eat his breakfast.

CALEB: (CALMLY) And don't be afraid to call me Caleb. Sometimes, the formality becomes annoying.

ELISA: (TURNS TO CALEB) I wouldn't do that if I were you.

CALEB: (TURNS TO ELISA) Why do you say that?

ELISA: Well, if you give me permission to call you by your first name, that sort of gives me the idea that you trust me. (LOOKS AT CALEB) Are you beginning to trust me, Officer McEntire?

Caleb stops eating and takes a moment to determine the answer to Elisa's question as he slowly turns to the half-eaten food on his plate.

CALEB: (SLIGHTLY SERIOUSLY) Is there something in this food that I should know about, Ms. Graves?

Elisa goes up to Caleb and takes the fork from him to take some of the scrambled eggs, potato hash and baked ziti and eats it herself. She swallows everything that she chewed and simply shrugs.

ELISA: You tell me.

Elisa walks away from Caleb as he sits there, subtly astonished by her and himself, until he realizes that his fork is missing.

CALEB: I want my fork back, Ms. Graves.

Elisa gives Caleb back his fork and he returns to eating his breakfast.

INT. THE RH-C DEPARTMENT OFFICE OF REGIONAL HEADQUARTERS – MORNING

Mr. Popkin walks around the office to check on the IT staff who are fixing the computers that were affected by General Metallic's broadcast yesterday.

MR. POPKIN: (RUSHED) All right, gentlemen, you have only a few minutes left until the morning shift starts! I have employees who need their systems to be fixed pronto – and I need you all to solve this at once!

DANIEL: (COMES UP TO MR. POPKIN) Mr. Popkin.

MR. POPKIN: (RUSHED) Not now, Daniel! I'm trying to make sure these systems are up and running before the shift starts. (NOTICES HANK) And Hank! Where is everyone? How come you're the only one here?

HANK: (TURNS TO MR. POPKIN) I'm not sure, Mr. Popkin. There is a possibility that they are all lining up for coffee, but I guess they're afraid to come up here because of yesterday's incident with General Metallic. But don't worry, sir. I'll do my best to bring everyone here as soon as possible.

MR. POPKIN: (NODS) Yes. You do that while we try to figure things out up here.

Hank nods and makes his way out of the office, while Mr. Popkin huffs in frustration as he looks around to see that the IT staff are still fixing the computers.

MR. POPKIN: (GROWLS) Great, just what I need. Not only has that buffoon messed with these machines, but he has also managed to scare off my entire staff – just fucking great!

DANIEL: You do realize that we have another problem on our hands. Not only can this second occurrence no longer be considered a prank, but we have also experienced a decrease in efficiency.

Daniel shows Mr. Popkin the operations report. He is shocked to see how much efficiency has decreased since last week.

DANIEL: Have you thought about talking to the department supervisors about any possible transfers?

MR. POPKIN: (TURNS TO DANIEL) Of course not. I had hoped that I would never have to speak to them again after the Entertainment Hall gathering that night. But this is impossible. We couldn't possibly be experiencing such low numbers, because we're only missing two people! And this isn't any of our doing – one just decided not to come back to work and the other decided to get herself arrested for no good reason. How is that any of our fault?

DANIEL: You have to understand that when those two were around, they managed to increase our efficiency by up to 70%, and without them, our efficiency is not even close to the rates of the other departments.

MR. POPKIN: (SCOFFS) Please, it isn't as bad as you think – the others just need to work harder, that's all.

DANIEL: (ARGUES) They have been working hard, and they haven't come close to the average rate! You have no other choice but to take this seriously. A 40% drop in efficiency is not as good as a 40% Tint Level.

MR. POPKIN: (IMPATIENT) All right, all right! You made your point. Just talk to the department supervisors, so we can get this situation solved.

DANIEL: That's another thing, sir. I was hoping to talk to you about this next matter privately, as I wish to take a leave of absence from now on.

Mr. Popkin turns to Daniel in shock as he mentally prepares for the worst.

MR. POPKIN: (DISAPPOINTED) Oh no ... not you too. Honest to Almighty – (UPSET) I'm getting sick and tired of people not being here when they are supposed to be! We have every person in this building trying to do the same thing because of this General Metallic person. Why should you be granted a leave of absence out of the rest of us?

DANIEL: To be honest, sir, my head hasn't been in the right place for the past few days – especially how I reacted to one of the employees the other day. I just want to take some time to clear my head for a while until I'm ready to come back.

MR. POPKIN: (BEGS) Daniel, please, you can't leave now. Not when everybody else is all stressed out! You're the only person they turn to during these troubling times.

DANIEL: I understand that, sir and I will continue to be that person if I'm given this break. Please, Mr. Popkin – I promise that I won't even take that long.

MR. POPKIN: I'm sorry, Daniel ... I can't let you take a leave of absence – not now – not when you're greatly needed here.

DANIEL: (SERIOUSLY) If you deny my request, I have no choice other than to bring this to the Head Council.

MR. POPKIN: Well, if you do that, I'll give the Head Council every reason to stand by my decision. (SERIOUSLY) Trust me, the last thing you want is to start a war with me, especially when I have everything I need to put an end to your career.

Outraged, Daniel looks at Mr. Popkin but continues to hold his ground.

MR. POPKIN: (SERIOUSLY) Now please talk to the supervisors about the employee transfers and forget that we ever had this conversation. (WALKS AWAY AND TURNS TO THE IT STAFF) And hurry up with those fucking computers! Time is not on your side!

The IT staff try their best to fix the monitors as quickly as possible, while Daniel stands there frustrated with everyone, including himself.

DANIEL: (QUIETLY ANGRY) Where are those damn two when you need them?

Several Hours Later

▎ INT. ELISA'S APARTMENT – EVENING

Elisa and Caleb spend the entire day sitting on the floor reading the books that were inside the box as well as those inside the chest. When Elisa finishes reading *Northern Light* and Caleb finishes reading *The Institute*, each puts their books in their own separate finished piles. Caleb moves to start another book until he stops and sees Elisa's finished pile as she begins to read *Northanger Abbey*.

CALEB: For crying out loud, woman. Are you planning to take a break anytime soon?

Elisa lets out a brief laugh and puts down *Northanger Abbey*. Caleb, however, stares at her finished pile with round eyes.

CALEB: How were you able to finish those books that fast? (LOOKS AT HIS FINISHED PILE) My pile doesn't even compare to yours.

ELISA: (THINKS) I guess because it was the only thing I ever enjoyed when I was younger. Once I was done with one story, I simply wanted another one (LOOKS AT HER FINISHED PILE), which could explain the large pile of books. Plus, my job requires me to read things quickly so that I can move on to the next assignment.

CALEB: I don't understand how you survive working at that place. I think I would instantly have Tint Brain if I were given an office job.

Elisa lets out a laugh along with Caleb as he starts thinking about *Our Souls at Night* and wonders why the book is not on Elisa's finished pile.

CALEB: (CONFUSED) But here's what I don't understand. Why waste no time whizzing through all of those books (POINTS TO THE BOOK) and not even attempting to finish that one in a day?

ELISA: That's because I want to take my time finishing that book. Knowing that I'm going to be stuck here for a while, I decided to read one chapter every day, as this book brings me peace of mind and helps me obey the rules of this house arrest.

CALEB: Well, do you mind starting that now before it's time for me to go? I want to know what's so interesting about two old people falling in love.

ELISA: Well, let me enlighten you, Officer McEntire.

Elisa picks up *Our Souls at Night*, finds the page that Caleb marked for her last night and prepares to read aloud. Caleb sits there wondering about the writing of the book but pays attention to Elisa's voice instead as he simply stares at her and watches her read aloud. Elisa continues reading until she gets startled when she hears Caleb's Timer beeping. He immediately turns it off but remains seated.

ELISA: I guess you have to go then.

CALEB: (SHAKES HIS HEAD) Don't worry about it; just keep going.

Elisa nods as she turns the page and starts reading again until they both hear a Notification Alert go off.

LIFE BAND AI: Notification Alert! It has been detected that you are five minutes over your standard monitoring time. An automated request has been set to notify a Steels colleague to enter the premises in case of an emergency –

CALEB: (PRESSES THE MONOGRAM) Dismiss automated request.

LIFE BAND AI: Automated request dismissed.

ELISA: (CONCERNED) I really think you should start going.

CALEB: (SHAKES HIS HEAD) Ignore that and keep going. It's only about four pages, right? You don't have to worry about me; just continue reading.

Elisa nods as she finishes reading the chapter before marking the page for herself and closing the book. She puts away *Our Souls at Night*, while Caleb immediately snaps back into focus.

CALEB: See? I told you that you had nothing to worry about, and after listening to a whole chapter, I still don't get the interest.

ELISA: (GIGGLES) Maybe you will once we get to the middle of the book.

CALEB: (SLIGHTLY UNCONVINCED) Yeah, let's see how long I even stay interested in this book.

Elisa laughs for a moment as she looks around. Seeing all the books that are scattered everywhere, she thinks about Garreth.

ELISA: You know, my dad actually bought these books for the both of us to read together. He actually spent years trying to get that case solved ... (SOLEMNLY) too bad these books were found after he passed away.

CALEB: (CONCERNED) Have you ever thought of figuring out who was responsible for your father's death?

ELISA: (SHAKES HER HEAD) I don't think I'm ready to open old wounds ... plus I know my mother wouldn't like it if I did either. She would rather stick with the closure she got five years ago than go digging for answers.

CALEB: I see. It's the first time I ever heard you speak about your mother. Why is that?

ELISA: My mother and I aren't on the best terms ... (THINKS ABOUT CARMAN) We haven't spoken to each other since I moved here. I'm surprised she hasn't even called me – I thought she would at least say something about me getting arrested ... or anything outside of myself.

CALEB: Have you ever thought of calling her? You have permission to do that.

ELISA: I've tried calling her before ... she never answers, and something tells me if I call her now, I'm going to face bigger rejection than what I've been receiving for the past five years. (SIGHS) But it is what it is ... maybe it's best not to call her at this time.

CALEB: I think you should try contacting her again. Regardless of your situation, she's the only parent you have. You should consider reaching out to her.

ELISA: (PAUSES) We'll see once I'm brave enough to try again.

Caleb feels slightly satisfied with Elisa's answer. Then, they both hear an aggressive knock on the door.

ELISA: That knock sounds like one of your colleagues is here.

CALEB: (UNINTERESTED) Well, whoever it is will have to wait. I'm not in a rush to leave this instant and they can radio me anytime if I'm needed back in the station.

ELISA: Don't take it that far. I wouldn't want you to get into trouble with Officer Drupal – not to mention Officer Webber.

CALEB: (CERTAIN) I've handled them both in one room at the same time. I'm certain I can handle either one of them if they have decided to come here.

ELISA: If you say so, just so long as you go back to the station. (THINKS ABOUT TEGAN) For a moment when Officer Drupal came here, I thought she was your girlfriend.

CALEB: (SHAKES HIS HEAD) Officer Drupal is not my girlfriend; she's my partner. We knew each other for five years before we started working together.

ELISA: I thought Officer Stanford was your partner.

CALEB: Officer Stanford is my mentoree. He works under me until he reaches his five-year mark, at which time he'll have to find his own partner. (CURIOUS) But why would you immediately think that she's my girlfriend, without even asking?

ELISA: How often does Officer Drupal show up to people's houses after your monitoring hours?

Caleb goes silent and nods as he thinks about Tegan's numerous visits.

ELISA: And isn't that what a normal person would think after coming across a person they don't know?

CALEB: I see what you mean, but I can guarantee you that there's nothing going on between me and Officer Drupal.

Elisa is startled to hear another aggressive knock on the door. Caleb starts to become irritated.

CALEB: (STERNLY) I can also guarantee that something will happen between me and the person behind that door if they don't find their patience.

Caleb gets up and goes to answer the door and he and Elisa see Tegan standing there wearing a protective vest.

CALEB: Well, if it isn't the person I expected from the first knock. We were just talking about you earlier. But I have to ask, isn't the vest a bit too much?

TEGAN: (UPSET) Are you absolutely kidding me? I mean hello – you are fifteen minutes over your staying period, and you expect me not to be worried about this! C'mon, I literally had to fight someone to get this on because I thought something had happened to you – but now that I come here (GESTURES TO ELISA'S APARTMENT), I see that you were just wasting time having a book party?

Elisa looks around at all the books scattered on the floor but remains silent as Tegan and Caleb continue to argue.

CALEB: (ADJUSTS TEGAN'S PROTECTIVE VEST) That's probably why your vest is on so crooked. But you know, if anything happened to me, I would've just called you right away. I wouldn't have you wait for hours just to let you know that something is going on.

TEGAN: (UPSET) Well, this better not happen again (TURNS TO ELISA), or penalties will be placed for keeping an officer after their monitoring hours.

CALEB: (TURNS TO ELISA) You don't have to worry about that. Those penalties are usually for the officers rather than the detainees and are usually a fine rather than an actual punishment. (TURNS TO TEGAN) I'm just about done here anyway, so let me pack up and I'll meet you outside.

TEGAN: (SERIOUSLY) We don't have time for that, Caleb. We are needed back at the station right now.

CALEB: (CONFUSED) What do you mean?

TEGAN: (SERIOUSLY) Deputy Reign said that he's found something that was related to yesterday's incident. He thinks this could lead us to General Metallic.

Caleb looks at Tegan in shock, while Elisa stands up in shock as well.

TEGAN: (UPSET) Yeah! So, say your little goodbyes already and let's go so we can figure this out. (TUGS ON CALEB'S ARM) C'mon.

CALEB: (YANKS HIS ARM BACK) All right, I'm coming. You don't have to be like this.

ELISA: (GOES UP TO CALEB) I'm willing to take the books back to the station if you want me to.

CALEB: (TURNS TO ELISA) It's okay, Ms. Graves. As appreciated as that is, you must remember that you're not allowed to step out of this building.

ELISA: (LOOKS AT HER ANKLE MONITOR AND REMEMBERS) Oh … I completely forgot about that. I'm sorry.

CALEB: It's okay, Ms. Graves. We tend to forget sometimes. You don't have to worry about the books; I'll bring them back to the station tomorrow.

Elisa nods in understanding as Tegan continues to lose her patience.

TEGAN: (UPSET) C'mon, we have to go.

CALEB: (BEGINS TO LEAVE) I'm stepping out of the apartment as we speak. Are you happy now?

Tegan huffs impatiently and walks away from Caleb. He gives Elisa an apologetic look and exits the apartment while she stands at the door.

ELISA: Tell Officer Drupal that I said good night.

CALEB: (CHUCKLES) I'll make sure she gets the message.

ELISA: You have a nice night as well, Officer McEntire.

CALEB: You too. (WAVES GOODBYE) Bye.

Elisa waves goodbye to Caleb and watches him leave as she closes and locks the door. She stands there for a moment, thinks about the day she had with him and then turns to the books that are scattered all over the floor. She begins sorting the books that have the red tags and the green tags, as well as the ones that came from the chest. She continues to organize the books on the floor until she comes across Caleb's finished pile and sees that he read five books. She goes through his pile and sees that he read *The Institute*, *Treasure Island*, *Milk and Honey*, *Gulliver's Travels* and *Gone Girl*. She picks up *The Institute* and thinks about reading it for the night. However, she feels her cheeks get hot again and wonders if she is starting to have feelings for him.

FIFTEEN

A Few Days Later

▌ INT. REGIONAL HEADQUARTERS COURTYARD – MORNING

Everyone takes their time to scan their Life Band through the entrance portals and head straight to the courtyard to meet up with friends and colleagues as they go about their business.

FEMALE EMPLOYEE 2: (COMPLAINS) This has got to be the worst week ever! Honestly, I just want things to go back to normal. I have never seen this place as hectic as it is today.

FEMALE EMPLOYEE 1: C'mon, it's not as bad as you think. Are you just saying that because of the General Metallic situation?

FEMALE EMPLOYEE 2: (COMPLAINS) No! I could care less about what that dude does! I'm talking about these missing employees; it's like every day someone has decided not to show up to work.

MALE EMPLOYEE 1: But hearing that a large number of people are not showing up to work does sound quite jarring. I believe this place has a bigger issue on their hands.

FEMALE EMPLOYEE 2: (COMPLAINS) Not as big as having us work overtime every single day. Plus, these transfers are getting out of hand! Listen, I had this chick who was the all-time star in our department

– smart girl who can do just about anything! Then, one day, they asked if she wanted to be transferred to a different department. She said yes and they moved her right away and did not even hesitate. Plus, our supervisor is quite the pervert, so she second thoughts about the move, either. The next day, she tells me about her new working space and how she enjoys being there and she hopes that she could earn a few brownie points from her new supervisor so that she could stay there longer. But just as soon as she got comfortable for about a week – they asked her to go back to her previous department. Can you believe that? What's the point of transferring these employees if you're not going to keep them for long?

The employees continue to talk until they notice a commotion going on near the entrance portals. Many employees turn in shock to see Elisa scanning her Life Band through the entrance portals and making her way to the RH-C Department Office.

FEMALE EMPLOYEE 1: (SHOCKED) What in the world?

MALE EMPLOYEE 1: (SHOCKED) If I have to be honest, I didn't expect to see her again.

FEMALE EMPLOYEE 2: (SHOCKED) But what is she doing here? I thought she was supposed to be in jail!

MALE EMPLOYEE 1: (SHOCKED) I guess she was given a lighter sentence and was allowed to come back.

FEMALE EMPLOYEE 1: (NOTICES ELISA'S ANKLE MONITOR) But she has an ankle monitor on, so I don't think she's off the hook yet.

Many employees take the chance to stare at Elisa's ankle monitor as she walks past them all.

FEMALE EMPLOYEE 2: (CONFUSED) This is ridiculous. What is she even doing here? Didn't she just beat up a person for no reason?

FEMALE EMPLOYEE 1: (TURNS TO FEMALE EMPLOYEE 2) We don't know that for sure; plus, we weren't there to know what actually happened.

FEMALE EMPLOYEE 2: (CERTAIN) It doesn't matter! A wrong is a wrong, and it should never go unpunished! (LOUDLY AT ELISA) You have a lot of nerve coming here! Shouldn't you be spending some time in prison?

Elisa continues walking without reacting to anyone's remarks about her.

MALE EMPLOYEE 1: (SMIRKS) Looks like she doesn't care what you have to say. From what I see, she looks like she's on a mission and isn't going to allow anyone to stop her.

The female employee scoffs in disbelief as she and her co-workers watch Elisa continue to make her way to the RH-C Department Office.

▌ INT. THE CORRIDOR OUTSIDE THE RH-C DEPARTMENT OFFICE OF REGIONAL HEADQUARTERS – MORNING

Daniel slowly paces back and forth near the entrance of the office, as everyone inside gets prepared for work. He continues to pace back and forth until he stops and sees Elisa exit from the elevator and make her way to the office.

DANIEL: (COMES UP TO ELISA) You're here.

ELISA: (STOPS MIDWAY) Yes, I am. Did I take too long to arrive?

DANIEL: (SHAKES HIS HEAD) No, that's just me wanting to make sure things are running smoothly – especially your arrival. Did you have any trouble getting in?

ELISA: (SHAKES HER HEAD) No, I managed to get in okay without any complications. Plus, having people staring at you for hours is nothing new in this building. It's good to see you again, Mr. Morin.

DANIEL: (HONESTLY) It's good to see you too, Ms. Graves ... to be honest, it was tough not having you around – especially when this office needed an extra hand with paperwork and corporate meetings.

ELISA: (NODS IN AGREEMENT) I can only imagine. I am truly sorry for what happened –

DANIEL: (HONESTLY) It's okay. You don't have to apologize. What happened is clearly none of my business, but Mr. Popkin would like to see you in his office before the shift begins.

Elisa nods in understanding and she and Daniel head inside the office.

▌ INT. MR. POPKIN'S OFFICE – MORNING

MR. POPKIN: (ON HIS WIRELESS EARPIECE) For the last time, we are no longer taking on any new transfers – as much as we enjoyed the extra help, there is no way that our office has the capacity to accept any more employees! Unless you have men who can build a dozen cubicles in five seconds … then there's no point in having this conversation!

Daniel lets himself and Elisa in the office. They both watch Mr. Popkin speak to one of the department supervisors through his Wireless Earpiece.

DANIEL: Mr. Popkin –

MR. POPKIN: (NOTICES DANIEL) Oh good, you're here. I was beginning to wonder when you would show up (NOTICES ELISA), and I see that you were able to complete your mission. Looks like I don't have to deduct your salary, after all.

Daniel attempts to say something, but Mr. Popkin holds his finger up as he tries to listen to the department supervisor through his Wireless Earpiece.

MR. POPKIN: (ON HIS WIRELESS EARPIECE) No, I wasn't talking to you! Even if I had the utmost desire to do that to yours, I highly doubt that the Head Council would give me that kind of power. (WAITS TO RESPOND) Well, good for you. Now, hang up the damn phone already! I need to make sure that my staff are ready –

Daniel and Elisa look at each other with concern, as they continue to watch Mr. Popkin argue with the department supervisor through his Wireless Earpiece.

MR. POPKIN: (ON HIS WIRELESS EARPIECE) Then find someone else to talk to. Life Band, end this call right now!

LIFE BAND AI: Call ended.

MR. POPKIN: (SIGHS) Remind me to never collaborate with those idiots again. They are seriously getting on the last of my nerves. (TURNS TO ELISA) Employee #263! You have some nerve being absent these past few days.

ELISA: (SUBMISSIVELY) Believe me, sir, it wasn't intentional.

MR. POPKIN: I figured that, since you don't seem like the violent type. However, you can spare me the details since the Steels Services has already notified me about everything. The only reason you were allowed back so early was because of your good behavior. But don't abuse this opportunity; if you did, you would again be the responsibility of the Steels officers' and facing further charges.

ELISA: (SUBMISSIVELY) Understood, sir.

MR. POPKIN: Now, I would allow you to go to work, but first, I have to make sure that you are aware of the restrictions in this office.

ELISA: (CONFUSED) What other restrictions?

A Few Minutes Later

INT. THE RH-C DEPARTMENT OFFICE OF REGIONAL HEADQUARTERS – MORNING

Mr. Popkin stands in front of the office with Daniel and Elisa, as the entire staff surrounds them at a safe distance.

MR. POPKIN: Pay attention, everyone, because this is important information that you all need to put into your heads. And since this is the first time this has ever happened, it is important to take this moment as an example of what will happen to you if you get involved with Steels Services. Not only will you be following restrictions by Steels Services, but you will also be following restrictions that have been set by this office. Whenever an employee has committed a criminal offence and is allowed to return to work in this building, he or she gets tagged.

Mr. Popkin pulls out his TagIt! Machine, as everyone stands there nervously, along with Daniel. He staples a red tag on Elisa's Life Band. She flinches at the sound of the device and looks at the red tag on her Life Band.

MR. POPKIN: The employee is required to wear this tag as an indication to others that he or she is under the watchful eye of the Steels Service. If this tag were to ever be removed without our permission, then they will go back to being the Steels' concern and will no longer be permitted to work here for the rest of their life – and trust me, I will know, as I have the only device that will be able to safely remove the tag. Until he or she is no longer part of the Steels' interest, this also allows everyone to keep an eye on this employee – especially if an incident were to occur. If the tagged employee is caught doing something outside of their restrictions, it is your responsibility to report it to either me, the Head Council or the Steels Services themselves so that the employee will go back to facing incarceration. However, if you have provoked a tagged employee to cause the incident, then you will be facing the consequences and possibly lose your job while the tagged employee continues to work his or her hours. This is a serious matter, everyone, meaning I want no funny business happening in this office. You may not have fully paid attention to what I said because you think this matter doesn't concern you, but believe me, you will find out immediately if you ever try anything silly during this situation ... and every single one of you knows that I will not hesitate to let go of anyone if they ever decide to cause foolishness in my office. Is that understood?

EVERYONE: (IN UNISON) Yes, sir!

MR. POPKIN: Good. Now clear the way so that the young lady can get to her cubicle.

Everyone clears the way for Elisa to go to her cubicle. However, she is slightly nervous and hesitates to make a move.

MR. POPKIN: (TURNS TO ELISA) Go on, Employee #263 – we don't have all day. You are welcome to go to your cubicle at this time.

From Elisa's perspective, everything moves slowly as she makes her way to her cubicle. She tries her best not to read the energy in the room, as some employees quickly move away from her, while others take a chance to whisper about her. Some employees (including Thomas) shake their heads in disapproval, while others openly enjoy the punishment she is receiving. Elisa tries her best not to let her nerves get to her until she comes across Gillian's cubicle and sees that it is still empty. She finally takes a seat at her cubicle and gets herself set up for work, while everyone else goes back to their cubicles to do the same.

MR. POPKIN: Your job begins in three! Two! One!

The Countdown Clock buzzer goes off and everyone simultaneously puts their headsets on and begins answering calls, answering emails, completing previous documents and writing reports.

A Few Hours Later

INT. THE RH-C DEPARTMENT OFFICE OF REGIONAL HEADQUARTERS – MORNING

Everyone in the office continues to answer phone calls, answer emails, complete previous documents and write reports without supervision for the day. Elisa wastes no time finishing all the work that was left for her. However, a few colleagues are annoyed by the sound of her rapid typing (which, practically speaking, is much quieter than anyone else's on a normal day).

MALE COLLEAGUE 1: (QUIETLY ANNOYED) Sounds like someone really needed to notify us of their presence.

FEMALE COLLEAGUE 1: (QUIETLY ANNOYED) Just shut up before you get yourself in trouble again.

The male colleague grimaces in surprise before going back to work. Elisa finishes up a report and is attempting to print it out when she receives a Notification Alert.

SYSTEM AI: Notification Alert! The printer is currently unavailable due to a paper shortage. Please cancel your print request and try again later.

FEMALE COLLEAGUE 2: (CONFUSED) Hey! Is someone going to fix the printer or something?

Elisa looks to see no one near the printing station, so she gets up to go fix it herself until she sees Zach on the floor trying to get the paper tray to open.

ELISA: (STARTLED) Oh my goodness!

ZACH: (LOOKS UP) I'm so sorry. I'm trying my best to get this thing to work, but I'm struggling. I promise I will be out of the way as soon as I figure this out –

ELISA: (TAKES A BREATHER) No, I should be apologizing. I didn't know that someone else was already here.

ZACH: (KINDLY) It's okay. I didn't mean to scare you ... but as far as I'm concerned, I think it's best if I allow someone else to take over.

Elisa tries to remember if she has seen Zach before in the office while she notices that his Tint Level is quite lighter than everyone else's. She tries her best not to stare at Zach for too long as he gets up from the ground and straightens out his clothes before giving up on the printer completely.

ZACH: I've been at this thing for quite some time now, but, as you can see, I'm not quite successful as a handyman and, to be honest, I am quite shocked that this office still uses paper, knowing how far advanced we are.

ELISA: (KINDLY) Some people have that exact same feeling, too, when it comes to the printer. However, it is the only thing that keeps track of all the documents, since Mr. Popkin doesn't trust electronic storage systems.

ZACH: But what happens if a fire breaks out and destroys all the printed documents in this building?

ELISA: I'm pretty sure this building is well advanced to prevent such incidents from happening in the first place; plus, electronic storage systems can be destroyed as well.

ZACH: (THINKS AND NODS) You've got a point there. (SIGHS IN FRUSTRATION) I just wanted to get this report handed in to Mr. Popkin before break, but I couldn't even figure out how to get the paper tray to open.

ELISA: (SMILES) It's okay, really. At least you tried. Usually, when it comes to finding the paper tray, there's no need to get on the ground to search for it. All you need to do is find the bottom hinge to get it open.

Elisa goes to the printer to search for the hinge without crouching down. She pulls the paper tray open with enough force as Zach looks on, dumbfounded.

ZACH: Wow, it was just as simple as that.

ELISA: (TURNS TO ZACH) You'll get the hang of it once you've done it a couple of times. (CHECKS THE INK LEVELS) Looks like the ink levels are low as well, so those have to be replaced.

Elisa opens the supply cabinet and takes out a fresh stack of printing paper, along with new ink cartridges. Zach stands there in awe as he watches Elisa fill up the paper tray and replace the old ink cartridges with new ones.

ELISA: There, that should do it.

Elisa turns on the printer, and it starts printing all the documents that were previously requested (including her report). Zach stands by, even more impressed than before.

ZACH: (TURNS TO ELISA) Thank you so much. You have no idea how much time you have saved for me.

ELISA: (TURNS TO ZACH) You're welcome. It's the least I can do.

ZACH: Now that that's done and over with, how are we supposed to know which one is which?

ELISA: All we have to do is look through the pile and sort them out.

Elisa waits for the printer to finish, and then she takes all the printed documents and gives half the pile to Zach to start sorting. He takes the time to look through the documents to find his own. He turns to see Elisa effortlessly sorting out all the documents in her pile and putting everything in order at the same time.

ZACH: (IMPRESSED) How are you able to do that so quickly?

ELISA: All documents have the employee's ID written on the header, so it's easy to tell which document belongs to who and just prepare them for submission.

ZACH: And then what? Are we supposed to give these documents to each employee?

ELISA: (GIGGLES) No, we leave them here and allow them to come pick them up for themselves. Distributing to the owners used to be allowed, but then Mr. Popkin realized that only a few people were willing to take on the task.

ZACH: (QUIETLY) Makes sense. It's about time everyone else got up off their asses.

Elisa tries her best not to laugh as she continues to sort out the printed documents in her pile. Zach attempts to do the same with his pile until he stops and realizes that he and Elisa have not truly introduced each other.

ELISA: (TURNS TO ZACH, CONFUSED) What's wrong?

ZACH: (OFFERS A HANDSHAKE) Zach Vault, kindly at your service.

ELISA: (SHAKES ZACH'S HAND) Elisa Graves. It's nice to meet you, Mr. Vault.

ZACH: (SMILES) It's nice to meet you, too, Ms. Graves.

Elisa and Zach continue to sort out the printed documents, while Daniel comes over to see what is going on.

DANIEL: (WALKS IN) Have you managed to get everything done, Employee #491?

ZACH: (TURNS TO DANIEL) Yes, I have. I just need to look through these documents to find my report first. I did have some trouble figuring out how the printer works, but luckily (GESTURES TO ELISA), I had some assistance.

DANIEL: Fine, then. Mr. Popkin has set some high expectations for you.

ZACH: I'm well aware of that.

DANIEL: So, you better have that report ready before break begins.

ZACH: (CONFIDENTLY) I'll make sure it gets done before the second hour begins.

Daniel goes back to his office while Elisa and Zach finish sorting through the printed documents for the other employees.

ZACH: (KINDLY) Well, I didn't see my document in this pile, so I guess I'll just have to print it again. Thanks again for your help, Ms. Graves.

ELISA: (KINDLY) Any time, Mr. Vault.

Elisa grabs her report and goes back to her cubicle to start on her other reports until she sees Zach sitting in Gillian's cubicle. She tries her best not to get too upset about the situation and continues working with everyone else in the office.

A Few Hours Later

INT. THE RH-C DEPARTMENT OFFICE OF REGIONAL HEADQUARTERS – AFTERNOON

Everyone in the office continues to answer phone calls, answer emails, complete previous documents and write reports under Mr. Popkin's observation until the Countdown Clock finishes going down and the Break Bell rings.

MR. POPKIN: (TURNS TO EVERYONE) All right, everyone! It's breaktime! Make sure to be back in an hour.

Everyone shuts down their systems temporarily and attempts to make their way out of the office as they head toward the cafeteria. Elisa attempts to do the same until Mr. Popkin stops her.

MR. POPKIN: Not you, Employee #263. You know the restrictions – you're not supposed to be eating in the cafeteria.

ELISA: (CONFUSED) But you never said that in your list of restrictions this morning.

MR. POPKIN: I didn't? Well, I'm saying it now that you should not be eating in the cafeteria, since I don't want to hear about any more incidents. Instead, you will be having your break here, where you can easily be monitored. I know this may seem like a lot to you, but don't blame me. These are just part of the rules.

ELISA: (SIGHS) Understood, sir.

MR. POPKIN: Good. Now, go to the kitchen and get yourself something to eat. I'm certain there's something in the fridge for you to munch on.

Elisa nods in understanding as Mr. Popkin goes back to his office, while a few employees smirk in satisfaction before going to the cafeteria. She begins to go to the kitchen, but then goes to her cubicle instead. She is about to start working when she finds a note on her keyboard.

ELISA: (READS) Meet me at the terrace. I think it's about time we got to know each other.

Elisa hesitates, confused and nervous, as she wonders who gave her the note.

EXT. THE ROOFTOP TERRACE OF THE RH-C DEPARTMENT OFFICE – AFTERNOON

Elisa takes her time entering the rooftop terrace, while Zach looks at the view of the entire Tint Valley. He stands there for a moment until he hears her heels clicking on the floor and turns to see her.

ZACH: (HAPPILY) And she arrives!

Elisa notices Zach standing near the railing, smiling at her arrival.

ZACH: (COMES UP TO ELISA) For a moment, I thought about sending you a Peer Request, but who would've thought that a simple pen and paper note would do the trick.

ELISA: (COMES UP TO ZACH) I didn't even know this place existed.

ZACH: (SMILES) Well, that's what you get for staying in one place for too long, and from watching you earlier, you rarely move around much.

ELISA: (SLIGHTLY TAKEN ABACK) Right ... (THINKS ABOUT GILLIAN) Why does watching me seem like a habit for everyone these days?

ZACH: (CLARIFIES) Don't take it personally. I wasn't trying to be offensive.

ELISA: (CLARIFIES) No, no, it's not you; it's just ... I don't think I'm supposed to be here.

ZACH: Well, one thing I know about your boss is that he's terrible at explaining things fully, and as long as you're within the office premises, you should be okay. Trust me, you're not the only employee who has been arrested before.

ELISA: How do you know all of this?

ZACH: I've seen it with my own eyes. Don't think I'm just some new recruit who arrived from the Outskirts. (WALKS AROUND) I've witnessed many things that have happened at the Regional Headquarters: office fights, secret relationships, terminations, loads of employee defamation – even this current trend of missing employees. This has happened before, but the reasoning behind this trend seems different from previous times.

ELISA: So, you, too, realize that something is off with the number of employees present?

ZACH: (TURNS TO ELISA) Of course, I do. It's the main reason why I'm here. I was transferred to this department. Otherwise, I would still be working in my own department and would not have to worry about fixing a printer.

Elisa smiles and begins to understand Zach's presence as he notices her relaxing for a moment.

ZACH: I know this is new for you, but if you have any other questions, feel free to ask. I'm willing to answer them right away.

ELISA: Why did you ask me to meet you here?

ZACH: Because there is something that I find intriguing about you. I was told by Mr. Popkin that I needed to find a mentor, since your department is clearly different from what I'm used to. Usually, we let the IT guys deal with those things and we have our own printer at our cubicles. However, I do like the fact that we get to move around a little more in the office. To cut this short, I'm obviously unaware of the work culture here and after what I was able to witness with today's struggle, I would like to ask you to be my mentor.

ELISA: (PAUSES) I'm not sure if that's a good idea.

Zach grimaces in confusion while Elisa looks down at her ankle monitor and red tag to remind herself of her current situation.

ELISA: In my current situation, I doubt that I'm allowed to mentor anyone at the moment.

ZACH: I don't think that should be an issue. You can even read the RH Guidebook to see that tagged employees are allowed to mentor their peers, if you like.

ELISA: Have you tried asking someone else? What about Thomas Dewberry? He has mentored newcomers before.

ZACH: Yeah, I don't think that's a good idea. I had a previous run-in with Mr. Dewberry, and he doesn't seem like someone I would ask to mentor me or a nice person to be around. But it looks like I have no other choice, since the one person I want to mentor me is scared –

ELISA: (DEFENSIVELY) It's not that I'm scared. I just have never mentored anyone (STOPS HERSELF AND BREATHES) ... Why do you want me to mentor you, anyway?

ZACH: (GENUINELY) Because you're the only one who sees me as a person. People get easily intimidated by me because of this Tint Level. I struggled for hours trying to figure out how to fix the printer and no one came to help me out. I can't even ask for help around here, because everyone expects me to know everything. But when you came in and simply showed me what to do without any preconceptions about me, why wouldn't I want to ask you to be my mentor?

Elisa is astonished by Zach's answer as she contemplates accepting his offer.

ELISA: (SIGHS) Fine. If it's not an issue with Mr. Popkin, then I will agree to be your mentor. I've given you the answer you wanted – are you happy now?

ZACH: (SMILES) Never been happier in my life. Now, all that's left is to celebrate this new union as I treat you to lunch.

ELISA: Actually, you don't have to do all that. I was planning on getting back to work in the meantime.

ZACH: (CONFUSED) Are you sure that's a good idea? You're not going to have anything to eat before you start working again?

ELISA: It's not that much of a big deal, I've –

LIFE BAND AI: Notification Alert! It has been detected that you have low nutrient levels in your body. It is advised to start the day with –

ELISA: (PRESSES THE MONOGRAM) Dismiss all notifications.

LIFE BAND AI: Notifications dismissed.

Elisa is slightly irritated with her Life Band AI, while Zach waits patiently for her to accept his offer.

ELISA: (GESTURES TO THE DOOR) Lead the way, Mr. Vault.

ZACH: (SMILES) My pleasure, Ms. Graves.

Zach makes his way to the kitchen, while Elisa feels as if she has no other choice but to follow him.

A Few Minutes Later

INT. THE RH-C DEPARTMENT OFFICE OF REGIONAL HEADQUARTERS – AFTERNOON

While returning to the office to go to the kitchen, Elisa and Zach stop upon seeing the IT staff attaching a trainee desk next to Elisa's cubicle, while Mr. Popkin supervises.

MR. POPKIN: (FIRMLY) Make sure that you get this done before the second shift begins, and try not to break the cubicle while you're installing that desk; it costs a lot more than you could ever earn in your lives.

ELISA: (COMES UP TO MR. POPKIN, CONFUSED) What's going on?

MR. POPKIN: (NOTICES ELISA) Ah, there you are. I hope you don't mind what we're doing to your cubicle, because you're about to take on an important task. I'm assigning you with Employee #491, and you will be mentoring him for the next few days. I'm confident that this will keep you busy while you're under these restrictions.

ELISA: Did you think to talk to me about this first?

MR. POPKIN: Obviously, I wanted to speak to you about this right away, but since you weren't in the office, I took matters into my own hands knowing that I could inform you afterwards. But we can talk about this more in my office if you don't like the arrangements –

ZACH: (STEPS IN) Actually, we just had a conversation about it outside, and Ms. Graves has already agreed to be my mentor.

MR. POPKIN: (TURNS TO ZACH) Is that so? Then there's no point in wasting any more time. (BEGINS TO LEAVE) Make sure he knows everything by the end of the week! I'm counting on you, Employee #263!

Mr. Popkin goes to his office, leaving Elisa in complete shock about what just happened. Zach leans toward her slightly.

ZACH: (PLEASANTLY) Looks like you're stuck with me, Ms. Graves.

Slightly annoyed, Elisa turns to Zach as he smiles and heads to the kitchen. Smirking in disbelief, she follows him.

SIXTEEN

▌ INT. THE HOUSE OF THE REIGN FAMILY

In the kitchen, **Stela Reign (mid-forties)** makes beef stroganoff and a few other dishes, while Malcolm enjoys a glass of whisky and dances to jazz music. He comes over to the kitchen to bother Stela, as she tries her best to finish cooking.

STELA: (SLIGHTLY ANNOYED) Oh, would you go away, Malcolm! Dinner's not ready yet!

MALCOLM: (MERRILY) I know that! I'm just enjoying the first day off I've had in weeks, while I finally get to enjoy a meal made by my lovely Stela while savouring a glass of whisky! Oh, the feeling that freedom brings to a person!

Malcolm gives Stela a few kisses, who squeals excitedly but tries to remain focused so as not to burn the food.

STELA: (SLIGHTLY ANNOYED) Oh, stop that, why don't you! Go help Jaina set the table while I get the food ready!

Malcolm surrenders and leaves the kitchen. He goes to **Jaina Reign (early-teens)** as she sets the table for dinner.

STELA: (FROM THE KITCHEN) And don't drink too much whisky – I don't want you spoiling your dinner!

MALCOLM: (TO THE KITCHEN) I promise not to drink too much. How could I ever spoil my appetite for my wife's cooking? (LEANS OVER TO JAINA) Unless she nags me every five seconds, that's how.

JAINA: (LAUGHS AND COUNTS THE TABLE SETTINGS) Dad, how come there's five table settings? Are we expecting someone?

MALCOLM: (HAPPILY) Yes, we are, and we are expecting her at any moment – (HEARS THE KNOCK ON THE DOOR) looks like she's here now!

Malcolm goes to answer the door and smiles as he sees Elisa standing outside carrying a dish of pastry hors d'oeuvres.

MALCOLM: (HAPPILY) Elisa! (GIVES ELISA A HUG) You finally made it!

ELISA: (KINDLY) Malcolm, how are you?

MALCOLM: (HAPPILY) I'm fine – I'm doing just splendid! Don't mind the whisky – I'm nowhere near as drunk as my wife thinks I am.

ELISA: (KINDLY) Well, you're certainly a lot happier than the last time I saw you. It's nice to see you like this.

Stela finishes cooking and comes over to see what is going on. When she sees Elisa standing by the door, she gasps with delight.

STELA: (EXCITEDLY) Oh, Elisa! (GOES TO GIVE ELISA A HUG) There's no way that's you! It's been too terribly long!

ELISA: Nice to see you, too, Mrs. Reign. (GESTURES TO THE DISH) I actually brought some appetizers.

STELA: (GASPS IN EXCITEMENT) You are far too kind. You definitely have your mother's manners.

MALCOLM: She also has her mother's temper, so you better watch out.

STELA: (SMACKS MALCOLM'S SHOULDER) Oh stop it, Malcolm! It's already embarrassing enough for the girl to walk around with this ankle monitor! Don't make her feel any worse.

MALCOLM: (DEFENSIVELY) I wasn't –

STELA: (SHAKES HER HEAD AND TURNS TO ELISA) Forgive him, Elisa. He usually doesn't know when to shut up when he drinks!

MALCOLM: (DEFENSIVELY) I'm not that drunk –

STELA: (TURNS TO MALCOLM) That's what you say every time you're on the verge of drunkenness. I'm afraid I'm going to have to start you on water before dinner begins!

JAINA: (RUSHES TO GIVE ELISA A HUG) Elisa!

ELISA: (HAPPILY) Jaina!

JAINA: (HAPPILY) I can't believe you're here. I missed you so much! Why did you take so long to visit us?

STELA: (TURNS TO ELISA) Yes, it has been a while since we saw you last, at your father's funeral. And you have become so beautiful. It's a shame that we didn't get to see you more often.

MALCOLM: (SINCERELY) Now, don't make her feel guilty. She has been through a lot, dear ... we all have ever since that day. It should make sense that we haven't seen her all this time. Plus, she's a working woman. She has to do whatever she can to take care of herself and her family. Let's just try to have a good time while we start dinner.

STELA: (HAPPILY) Yes, we should. (TAKES THE DISH FROM ELISA) Let me take care of that for you while you help Jaina set the table.

MALCOLM: (DEFENSIVELY) I thought I was helping Jaina.

STELA: (TURNS TO MALCOLM) Not until you put down that glass, Malcolm!

Stela goes back to the kitchen as Jaina takes Elisa's hand and brings her to the dining table. Malcolm stands by in disbelief before shrugging it off and taking another sip of whisky.

A Few Minutes Later

❚ INT. THE REIGNS' HOUSE – EVENING

Malcolm, Elisa and Jaina sit around the table while Stela brings out all the dishes, including the beef stroganoff and the pastry hors d'oeuvres. She takes a seat beside Malcolm as he begins drooling over the food on the table.

MALCOLM: (HAPPILY RUBS HIS HANDS TOGETHER) All right! Let's get started!

Malcolm attempts to reach for a spoon before Stela smacks his hand to stop him from taking any food.

MALCOLM: (CONFUSED) What?

STELA: (FIRMLY) Where are your manners? Have you forgotten that we've always let our guests go first? (TURNS TO ELISA) Go ahead, Elisa dear – don't mind the rest of us.

MALCOLM: (ARGUES) But I'm starving.

ELISA: (KINDLY) It's okay, Mrs. Reign. I'm willing to wait for everyone to serve themselves. (PAUSES NERVOUSLY) Will Rueben be joining us for dinner?

Malcolm and Stela stop arguing and freeze as Elisa and Jaina wait for an answer.

ELISA: (KINDLY) The last thing I want is to start dinner without a member of your family around ... I think it would be wrong for me to do that since this is not my house.

STELA: (GENUINELY) That's very considerate of you, Elisa ... it's a shame that there is no one else like you.

JAINA: (GETS UP) Should I go get him, Mom?

MALCOLM: (SERIOUSLY) Don't bother your brother. Now's not the time.

Jaina sits back down, while Stela turns to Malcolm in concern.

MALCOLM: (SERIOUSLY) All I want is to have a peaceful dinner without any trouble. I already deal with that at work; I don't want to deal with it at home. It's nice of you to want to include him, but you don't need to worry about Rueben ... this is my house, so he'll come when he wants to join us.

Rueben Reign (early-twenties) stands quietly in the corridor of the house as he watches Elisa interact with Malcolm, Stela and Jaina at the dining table.

MALCOLM: (SERIOUSLY) Let's just start dinner. Jaina, please sit beside Elisa if your brother decides to join us.

STELA: (GETS UP) I'll plate his food for him. I know he likes his momma's sweet potatoes!

Stela takes a serving spoon to scoop up some sweet potatoes for Rueben, while Jaina goes to sit beside Elisa at the dining table. She helps herself and Jaina plate their food, while Malcolm does the same for Stela and himself. As Stela finishes plating Rueben's food, Malcolm tastes the beef stroganoff and smiles.

MALCOLM: (PLEASANTLY) Now that's what I call good cooking.

STELA: (SMILES) Well, thank goodness. I thought that scowl was going to stick on your face forever!

MALCOLM: (PLEASANTLY) Not when it comes to your beef stroganoff – it's simply the best.

Stela gives Malcolm a kiss as she, Jaina and Elisa start eating. Rueben continues to watch them have dinner together until Jaina notices him standing in the corridor.

JAINA: (EXCITEDLY) He's here!

Both Rueben and Malcolm tense as Jaina gets up to give Rueben a hug and Stela rubs Malcolm's arm to calm him down.

JAINA: (EXCITEDLY) He finally came out of his room – we can have dinner as a family! Are you going to join us, Rueben?

Rueben and Malcolm remain silent as Stela and Elisa prepare for the worst.

RUEBEN: (DULLY) If it's only okay with Father, then I'm willing to stomach through sitting with you guys.

MALCOLM: (SERIOUSLY) Of course you can, Rueben. It's your house, too, since you're a part of this family … come join us for dinner, son.

JAINA: (EXCITEDLY) Come sit with us, Rueben!

Rueben relaxes slightly as he allows Jaina to bring him to the dining table, while Malcolm also tries to relax. Rueben takes a seat between Jaina and Malcolm and everyone begins to eat dinner.

JAINA: (EXCITEDLY) Mom made your favourite things – and look, Elisa came to visit us today! Aren't you happy to see her?

Rueben gives Elisa a look that makes her feel uncomfortable, although she tries her best not to show it in front of everyone.

STELA: (QUIETLY) Now, Jaina, there's no need to make a fuss. Let's just have dinner quietly and try not to anger anyone, okay.

JAINA: (WHINES) But Mom, I wasn't doing –

ELISA: (KINDLY) Listen to your parents and everything will be okay.

Jaina nods in understanding and begins eating, along with everyone else. Meanwhile, Rueben stares at his plate of food.

STELA: So how was work today, sweetie? I know I forgot to ask when you came in earlier.

RUEBEN: (DULLY) Today was all right. The workload seems to be slowing down, but it's the same every day … What's so exciting about butchering different animals?

Everyone around the table sits quietly as Rueben grabs a pastry hors d'oeuvre and gives it a taste before anyone can start eating again.

RUEBEN: (DULLY) I didn't know you went back to baking, Mother. What happened to your mantra of pastries causing your skin to break out?

STELA: I didn't make those, son. Elisa brought them over for dinner.

Rueben tosses the half-eaten pastry hors d'oeuvre back in the dish, while everyone else around the table looks on in slight disbelief.

STELA: (SLIGHTLY FIRMLY) Can you at least show some respect to our guest? She did bring them over just for us.

ELISA: It's okay, Mrs. Reign. I'm happy to take them back if no one likes them.

MALCOLM: Nonsense, you will do no such thing. You are our guest, and you deserve to be treated with respect, just like the rest of us at this table.

JAINA: (HAPPILY) I'll eat it!

Jaina grabs the half-eaten pastry hors d'oeuvre from the dish, along with a few more and eats it without hesitation.

JAINA: (HAPPILY) Mm! These are excellent! (TURNS TO ELISA) Did you make them yourself, Elisa?

ELISA: Yes, I did, especially for you.

JAINA: (HAPPILY) Well, I really like them! (TURNS TO RUEBEN AND POUTS) Shame on you, Rueben. How dare you throw away a pastry.

STELA: (TASTES A PASTRY HORS D'OEUVRE) These definitely remind me of the pastries Mrs. Graves used to make at the Outskirts. You were clearly given her skills in baking. (TURNS TO ELISA) How is your mother doing, by the way, Elisa?

ELISA: (PAUSES SLIGHTLY) I bet she's doing okay. Knowing her, she will only call when something serious is happening.

STELA: (CONFUSED) But I don't understand. Why?

MALCOLM: (QUIETLY) It's quite a sensitive topic for her, Stela. So, please don't push it.

RUEBEN: (DULLY) Especially when we all know that her mother never wants to see her again.

Elisa begins to feel slightly ashamed about her distant relationship with Carman, as Malcolm gives Rueben a cold look. Stela immediately reads the energy in the room and tries to think of ways to change it.

STELA: All right, let's focus on something else. So, how do you enjoy working at the Regional Headquarters, Elisa? I heard it's a pretty tough job for a lot of people – especially for all of my friends' daughters.

ELISA: You can say something like that, but it does pay well, and I get to live near my workplace as well, so ... it's not bad at all.

MALCOLM: (PLEASANTLY) That's always the best thing about Tint Valley; everywhere is close by. Thank goodness that we decided to move. I don't know what I would've gotten myself into if we were still living in the Outskirts.

STELA: (HAPPILY) All right, trying to steer away from the topic of work. Are you dating anyone, Elisa?

ELISA: (SLIGHTLY EMBARRASSED) Um – no, Mrs. Reign. I'm not dating anyone at the moment.

STELA: (GASPS IN DISBELIEF) Really? That can't be true!

MALCOLM: (CHUCKLES) I know a lot of Steels officers at my station who are willing to take you out on a date. They might not be brave enough to say it to your face, but they are waiting for the moment when you take off that ankle monitor –

STELA: (SMACKS MALCOLM'S SHOULDER) Oh! Now, you stop it! There is no way that's happening – how could you say such a thing?

MALCOLM: (DEFENSIVELY) But it's the truth! One of my rookies couldn't stop asking about her –

STELA: (ARGUES) Oh please, Malcolm. Don't try to write off her future! She will not become a Steels wife just to deal with the fear of her husband not coming home! (CONFIDENTLY) Instead, she will marry a hardworking man who will come home every day, fill her up with babies and treat her like the princess she deserves to be.

MALCOLM: (DEFENSIVELY) Now you're just contradicting yourself – How could you say such a thing when you're a Steels wife yourself?

STELA: (ARGUES) That doesn't change the worries I have for you every day, Malcolm – especially with your new position as Deputy. There are times when I never see you home for a full week.

MALCOLM: (CHUCKLES) Then just tell me you miss me, and I'll be home with you for a full month.

Elisa enjoys watching how Malcolm and Stela love each other. He gives her a few kisses and she does not resist kissing him back.

RUEBEN: (DULLY) Maybe a year if he gets injured.

Malcolm's smile quickly fades, and he stiffens in anger, while Stela turns to Rueben in shock.

STELA: (FIRMLY) Now, Rueben, there's no need to wish such a thing on your father. (HOLDS ONTO MALCOLM) I love him anyway – especially when he knows how to make a girl blush. (TURNS TO ELISA) But really, Elisa, I'm surprised that you don't have a line of men just flocking for your attention. You're so beautiful – who wouldn't want to date you?

RUEBEN: (DULLY) Many people wouldn't. Can't you see?

Elisa remains silent as Stela looks on in disbelief and Malcolm begins to lose his patience.

RUEBEN: (DULLY) Who would want to date her when she has on that atrocious Tint Level? Just the thought of it would cause anyone to jump off a cliff. Who would want to deal with such an inconvenience. (TURNS TO STELA) That's why you have to be thankful that Jaina is not in that position, Mother (POINTS TO ELISA), because she wouldn't even last a day with the amount of hate she would receive if she were her! (TURNS TO ELISA COLDLY) I just wish that we could go back to the times when Slates were easy to get rid of – that we never had to see them again after one day of being part of their disgusting presence! I want to go back to those times already because who wants to ever be around a Blank –

MALCOLM: (STANDS UP AND SCREAMS) That's enough, Rueben!

Everyone turns to Malcolm in shock, who stands in anger and looks at Rueben with distorted features.

MALCOLM: (ANGRILY) The only person who wanted you to be part of this dinner was her, and the only person who always has a disgusting presence is you! If you think that I'm just going to let you sit here and disrespect her – then you have no reason to be a part of this family in the first place! Until some sense comes back into your head, I want you to leave this table now and do whatever you can to get out of my sight. (SCREAMS) Now!

Just as angry himself, Rueben glares at Malcolm, gets up furiously and storms to his room, where he slams the door. Stela, Jaina and Elisa look at Malcolm worriedly as he tries his best to calm himself down.

STELA: (CONCERNED) Malcolm.

MALCOLM: (SERIOUSLY) Let's just have a peaceful dinner, please … I'm not in the mood to deal with any more trouble.

Malcolm calmly sits back down to eat his dinner while Stela, Jaina and Elisa hesitate to do the same without Rueben.

A Few Hours Later

❙ INT. THE REIGNS' HOUSE – EVENING

Elisa washes the dishes in the kitchen while Malcolm, Stela and Jaina spend the rest of the time in the living room listening to jazz music.

STELA: (FROM THE LIVING ROOM) Oh, Malcolm! Would you put that glass down already?

MALCOLM: (FROM THE LIVING ROOM) Oh, Stela! Can't you see that I'm having a good time!

JAINA: (FROM THE LIVING ROOM) Mom, I think Dad's drunk again!

MALCOLM: (FROM THE LIVING ROOM) I'm not drunk! I'm just finally at peace with my two favourite people in the world!

Elisa smiles as she enjoys listening to the positive commotion coming from the living room and continues to wash the dishes.

RUEBEN: (DULLY) That's fine porcelain, so I would be careful with that if I were you.

Startled, Elisa almost drops a plate. She turns to see Rueben standing in the entry. She takes the time to regain her composure as she continues to wash the dishes and ignores Rueben.

RUEBEN: (DULLY) You got some nerve coming here with that thing around your ankle. I'm concerned that we might see squad cars at any moment now.

ELISA: (FIRMLY) I'm still within the five-hundred-kilometre radius. Plus, it was your father who invited me to this dinner, so you don't have to worry about Steels showing up anytime soon.

RUEBEN: (DULLY) Unless you decide to commit a second offence.

ELISA: (FIRMLY) Just go away, Rueben.

RUEBEN: (DULLY) Why? What would you do if I didn't? My father did say that you wanted me to stay ... I just came here to fulfill your wishes.

Beginning to feel uncomfortable with Rueben's presence, Elisa tenses as she feels a knife under the soapy water in the sink.

RUEBEN: (DULLY) But I knew you only said that just to be nice ... not realizing that's the worst thing you can do to a person, and I can't forgive you for that. (NOTICES ELISA'S HANDS) And that knife in the sink is not going to help you either way.

ELISA: (FIRMLY) I will do anything to protect myself.

RUEBEN: (DULLY) You know, you were way too young when the Metallic Order was first established. You wouldn't have been able to remember how the soldiers used to conduct an obstacle course called the Loyalty Trials.

ELISA: (FIRMLY) I don't have time for your stories.

RUEBEN: (DULLY) The soldiers would play a simple game with the entire population where they got to see who was the strongest and who was the weakest. Do you want to know what happened to people who were the weakest?

Elisa clenches the knife inside the sink as she feels Rueben moving until Malcolm walks in to see what is going on.

MALCOLM: (IN DISBELIEF) Oh my goodness, Elisa.

Elisa releases the knife inside the sink as Malcolm comes up to her to see that she has done most of the dishes, while Rueben stays where he is.

MALCOLM: (GRATEFUL) I cannot believe this with my own eyes. How dare you believe that we would ever let you do the dishes? You're our guest; you shouldn't have to do such a thing for us.

ELISA: (SMILES) It's okay, Malcolm. It's the least I can do.

MALCOLM: (GRATEFUL) No, it's not okay, Elisa. Now I'm completely indebted to you, especially since it was my turn to do the dishes.

Elisa smiles and begins to relax as Malcolm turns to Rueben with a serious look on his face.

MALCOLM: (SERIOUSLY) I knew there was a reason for me to come here. What are you doing here? I thought I told you to go to your room? Are you here to apologize or are you really trying to bring out the deputy in me? Because I'm already sick and tired of what you did at the dinner table. Don't think that I will allow you to continue this behavior by harassing her!

RUEBEN: (DULLY) You can't protect her forever.

MALCOLM: (SERIOUSLY) Oh, I can, and I will! You had all the years to prove to me that you were better than this and failed every single time, meaning that I will do everything necessary to protect her – even if it means arresting my own son! Don't you dare tempt me, Rueben!

Rueben gives Malcolm a dirty look and then walks away to go to his room. Elisa worries about Malcolm as he lets out a deep sigh of exhaustion.

ELISA: (SOLEMNLY) Sorry about that, Malcolm ... maybe it was a bad time for me to come.

MALCOLM: (CALMLY) No ... no, it wasn't ... You're not the problem; he is. It hurts to say, but he always has been. (HONESTLY) Just thinking about what he said about your mother ... he and I live in the same house, and we can go an entire week without speaking to each other.

Elisa nods in understanding as she worries about Malcolm's relationship with Rueben.

ELISA: I thought he was getting better after what happened.

MALCOLM: (SIGHS) Yeah, I thought so too ... that was, until he stopped getting help and started again and stopped again and – (STOPS HIMSELF AND BREATHES). All I know is that, ever since the incident, he has never been the same. And, unfortunately, he's taking it out on you, because he never got a chance to prove your father wrong before he died. Now, all he ever talks about is the dark times. It's just soul-crushing to be around him these days. (SOLEMNLY) I spent my entire life solving cases, eliminating threats and ensuring people's safety at my job, and I can't even make things right with my own son ... It's quite sad now that I say it out loud.

ELISA: I'm really sorry to hear that.

MALCOLM: (CALMLY) It's okay, Elisa. I guess it goes to show that we're all human; we all have our issues with family. Hopefully, a full day of work will help me get over what just happened at dinner – I have to apologize to you on his behalf.

ELISA: It's fine, really. (HONESTLY) I was prepared for it anyway, so you don't need to worry.

MALCOLM: I also wanted to tell you that I've been checking the database of our missing person reports on a daily basis. So far, no information has been found about your friend but not to worry. We'll continue to look into it. We have heard that a large number of people have stopped going to work at Regional Headquarters.

ELISA: Thanks again for your help, Malcolm.

MALCOLM: Any time, Elisa. From the looks of it, we have a serious issue on our hands, but I trust that the team will have it figured out in no time. Right now, all I need to think about is taking you home.

STELA: (FROM THE LIVING ROOM) Oh no, Malcolm! You're not going anywhere!

MALCOLM: (TO THE LIVING ROOM) But how is Elisa going to get home? She needs to be at work in the morning, and you can't drive!

STELA: (FROM THE LIVING ROOM) I know I can't, but you know too damn well that you can't be trusted behind the wheel after having a glass of whisky! Just call one of your trusty friends at the station, and I'm sure they'll get her home safely!

Malcolm sighs in exhaustion, while Elisa smiles in understanding.

SEVENTEEN

▎ EXT. OUTSIDE THE REIGNS' HOUSE – EVENING

A Steels officer opens the door of the back of his squad car for Elisa as Malcolm, Stela and Jaina step outside of their house to wave goodbye to her.

MALCOLM: (HAPPILY) Thanks again for coming to dinner, Elisa!

JAINA: (HAPPILY) Bye, Elisa! It was so nice to see you again!

ELISA: (TURNS TO JAINA) It was nice seeing you too, Jaina! I hope we see each other again soon!

STELA: (HAPPILY) Bye, Elisa dear – I hope that you come by soon! (REMEMBERS) Oh, and don't worry about your dish – I'll make sure Malcolm brings it over for you.

ELISA: (KINDLY) It's okay, Mrs. Reign! I doubt that I'm going to use it again, so I'll let you keep it for the time being!

STELA: (GASPS IN EXCITEMENT AND TURNS TO MALCOLM) You hear that, Malcolm? We get a free dish – we get a free dish!

MALCOLM: (UNINTERESTED) Yeah, I'm sure we do. (HAPPILY) Bye, Elisa. I'll see you another time!

ELISA: (HAPPILY) Same to you, Malcolm! Goodbye, everyone! (WAVES GOODBYE) Thanks again for dinner!

Malcolm, Stela and Jaina wave goodbye to Elisa as she gets into the backseat of the squad car and the Steels officer closes the door for her.

MALCOLM: (LOUDLY) Make sure you get her home safe!

The Steels officer nods as he gets in the squad car to start driving. Elisa waves goodbye to Malcolm, Stela and Jaina as they watch the squad car leave the area while the Steels officer drives her home.

STELA: (HAPPILY) Aw, such a sweet girl.

MALCOLM: She is. It's such a shame that she lives by herself.

STELA: (GASPS IN SHOCK) By herself? Oh, why didn't you tell me that she was living by herself? She wouldn't have to deal with such a thing if she were living with us! I knew she would've been happier if you'd allowed those two to get married; then Rueben wouldn't be the person that he is today.

Stela goes back inside the house with Jaina, while Malcolm sighs and thinks about the days when his family and Elisa's family still lived in the Outskirts.

Nine Years Prior

EXT. OUTSIDE TINT VALLEY MIDDLE SCHOOL – AFTERNOON

Twelve-year-old Elisa sits on the stairs of an empty portable while every other student takes the chance to leave Tint Valley Middle School after their last day of school. She spends the time making "paper ammo" with the pages of her notebook and practices her shooting skills with some small soda cans and a rubber band. Twelve-year-old Elisa uses the rubber band as an arrow to shoot down the soda cans with the paper ammo she made.

TWELVE-YEAR-OLD ELISA: Why did Dad take so long to show me this trick? It would've saved me a lot of trouble with those eighth graders.

Thirteen-year-old **Stacy Danvers** and her friends leave a portable to make their way to the front of the school. They talk about the end of the school year, while twelve-year-old Elisa continues to shoot down the soda cans.

THIRTEEN-YEAR-OLD STACY'S FRIEND 1: (NOTICES TWELVE-YEAR-OLD ELISA) Don't look now; bad luck, just up ahead.

THIRTEEN-YEAR-OLD STACY: (CONDESCENDINGLY) You know what they say. If you stare at a Slate for too long, you might get coal for Christmas.

Thirteen-year-old Stacy's friends laugh at her remark, while twelve-year-old Elisa ignores them and continues to practice her targeting skills.

THIRTEEN-YEAR-OLD STACY'S FRIEND 2: (CONDESCENDINGLY) She's such an embarrassment. What is she doing anyway?

THIRTEEN-YEAR-OLD STACY: (CONDESCENDINGLY) I don't know, maybe practicing how to kill her parents.

THIRTEEN-YEAR-OLD STACY'S FRIEND 1: (NOTICES TWELVE-YEAR-OLD ELISA) I'm surprised that she's not practicing how to kill herself. However, it's about time her parents get put out of their misery.

THIRTEEN-YEAR-OLD STACY: (CONDESCENDINGLY) Maybe just her mother; her dad's job might take him out first before she gets a chance.

Hearing this, twelve-year-old Elisa stiffens in anger, gets up and turns to thirteen-year-old Stacy and her friends as they are walking away.

TWELVE-YEAR-OLD ELISA: (DETERMINED) Hey Stacy.

THIRTEEN-YEAR-OLD STACY: (TURNS TO TWELVE-YEAR-OLD ELISA HARSHLY) What, you loser!

Twelve-year-old Elisa shoots a paper ammo at thirteen-year-old Stacy, which strikes her in the eye; she screams in agony.

▌ EXT. OUTSIDE THE GRAVES' HOUSE – AFTERNOON

Twelve-year-old Elisa makes her way home alone and finds Carman sweeping the driveway and the front porch.

TWELVE-YEAR-OLD ELISA: Mom, I'm home! How was your day?

Carman does not respond, as she continues to sweep the driveway and the front porch.

TWELVE-YEAR-OLD ELISA: (CONCERNED) Mom, are you okay? Did someone make you angry today?

Twelve-year-old Elisa waits for Carman to respond as she continues to watch her sweep the driveway and the front porch.

TWELVE-YEAR-OLD ELISA: Well, I had a great day today. I didn't make any of my teachers angry with me, and I got an A+ on my math test.

Carman does not respond, but continues to sweep the driveway and the front porch. Meanwhile, Twelve-year-old Elisa tries her best not to lose her patience.

TWELVE-YEAR-OLD ELISA: Mom, are you even listening to me?

Carman continues sweeping until she and twelve-year-old Elisa turn to see a silver convertible speeding down the street. The car stops abruptly near their house and **Mrs. Ortica Danvers (mid-forties)** gets out of the car and begins looking around angrily for twelve-year-old Elisa.

MRS. DANVERS: (LIVID) Where is she? Where is that little bitch?

Seeing twelve-year-old Elisa, Mrs. Danvers, whose features are lividly distorted, goes up to her and grabs her by the arm. Seeing this, Carman drops the broom and goes over to intervene.

MRS. DANVERS: (LIVID) Did you really think you were going to get away with what you did?

CARMAN: (CONFUSED) Whoa–whoa – just hold on for a second. What is going on here?

MRS. DANVERS: (LIVID) You should be asking your daughter that.

CARMAN: (FIRMLY) Well, I would love to be told in a more civil manner, if you will just take your hands off her.

Carman yanks Mrs. Danvers's hand off twelve-year-old Elisa and pulls her daughter to stand behind her for the time being.

CARMAN: (FIRMLY) Now, would you mind telling me what on earth is going on? Because I'm not in the mood to deal with lunatics coming to my house.

MRS. DANVERS: (ANGRILY) The only lunatic here is your daughter, who is obviously out to cause trouble again! Did she get a chance to tell you what she did today? Do you know what your daughter did to my daughter after school?

CARMAN: (UNINTERESTED) I don't know, Mrs. Danvers. This won't be the first time our children have fought with each other. What's different now?

MRS. DANVERS: (SCOFFS) It's like you Slates don't even care about the consequences of your actions! How do you expect us to be civil when you can't even properly train your children to know their place! Do I have to show you what your daughter caused?

Mrs. Danvers goes to bring thirteen-year-old Stacy out of the car and comes back to Carman and twelve-year-old Elisa, who both see that the girl is wearing a patch over her right eye.

MRS. DANVERS: (ANGRILY) Because of this bastard child, my Stacy came home with a red eye! We even had to take her to the clinic because she had an allergic reaction to whatever she threw at my daughter's eye! (TURNS TO THIRTEEN-YEAR-OLD STACY) Tell her what she did to you, Stacy.

THIRTEEN-YEAR-OLD STACY: (CRIES) She hit me in the eye with that stupid paper bullet of hers! Her dirty hands were touching the grass. That's how my eye turned out like this!

CARMAN: And what were you expecting us to do by coming here?

MRS. DANVERS: (ANGRILY) Give an apology, of course! She needs to take ownership of her actions and apologize to my daughter! We also demand that you give us compensation for the damages she caused to Stacy, along with the medical bills, to get this resolved.

Carman sighs in exhaustion and turns to twelve-year-old Elisa for an explanation.

CARMAN: Elisa, did you do this to her?

TWELVE-YEAR-OLD ELISA: (SUBMISSIVELY) Yes, Mom.

CARMAN: And why did you do it?

TWELVE-YEAR-OLD ELISA: (SUBMISSIVELY) Because she said something bad about you and Dad. She and her friends said that I was practicing my targeting skills to kill you and Dad, when that wasn't even true. She even mentioned that Dad's job would kill him before I ever got a chance. That's why I shot the paper bullet at her.

Carman nods in understanding and slowly turns back to Mrs. Danvers and thirteen-year-old Stacy.

CARMAN: I see ... so she had every reason to put that eye patch on your eye.

MRS. DANVERS: (IN DISBELIEF) You're not seriously condoning this behavior, are you?

CARMAN: To be fair, your daughter did leave my daughter with a bloody lip, but did we come tearing up your neighbourhood, demanding compensation and an apology? No, we went to the school and spoke to the principal about it, while they both faced their consequences. (ARGUES) And how could she have known that your daughter is allergic to grass if they're not even friends? Was there a sign to tell the entire school that she has allergies? No! All I know is that your demand for compensation is entirely bullshit, and I will get my husband involved if you do not get the fuck off my property right now.

MRS. DANVERS: (ANGRILY) We're not leaving until this bastard Slate faces the consequences!

CARMAN: (SHRUGS) All right. I'll play your little game with you, Mrs. Danvers ... but since everyone knows that you have an apprehension about dust.

Carman goes to pick up the broom and rips a handful of grass from the front yard as Mrs. Danvers begins to panic.

MRS. DANVERS: (FRANTICALLY) Almighty – let's get out of here! We can't stay here with these uncivilized people!

Carman stays where she is, as she and twelve-year-old Elisa watch Mrs. Danvers and thirteen-year-old Stacy rush back to the car.

MRS. DANVERS: (LIVID) This isn't over, Mrs. Graves!

Mrs. Danvers drives off as Carman watches the car leave the area until she takes a breather and turns to twelve-year-old Elisa.

CARMAN: Get inside. I'll have a word with you later.

Twelve-year-old Elisa nods sheepishly. She is heading inside the house when she and Carman see another convertible heading toward the house in a more civilized manner, and it stops near the driveway. Looking excited, Stela gets out of the car with fourteen-year-old Rueben, followed by Malcolm, who looks noticeably less excited.

STELA: (HAPPILY) I believe we're in the right place! (TURNS TO MALCOLM) Don't you think so, honey?

MALCOLM: (SLIGHTLY NERVOUS) Yeah, we're definitely in the right place. (WAVES TO CARMAN) Hey, Carman, how's it going? Are you having a good day?

CARMAN: (COMES UP TO MALCOLM) I wish I could tell you that, if I was expecting a visit. What's going on, Malcolm? Why have you come here today?

MALCOLM: Take it easy. We just came to talk to you about something – plus, I don't think you've met my wife.

STELA: (SHAKES CARMAN'S HAND HAPPILY) Hi! It's so nice to meet you. I'm Stela! But please call me Mrs. Reign. (HOLDS ONTO MALCOLM) I need to let everyone know that I'm married to this hunk of handsomeness!

MALCOLM: (CHUCKLES) That's one way to make me feel better. (QUIETLY) Focus on your task, dear.

STELA: (GESTURES TO FOURTEEN-YEAR-OLD RUEBEN) And this is our dashing son, Rueben. I believe he and your children go to the same school together.

FOURTEEN-YEAR-OLD RUEBEN: (KINDLY) It's nice to meet you, Mrs. Graves.

CARMAN: (UNCERTAIN) Nice to meet you both. May I ask, what's going on here?

STELA: Well, you see, we came here to raise a serious topic with you and your husband – which, I know he's still at work, but I wanted to address this to you anyway. You see, we're actually here for your daughter.

CARMAN: (BLUNTLY) I have two. Which one are you talking about?

STELA: I'm aware that you have two daughters, since Malcolm talks about your family all the time, and even though it sounds unorthodox (GESTURES TO TWELVE-YEAR-OLD ELISA), we actually want to speak with your youngest daughter, Elisa.

CARMAN: (CONFUSED) Elisa? What did she do this time? (TURNS TO TWELVE-YEAR-OLD ELISA HARSHLY) How many times are you going to get yourself into trouble? You almost got punished by Mrs. Danvers and now you manage to cause trouble with Malcolm's family –

MALCOLM: (CLARIFIES) Whoa, whoa, Carman! Calm down. That is not what we're here for. Elisa didn't cause us any trouble – we can assure you of that.

STELA: (CLARIFIES) My husband is right; she didn't do anything wrong to us. It's my fault. I didn't make myself clear enough.

MALCOLM: (TURNS TO STELA) It's okay, honey. Just finish what you have to say.

STELA: (CLARIFIES) We definitely came here on good terms, especially since this meeting will be good for both of our children. You see, we didn't come here to punish her; we came because we have a proposition for her.

CARMAN: (CONFUSED) Proposition?

Malcolm sighs with concern as Carman and twelve-year-old Elisa look on, confused.

A Few Minutes Later

▌INT. THE GRAVES' HOUSE – AFTERNOON

Sixteen-year-old Deidre and fourteen-year-old Fredrick sit quietly near the window as they both watch Carman talk to Stela about the proposition they have for twelve-year-old Elisa.

SIXTEEN-YEAR-OLD DEIDRE: (WHINES) This is not fair!

FOURTEEN-YEAR-OLD FREDRICK: (CONFUSED) Why are you so upset? This has nothing to do with you.

SIXTEEN-YEAR-OLD DEIDRE: (WHINES) That's exactly why it's not fair! Why does Elisa get a chance to get married before me?

FOURTEEN-YEAR-OLD FREDRICK: Maybe this is a good thing for us. If she gets married right away, we'll never have to see her again. Then, we can finally have our parents' attention to ourselves and never have to think about having a little sister ever again.

SIXTEEN-YEAR-OLD DEIDRE: (SCOFFS) You're such a jerk, Fredrick.

Sixteen-year-old Deidre walks away from fourteen-year-old Fredrick and goes upstairs, leaving him sitting in disbelief at her response.

FOURTEEN-YEAR-OLD FREDRICK: (OFFENDED) Hey! Come back here!

Fourteen-year-old Fredrick leaves the window to follow sixteen-year-old Deidre upstairs.

▌ EXT. OUTSIDE THE GRAVES' HOUSE – AFTERNOON

Carman serves Stela some tea before taking a seat with her, twelve-year-old Elisa and fourteen-year-old Rueben as they talk about the proposition.

STELA: (KINDLY) Thank you so much.

CARMAN: You're welcome. So, explain to me what this whole arrangement is all about.

STELA: (HAPPILY) Well, the neighbourhood mothers and I came together and discussed the future of our children. Since some of our children haven't reached a 60% Tint Level, we thought it would be nice if we took matters into our own hands and matched our children with their potential life partners.

CARMAN: (CONFUSED) You're talking about arranged marriage.

STELA: (HAPPILY) Well, I wouldn't say it like that, but yes, it's exactly that.

Carman looks at Malcolm in disbelief, while he shrugs hopelessly and gestures to Stela as she takes a sip of tea.

STELA: (GIGGLES) Oh, my goodness, I don't want to embarrass my son here, since this is personal for him. But when he told me about the day he saw your daughter walking home by herself, he literally couldn't contain himself and fell off his seat on the bus just at the sight of her. The way his eyes gleamed when he talked about her beauty, I just knew she would be the perfect match for him, since that exact day made him so happy.

Carman notices fourteen-year-old Rueben staring at twelve-year-old Elisa. He waves hello to her and she does the same, then quickly turns away from him and sits there quietly.

CARMAN: (CAUTIOUS) I see ... and he wouldn't mind marrying her, even if she continues to have this Tint Level?

STELA: (CERTAIN) Of course he wouldn't mind! We would definitely love to take her into our family! Plus, he's been working hard at the Steels Services Academy, so he'll definitely be the right partner for your daughter.

FOURTEEN-YEAR-OLD RUEBEN: (CONFIDENTLY) I promise that I'll do everything I can to protect your daughter and give her the love she needs to be a happy wife.

CARMAN: (CAUTIOUS) Yeah, I bet you will ... (TURNS TO MALCOLM) Malcolm, does Garreth know about this?

MALCOLM: (SHAKES HIS HEAD) Unfortunately, no. We were hoping to come by later to discuss this with both of you, but to my knowledge, he chose to stay back to work on a case. Also, Stela was really excited to meet Elisa for the first time.

STELA: (HAPPILY) Yes, I was (TURNS TO TWELVE-YEAR-OLD ELISA), and she is such a beautiful girl – she matches Rueben's testimony completely. Obviously, we want to wait until both kids graduate from high school, but I hope that we can start the process as soon as possible so that our children get to know each other in the time being. We really would like to have Elisa over one day.

CARMAN: (PAUSES) Well, I don't want to jump into saying yes just yet ... but I can't help but think that this might actually be good for her.

While Carman is fairly sure how Garreth will react to Stela's marriage proposition, she takes the time to think about it. Twelve-year-old Elisa, however, thinks about the prospect of getting married at a young age and begins to freak out.

TWELVE-YEAR-OLD ELISA: (QUIETLY PANICS) Mom ... Mom?

CARMAN: (TURNS TO TWELVE-YEAR-OLD ELISA) What? (ANNOYED) What is it?

TWELVE-YEAR-OLD ELISA: (QUIETLY PANICS) Don't accept this proposition. I don't want to get married.

CARMAN: (QUIETLY HARSH) You seriously can't be doing this now when this boy is staring right at you.

TWELVE-YEAR-OLD ELISA: (QUIETLY PANICS) But Mom, I'm too young to have a husband. Please, Mom! I don't want to accept this proposition.

CARMAN: (QUIETLY HARSH) And I don't want you embarrassing our guests with your antics – especially after what you managed to cause earlier! If you don't want to carry the burden of a man's broken heart, then you better shut your mouth this instant and sit there quietly!

Twelve-year-old Elisa immediately goes quiet and pouts in silence, while Malcolm immediately understands how she feels.

MALCOLM: You know what, I think it's best if we take our leave. If Elisa is uncomfortable with the idea, then we won't continue with the proposition, but we will come back another time to discuss this when Garreth is here.

CARMAN: (TURNS TO MALCOLM CALMLY) No, Malcolm – there's no need for you guys to leave. She's just being childish. Just give her some time to think about it while we …

Carman stops herself as she sees Garreth's car pulling over to the house, where he parks in the driveway.

CARMAN AND MALCOLM: (QUIETLY) Oh shit.

Garreth gets out of the car and walks over with an expression of confusion when he sees Malcolm, Carman and twelve-year-old Elisa outside.

GARRETH: (TURNS TO MALCOLM) Is everything all right, Officer Reign?

MALCOLM: (COMES UP TO GARRETH) Everything's fine, Garreth. No need for you to be formal with me outside of work. We just came for a casual meeting.

GARRETH: (CONFUSED) What do you mean, we?

STELA: (COMES UP TO GARRETH HAPPILY) Hi there, Officer Graves! I hope you don't mind us intruding in your home! I'm Stela – Malcolm's wife!

GARRETH: (HAPPILY) Oh, so you're the famous Mrs. Reign! Malcolm has told me so much about you!

STELA: (EXCITEDLY) Really? Thank goodness! I know Malcolm likes to be casual with everyone, but I demand my respect as Mrs. Reign. (HAPPILY) It's so nice to meet Elisa's father.

GARRETH: (HAPPILY) It's nice to meet you too, Mrs. Reign (CONFUSED), but what's with this mentioning of my daughter? (CONCERNED) Did she do something wrong?

STELA: (CLARIFIES) Oh no, she is an absolute sweetheart.

GARRETH: (NODS IN AGREEMENT) Yeah, she really is ...

Garreth stops himself when he sees twelve-year-old Elisa sitting with fourteen-year-old Rueben, and his smile goes away completely.

GARRETH: (SERIOUSLY) What is this punk doing at my house?

Stela stands there cluelessly as Garreth immediately charges for fourteen-year-old Rueben and Carman does all that she can to stop him.

CARMAN: (CALMLY) Garreth, calm down. Please don't do this now – not in front of everyone.

MALCOLM: (COMES UP TO GARRETH) Take it easy, Garreth. What's going on? Why are you getting so angry with him?

Fourteen-year-old Rueben remains on edge as Garreth stops resisting and turns to Malcolm in disbelief.

GARRETH: (SERIOUSLY) Don't tell me that boy is your son, Malcolm.

MALCOLM: (NODS) Yes, he is, actually. (CONFUSED) What exactly is going on here? Did he do something wrong?

CARMAN: (STERNLY) Do you really have to be like this now?

GARRETH: (SERIOUSLY) Be like what, exactly? (TURNS TO TWELVE-YEAR-OLD ELISA) Elisa, come here this instant!

Twelve-year-old Elisa gets up and immediately goes up to Garreth, who holds onto her tightly before bringing her to face him.

GARRETH: (SERIOUSLY) Be honest with me, Elisa … Do you hang out with this boy at your school?

TWELVE-YEAR-OLD ELISA: (FRANTICALLY) No, Daddy, I don't! Mrs. Reign says she has a proposition for me, but I don't want to do it! Please, don't accept it, Dad – I don't want this proposition at all!

GARRETH: (CONFUSED) What proposition? (SHOUTS) Can someone please tell me what is going on here?

Everyone goes silent for a moment, and then Malcolm goes up to fourteen-year-old Rueben for an explanation of Garreth's anger toward him.

MALCOLM: (SERIOUSLY) For crying out loud, what did you do, Rueben?

FOURTEEN-YEAR-OLD RUEBEN: (DEFENSIVELY) I did nothing, Dad! I don't know why he's getting mad at me.

MALCOLM: (UPSET) Really? Because I've known this man my entire life and I know he doesn't get angry for nothing. So, you better not be lying to me.

FOURTEEN-YEAR-OLD RUEBEN: (DEFENSIVELY) I'm not lying to you, Dad – I swear I didn't do anything! (TURNS TO STELA, UPSET) Mom! Tell him already. He's ruining everything for me!

In a fury, Garreth looks at fourteen-year-old Rueben and again attempts to charge him, while Carman and twelve-year-old Elisa try to calm him down.

STELA: (COMES UP TO EVERYONE) All right, calm down, everyone! I can see that some things need to be cleared up right away!

GARRETH: (TURNS TO STELA, UPSET) Yes! Things definitely need to be cleared up right away! What is this proposition you have for my daughter?

STELA: (HAPPILY) Well, the main reason for our visit is because my son actually has an interest in your daughter.

GARRETH: (EXAGGERATED) Does he now! Oh, now I see what's going on here – he has a crush on my daughter! So I'm guessing you brought him to my house so that he can end that crush, right?

STELA: (SLIGHTLY TAKEN ABACK) Um – no, of course not. (HAPPILY) I was just telling your wife that a group of mothers and I teamed up to take charge of our children's futures, and we came here today specifically for Elisa just to see if she was interested in being Rueben's life partner in marriage.

GARRETH: (SHOCKED) Marriage? You mean, you want to set my daughter up for an arranged marriage?

STELA: (HAPPILY) Well, I wouldn't say it like that –

GARRETH: (UPSET) But it is that! It's exactly like that!

CARMAN: (UPSET) Would you show her some respect, Garreth? She doesn't deserve to be talked to like that! Why are you making such a big deal about this?

GARRETH: (UPSET) For Almighty sakes, Carman! She's not even nineteen to talk about marriage! Why on Earth would you even think about accepting this proposition?

CARMAN: (ARGUES) I thought this would be a good thing for our daughter, at least to give her a sense of stability before she finally gets out of 79%. But I wasn't going to give them a final answer without consulting you. I obviously wanted to talk to you about it after you came home!

GARRETH: (EXAGGERATED) Oh good! Sounds like an excellent plan! Well, I'm home now. We had the chance to talk about it, and as for my final answer (UPSET), it's obviously a no! (TURNS TO STELA, UPSET) I'm sorry if we wasted your time, Mrs. Reign, but Elisa will not be participating in any arranged marriages (GESTURES TO FOURTEEN-YEAR-OLD RUEBEN), especially involving that punk right there!

Malcolm takes the chance to come up to Garreth as he continues to charge at fourteen-year-old Rueben, who prepares to run away from him.

MALCOLM: (PLEADS) Garreth, please calm down! Don't do this to my son!

GARRETH: (PLEADS) Malcolm, you know you're the only true friend I have, but if you want me to respect you and your family (ANGRILY), then you better get him out of my face before I rip his trachea out of his throat! You don't know what he allowed to happen.

CARMAN: (UPSET) For Almighty sakes, Garreth! What did this boy do?

FOURTEEN-YEAR-OLD RUEBEN: (STANDS UP SHOUTS) I love Elisa!

Everyone goes silent, while Stela gushes with joy. Garreth is livid, glaring at fourteen-year-old Rueben as he approaches him.

FOURTEEN-YEAR-OLD RUEBEN: (DETERMINED) And I will do everything it takes to make her my wife! I will love her, protect her and care for her with all my might! Even if you hate me and won't accept me, I will do everything to be the best husband I can for her! I am man enough to tell you that!

GARRETH: (ANGRILY) But were you man enough to tell the truth to your parents? Were you man enough to stop your friends from what they did to that girl? Are you man enough now to let everyone know what you allowed to happen? Because I know everything, and I saw everything – I even spent the last hour prosecuting your friends for what they did to that girl! They're in the back of a transport vehicle on their way to prison, as we speak!

Fourteen-year-old Rueben stands frozen in shock, as Malcolm remembers the case he and Garreth were working on before he left.

MALCOLM: (STUNNED) Wait a minute. We were just working on that case before I left.

GARRETH: (CERTAIN) Oh yes! Rigdon Burns and Dornan Carse – they were finally proven guilty for assault! And they couldn't help but say that your son was an acquaintance of theirs as well.

MALCOLM: (TURNS TO FOURTEEN-YEAR-OLD RUEBEN, STUNNED) Rueben, I thought I told you to stop hanging out with those boys. (ANGRILY) These better not be the friends he's talking about!

FOURTEEN-YEAR-OLD RUEBEN: (ARGUES) Dad, how could you possibly believe everything this man says!

GARRETH: (ANGRILY) Because surveillance cameras do not lie! Not only do they show that you were there, but the surveillance footage also shows you cowering at the scene. Malcolm, he watched that poor girl suffering the consequences of what his friends did to her.

Malcolm stands in shock and turns to fourteen-year-old Rueben angrily while Stela looks on, confused.

STELA: (CONFUSED) Now wait a minute. He couldn't have been there when that incident happened. He told me himself that he was at the library studying for an exam –

Malcolm screams in pure anger and tries his best not to come after fourteen-year-old Rueben himself, while Stela looks on, even more confused.

STELA: (CONFUSED) Now why are you so upset? Your friend here is basically calling our son a liar.

MALCOLM: (ANGRILY) For Almighty sakes, Stela – that's because he did lie to you! He uses that as an excuse just to hang out with those boys (TURNS TO FOURTEEN-YEAR-OLD RUEBEN, UPSET), and I know because I saw him one time and told him not to do it again! (SHOUTS LIVIDLY) Do you realize what's in jeopardy for you? They'll kick you out of the Academy for being an accessory to a crime. How could you let this happen!

FOURTEEN-YEAR-OLD RUEBEN: (DETERMINED) I don't care if I get kicked out of the Academy! I'll find other ways to make money, as long as I get to be with Elisa!

GARRETH: (CHUCKLES OMINOUSLY) I don't think you know who you're messing with … you see, kid.

Garreth aggressively grabs fourteen-year-old Rueben by the collar as Carman, Stela and twelve-year-old Elisa look on in shock.

GARRETH: (ANGRILY) I don't think you ever had someone whoop your ass before, and I'm willing to be the first to do that now!

Carman and Stela rush over to stop Garreth as he continues to aggressively hold onto fourteen-year-old Rueben's collar.

CARMAN: (UPSET) Garreth, you need to stop this! Let go of him!

STELA: (UPSET) Release my son this instant! Malcolm, do something!

Malcolm, who is extremely disappointed in fourteen-year-old Rueben, does not make a move, while Garreth continues to aggressively hold onto the boy's collar.

GARRETH: (ANGRILY) You see – not even your father wants to help you out! (LIVID) Even your eyes can't hide the cowardice that's inside you! That's why you could never be considered a man to me! If you couldn't even protect that girl from what your friends did to her, then how do you expect me to let you protect my daughter!

Everything goes silent for twelve-year-old Elisa as she watches Garreth aggressively shaking fourteen-year-old Rueben by the collar, while Carman tries her best to break up the fight. Malcolm continues to absorb the news in disbelief as Stela tries to get him involved with the altercation. Twelve-year-old Elisa is in shock as she watches everyone fighting, screaming and getting angry with each other while she wonders if she caused all of this to happen.

Nine Years Later

▌INT. INSIDE THE STEELS SQUAD CAR – EVENING

STEELS OFFICER 3: And that's what happened?

ELISA: (NODS) Yeah ... that's what happened.

STEELS OFFICER 3: Well, no wonder Rueben behaves that way – anyone would've gone mad for a girl like you. Sorry for being nosey. I was just curious about what happened in that kid's past.

ELISA: It's fine, as long as you keep your promise.

STEELS OFFICER 3: Don't worry, I won't breathe a word to the other officers – I won't even tell Malcolm that you told me. But I will tell you this ... as much as it would've prevented a lot that is happening in his life and allowed you to have the best father-in-law in the world ... I'm glad you didn't marry his son.

ELISA: Yeah ... I'm glad, too.

Elisa sits in the back of the Steels squad car thinking about the incident that day as she wonders if everything would have changed if she had accepted the marriage proposition. At the same time, she begins to feel bad for Rueben and Malcolm, along with missing Garreth's presence as the Steels officer drives her home.

EIGHTEEN

The Next Day

▌ INT. REGIONAL HEADQUARTERS COURTYARD – MORNING

INFORMATION HUB AI: Access granted. Here is an overview of all of your e-transfers. Your recent e-transfer status of one hundred thousand dollars sent to CARMAN GRAVES has been updated to: DECLINED. What would you like to do with this e-transfer?

ELISA: Transfer funds back to my account.

INFORMATION HUB AI: Transferring funds. (LOADING) Request granted. One hundred thousand dollars has been successfully transferred to the account of ELISA GRAVES. Is there anything else I can do for you today?

ELISA: Dismiss complete access.

INFORMATION HUB AI: Dismissing complete access. (LOADING) Request granted. Please remove your Life Band from the ID slot to complete your request.

Elisa removes her hand from the ID slot, as the Information Hub removes her information and resets itself for the next user.

INFORMATION HUB AI: Thank you for using the Information Hub. Have a great day. (LOADING) Welcome. Please scan your Life Band through the ID slot.

The Information Hub repeats its greeting as Elisa stands there and takes a moment of silent frustration while the female employee behind her waits for her to leave.

FEMALE EMPLOYEE 1: (TAPS ON ELISA'S SHOULDER) Excuse me, are you done?

ELISA: (SNAPS INTO FOCUS) Oh yes – sorry about that.

Elisa steps out of the way to allow the female employee to use the Information Hub while she makes her way to the RH-C Department Office.

INT. THE RH-C DEPARTMENT OFFICE OF REGIONAL HEADQUARTERS – MORNING

Zach stands near the printer drinking a cup of coffee and waits for Elisa until he sees her entering the office and making her way to her cubicle without noticing him.

ZACH: (SMILES) Morning, Ms. Graves.

ELISA: (STOPS AND TURNS TO ZACH) Morning, Mr. Vault. How are you today?

ZACH: (HAPPILY) I'm doing just fine now that you're here. You're actually just in time because I want to show you something – watch this.

Zach puts his coffee away as he takes out a fresh stack of printing paper from the supply cabinet. He manages to find the paper tray by himself, pulls it open and fills it up with the stack of paper before closing it. Zach also takes the time to replace the ink cartridges before turning the printer on, as Elisa looks on, impressed when she sees the printer working.

ELISA: (IMPRESSED) Wow. In just one day, you showed major improvement.

ZACH: (HAPPILY) Thanks, Ms. Graves. I know I'm a fast learner, but I couldn't have done it without my mentor.

ELISA: (IMPRESSED) Well, I'll be more than honoured to teach you more things.

XAVIER: (RUSHES IN) Ms. Graves, there's something I need to tell you!

Slightly perplexed, Elisa turns to Xavier, while Zach, confused and upset by being interrupted, looks on.

ELISA: (CONFUSED) Sure, Mr. Cunes. What is it that you need to tell me?

XAVIER: (SHEEPISHLY) I just wanted to say ... (SINCERELY) Thank you for what you did at the Plaza that day. You're one of the bravest Tints that has ever walked into this office! No one has ever been able to confront those lemonheads the way you did, and it's nice to be in the presence of someone who could stand up for herself and inspire others like us to do the same ... and you definitely inspired me to be a better person to myself ... I want to thank you for doing that.

ELISA: (SPEECHLESS) I ... honestly don't know what to say ... Thank you, Mr. Cunes. It was really nice of you to say that.

XAVIER: (SINCERELY) You're welcome, Ms. Graves – I meant every word I said!

Zach rolls his eyes in annoyance while Elisa stands there, touched by Xavier's kind words.

XAVIER: (GUILTILY) I also wanted to apologize for what I said the other day ... I know it was wrong of me to use that word to you and the other lady (SINCERELY), and I promise I won't use it again from now on, and I hope I can make it up to you if ... you can be my mentor.

ZACH: (STEPS IN FRONT OF ELISA) Sorry, kid, but she's with me. You're going to have to find someone else.

ELISA: (TURNS TO ZACH) Now wait a minute. There's no need to be like that, and I can speak on my own, thank you very much. (TURNS TO XAVIER) Unfortunately, I can't take on another student due to the restrictions, but if you ever need any assistance, feel free to ask me and I'll lend you a helping hand.

XAVIER: (SINCERELY) Thank you, Ms. Graves! I promise to do that from now on!

Xavier rushes back to his cubicle as Elisa stands there, impressed by his new attitude.

ZACH: Someone is sure popular today.

ELISA: (SMILES) Well, that doesn't matter. I'm just surprised that he managed to improve during the last few weeks (TOUCHED), and his words were truly sweet.

ZACH: (OFFENDED) Hey, he tried to steal my mentor from me.

ELISA: (TURNS TO ZACH) He did no such thing, and you should learn how to respect your own colleagues.

ZACH: (SINCERELY) Well, the only colleague I respect in this office is you. Not just because you're my mentor, but you actually deserve respect in so many ways.

ELISA: (SMILES) Well, Mr. Vault, if you want to continue respecting me (GESTURES TO ZACH'S COFFEE), then get rid of the coffee first. Mr. Popkin is not going to like seeing that.

Zach is a bit dumbfounded and releases Elisa to go to her cubicle to get herself set up for the morning shift.

ZACH: Did my words at least have the same effect as his?

Zach takes his cup of coffee and tries to drink it quickly as he follows Elisa to her cubicle, while everyone else gets ready for work.

A Few Hours Later

INT. THE RH-C DEPARTMENT OFFICE OF REGIONAL HEADQUARTERS – AFTERNOON

Everyone in the office continues to answer phone calls, answer emails, complete previous documents and write reports under Daniel's supervision. A few colleagues try to focus on their work but cannot help but turn to Elisa and Zach. They are taken aback to see how their typing skills match each other perfectly, enabling them to finish their reports at the same time.

ZACH: (WHISPERS) I beat you again, Ms. Graves.

ELISA: (WHISPERS) I'd rather you focus on your next task than pay attention to what I'm doing.

ZACH: (WHISPERS) Well, where's the fun in that? I thought we were enjoying our little competition.

ELISA: (WHISPERS) By focusing on what others are doing, you will only slow down your progress, which can actually affect the entire office's productivity. But if you only focus on your own tasks, you'd be surprised at how much you get done in two shifts.

ZACH: (WHISPERS) Well, these two shifts are definitely long. How do people survive these long hours of just sitting in one spot? I surely need a break, after all this.

Zach secretly takes a sip of his coffee, which he has been hiding under his desk the entire time. However, Elisa notices it immediately and sighs in disbelief.

ELISA: (WHISPERS) What did I tell you about the coffee?

ZACH: (WHISPERS) I'm sorry, Ms. Graves – but if you ask me, it's kind of hard to chug down a drink that's hotter than a hundred and sixty degrees.

ELISA: (WHISPERS) Unless you want that a hundred and sixty degrees to splash all over the floor, I suggest you take your time to finish it in the kitchen. You can have your coffee anywhere else during the shift, but it can't be near the computers – and he will know for sure.

Zach grimaces in confusion when Elisa is displeased to see him sitting there.

ELISA: (WHISPERS) Go.

ZACH: (WHISPERS) Okay, I'm going.

Zach gets up with his coffee and makes his way to the kitchen while Elisa moves on to her next task without noticing Daniel approaching her.

DANIEL: Employee #263.

ELISA: (GETS STARTLED AND TURNS TO DANIEL) Yes, Mr. Morin.

DANIEL: Where's your student? I thought I just saw him leave.

ELISA: (STUTTERS SLIGHTLY) Um, he's – taking a brief break in the kitchen. He felt sort of dazed by the long hours and wanted to revitalize himself with something to drink.

DANIEL: That's fine, as long as he returns to this desk after his break. Mr. Popkin expects him to be on top of his game by the end of the week.

ELISA: I'll make sure that happens, sir.

Daniel begins to leave as Elisa attempts to focus on her new task until she catches a glimpse of Gillian's empty cubicle and tries to recall what time it is.

ELISA: (GETS UP) I also want to take a quick break for myself.

Daniel stops and turns to Elisa in confusion, along with a few colleagues, as she realizes how abruptly she got up.

ELISA: I was wondering if you would allow me to do so.

DANIEL: It's okay, Employee #263. You never had to ask either of us to take a break before.

ELISA: I know. (GESTURES TO HER RED TAG) I just thought I had to, knowing the restrictions.

DANIEL: (REMEMBERS) I understand now. You're welcome to take your break, but be sure to be back after fifteen minutes.

ELISA: Thank you, sir.

Elisa takes off her headset and rushes out of the office, while Daniel, along with everyone else, begins to wonder what she is really up to. Zach returns from the kitchen and goes back to his trainee desk just to see her leaving.

ZACH: (CONFUSED) Where is she going?

DANIEL: (TURNS TO ZACH) She's going to take a break, but she'll be back after fifteen minutes. Get back to work, Employee #491.

Daniel returns to his supervising duties, while Zach remains confused by Elisa's decision to take a break.

A Few Minutes Later

▌ INT. THE RH-C DEPARTMENT BREAK ROOM – AFTERNOON

All the janitors of the RH-C Department have their usual weekly feast, as a variety of brunch dishes are placed on the table. Elisa enjoys eating a Cubano sandwich with Hank, as he explains to her what has been happening during her absence.

HANK: They were just about to start the day when that General Metallic guy showed up out of nowhere again and shut down most of the computers. Everyone was so scared that they remained downstairs the entire time while the IT guys spent all day fixing the systems. That's why the supervisors decided to start transferring employees and Head Council began to notice the dwindling numbers. (GESTURES TO ELISA'S SANDWICH) How are you enjoying that sandwich, Ms. Graves?

ELISA: (WITH HER MOUTH FULL) It's amazing. I never had anything like this before.

HANK: (POINTS TO GORDAN) Gordan is the one who made them. He actually spends his weekends making these sandwiches for his entire neighbourhood. (TURNS TO GORDAN) Isn't that right, Gordan?

GORDAN: (IN ESPERANTO) Kompreneble, Hank. Se mia komunumo iam pensus pagi al mi por la manĝaĵoj, kiujn mi preparas por ili, mi antaŭ longe estus forlasinta ĉi tiun laboron nur por foriri de la infaneto de Sinjorino Popkin.

Of course, Hank. If my community ever thought to pay me for the food I make for them, I would've quit this job a long time ago just to get away from Mrs. Popkin's toddler.

Hank and the rest of the janitors laugh hysterically along with **Gordan Sanchez (mid-fifties)**, as Elisa joins along as well.

ELISA: (TURNS TO HANK, CONFUSED) What on earth did he just say?

HANK: (SHAKES HIS HEAD) We have no idea. His wife is usually here to translate for us, but she hasn't gotten the chance to come by since she has to work full time. Everyone has been affected by these changes – you should've seen what this office was like during your absence, coffee spills everywhere while everyone was freaking out about Office Requests. Even Mr. Morin wanted to leave at one point.

ELISA: That's a shame to hear. Do you think General Metallic might have something to do with the dwindling numbers.

HANK: (SHRUGS) I don't know, though I can't help but think that. Even with all this going on, I still haven't seen Ms. Grant, which has really got me worried over the past few weeks.

ELISA: (SIGHS IN WORRY) I can't help but worry myself.

HANK: Mr. Morin hasn't been harassing you about her disappearance, has he?

ELISA: (SHAKES HER HEAD) No. He asked me about her after the first cyberattack had happened, but that was the only time. (TURNS TO HANK, CONFUSED) Why would you say that?

Hank looks around carefully to see that the rest of the janitors are talking amongst themselves, while Elisa continues to eat her sandwich.

HANK: (QUIETLY) I'm not supposed to be telling you this because I'm not regularly a gossip, but I need you to be aware in case it happens again. Mr. Morin only came to you because you're the only one who was ever close to her, not just for a routine checkup, but because he is romantically involved with Ms. Grant.

Elisa almost chokes on her sandwich as Hank and a few other janitors turn to see if she is okay.

HANK: (CONCERNED) Are you all right, Ms. Graves?

ELISA: (CLEARS HER THROAT) Yeah, I'm okay. (QUIETLY IN SHOCK) But, no kidding – Gillian and Mr. Morin?

HANK: (QUIETLY) Yes, it's been happening for almost a year now. I was surprised that an office relationship could ever last that long – especially when it's been kept a secret.

ELISA: (QUIETLY) Did she tell you about this?

HANK: (QUIETLY) I wish she had, so I would have been better prepared. Unfortunately, I caught them both here in an uncomfortably exposed state, but luckily, I helped them sneak out before the boys came in to start our feast. It's not like I haven't seen this happen before, but I was shocked to see Mr. Morin involved with anyone – he's usually very reluctant with relationships. And I kept my word and promised not to say anything about it, so please don't tell anyone.

ELISA: (QUIETLY) Of course not. You know I'm not into gossip, Hank.

HANK: (QUIETLY) I know. I trust you more than anyone else in the office – not even Gordan can keep a secret. Once I was aware of the situation, Ms. Grant was more open to telling me about everything: the good times, the bad times, and the X-rated times.

Elisa laughs as she imagines Gillian telling Hank about her X-rated times with Daniel.

HANK: (QUIETLY) You could definitely tell that she was in love with Mr. Morin ... but she was also sad about it as well.

ELISA: (QUIETLY) Why would she be sad about being in love with Mr. Morin?

HANK: (QUIETLY) Think about it, Ms. Graves. It all has to do with the position Mr. Morin is in. He's basically Mr. Popkin's right-hand man – he's the only person that man can ever depend on. However, because of his high maintenance, it always ends up in a fight between Ms. Grant and Mr. Morin. They can't even have a simple makeout session in secret without Mr. Popkin bothering him for something. It's a terrible situation for the both of them – she even considered breaking up with him and told him that before the Gala began.

ELISA: (QUIETLY) I guess that's why she wanted to go out that day before her mother called, but I highly doubt that she would leave her job completely because of a fight.

HANK: (QUIETLY) Believe me, Ms. Grant does have the tendency to do things out of spite if you allow her to. But she knows better than to put her job into jeopardy, especially since she hasn't reached 60% yet.

ELISA: (QUIETLY) And how does Mr. Morin feel about her disappearance? He hasn't been very vocal about it lately.

HANK: (QUIETLY) That's because he can't, especially when he has Mr. Popkin watching him like a dog. He's also very talented at hiding his emotions, but he has been slowly losing it these days – especially the time that young man broke your keyboard.

Elisa remembers the incident she had with her colleagues, as she also recalls Daniel's anger that day.

HANK: (QUIETLY) It's rare to see Mr. Morin showing any form of anger, but deep down, you can tell that he's hurting on the inside too. The fact that Mr. Popkin denied his request to take a leave of absence has definitely put him on edge.

ELISA: (QUIETLY) Does he come here to talk to you about things as well?

HANK: (CERTAIN) Of course he does. Everyone does when they are in a bad mood. Why do you think this place is so popular?

ELISA: (GIGGLES) I guess I should come here too when I'm in a bad mood.

HANK: (KINDLY) You're always welcome to join us. We'll keep you fed and everything. Plus, I would like to hear what's going on from you instead of from someone else.

Elisa grimaces in confusion, while Hank sighs guiltily.

HANK: (QUIETLY) Ms. Grant managed to tell me about your life as well as your current situation with your mother. I obviously thought of telling you before things went further, but I didn't want to break the bond, as she has taken a liking to you.

ELISA: (PAUSES) As I've taken a liking to her as well …

HANK: (KINDLY) You obviously don't have to tell me everything now, since I've already breached a couple of people's trusts. But when you are ready to talk about it, feel free to come by anytime … I'm always here to talk, if you want.

ELISA: (SMILES) Thanks, Hank … I really appreciate that.

HANK: (KINDLY) You're welcome, Ms. Graves. You have no idea how terribly missed you have been – I can't help but be happy that you've finally become part of these feasts.

ELISA: (KINDLY) You know I always keep my promises.

HANK: (KINDLY) Yes, and I'm very glad that you have. (POINTS TO THE SAUSAGE ROLLS) Here, try some of these sausage rolls.

Elisa takes a few sausage rolls and tries one for herself. She immediately enjoys the taste, which makes Hank smile gleefully.

ELISA: (WITH HER MOUTH FULL) These are so good. Did Gordan make these as well?

Gordan notices Elisa trying the sausage rolls and nods happily, as everyone in the room lets out a pleasant laugh.

A Few Minutes Later

INT. THE CORRIDOR OUTSIDE THE RH-C DEPARTMENT OFFICE OF REGIONAL HEADQUARTERS – AFTERNOON

Elisa leaves the breakroom and rushes back to the office while quickly eating a sausage roll and brushing off crumbs along the way.

INT. THE RH-C DEPARTMENT OFFICE OF REGIONAL HEADQUARTERS – AFTERNOON

As Elisa returns to the office and rushes to her cubicle, Zach turns to see her taking a seat before preparing herself to get back to work.

ZACH: (WHISPERS) Where have you been?

ELISA: (WHISPERS) Went to get something to eat. Here, have this.

Elisa gives Zach a rolled-up napkin, which he opens to see the sausage rolls inside.

ZACH: (WHISPERS HAPPILY) Sweet! Actual food for once!

ELISA: (WHISPERS) Eat it quickly before Mr. Popkin comes. And no crumbs.

Zach nods as he quickly eats a sausage roll and immediately enjoys the taste, while encouraging Elisa to have some for herself. They both finish the sausage rolls that were in the napkin and discreetly brush off any crumbs. Elisa tosses the napkin into the garbage before Mr. Popkin leaves his office with Daniel by his side.

DANIEL: (CONCERNED) I'm not sure if this is a good idea on your end. Are you sure you should be doing this, sir?

MR. POPKIN: (UNCERTAIN) I don't know. Everything has gone to the shits since that hacker decided to make a name for himself. And I don't think I'm comfortable releasing a project when there's a possibility of him stealing our information ... there's no other choice but to put the project on hold. I honestly wish that none of this was happening at the moment.

Hearing himself step on a crumb, Mr. Popkin stops as Daniel does also to see what is going on. He sees Mr. Popkin slowly stiffening in anger as he takes his time to see that he has stepped on a crumb.

MR. POPKIN: (SCREAMS) Who has left crumbs in my office?

Everyone in the office is startled frightfully and immediately stops working, as Mr. Popkin stands there in anger. Daniel prepares for the worst, as they both turn to see that the crumbs are near Zach's trainee desk.

MR. POPKIN: (SCREAMS) Employee #263!

ELISA: (GETS UP QUICKLY) Yes, sir.

MR. POPKIN: (TURNS TO ELISA ANGRILY) Explain to me why there are crumbs near your area? Have I entertained the idea of eating and drinking inside your cubicles?

ELISA: (SHAKES HER HEAD) No, sir.

MR. POPKIN: (SCREAMS) Then explain the crumbs on the floor!

Everyone remains silent and prepares for the worst as Elisa tries to figure out what to say. Thomas relaxes in his cubicle and enjoys watching Elisa panic as Mr. Popkin waits angrily for an answer.

ELISA: (SLIGHTLY NERVOUS) Well … you see, Mr. Popkin –

ZACH: (GETS UP QUICKLY) It was me, Mr. Popkin … I was the one who dropped the crumbs on the floor.

Elisa turns to Zach in shock, along with everyone else in the office. Thomas is in disbelief that he would choose to stick up for her.

ZACH: I got a little peckish during the shift, so I thought to bring some snacks over to keep me awake for the time being.

MR. POPKIN: (PAUSES ANGRILY) Are you sure what you're saying is true?

ZACH: (NODS QUICKLY) It definitely is, sir.

Mr. Popkin stares at Zach just to see if he will flinch, but he maintains a straight face the entire time.

MR. POPKIN: (FIRMLY) All right then … since this is the first time you have allowed this to happen, I'll let you off for now. (TURNS TO ELISA ANGRILY) But believe me when I say this, Employee #263, if your student does this sort of thing again, I will have the both of you stay after work just for you to see what the janitors have to deal with at night! (SCREAMS) Do I make myself clear?

ELISA AND ZACH: (IN UNISON) Yes, sir.

MR. POPKIN: (FIRMLY) Good. Now, let's carry on, Mr. Morin.

Mr. Popkin walks away from Elisa and Zach as Daniel shoots them a stern look before catching up to him. They both give a quiet sigh of relief, while everyone else slowly goes back to work.

ZACH: (QUIETLY) Holy shit! I did not expect him to get that angry.

ELISA: (QUIETLY) It's okay. Let's just get back to work.

Elisa and Zach take a seat, as they both return to work and focus on their new tasks.

ELISA: (WHISPERS) Thank you for what you did just now.

ZACH: (WHISPERS) You're welcome, Ms. Graves. I'm always willing to do anything for you.

ELISA: (WHISPERS) I appreciate that. (PAUSES) I did say no crumbs.

ZACH: (WHISPERS) And I did just save your ass back there after you brought food into the office.

ELISA: (WHISPERS) Which I brought back for you so you wouldn't continue to be groggy.

ZACH: (WHISPERS) So either way, this makes us even.

ELISA: (WHISPERS) Yes, this actually does.

Elisa and Zach turn to each other and smile as they continue their work. Thomas sits in his cubicle, silently furious that the two of them are getting along so well. However, he has no other choice but to go back to work.

NINETEEN

| INT. THE STEELS PROTECTION SERVICES STATION – AFTERNOON

Vance is looking through the surveillance footage of the Tint Valley Residence incident when Caleb comes up to him after finishing an interrogation.

CALEB: Find anything yet, Officer Stanford?

VANCE: (TURNS TO CALEB AND SHAKES HIS HEAD) No, not yet. I thought I would spend the time looking through the footage while we waited for Deputy Reign to come back, but so far, nothing.

CALEB: Well, hopefully, when Deputy Reign comes back, we will be able to get the answers we need to solve this.

Caleb looks through the surveillance footage of the incident, as Vance notices that something is off about him.

VANCE: (JOKINGLY) So, you seem awfully quiet after finally coming off monitoring duties. How does it feel not to have to watch over Ms. Graves anymore?

CALEB: (SHRUGS) Okay, I guess. Why do you ask?

VANCE: (CONFUSED) You're usually a lot happier about it when you don't have to monitor a detainee anymore. Officer Webber even modified the restrictions for you so that Ms. Graves could go to work by herself. I'm surprised that you're not thrilled about this more than anyone else in this room – I know Tegan is celebrating before you even have a chance.

CALEB: (SIGHS IN ANNOYANCE) Yeah, I'm glad that I don't have to monitor her anymore (HONESTLY), especially since she was the most boring detainee I ever had to monitor in my life. There were even times when I attempted to call in just to leave early.

VANCE: (SUSPICIOUSLY) Yeah, but there were times when you arrived late after you finished monitoring Ms. Graves. Something tells me that you managed to find something to do while you were there.

Caleb goes silent as he thinks about the times he read books with Elisa, as Vance carefully pays attention to his facial expressions.

VANCE: (DUMBFOUNDED) Dude, do you actually like her?

CALEB: (SNAPS INTO FOCUS) What? (DEFENSIVELY) Now, you're just talking foolishness.

VANCE: (SURRENDERS) I'm just asking you a question. You're the one who's getting defensive. (SMILES) I think you seriously like Ms. Graves.

CALEB: (DEFENSIVELY) I don't like her, and I never will like her – so you better get that thought out of your head this instant!

VANCE: (DUMBFOUNDED) Oh, my goodness, Caleb McEntire actually has a crush on a girl ... (LAUGHS) and it's a first offender, of all people.

CALEB: (STERNLY) You better shut your mouth –

VANCE: (HONESTLY) You have to admit, Ms. Graves is quite a looker. She is insanely hot – you're going to have to admit that.

MALCOLM: (WALKS IN) Ah, it's nice to see you both here on time. Now we can get started.

VANCE: (SINGS) Deputy, Caleb has something to tell you.

CALEB: (TURNS TO VANCE) Come off it already, Vance.

MALCOLM: (STERNLY) For Almighty sakes, gentlemen – we're dealing with a serious matter here!

Vance immediately stops fooling around with Caleb as they both fix their stances on military style.

MALCOLM: (STERNLY) There's no time to horse around like children. I need you both to take this seriously. Do you understand what I'm saying?

CALEB AND VANCE: (IN UNISON) Yes, sir. Sorry, sir.

MALCOLM: (SERIOUSLY) Now that we got that out of the way, there's something I need to show you both.

Caleb and Vance step aside for Malcolm, as he pulls out all the short clips and screenshots for them to see.

MALCOLM: While looking through the footage with Officer Webber, we managed to capture a few screenshots and found this.

Malcolm opens a screenshot of CX on the screen, while Caleb and Vance look at the photo in confusion.

CALEB: (CONFUSED) It's just a guy wearing a helmet. We've seen those guys all the time at the Debris Crest. (TURNS TO MALCOLM) What does he have to do with this case?

MALCOLM: Watch carefully.

Malcolm clicks on the screenshot as it plays a video of CX shooting at the crowd during the incident, as Caleb and Vance stiffen in anger.

VANCE: (SERIOUSLY) So, he must've been the one responsible for the shooting that day. (CONFUSED) He could be one of those Night Riders at the Debris Crest, but why on earth does he have CX on his helmet?

MALCOLM: (SERIOUSLY) Look closely. (DEMANDING) Pay attention to every detail on this next shot.

Malcolm pauses the video and zooms in for Caleb and Vance to see the old Metallic Order badge stitched on CX's suit.

VANCE: (STUNNED) He's wearing a Metallic Order badge on his suit (PAUSES). But that can't possibly be General Metallic. (TURNS TO MALCOLM) He wouldn't dare to expose himself in broad daylight. (POINTS OUT) Plus, the helmet he was wearing in those holograms is completely different from the one in this picture.

CALEB: Unless he has an accomplice.

Surprised, Malcolm and Vance turn to Caleb, as they both realize that he might be on to something.

MALCOLM: What made you come to that conclusion?

CALEB: It's like every bad guy movie out there. General Metallic does all the evil planning, while the sidekick does all the dirty work. (CONFUSED) However, this incident doesn't make any sense at all.

Caleb goes up to the screen and replays the footage to see CX not aiming to kill or hurt anyone as he shoots toward the crowd.

CALEB: (CONFUSED) If this person is really working with General Metallic, then why would he just randomly shoot near a crowd without actually killing anybody or causing injury? What would be his reason for having an accomplice in the first place?

The video stops playing as all the lights and computers begin acting up. The hologram of General Metallic appears on every screen at the Steels Protection Services Station.

GENERAL METALLIC: (DISTORTED) Yes, why on earth would I have someone to do the dirty work for me … when I'm obviously capable of doing it myself? It's just much easier.

VANCE: (SHOCKED) The fuck?

MALCOLM: (DEMANDING) Check the system controls! Do whatever you can to neutralize any connections at this moment!

All the Steels Technicians rush over to the system control room while everyone at the station tries their best to plug any devices necessary to disconnect General Metallic's live broadcast while Malcolm, Caleb and Vance remain on edge.

GENERAL METALLIC: (DISTORTED) Oh, try all you want, deputy. There's no way you can break this connection … especially when this live broadcast is specifically just for you and every Steels Protection Services Station out there.

MALCOLM: (ANGRILY) What is the meaning of this? What is it that you're trying to do, exactly?

GENERAL METALLIC: (DISTORTED) There's no need to be hostile, Deputy. I just thought that you needed to be aware of some information that has managed to go over everyone's heads recently. Since everyone is so interested in what I'm up to.

The entire Steels Protection Services Station suddenly goes dark for a moment until all the screens come back on to show all the profiles of every Tint Valley citizen who has gone missing over the past month. Malcolm stands there in shock to see Gillian's profile on the screen as well while Caleb, Vance and the rest of the Steels officers remain on edge.

GENERAL METALLIC: (DISTORTED) Perhaps I will give you the bigger picture of my plan just for the fun of it.

MALCOLM: (DEMANDING) What is all this? Why are you showing me these people?

GENERAL METALLIC: (DISTORTED) My goodness, Deputy, I actually thought you cared for once – especially when these are the people that you've been searching for the entire time. I know where they are, but I can't tell you where. However, there's no need to worry, everyone. I'll make sure you see them again very soon.

NOLAN: (ANGRILY) This has gone way too far!

Everyone turns to see Nolan coming out of the interrogation room as he walks in angrily to face the screen.

NOLAN: (ANGRILY) Now listen to me, you son of a bitch! You better tell me where you're hiding these people or I swear, once I find you –

GENERAL METALLIC: (DISTORTED) I'm afraid you haven't been listening, Officer, as I can see you've come late to the party. Plus, if you haven't succeeded in tracking down these people's whereabouts in the past month, how exactly do you expect to find me? But that's not all that I wanted to show you.

The collage of citizens' profiles automatically grows as new profiles begin to appear on the screen. Everyone stands and looks on in alarm as they begin to realize that the people shown on the screen have a Tint Level between 80% and 70%.

GENERAL METALLIC: (DISTORTED) Not only do I get to show you the people who have already gone, but the people who are still yet to come. That's probably the only reason why I have an accomplice: there are quite a lot of citizens in this country.

The many Steels officers are immobilized by their reactions as they see profiles of their loved ones on the screen. Malcolm cannot help but be beside himself when he sees Rueben's profile on the screen, along with others whom he knows personally.

GENERAL METALLIC: (DISTORTED) Even your son is a part of this list, Deputy – you might wanna keep an eye on him if you don't want him out of your sight.

MALCOLM: (ANGRILY) What are you planning to do with these people?

GENERAL METALLIC: (DISTORTED) The one thing that your late Commander-in-Chief could never have done during his time – neither your current leadership, the Steels Protection Service nor the entire country of Bartlett's Piece – can stop this from happening.

Caleb remains transfixed along with Vance, as they both see Elisa's profile on the screen, while Malcolm trembles in complete anger.

GENERAL METALLIC: (DISTORTED) You have failed everyone on this list with your crooked system. Now, we will help them rise to bring this system to annihilation!

General Metallic bursts into an ominous laugh while Malcolm, Nolan, Caleb, Vance and the rest of the Steels' officers stare at the collage of citizens' profiles on the screen. They are consumed by worry about the entire situation, along with the people who might fall as victims of General Metallic's master plan.

A Few Hours Later

▌ EXT. PRIMETIME PLAZA – EVENING

PRIMETIME PLAZA AI: Attention all consumers. All stores at Primetime Plaza will officially close due to an Environmental Emergency. Please make your final purchases, as the plaza will be under Lockdown Mode in the next five minutes. Thank you for shopping at Primetime Plaza and have a good day.

Everyone at Primetime Plaza wastes no time making their way home, as they all pay attention to the clouds and realize that a storm is coming.

▌ EXT. OUTSIDE THE TINT VALLEY RESIDENCE – EVENING

Many citizens outside the Tint Valley Residence quickly make their way inside to avoid the heavy rain as the storm worsens. A few other citizens who have reached their Canvas Phases stand outside for a moment to be soaked in the rain. One girl tries her best to withstand the heavy rain and strong winds, while her mother urges her to come inside the building.

CONCERNED MOTHER: (SCREAMS) For goodness's sake! Would you come back inside already?

CONCERNED MOTHER'S DAUGHTER: (SCREAMS) Not until I change into a Hue!

CONCERNED MOTHER: (SCREAMS) You have to be absolutely out of your mind – this is not even the Rain of Passion! It's a bloody storm out there! You must come inside this instant!

CONCERNED MOTHER'S DAUGHTER: (SCREAMS) No, Mom! I've been waiting my whole life for this moment to come, and I won't miss another chance! I need to know what Hue I'll become!

CONCERNED MOTHER: (SCREAMS) You're going to get hurt if you stay out there!

CONCERNED MOTHER'S DAUGHTER: (EXCITEDLY) It's happening!

The daughter's white dress slowly turns orange with every single raindrop as her mother watches her turn into an Economical Hue.

CONCERNED MOTHER'S DAUGHTER: (EXCITEDLY) Yes! I'm a Hue now! (JUMPS HAPPILY) I'm finally a Hue – I'm finally a Hue –

The daughter stops celebrating as she gets spooked by a trash bin falling nearby. The mother rushes outside to protect her from any flying debris.

CONCERNED MOTHER: (ANGRILY) For goodness's sake! When will you ever listen? I don't care if you are a Hue; you're still my child!

The mother drags the daughter inside the building and she quickly closes the door to protect them from the storm.

A Few Hours Later

█ INT. ELISA'S BEDROOM – NIGHT

As the storm continues to get even worse, Elisa remains fast asleep in her bed. Lightning begins to flash inside the room, and a loud clash of thunder wakes her up instantly. Elisa immediately sits up and looks around in fright before turning to the window to see the storm intensifying while she trembles in fear.

GARRETH: (IN ELISA'S HEAD) It's okay, Elisa. There's nothing to be afraid of. It's just a storm. It'll soon pass.

EIGHT-YEAR-OLD ELISA: (IN ELISA'S HEAD) But Dad, what if the storm wants to hurt us? What if it's angry with us?

GARRETH: (IN ELISA'S HEAD) You don't know that for sure, sweetie. Just because you're afraid of something doesn't mean it intentionally wants to hurt you … it probably wants to talk to you.

Elisa tries to control her trembling as she lies back down and tries her best to listen to the storm, while Garreth's words continue to play in her head.

GARRETH: (IN ELISA'S HEAD) All you have to do is relax and listen to what the storm is trying to say to you.

Elisa closes her eyes and tries to go back to bed, when suddenly she is again startled when she hears a heavy knock on the door.

CALEB: (THROUGH THE DOOR) Elisa? Elisa, are you there?

Elisa immediately recognizes Caleb's voice and she quickly gets out of bed to answer the door.

▌ INT. ELISA'S APARTMENT – NIGHT

Elisa navigates her way through the dark while Caleb continues to knock on the door.

CALEB: (THROUGH THE DOOR) Elisa, please open this door! It's vital!

Elisa makes it to the door and quickly opens it, and she is shocked to see Caleb standing there wearing a protective raincoat.

ELISA: (SHOCKED) Officer McEntire? What are you doing here? How did you manage to get here during a storm?

CALEB: (RUSHED) That's not important right now. I only came here because there's something I need to tell you.

ELISA: (WIDENS THE DOOR) Why don't you come inside, so we can talk about it?

CALEB: (FURIOUSLY) There's no time for that, Elisa – especially when it's past curfew!

Completely taken aback, Elisa waits while Caleb tries to maintain his composure.

CALEB: (SERIOUSLY) Listen to me; you have to stop going to work.

ELISA: (PAUSES IN SHOCK) What?

CALEB: (SERIOUSLY) Do not go to work tomorrow – or any other day, if possible! I'm begging you to just stop going to work.

ELISA: (CONFUSED) Why? Why are you telling me this? Did something happen?

CALEB: (RUSHED) I can't tell you everything. That's why you're just going to have to listen to me on this point!

Elisa stands there even more perplexed, unaware that Caleb wishes to tell her about General Metallic's live broadcast at the Steels Protection Services Station but cannot.

CALEB: (RUSHED) Just hear what I have to say! I don't care if you call in sick, fake an injury or stop going entirely – you're just going to have to stop going to work. Just don't go to work anymore. Do you understand me?

ELISA: (UPSET) No! I don't understand you at all! I don't understand why you're telling me not to go to work! What exactly is going on here?

RESIDENCE SECURITY GUARD: (FROM AFAR) Hey! You're not supposed to be here!

ELISA: (PANICKED) Please tell me what's going on. You're really scaring me.

CALEB: (GRABS ELISA BY THE SHOULDERS) Hey, there's nothing to be scared about. Everything will be all right if you just listen and do as I say. (DEMANDING) So, when I tell you not to go to work – do not go to work!

Elisa stands there speechless as she begins to take in how close she is to Caleb, as he begins to realize it as well and releases his grip from her shoulders.

CALEB: (BACKS AWAY FROM ELISA) We better not see each other when we wake up tomorrow.

ELISA: (PANICKED) Wait, Officer McEntire –

CALEB: (BEGINS TO LEAVE) I have to go now. Just trust me on this one!

Dizzied by a mix of emotions, Elisa sticks her head out the door to see Caleb trying to avoid the residence security guard while he leaves the Tint Valley Residence.

ELISA: (LOUDLY) Officer McEntire? Officer McEntire!

RESIDENCE SECURITY GUARD: (PASSES BY STERNLY) Go back inside, ma'am! Or you will face the consequences!

Remembering the ankle monitor she has on, Elisa goes back inside her apartment and closes the door. She locks the door immediately but stands there, confused and scared at the same time as she thinks about Caleb's demand for her to stop going to work.

The Next Day

▌ INT. ELISA'S APARTMENT – MORNING

Elisa leaves the TV on the news channel while she sits in the living room and talks to the Head Council at the Regional Headquarters through her Wireless Earpiece.

ELISA: (ON HER WIRELESS EARPIECE) I understand that completely. I just thought it would be best if I stayed home today. I'm not feeling well at the moment, and I don't think it's best for me to come in today. I don't want to infect anyone at the office. Yeah, I'm aware that I've taken on a student recently. I'm certain that there's someone else who could take my place and teach him everything he needs to know while I'm absent. I can guarantee that for sure. Thank you for accepting. You too, bye.

LIFE BAND AI: Call ended.

Elisa takes off her Wireless Earpiece and sighs in frustration as she watches the news and takes the time to think about Caleb's unexpected visit last night.

TO BE CONTINUED ...

SPECIAL THANKS TO

Scribendi

mdcreation

Wordzworth

Cre8tive Eye Designs

IngramSpark

Beautiful Women Society

My Family and Friends

IN
HUE'S EARTH
PHASE 2

COMING SOON!